Titles by Jayne Ann Krentz writing as Jayne Castle

The Guinevere Jones Novels

Titles by Jayne Ann Krentz writing as Amanda Quick

Other titles by Jayne Ann Krentz

DREAM EYES	SOFT FOCUS
COPPER BEACH	ECLIPSE BAY
IN TOO DEEP	EYE OF THE BEHOLDER
FIRED UP	FLASH
RUNNING HOT	SHARP EDGES
SIZZLE AND BURN	DEEP WATERS
WHITE LIES	ABSOLUTELY, POSITIVELY
ALL NIGHT LONG	TRUST ME
FALLING AWAKE	GRAND PASSION
TRUTH OR DARE	HIDDEN TALENTS
LIGHT IN SHADOW	WILDEST HEARTS
SUMMER IN ECLIPSE BAY	FAMILY MAN
TOGETHER IN ECLIPSE BAY	PERFECT PARTNERS
SMOKE IN MIRRORS	SWEET FORTUNE
LOST & FOUND	SILVER LININGS
DAWN IN ECLIPSE BAY	THE GOLDEN CHANCE

Specials

THE SCARGILL COVE CASE FILES

Anthologies

CHARMED
(with Julie Beard, Lori Foster, and Eileen Wilks)

Titles written by Jayne Ann Krentz and Jayne Castle

NO GOING BACK

DESPERATE
AND
DECEPTIVE

THE GUINEVERE JONES COLLECTION, VOLUME 1

JAYNE CASTLE

BERKLEY BOOKS, NEW YORK

THE BERKLEY PUBLISHING GROUP
Published by the Penguin Group
Penguin Group (USA) LLC
375 Hudson Street, New York, New York 10014

USA • Canada • UK • Ireland • Australia • New Zealand • India • South Africa • China

penguin.com

A Penguin Random House Company

DESPERATE AND DECEPTIVE

Berkley trade paperback ISBN: 978-0-425-27183-4

An application to register this book for cataloging has been
submitted to the Library of Congress.

PUBLISHING HISTORY
The Desperate Game Dell Books edition / June 1986
The Desperate Game InterMix eBook edition / July 2012
The Chilling Deception Dell Books edition / August 1986
The Chilling Deception InterMix eBook edition / July 2012
Berkley trade paperback omnibus edition / January 2014

PRINTED IN THE UNITED STATES OF AMERICA

10 9 8 7 6 5 4 3 2 1

Cover background photo © Shutterstock.

CONTENTS

Dear Reader:

If you've been keeping track of my titles, you probably know that a while back I did a four-book series featuring an amateur sleuth named Guinevere Jones. (No relation to the Arcane Joneses—at least I don't think so). The books are all straight-up romantic suspense and they were written under my Jayne Castle name. They have been out of print for some time but now I am delighted to tell you that my publisher is making them available again. The first two titles, The Desperate Game *and* The Chilling Deception, *are contained in this book,* Volume One of the Guinevere Jones Collection.

I hope you enjoy the ride with Guinevere Jones as she solves crimes and falls in love with the sexy, mysterious Zac Justis.

Sincerely,
Jayne Ann Krentz
(aka Jayne Castle)

DESPERATE
AND
DECEPTIVE

THE
DESPERATE
GAME

CHAPTER 1

He was the ugliest man in the bar, and he had his eye on her.

It figured, Guinevere Jones decided as she swept up an empty bottle of imported British ale. Give her one entire evening in the trendiest yuppie bar in Seattle, and she would end up attracting the attention of the only nontrendy, nonyuppie in the room. Deliberately she avoided looking at the corner table where he sat brooding under a huge fern.

Deftly she replaced the empty bottle with a full one, made change with a charming smile, and thanked the attractive young urban professional male who had just ordered the ale. It took an effort to project her voice over the monotonous din of music currently considered hot. By the time the bar closed for the night she would be hoarse.

She was also going to have very sore feet. The black pumps that were a part of the cocktail waitress uniform had become uncomfortable five minutes after she'd stepped into them. The pencil-slim black skirt and the mauve blouse weren't as unpleasant as the shoes, but Guinevere felt conspicuous. Skirts cut as narrowly as the one she wore were designed for what the fashion industry termed the *junior* figure. She knew her derriere had not fallen within the junior parameters since she was twelve years old. Unfortunately the blouse seemed to have been styled for a Hollywood starlet, and her bustline had maintained its petite dimensions even though she was now thirty.

Ah, well. Such was the price one paid for the joys of being one's own boss. She'd spent worse evenings. The client was happy, and the image of being totally dependable had been maintained. One always had to consider the image.

Guinevere made her way to the next tableful of fashionably casual up-and-comers and dutifully took their orders for California wines and an imported light beer. Sooner or later she was going to have to go back to the table in the corner. The nonyuppie had almost finished his small glass of tequila. It was after she'd taken his order the first time that she'd become aware of his intent scrutiny. Might as well get it over and done. Resolutely Guinevere headed for the fern-shrouded table.

"Another tequila?" She kept her voice bright and her smile brilliantly professional.

He nodded once and swallowed the last sip in the small glass. Guinevere stifled a shudder.

"When do you get off work?"

The low, dark shade of his voice surprised her for some reason, perhaps because it didn't sound in the least affected by the tequila.

"I don't. I work twenty-four hours a day. No time off for good behavior. Or bad either." She made her response polite but firmly discouraging.

"Just one long hustle, hmmm?"

"A woman's work is never done." She scooped up the little glass, her tone dropping several degrees in temperature. "I'll be right back."

"I put in a lot of twenty-four-hour days myself. Or at least it seems that way sometimes."

"Fascinating. Excuse me." Without another word she took the glass and hurried back to the long, ornate bar at the far end of the room. In all fairness the man wasn't really ugly. It was just that in this terribly chic environment he tended to stand out. Like a sore thumb.

For one thing, he was definitely older than almost everyone else in the room, probably near forty. The typical young, upwardly mobile urban professional tended to be around thirty—a good age for making it big or at least living well so that everyone was convinced you were making it big. Same difference.

The man crouching like a malevolent frog under the fern was dressed much more conservatively than those around him. His white shirt and bland tie were definitely nondesigner, and his short, no-nonsense haircut was not the product of a blow dryer. She hadn't peeked under the table, but Guinevere was willing to bet the shoes would be wing tips.

In the dimly lit room it was difficult to get a good look at his face, but she'd seen enough to know the frog drinking tequila among princes had not been cloned from the same designer genes as the rest of the crowd in the bar.

And the heavy-handed pass he was attempting to make could have used some social polish, to say the least.

"Order in," Guinevere called to the busy bartender. Jerry nodded once to show he'd heard and went on blending the frothy pink strawberry daiquiri someone had ordered. His expression was polite, but she had a hunch what he was thinking. Bartenders, Guinevere had learned, were very disdainful of people who ordered fluffy drinks. She waited patiently until he was done.

"Two more chardonnays, three draft bitters, and another tequila straight."

"Who's the guy drinking the tequila?" Jerry smoothly poured the white wines.

"A frog that never metamorphosed into a prince."

"Huh?"

"Never mind. Don't they ever turn that music down, Jerry?"

"Nope. It's after midnight. The meat-market action is going to be getting very intense soon. The music helps."

"Helps what?"

Jerry shrugged with the wisdom of bartenders the world over. "Helps make it all right, I guess. How are you holding up?"

"My feet are killing me, but I'll last."

"You get used to it after a while." Jerry grinned abruptly. "But I guess that bit of information doesn't matter much to you. You're here only for the night."

"Thank heaven. I think I'm getting too old for this sort of thing. Be back in a few minutes."

Guinevere picked up the drink-laden tray and moved back into the crowd. Jerry was right. The action was getting intense. There was an air of urgency hanging over some of the participants. It was Friday evening, and a lot of the people in the room were going to be facing a lonely weekend if they didn't connect with someone soon.

She would have found the whole scene sociologically interesting if she hadn't been so tired, Guinevere realized. And if her feet weren't hurting so much. She saved the tequila order for last.

"You didn't answer my question," the man under the fern said just as if their earlier conversation hadn't been terminated.

Guinevere set down the tequila. "Seven, please."

"What time do you get off work?" He pushed eight dollar bills toward her. They were left over from the change she had made on his first drink.

"I told you, never. They lock me up in a little cage in the back room from two A.M. until six. Then I start all over again." Guinevere found fifty cents in change and set it in front of him. "Thank you." She turned to leave.

"I'm thinking of locking you up in a cage myself." He gave her a contemplative glance, ghost gray eyes moving over her with grave consideration.

Guinevere knew she was close to losing her temper. Only the necessity of maintaining a good image in front of the client kept her from dropping the tray on the Frog's head. Smiling very sweetly, she leaned a little closer.

"Allow me to point out that you have wandered into the wrong pond tonight, sir. This is trendy, young, go-getter territory. Not really suited for frogs. Try your luck in one of the big hotel bars downtown or out on the airport strip. I think that would be more your style. Better hurry. It's getting late."

"Whatever luck I'm going to have will be here." He picked up the tequila. "You see, I'm not looking for just any woman tonight. I'm looking for you, Guinevere Jones. And I've found you."

She drew in her breath slowly, hiding the jolt he had given her. The fact that the Frog knew her name introduced a vaguely alarming element into the atmosphere. She wished he looked more like a drunken businessman attempting a clumsy pass. She didn't care for the steady regard of those dark eyes.

"Just what," she said calmly, "did you intend to do with me after you found me?"

"I told you. Put you in a cage."

There was always the possibility, of course, that he was simply crazy. But Guinevere couldn't find any sign of obvious insanity in the unrelenting face of the man under the fern. It was the fact that he knew her name that really disturbed her.

"Would you care to explain yourself so that I can make a decision?" she inquired politely.

"Make a decision about what?"

"About whether to call the cops or the mental health folks."

A faint smile flickered briefly at the edge of his grim mouth. "I don't think you want to call either crowd, Miss Jones. The police would be an embarrassment to you, and the mental health people have more important things to do."

Guinevere went still, the tray balanced precariously on one hand as she eyed the Frog. "Why," she asked distinctly, "would the cops prove embarrassing?"

Looking thoughtful, he tasted the tequila and then reached up to push aside a trailing piece of fern that seemed to be trying for a sample of his drink. "Because then I would have to go into long and rather detailed explanations about who I am and why I'm spending an evening fighting off a fern and making threats to a particular cocktail waitress, all of which would be awkward for a supposedly upright, tax-paying small businessperson such as yourself."

The tray wavered a bit on her hand. Guinevere steadied it. "Okay, I'll ask the obvious. Who are you?"

"Zachariah Justis. You can call me Zac."

"Why would I want to call you Zac?"

"Because you'll soon be working for me and I'd like to try for a certain degree of informality on the job. I've heard it, uh, lubricates the channels of communication. Smooths the ripples in the chain of command. Makes for an atmosphere of teamwork. That sort of thing."

Guinevere was aware of a growing sensation of light-headedness. Frantically she kept a hold on the tray and her nerves. Her throat felt a little dry. "Where did you hear that, Mr. Justis?"

He opened one large, square hand in a negligent gesture. "I think I read it in a recent issue of some business management magazine."

"You read a lot of those?"

"Not as many as I should, I'm afraid." There was no real note of apology in the words. "I find them irritating."

"I'll just bet you do." He looked like a man who would in general find irritating excessive demands for polite, socially acceptable behavior, let alone the courtesies of modern management.

"How soon can you leave?" he asked, ignoring her comment.

"You have a one-track mind. I'm not going anywhere with you, Mr. Justis."

"This is where I get to say the magic word."

"Which is?"

"StarrTech."

Guinevere let out the breath she hadn't realized she'd been holding. A small, nasty sensation of prickly awareness went down her spine. "For a frog you know some interesting magic words."

"I thought you'd appreciate that particular one. Can you leave now?"

She shook her head instantly. "No."

"When?"

"Not until two."

He glanced at the clock over the bar. "That's another hour."

"Don't let me keep you. If you're bored with waiting, feel free to leave." She swung around and started for the next table.

"I'll wait," he said behind her.

Guinevere didn't doubt it.

Zac watched her as she moved off into the crowded room. She'd handled it well. When he'd mentioned StarrTech, there had been no furious denials, no loud exclamations of angered innocence, no contrived demands for an explanation. She had assessed the single word and figured out for herself all the ramifications. She'd be going home with him at two.

He appreciated that kind of direct acceptance of reality. He hadn't expected to find it in Guinevere Jones. But, then, she was a small businessperson, just as he was, and people struggling to keep small businesses afloat learned in a hurry to deal with reality.

It was an interesting concept, Zac decided, this notion of having something in common with Miss Guinevere Jones. He wondered how she'd react to the idea. Probably wouldn't be thrilled. What was it she had called him? A frog. That was it. Absently he shoved the fern frond off his shoulder. The damn thing seemed to be alive, the way it was attempting to climb into his drink. Suddenly he realized how he must look sitting in this dark corner under the overly healthy plant. Rather like a frog.

Miss Jones, on the other hand, didn't look at all like a frog. She also didn't look like the stereotype of the young urban professional either, although she was about the right age. Zac was willing to bet his IRS deductions for an entire year's office expenses that Guinevere Jones had never been a cheerleader in high school or homecoming queen. That pleased him in a vague sort of way. He had never been captain of the football team or homecoming king. Something else in common.

Her hair was longer than that of most of the other women in the room. Every other female seemed to be wearing a sleek, expensively styled cut that probably cost a fortune and looked as if it had come out of *Vogue* magazine. Guinevere's below-shoulder-length hair was braided and coiled at the nape of her neck in an old-fashioned style that was timeless in its simplicity. Zac liked its coffee-brown color.

It annoyed him that he was trying so hard to analyze her, but he couldn't deny his own curiosity. He'd spent a lot of time deciding whether to move in on her and even more time figuring out how to do it. It was his nature to take his time reaching conclusions. During the hours he'd spent making his decisions, Zac had also had plenty of opportunity to wonder about the woman he was planning to cage.

The first thing he'd noticed when he'd finally identified her in the shadowy bar was that she seemed to be wearing a skirt that was a size too small and a blouse that was at least a size too big. It was probably the tequila that made him want to reach out and explore firsthand both ends of the spectrum.

It was amazing how professionally she handled the cocktail waitress role. Apparently she'd filled the job at StarrTech just as easily. Zac was impressed. He'd have to ask her where she'd learned the knack of blending into such varied situations. It was a talent he could use.

She didn't return to his table for the rest of the remaining hour. But Zac knew Guinevere was aware of his watching her. There was a hint of tension in the way she held her shoulders and in the scrupulous way she avoided his eyes. But he was certain she wouldn't run. Guinevere Jones was the kind who held her ground and went down fighting. Zac knew he lacked finesse when it came to handling people, but his instincts about them were usually sound. He winced as another round of prerecorded music hit the speakers. It seemed to him that someone was deliberately turning up the volume.

At closing time Guinevere considered her options and realized she really didn't have any. If the Frog had put her name together with StarrTech, Inc. so long after she'd quit working there, he definitely knew too much. There was no safety in running. Hiding her head in the sand wasn't going to make this particular frog disappear. She could tell that by the way he sat under the fern with such lethal patience. By the time she had collected her oversize red canvas tote and made her way out onto the sidewalk, she was prepared for the fact that Zachariah Justis would be waiting.

"Do you want some help with that?" He stepped out of the shadows and indicated the tote.

"No, thanks. I can carry my own purse," she told him tartly.

"Purse? I thought it was a piece of luggage." His hand dropped quickly. He shoved it and his other fist into the front pockets of the tweed jacket he wore. "What the hell have you got in there?"

"A very large assault rifle."

He nodded, walking toward a cab that waited at the curb. "I understand that a woman living alone has to protect herself."

Guinevere gritted her teeth and got into the cab without protest. "You seem to know a great deal about me, Mr. Justis."

"I try to learn as much as possible before attempting to blackmail someone, Miss Jones. May I call you Gwen?"

"No." Blackmail? That wasn't quite what she had been expecting. Guinevere's palm was damp against the soft red leather of the tote. For a moment she wished devoutly for the assault rifle she'd told him was inside her bag.

"Every report I have on you implies that you can be a very warm and charming woman, someone who wouldn't hesitate to let another person call her by a short form of her name," Zac said as the cab swung away from the curb.

Guinevere noticed that the driver already seemed to have the address. The cab was speeding along Western Avenue toward the Pioneer Square area. In other words, she was being taken home. That information brought an element of relief but not much. Out on the darkness of Elliott Bay a huge cargo ship was making its way cautiously into the port of Seattle. She caught glimpses of its lights between buildings as she looked out through the cab's windows.

"I limit my warmth and charm to people who aren't prone to kidnapping and blackmail," Guinevere said finally. The backseat of the cab felt crowded. Zac Justis was a little less than six feet in height, and she hadn't noticed any fat on him, but he somehow seemed to fill up all the available space. She felt he was pushing her in more ways than one.

"Aren't you worried about limiting your circle of acquaintances?"

"I have a feeling that I've got more friends than you have, Mr. Justis." She kept her eyes on the night-darkened scene visible through the cab's windows.

"You're probably right," he admitted dryly. Then he leaned forward to tap the driver's shoulder. "That's the building there on the left."

Guinevere resisted the urge to comment scathingly on his knowledge of her address. He was probably trying to impress her with just how much information he had. She wouldn't give him the satisfaction of demanding further explanations.

Without a word she stepped out of the cab and waited stoically while her unwanted escort paid the driver. She noticed out of the corner of her eye that he tipped carefully but not at all lavishly. A man who watched his money. She could identify, however unwillingly, with that. Sighing, she fished her key out of a zippered pocket on the tote.

"I suppose you intend to come upstairs?" she muttered as Zac walked toward her.

"How can I turn down such a generous invitation?"

Closing her teeth very firmly against the retort that hovered in her throat, Guinevere led the way through the well-lit entrance of the brick building and up one flight of stairs. The façade of her apartment building was a stately design of arching windows and ornamental detail that dated back to the turn of the century. The inside had been gutted and completely renovated with the goal of capturing the attention of the new urban pioneer: the single person who wanted to live downtown and demanded something more interesting than a bare box.

"All right, Mr. Justis," Guinevere said as she opened the door of her apartment, "let's hear what you have to say about blackmail and StarrTech. And then you can leave."

His mouth curved slightly at one corner and there was a reluctantly appreciative expression in his eyes as he followed her through the door. He came to a halt on the threshold and absorbed the brilliant impact of color that greeted him.

"Somehow it looks like you. Unexpected."

He walked toward the floor-to-ceiling bookcase, which was painted with yolk-colored enamel. En route he noticed slate gray carpets bordered in red. There was more red throughout the apartment: a red window seat, a red-painted desk with red bookcases behind it, and a red shelf in the entrance hall. The yellow reappeared elsewhere in the shape of a tea cart and a trash can beside the desk. The room seemed to be anchored by the few pieces of furniture, all of which were in black. The night was locked out with miniblinds custom-designed to fit the high, arched windows.

"I'm surprised you find anything about me unexpected. You seem to have done a fairly thorough job of snooping." Guinevere tossed her tote bag onto the tea cart and stepped out of the pumps with an exclamation of relief. Barefooted, she lost a couple of inches of height, but a few centimeters weren't enough to make her feel any more in charge of the situation anyway, so why suffer? She walked to the black leather love seat and threw herself down into a corner. "My God, I'm exhausted. Say what you have to say and then leave, Mr. Justis."

"You've had a long day," he observed mildly. He took the black-wire diamond-shaped chair across from her and eyed her feet. "You were in the offices of Camelot Services at seven o'clock this morning, ate a sandwich at your desk for lunch, grabbed a bite of supper on your way to the bar, and then put in a full shift as a cocktail waitress."

"The woman who was assigned to take the waitress job phoned in sick at the last minute." Guinevere decided trying to keep him from using the short form of her name would be pointless. Another small battle lost. Sooner or later she was going to have to find a defensible position.

"Do you always sub for your people when they can't go out on one of the temporary assignments?"

"Someone has to do it. As you must know from your prying,

Camelot Services is still a very small operation. I didn't have any-one else I could call in at the last minute."

"And you didn't want to offend the client by being unable to meet the request for a temporary cocktail waitress," he said softly.

"When you're in the temporary help business, you can't come up with too many excuses or you'll lose clients."

"Yes. I know how important it is to please clients. Which brings me to the reason I'm here."

"I'm glad something is going to get you to explain yourself. Do me a favor and lay it all out in short, pithy sentences. I'm too tired to fence with you."

"I want to please one of my clients, Gwen. I think you can help."

She eyed him narrowly. "What client?"

"StarrTech."

"I see." She thought about that for several long seconds. Then she thought about the future of Camelot Services. It was the same as thinking about her own future. At the moment both were begin-ning to look shaky. "What, exactly, are you doing for StarrTech?"

"It's hired my firm to take a private, very quiet look at a problem it's been having with lost equipment shipments. The people there think the problem is originating within their computer department."

"Your firm?"

"Free Enterprise Security, Incorporated." There was a hint of satisfaction underlining the words.

Guinevere blinked. "You're an investigating agency? A private detective service?"

He shook his head. Then he frowned down at his hands. He'd clasped them loosely between his knees, his elbows resting on his thighs. "My firm offers consultations to businesses."

"What sort of consultations?" It was like pulling teeth, Guine-vere decided. But she was going to get some answers if it killed her. Perhaps a little more liquor would make him chattier. And heaven knew she could use a drink. She got to her feet, wincing a little. "Would you like some brandy?"

"Thank you." He watched her as she walked into the kitchen, but he didn't follow. When she reappeared, holding two small snifters of brandy, he accepted the offer with a polite inclination of his head.

"You didn't answer my question." Guinevere prompted him, resuming her seat. "Just what sort of consultations do you provide?"

"Security consultations."

"Ah." She swallowed some of the brandy. It might not make her guest any more comprehensible, but it certainly made it easier to sit here and deal with his presence in her apartment. She took another sip. "Ah," she said again, and wondered if it sounded any wiser this time.

"My firm provides very discreet services, Gwen. We're called in when management does not want to create a stir or make accusations. Generally corporate managements hate to create stirs or make accusations. Bad for the image and stockholders take a dim view of that sort of trouble. If we learn that there's something worth creating a stir about or decide that accusations should be made, we go ahead and make the recommendation. It's up to the client to pursue it into court."

"You keep saying 'we.' Just how big is Free Enterprise Security?"

He hesitated, then shrugged. The small movement emphasized the width of his shoulders. "You will have the distinction of being my first employee. I just got started a few months ago, and until now I've been a one-man operation. A small business, just like your own."

Guinevere stared at him and then seized on the most puzzling element in his explanation. "Your employee?"

"Ummm."

"I don't understand."

"Of course not. That's where the blackmail comes in." He lifted the snifter to his mouth and took a healthy swallow.

Guinevere placed her glass down very carefully on the table beside the small sofa. "Let me get this straight. You're not planning on impressing your client by dragging me in chains into StarrTech headquarters?"

"The image is intriguing, but frankly I've got bigger fish to fry. Your bit of finagling with StarrTech's computerized benefits program is not what I'm investigating."

Guinevere closed her eyes briefly. Hearing it put into words made it suddenly very, very real. This man knew what she had done during her short stint as a clerk in the computer department of StarrTech. "How did you find out?" she asked bleakly.

"Russ Elfstrom is a friend of mine." Zac was calm, almost placid. A man in control. "He came across your little maneuvers a couple of weeks ago. Just about the same time that management began to worry about bigger problems it had discovered."

Russ Elfstrom, Guinevere remembered, had been in charge of all computer systems at StarrTech. She hadn't liked the man. No one in the department did. The programmers had called him the Elf behind his back. He wasn't particularly short, but there was a kind of high-strung quality about the man. He smoked incessantly, and occasionally, while she was at StarrTech, Guinevere had seen him furtively pop a couple of small pills. Wiry and balding, with restless, pale eyes, the Elf had ruled the department with little regard for the delicate egos of programmers and even less for the hopeful computer operators who had dreams of using the machines as a way out of the clerical pool.

On the other hand, Russ Elfstrom was a good company man. He got things done. Management liked him, and as long as he was content to run a department that had a high turnover in personnel, management was content to leave him alone. Management didn't

really understand computers, anyway, let alone computer personnel. Results were all that mattered.

"So the Elf tossed me into your clutches," Guinevere murmured. "Why?"

"He was simply going through every detail he could think of
that might be helpful to me in my examination of the missing shipments. In the process he uncovered your manipulation of the benefits plan. He was on the verge of mentioning you to management.
I persuaded him to let me have you instead. I think you might
prove useful, Gwen."

"I sound like an odd little tool you've discovered and aren't
quite certain how to use," she snapped bitterly.

"Oh, I think I know how to use you. I'm offering to keep
your name clear at StarrTech if you'll give me a hand on this other
problem." Something a little fierce flared in his eyes for an instant.
"Keeping your name clean should be important to you, Gwen. After all, independent businesspeople have to maintain spotless
reputations, don't they? It wouldn't do at all to have potential clients thinking that you use your services as a cover for theft and
other assorted activities, would it?"

In spite of her resolve to stay absolutely cool, that stung. Guinevere sat upright, her hazel eyes narrowed, her mouth tight.
"Camelot Services is utterly reliable, Mr. Justis. There has never
been a complaint or a doubt about the ethics of my company!"

"Until your venture into StarrTech?" He leaned back in the
black steel-mesh chair, apparently satisfied with the results of his
accusation.

Guinevere fought a short, violent battle for control and surprised herself by winning. "My *venture* into StarrTech was a different matter. A private matter." She picked up the brandy, her grip
so savage that it was a wonder the glass didn't shatter. She forced
herself to drink.

"There was something different about your contract with

StarrTech?" Zac inquired benignly. "Something that set it apart from other short-term temporary assignments?"

"If you're going to make an accusation, I'll get a lawyer. If you're not, then I don't need one, do I? Either way, I don't intend to say anything further on the subject of my business at StarrTech."

Zac waited for a long moment, watching her. "I won't be making any accusations to StarrTech management, Guinevere Jones, because I think you're going to cooperate. Isn't that right?"

She made herself inhale slowly, seeking a way to calm herself. "Blackmail."

"Just as I promised."

"Do you always make good on your promises?"

"Keeping my promises is one of the few things in which I still believe, Gwen."

She focused on the massive yellow bookcase across the room. "What is it you want me to do in exchange for your silence?"

"I want you to go back into the computer services department at StarrTech, doing pretty much the same sort of clerical work you did the first time. But this time around you're going to be my eyes and ears in the department. I need some answers, and you're going to get them for me."

She moved her head in a vague denial. "What about the Elf? How do I know he'll keep quiet?"

"As I said, Russ is a friend of mine. He'll do whatever I ask him to do in this matter."

"Somehow I find it hard to imagine," Guinevere said.

"What? That you're being blackmailed?"

"No, that you and Russ Elfstrom are such close friends. You're not a friendly type, Mr. Justis."

"Russ and I go back a long way together."

"How unfortunate for you. That's just about the most depressing thing I've heard since the last time I talked to my sister's shrink."

Justis blinked owlishly, assimilating that information and try-ing to make sense of it. "What's this got to do with your sister?"

"Never mind. Tell me what you want, Mr. Justis. And then go back to your pond."

CHAPTER 2

"You're making a mistake, Zac. I wouldn't trust that woman to make brownies for a kindergarten bake sale, let alone be your inside man on this."

"My inside woman," Zac said mildly into the telephone. He leaned back in the used swivel desk chair that had been such a bargain six months ago when he'd spotted it on sale. At the time he'd been certain he could live with the squeak. Now he wasn't so sure. It was becoming increasingly annoying. "Don't worry about it, Russ. Everything's under control. I know what I'm doing." You had to sound confident. Image above all. He'd read that somewhere recently in one of those damn business journals he'd been forcing himself to peruse.

"I hope so. God knows she sure managed to slip one by me the first time she showed up in my department. The conniving little bitch."

Guinevere's success in outfoxing Russ Elfstrom even for a few months was something his friend was never going to be able to accept with any equanimity. Zac wondered why it bothered him to hear Russ call her a bitch, though. Theoretically he shouldn't care one way or the other what kind of language Russ used regarding Guinevere. Maybe it had something to do with the fact that he was now Guinevere's boss, Zac decided. Maybe one automatically felt some obligation to defend one's employees. An interesting development and one he hadn't expected.

Zac studied the bare walls of the tiny office suite he'd rented in the downtown high-rise. There was no view. The floor-to-ceiling windows along one wall opened onto the corridor. Across the hall there was another row of tiny office suites being rented by other small businesses.

The idea of condominium office space in a flashy glass and steel building was practical, allowing someone such as Zac to operate out of a much higher rent district than he'd normally be able to afford. Another brick in the wall that was his tiny but—he hoped—growing business image. The outside of the high-rise was as impressive to his clients as it was to the clients of the huge law firm that leased the entire top two floors of the building. But there was no getting around the fact that the tiny ten-by-ten room lacked something in the way of aesthetic appeal. Especially after you'd been in it a couple of hours. Fortunately in another forty-five minutes he'd be able to escape to lunch.

"Did she show up on time this morning?" Zac asked.

"Oh, sure. Along with a big sack of doughnuts for everyone. The staff went crazy. You'd think she was some long-lost member of the family instead of just a temporary clerk who'd been recalled."

"That's why I want her in there, Russ. She has a knack for blending in almost instantly. I watched her at work last night in a cocktail lounge. You'd have thought she'd been working there for years. The bartender was her good buddy by midnight, and the rest of the waitresses had included her in their gossip long before that. People like her. More important, from what you've told me, they talk to her. That's why I can use her." A tool. That's how he should regard Guinevere Jones: as a useful tool.

Russ made an unpleasant noise, the comment of a man who had never enjoyed a lot of spontaneous confidences from others. "Just see that you use her, and not vice versa."

"I'll keep her in line." For the sake of this lucrative contract with StarrTech he would learn to ride the tiger. Zac paused, aware of Russ inhaling deeply on a cigarette. Then he said earnestly, "I want to thank you again, pal, for recommending Free Enterprise Security to your management. Lord knows I need the clients. I just wish I knew more about computers."

"I can handle the technical end of things for you. I've told you, don't worry about that. It's just the personnel side that gives me trouble. If I knew a way to get these damn programmers to talk, I'd be able to solve the whole problem on my own. But if I ask 'em a question, they look at me as if their brains had gone as blank as a dead computer screen. I'm management. Nobody gossips to management. I just don't know if you can trust this Guinevere Jones to level with you, even if she does get some of the staff to confide in her or share the gossip."

"She'll do as she's told," Zac told him, wondering if crossing his fingers was unethical or demonstrated a lack of confidence. He did so anyway. Keeping Guinevere Jones on a leash was going to take some fast footwork. He didn't try to kid himself on that score. "I've promised her silence on our end if she helps us out."

"Well, I won't go to Hampton Starr with the details of her little scam until you give the okay."

"If she does what she's supposed to do in this investigation, I'm never going to give the go-ahead to turn her over to your boss, Russ. I want to be sure you understand that. I've made a deal with her. Think of this as plea bargaining or something of that nature. I'm more or less blackmailing her into this, and I intend to make good on my end if she keeps her promise to help me." There was more steel in his words than Zac had intended. He realized he'd meant what he said, and he wanted to be certain Russ understood.

Russ grumbled something that sounded uncomplimentary concerning the necessity of using thieves to catch thieves, but he didn't argue further. "I hope you know what you're doing. What cover are you going to use for hanging around Jones?"

"I'm posing as her current, uh, *significant relationship*. I believe that's the correct modern phrase." Guinevere had been disdainfully amused when he'd informed her of that plan.

"Her what? Oh, her lover."

"Yeah. I'm picking her up in forty minutes for lunch. It should all look fairly normal to anyone who happens to notice."

"I hope so. Management wants this matter resolved as soon as possible, as quietly as possible. Company image, you know. You've met Starr. You know how big he is on that sort of thing. I've got to run, Zac. We're shorthanded lately. One of my prima donna programmers hasn't seen fit to show up for work for more than a week. I'll talk to you later. Remember, I want to be kept up-to-date on your investigation. I'm supposed to act as your liaison. I'll keep Starr informed of progress. Just like old times, huh, Zac?"

"Just like old times." Zac recradled the phone and sat gazing out the windowed wall that revealed only the hallway and the row of offices on the other side. A salesman hurried past in the corridor, nodding aloofly at Zac before disappearing into his own cubbyhole. *Hell of a view*, Zac told himself for the hundredth time. Intimate. Pastoral, even, if you counted the time he'd seen someone carry a poodle past. He wondered what sort of view Guinevere Jones had from her office down on First Avenue. One of these days he'd invite himself over and take a look. It was a cinch she would never get around to issuing the invitation first.

He glanced at the black quartz watch on his wrist and decided that he had to work only another half hour before he could leave to meet

Guinevere for lunch. For some reason the thought gave him a shot of energy. He managed to fill out the entire application for a bank charge card for Free Enterprise Security before he left the office.

Promptly at noon Zac was waiting on the steps of the sleek high-rise on Second Avenue where StarrTech maintained its head-quarters. He glanced toward the revolving glass doors just as Guinevere Jones came out of the lobby. The sense of anticipation he'd been feeling for the past hour turned into a flare of satisfaction as he watched her come toward him.

Today Gwen's nicely rounded derriere was sheathed in a fash-ionable wool skirt that fitted better than the cocktail outfit had. On the negative side was the fact that it didn't reveal quite as much, he noted with disappointment. She looked very professional, very businesslike in the suit and leather pumps. Only the huge red tote seemed slightly out of place. Her hair was in its neat, braided knot, and as she raised an umbrella against the faint Seattle mist, Zac decided that no, she wasn't beautiful. She wasn't even outstand-ingly attractive. Nice eyes, but lots of women had nice eyes. He liked the animation in her gaze, though. Even when she was pro-jecting distinct antipathy, as she was now, she seemed very aware and very alive. Did she still see him as a frog?

A light rain suited the Frog, Guinevere decided as she hurried across the damp plaza in front of the stylish high-rise. Zac's dark hair was damp, and the shoulders of his dark tweed jacket were getting wet quickly. He waited, apparently oblivious of the weather, a solid, strong, monolithic shape in the middle of the grayed atmo-sphere. He nodded once as she walked toward him, and then he was stepping forward to take her arm in what probably appeared to others as an affectionate gesture. Only Guinevere was aware of the unnecessary strength in his fingers.

"Right on time," Zac observed politely.

"I usually am when someone else is picking up the tab for lunch. Where are we going?"

"Are you a big eater?" he asked warily.

"When someone else is paying for my food, yes." She smiled mockingly.

Zac sighed as he guided her across the street. "How about the place on the corner?"

"It's a hamburger joint. I refuse to play stoolie over a hamburger. I place a higher value on my personal sense of integrity than that."

"I see. Well, in that case, I guess I could go for the new oyster bar down on the wharf."

"Try again. I hate raw oysters. Besides, they're too cheap."

He slanted her an assessing glance. "The Italian place on First?"

"Sounds great."

"Try to keep the price tag on your integrity within reason, okay? I haven't convinced the bank to give me a charge card for the business yet."

"Really? How unfortunate. I got one two months ago. Perhaps the bank has learned about your rather unusual business practices. Blackmailing people into working for you might still be frowned upon in some circles."

Twenty minutes later she had managed by dint of careful ordering to drive the price of her personal sense of integrity well over thirty-five dollars. The Frog watched in stoic horror as she munched her way through a spinach salad, tortellini in basil sauce, hot rolls, espresso, and a spectacular walnut tart. The sight seemed to affect Zac's appetite, Guinevere noticed toward the end of the meal. He had barely touched the small pâté sandwich he'd ordered.

"Aren't you hungry?" she asked, trying to pretend concern.

"Not nearly as hungry as you are apparently."

She grinned. "Be grateful. The only reason I didn't order wine is that I think it makes a bad impression to come back from lunch with alcohol on one's breath. The image, you know."

"I'm well aware of the importance of maintaining the image."

Zac regarded the remains of her meal with a brooding expression. "I'm going to expect a fairly extensive report after all this."

"Don't hold your breath. I've been there only one morning. Spent most of the time finding out what's happened to the others during the months since I last worked for StarrTech. Catching up on office gossip. Have to lay the groundwork, you know. Can't rush this snitching business."

"Is that how you see yourself? A snitch?"

"Snitch, informant, stool pigeon, spy, whistle-blower, tattletale, squealer—"

"All right, all right." He held up a hand in disgust. "I get the picture. You don't see yourself as a female James Bond."

"Nothing that glamorous. I can tell you right off that my heart isn't in this, in case you haven't noticed. I've been drafted, remember? My personal feeling is that anyone who's found a way to rip off StarrTech should be quietly applauded, not exposed."

He looked at her with sudden thoughtfulness. "Why do you hate that company so much? Working there a few months ago was just another short-term contract for Camelot Services, wasn't it? Why did you risk so much to try to take them for a measly ten thousand dollars? Cash flow problem?"

Guinevere didn't look at him. She polished off the last of her walnut tart and then waved the fork significantly in the air. "Our deal last night did not require me to make a confession or provide any details of my relationship with StarrTech. You learned enough to blackmail me. Don't expect me to add any more information voluntarily. God knows what you'd do with further gory details."

"Are the further details that gory?"

"Forget it. I think I'll have another cup of espresso."

"There aren't any free refills on the espresso." He narrowed his eyes. "Only on the regular coffee. A second cup of the fancy stuff will cost five bucks."

"Why do you think I ordered espresso?" She beckoned the

waitress by raising the small coffee cup while Zac continued to eye the situation with brooding impatience. "Don't worry," Guinevere said blithely as the waitress took the cup and left the table, "I'll get the tip."

"Very generous of you." He took another bite out of his sandwich. "Speaking of generosity, I understand you brought in a sack of doughnuts this morning?"

"Programmers and operators go crazy over doughnuts and junk food. I think their systems are evolutionarily designed for the stuff. Twinkies, cola, and chips are the staples of the diet, with doughnuts and assorted candy bars and ice cream providing other essential nutrients. Just think of it, Zac, the entire computer revolution is being fueled by junk food. The interesting question, of course, is which came first. The revolution or the junk food? Hard to imagine one without the other. One of the great questions of human development."

"Too bad you aren't willing to dine on food from a machine. It would have cost a lot less than this place." Morosely he shoved aside his plate and folded his arms on the table. "Okay, you've had your feast. Let me have my first report."

"I've told you. There's really nothing to report yet. Zac, I've been back only a few hours. I'm still catching up on news."

"What news?"

"Well, Liz had her baby; a little girl. Jackson is still looking for another job and is beginning to get restless. Larry Hixon is back from vacation and feeling depressed—"

"Why?"

Guinevere shrugged. "Because his friend Cal hasn't been in to work for almost a week. He took off while Larry was on vacation and hasn't returned."

"So why does that depress Hixon?"

She groaned. "Zac, they're friends, and they've been working on a secret project."

"Secret project!"

Guinevere laughed at his astounded expression. "Don't get excited, Zac. Larry and Cal were secretly designing a computer game. Larry's been anxious for Cal to get back to work so they can finish it. The idea is to sell it to a software firm that will market it to all the kids in the nation who have their own home computers. Larry and Cal have plans to retire early on the proceeds."

"So why is it a secret?" Zac asked pointedly.

She explained painstakingly. "Because when they hired on at StarrTech, both Larry and Cal had to sign one of those cute little papers that say anything they invent on the job automatically becomes the property of StarrTech."

"Standard employment forms."

"Exactly. But neither Larry nor Cal has any intention of giving StarrTech rights to their new game. Why should they? StarrTech specializes in the manufacture and marketing of communication and test equipment, not children's games. Relax, this is no earthshaking conspiracy. Furthermore," Guinevere said coolly, "if you tell Elfstrom about the game, I will personally take pains to screw up your big investigation."

"I'm supposed to be the one threatening you if you'll recall." Zac paused as the waitress returned with the espresso.

"I haven't forgotten. But somehow I don't think you'll turn in Larry and Cal. They're not big enough fish, are they?"

Zac tilted his head thoughtfully. "Not unless they're the ones responsible for the missing shipments of test equipment."

Guinevere frowned. "They aren't."

"How can you be sure? They're in the right place to organize that kind of scam. They have access to the computerized shipping program, the accounting programs, the payroll programs, and the scheduling program. They could do all sorts of neat tricks."

"So could a lot of other people. Almost anyone could get into the computer room after hours."

"From what Russ has told me," Zac said, "it takes someone who knows what he's doing. From what we can piece together it looks like the day before a marked shipment is due to go out, someone issues address instructions via the computer and then goes back in and erases the instructions after the stuff has left the loading dock. There's no record left. The packing and shipping people just follow orders on the computerized forms they get with each shipment. The whole process is automated. Neat, simple, cost-effective. And almost nothing left in the way of a paper trail."

"StarrTech makes thousands of shipments a year. How did anyone even realize a few of the shipments were going astray?" Guinevere asked.

"A new inventory control program apparently turned up some discrepancies. Small differences the old program would never have caught. Some guy in accounting discovered them and brought them to Russ's attention. Russ told Hampton Starr what was happening."

"And Starr hired you to ask some discreet questions."

"Speaking of questions," Zac interrupted, "I've been curious about something."

"You're curious about a great many things," she said complainingly.

"I know, but this relates to you."

"I was afraid of that." She picked up the hot espresso cup and waited with a resigned expression. "What now?"

"You don't really know much about computers, do you? I mean, the work you do in the department is largely clerical."

"True. Most temporary help work is clerical. I'm terrific at typing and answering phones. Probably missed my calling. Could have been a full-time receptionist. Instead, I blew it and became a big-time industrial spy."

He moved his hand slightly, cutting off the sarcasm. "If you don't know much about computers, how did you manage the little trick you pulled on StarrTech? You drained ten thousand dollars out of the benefits program without anyone's realizing what had happened for months. Russ said if he hadn't been tearing things apart looking for answers to the missing shipments, he wouldn't ever have stumbled across your little project."

She smiled brilliantly. "I'm a quick study."

Which, translated, Zac knew, meant he wasn't going to get any more out of her on that score. Later, he promised himself. He was a patient man. Some even said he was on the slow side. But eventually he always got where he was going. One of these days he would answer the questions he was formulating on the subject of Guinevere Jones.

As far as Guinevere was concerned, the man could drown in his own curiosity. *Let him guess forever*, she thought. *Damned if I'll help him.* She had little enough as it was with which to retaliate against the man who was blackmailing her. Making him shell out for an expensive meal hardly counted as real vengeance.

The note waiting on her desk after lunch was predictable enough. She frequently heard from her sister during working hours. It didn't matter how many times she told Carla to call only in the event of a genuine emergency. That logic floundered because nearly every new development in Carla's life these days constituted an emergency. Glancing at the clock, Guinevere decided she had a few minutes left on her lunch hour, so reluctantly she dialed Carla's apartment.

"Carla? I got your message—"

"Oh, my God, Gwen, she's cutting off the Valium! I'll die. I will just lay down and die!"

"Carla, please. Calm down. I don't understand." But Guinevere was very much afraid she did comprehend. Completely. This was not going to be the kind of news she needed just now.

"You've got to talk to her, Gwen." Her sister's soft, husky voice was filled with despair and a threat of tears. "Explain to her that it's just too soon. I'm not ready for this. Gwen, you know I'm not ready. I'll really fall apart." Her tone took on aspects of a wail. "I can't handle it, Gwen!"

"Carla, listen to me. I'm sure Dr. Estabrook knows what she's doing. She's a very competent psychiatrist. You've told me you trust her—"

"It was all your idea to pick a woman therapist! You said she'd understand, but she doesn't, Gwen. She just doesn't know how hard this has been on me. She's trying to make me go cold turkey!"

Guinevere took a firm grip on her shaky temper. "Carla, this is my lunch hour, and it's almost gone. I'm not in the office. I'm at a client's. I have to watch this sort of thing. You know that. It's not good for a temp to be seen spending too much time on the client's phone. Now just calm down and wait until this evening. I'll talk to you then."

"Call her, Gwen. She'll listen to you. Please, call her for me. I just want one more renewal on the prescription. Is that too much to ask?"

"Dr. Estabrook obviously thinks so." But she'd heard the broken sound in her sister's words and was worried.

"Dr. Estabrook is some sort of radical feminist! She thinks all women should abandon men and live like amazons or something!"

Guinevere groaned. "Carla, she's a happily married woman herself."

"That's just it!" Carla replied triumphantly. "She tries out her theories on patients like me while in the meantime, she's got it all. Nice husband, expensive home, and a good career. I want to change psychiatrists, Gwen. I've had it with her."

Something clicked. Guinevere began to see where the conversation was going. "I don't think so, Carla. I think Dr. Estabrook is handling your case very well."

"Cutting off my Valium is not handling me well! Gwen, I want another doctor. I need a different one, someone who understands me, someone who is capable of some degree of empathy. I'm going to start phoning around this afternoon."

Guinevere shoved her red tote into the bottom drawer of the desk. It took some doing, but she finally managed to get the drawer closed. "You're welcome to shop around for a different psychiatrist," she told her sister very calmly, "but the only bill I'm picking up is the one from Dr. Estabrook."

A charged, furious silence greeted that bit of news. And then the phone went dead in Guinevere's ear as her sister hung up. Smiling wryly, Guinevere replaced her own instrument. Then, with five minutes left on her lunch hour, she quickly dialed the office of Diane Estabrook. She was put right through by a receptionist who knew her well. She ought to, Guinevere thought. It was Guinevere Jones's name on the monthly check that paid for Carla Jones's therapy.

"Hello, Gwen." Diane Estabrook's warm voice came on the line. "Heard from Carla already, have you?"

"How did you guess? Did you really cut off the Valium?"

"Of course. She's been on it long enough. We all know it. I started it only to help her get through the initial trauma. There was never any plan to keep her on it for more than a few weeks."

"I know you're right," Guinevere said. "It's just that things have been so much more pleasant while she's been on it!"

Dr. Estabrook laughed. "I can imagine. Things have been more pleasant for me during the past few weeks too. You should have heard the language in my office this morning when I informed her I was not renewing the prescription. But she has to take charge of her own life, Gwen. If she won't do it of her own accord, then we're going to have to force her to do it. She's become obsessed with that incident a few months ago. She's using it as an excuse for everything from failing to look for a job to chronic depression."

"All right. Thanks, Diane. Just thought I'd get the facts straight before I went home tonight."

"Yes, well, don't let her take it out on you, Gwen. You've got your hands full running your own life. Still paying Carla's rent as well as my bill?"

"You'd better believe it. It's worth every cent just to keep her from moving in with me!"

"Good. Whatever happens, I hope you won't offer her that alternative. She's got to be made to stand on her own two feet. Sooner or later you'd probably better tell her you won't be picking up either tab much longer."

Easy for you to say, Guinevere thought as she hung up the phone. For a moment she conjured up an image of Carla as a homeless waif, forced to seek shelter at one of the gospel missions along with the other picturesque Seattle derelicts. Carla might just be capable of acting out the whole scene for the sake of its dramatic impact.

"Hey, Gwen, any doughnuts left?" Larry Hixon sauntered through the door, tossing aside an empty can of cola.

Guinevere eyed him with an affectionate smile. "A chocolate one, I think. You're going to have to watch the calories, Larry."

"I know." He patted his stomach. "Programmer's paunch." He threw himself down in front of his littered desk and idly tapped a couple of keys on his keyboard. "I think I'm eating too much because of incipient depression."

"You should meet my sister," Gwen muttered wryly.

"Huh?"

"Nothing. My sister's feeling a little depressed lately, that's all. It just occurred to me that the two of you have something in common."

Larry brightened. "Oh, yeah? She into computers?"

"Unfortunately she's not into anything at the moment. She used to work as a secretary, but . . ." Guinevere let the sentence disintegrate. It was not a safe topic around StarrTech. "Still worrying about finishing the game? Can't you go any farther without Cal?"

"Yeah, I could, I suppose, but I didn't want to mess with Cal's end of things. This was supposed to be a joint effort, you know. He'd be pissed when he got back if he thought I'd gone on ahead without him. It's just that we were so close to finishing this week. I thought we'd be done by Friday. I want to get the program out to a software house. I'm sure it'll be snapped up right away. It's brilliant, even if I do say so myself. Now it looks like we'll have to postpone the big *Take This Job and Shove It* scene for a while." Larry exhaled loudly. "I'm really looking forward to that scene, Gwen. I have such fantasies," he went on dreamily. "First I'm going to come in real late that last day and wait until the Elf starts into his usual lecture on the unreliability of idiot savant programmers. Then, about halfway through, I'm going to tell him I really can't bear to cause him one more day of grief."

Guinevere picked up a pile of papers on her desk. "And then you'll turn around and wave good-bye forever, leaving him with that month's payroll half done, right?"

"Something along those lines." Larry straightened as his computer began talking silently back to him. "The bastard ought to be grateful to me. After all, Cal and I are going to immortalize the sucker."

Arching one eyebrow, Guinevere slid him a questioning glance. "How?"

Larry grinned evilly. "Know what we're calling the game?"

"I think I'm getting a horrible premonition."

"Elf Hunt."

"Oh, Lord."

Guinevere swung around to her computer and began the laborious task of inputting a six months' backlog of sales figures. It was the clerical job Elfstrom had assigned her this morning, and she was fairly certain he'd done it out of sheer spite. The monotonous task was sure to deaden the brain of one of the less advanced species of worms, let alone a human being.

There was a wide spectrum of jobs that needed doing in the brave new world of computers, and a lot of them lacked anything resembling challenge and creativity, advertising to the contrary notwithstanding. Many of the jobs were, in fact, just routinely clerical, the same as they had always been. They were also somewhat painful. Guinevere's lower spine already ached a bit from this morning's session in front of the computer. Russ Elfstrom did not believe in wasting StarrTech's money on computer furniture designed to ease the strains of his employees.

"You know, I'm really beginning to wonder what Cal's up to," Larry said wearily as he went back to work. "I can't even get him on his home phone. He's a natural-born loner, but sometimes he takes it to extremes."

It was another voice that answered, that of Liz Anderson, a computer operator. As she walked back into the room she swung her purse down from her shoulder. "Maybe he took an impromptu vacation after the last time Elfstrom yelled at him. Cal worked hard on that new inventory control program, you know, and the Elf didn't even tell him he'd done a good job." She poured herself a cup of coffee from the machine that sat in the corner, smiled at Guinevere, and took a seat in front of some printouts on her desk. "For crying out loud, you act like he's a missing brother, Larry. What do you think happened to him?" An attractive woman in her late twenties, Liz was still carrying some weight left over from her pregnancy. She stuck scrupulously to diet colas and coffee. She'd even limited herself to half a doughnut earlier.

"Maybe he ran off to California to join a commune," said Jackson. "He used to talk about how it was too bad he was born too late to be a hippie. I can just see him starting a whole new trend—computerized communes, complete with inventory control and automated donation-gathering procedures."

Jackson, an energetic programmer fresh out of college and still wearing signs of acne, had traipsed in through the door. He was unpeeling the wrapper on a Twinkie.

He was dressed, as Larry was, in a pair of jeans that were too short, white socks, sneakers, and a polyester shirt. He also had a pair of classic nerd glasses and the familiar nerd pack of pens and pencils in his left shirt pocket. He offered Guinevere a bite of the Twinkie as he passed by her desk.

"No, thanks." She smiled. "Had a big lunch."

"Cal hasn't run off to some commune, and you know it." Larry glared at his screen.

"Yeah? Then where is he? Visiting his mother?" Jackson dropped into his chair and stabbed at the keyboard in front of him.

"He hasn't got a mother," Larry muttered, hunching over his own keyboard.

"That's an interesting notion." Guinevere grinned across the room at Liz. "Are they hatching programmers directly out of computers these days?"

Larry glared at her. "You know what I mean. His folks are dead. He hasn't got any close relatives."

Liz made a notation on the printout she was studying. "Unless you count the rather unnatural relationship he has with his home computer."

"For Christ's sake, Liz, will you stop making a joke out of it?"

Liz tossed Guinevere a meaningful glance.

Jackson made a valiant effort to change the topic. "Looks like the snow in the mountains is going to be late this year. Here I am sitting on a new pair of skis, and the resorts are saying they won't be able to open until December."

Everyone took the hint and stopped discussing Cal Bender.

It was difficult to concentrate on the detailed work of data entry while mulling over her own problems, and Guinevere didn't make much progress on the latter. The shock of finding herself blackmailed back into StarrTech had faded, and with her customary forthrightness she was facing reality.

Several major problems loomed on the horizon. The first was her concern over whether the Frog would keep his end of the deal. He had promised her absolute silence on the matter of her computer tampering. For some odd reason she was inclined to think he'd stick by the bargain. Her short acquaintance with Zachariah Justis had left her with a strange conviction that he would keep his word. There was something about the man that seemed solid and dependable.

But what about Russ Elfstrom? What sort of relationship did the Elf have with Zachariah Justis? Apparently Zac was sure enough of the friendship to guarantee his friend's silence in addition to his own. And Elfstrom had said nothing about the ten thousand dollar drain on the benefits program this morning when she'd reported to work. That had surprised Guinevere. It made her realize that there must be an unusually strong bond between Elfstrom and Zac. She wondered what lay at the bottom of the association.

For some reason she didn't quite see the Frog and the Elf as lifelong friends.

The other factor that had her really worried was the problem of what would happen when Zac learned that Guinevere was probably going to be useless as a spy. She was certain that even if there was something highly illegal going on in this department, she wasn't likely to discover what it was.

After that her list of problems went downhill rapidly. There was the issue of how to handle Carla, keeping the Camelot Services office staffed while the boss was working at StarrTech, and, last but not least, dealing with Zac Justis.

She had been startled when he'd informed her that he was going to pose as her "significant relationship" during the course of her investigation.

"What's that mean?" she'd demanded warily.

"Guess."

"Oh, hell," Guinevere remembered saying. That had been last night, when he'd briefed her on the assignment. Today she had to admit the cover did make it easy to meet with him whenever it was required.

What she didn't like was the uneasy feeling it gave her to think of Zac Justis in terms of a lover even when the entire scene was a sham. There was something infinitely disturbing about the thought of kissing a frog.

In certain historical instances women had been shocked to learn there was no prince beneath the froggy exterior. Guinevere didn't like surprises.

CHAPTER 3

The small tavern just off First Avenue had been designed to appeal to the crowd that worked in the neighboring government offices and financial institutions. It styled itself a pub, offered an interesting selection of locally brewed ales as well as the imported kind, and featured a great deal of furniture that appeared to have been rescued from a 1930s yard sale. It was the younger, lower-level, but still upwardly mobile types who came in here after work. The older, more established executives who drank martinis instead of imported beer and wine and who would always view women in business as secretaries regardless of their incomes or clout didn't hang out here. They headed for the stylish ambience of one of the hotel bars a few blocks away. The pub was for people like Guinevere and Larry Hixon.

Guinevere hadn't started out to spend the after-work tavern hour commiserating with Larry. She had intended to spend the time trying to talk sense into her sister, whom she had arranged to meet in the pub at five. Unfortunately, as Guinevere walked in the front door and stood for a few seconds searching out a free seat, Larry Hixon's morose face was the first thing she saw. He was sitting by himself, sprawled in an overstuffed couch that should rightfully have been used to seat three people instead of one in such a crowd. Apparently Larry's brooding expression had been sufficient to keep would-be couch sharers' circling instead of landing. His eyes met Guinevere's, and he motioned for her to join him.

Stifling an inward sigh, Guinevere summoned up a reasonably cheerful smile and headed across the room. Perhaps she should be grateful, she told herself. After all, there wasn't another free seat in the place.

"Hi, Larry. I didn't know you were planning on dropping in here. We could have walked down from StarrTech together." Guinevere caught the harried waitress's eye and smiled. The waitress smiled back and mouthed "The usual?" Guinevere nodded.

"I felt like having a few beers," Larry informed her in a morbid-sounding tone.

"I see. No word from Cal, hmmm?" Guinevere knew very well there had been no word from Cal Bender. Larry had been moping about the fact since she had arrived at StarrTech days ago. Tonight was Tuesday. For the three workdays she had been at the company no one had heard from Cal.

"Maybe he just got pissed off and split," Larry muttered. He drained half the beer in his glass. "Couldn't blame him. The Elf has really been on his ass lately."

"You're probably right. Stop worrying about it, Larry. Cal will be back when he's ready. In the meantime, you're only going to make Elfstrom more irritated than ever if you don't at least try to look efficient at work."

"I don't give a damn what the Elf thinks. Let him bring someone else in to do my job if he doesn't like the way I'm handling it. I'd like to see him figure out the payroll program by the end of the week."

"Now, Larry, you've told me yourself that you need the job until you hit it big with your software game."

"Maybe I'll just take my chances and quit." Larry gazed forlornly into his beer mug. "I could finish the game on my own, Gwen. God knows it was supposed to be a team project. Cal and I were going to make it together, but if he's flipped out on me, I'll just have to think about going ahead alone." He raised frustrated, uncomprehending eyes to meet Guinevere's sympathetic gaze. "Why would he do it, Gwen? Why would he just leave without even telling me he was going? God knows he was never the confiding type, but to walk out in the middle of a business arrangement doesn't fit. Cal wanted to finish that game and get it into the market as much as I do."

Guinevere leaned forward to touch his hand just as the waitress set down her glass of California bulk burgundy. "Larry, you've got to stop fretting like this." She glanced up. "Thanks, Jan. Can I start a tab?"

"Sure. How's it going, Gwen?" The young woman who had just delivered the wine was attractive in an artsy sort of way. She wore her dark hair cut in a trendy style that was carefully designed to stay on the safe side of outrageous. Her clothes fell into the same category. In real life Jan was attempting to make it as an interior designer. She was trying to accomplish that goal in a city that was already teeming with designers. Hence the part-time job as a pub waitress. Jan had once spent a quiet evening in the pub explaining to Guinevere just how tough it was going to be to become successful. After that a limited friendship had sprung up between the two women.

"I'm surviving," Guinevere told her easily. "Things have been hectic lately. Have you seen my sister? She's supposed to be here by now."

"Nope. But I'll keep an eye out for her." From her vantage point Jan swept the room with a practiced gaze. "Looks like someone else is headed this way, though."

Guinevere glanced toward the door. "Oh, hell."

"Know him?" Jan asked interestedly.

"Unfortunately." From across the room Zac Justis saw her and started forward with unerring accuracy. "You'd think I'd planned a party and everybody decided to come."

She watched Zac's approach with a feeling of impending doom. She didn't know anyone else on the face of the earth who inspired such a sensation, not even her accountant. But there was something about Zac that gave her the feeling of sinking into quicksand.

She hadn't seen him since lunch the previous day, when she'd blithely informed him yet again that she had absolutely nothing to report. She'd tried to impress upon him the futility of the under-cover project while making her way through the most expensive items she could find on the menu. It had been hard running up a big tab at the pizza place Zac had chosen, but she had managed it through determination and attention to detail. It wasn't that she'd actually wanted to eat the extra-large "kitchen sink" pizza, a salad, and garlic bread. Rather, it had been an attempt to convince Zac that taking her to lunch every day was going to prove more than his fledgling business could afford.

Larry spotted the newcomer. "That's the boyfriend, isn't it?"

Guinevere blinked. "Somehow I never think of him as boyish."

Larry flushed, embarrassed. "Sorry. Have they got a good word for boyfriends who look like they're pushing forty?"

Before Guinevere could answer, Zac was upon them. "That's an interesting question. Have you got a good word for me, Gwen?" He smiled at Guinevere as he sank down onto the couch beside her. The cushions gave considerably beneath his weight, and she found herself tilting precariously against Zac's side.

"Nothing printable." She kept her balance with an effort. Zac didn't look as though he had anything resembling fat anywhere on his body, but he must have weighed a ton to create such havoc with the springs at the end of the old couch. "What are you doing here, Zac, besides destroying the ecological balance?"

"Some helpful soul on her way out the door at StarrTech obligingly mentioned that you might be headed for this place. I was very grateful for the advice. Otherwise I might have stood around in front of StarrTech until midnight waiting for you to get off work." The cool chastisement in his gray eyes totally belied the Frog's smile. Justis was not pleased at having been stood up.

Guinevere took heart from the small victory. "Loitering in front of a building until midnight is a good way to get yourself picked up on suspicion of prostitution."

As Zac extended an arm along the back of the couch, "Would you have posted bail for me?"

"Not unless I could have deducted it from my income taxes." Guinevere tried to edge away from the arm that seemed to be imprisoning her even though it wasn't touching her. "Zac, have you met Larry?"

Zac nodded gravely at the younger man, who inclined his head and mumbled something relatively polite before taking another swig of beer.

"Larry's had a hard day," Guinevere said dryly.

"We all have." Zac studied her face. "Speaking for my own hard day, I can tell you it wasn't made any easier by having my plans for the evening disrupted."

"I didn't know you had plans for the evening." Guinevere caught sight of a familiar blond head and lifted a hand to get her sister's attention. "It's about time Carla got here. Larry, I don't believe you've met my sister, have you? Neither have you, Zac."

Smiling with a mockingly gracious air, Guinevere used Carla's appearance to dissipate the thickening atmosphere that had arrived along with Zac. Carla's quietly tragic green eyes, delicately sculpted features, and well-proportioned body made her a very useful diversion. Carla was saved from the kind of perfection that terrifies many men by the sprinkling of freckles across her nose and an aura of fragility. She looked in need of protection and had looked that way since she was five years old. Even Guinevere, who had known her since she was born, still wasn't certain just how much protection her sister really did need. Some of the fragility in Carla was all too real.

Zac acknowledged the introduction coolly, his gaze speculative. Larry, still lost in his own pit of depression, managed another polite nod. Then he hesitated as Carla seated herself gracefully on the small padded hassock at his feet. "Uh, would you rather sit on the couch?"

"Oh, no, this is fine, thank you." Carla treated him to a grateful smile. She looked very delicate and gentle curled on the hassock. She was wearing a green silk blouse and a pair of pleated wool trousers. Her blond hair was parted in the middle and cut bluntly along the line of her jaw, serving as a subtle curtain when she bent her head. "You're a friend of Gwen's?"

"Yeah, I, uh, work at StarrTech." Larry fumbled a bit at first but seemed to pick up the ball quickly. "Would you like a beer?"

"That sounds marvelous. It's been such a long, dreary day."

"You can say that again," Larry said feelingly. He waved a hand for the waitress.

Guinevere watched the scene with a sense of resignation. Larry hadn't bothered to think of ordering anything for her when she'd arrived. He'd been too deeply mired in his own thoughts. She eyed her sister. "Just what did you do today that made it seem so long and dreary, Carla?"

"I took a walk along the waterfront after seeing Dr. Estabrook," Carla began wearily. She stopped and looked pointedly at her sister. "I'm afraid Dr. Estabrook didn't have good news, Gwen."

There was a moment of embarrassed silence as Larry and Zac dealt with the unexpected introduction of such a personal topic.

Larry frowned worriedly. Zac said quietly, "Your sister didn't mention that you were ill. I'm sorry to hear it, Carla."

Carla swung her wide, tragic gaze to his face. "I'm afraid my sister doesn't think of me as being ill, Zac. Dr. Estabrook is my psychiatrist. I've been going to her for counseling for the past few months."

"I see." Zac glanced at Guinevere's composed features.

Larry Hixon looked very relieved. "I'm glad it's that kind of problem and not a, uh, medical one."

Carla smiled sadly. "Don't you think depression is a serious problem, Larry?"

He nodded vigorously. "Oh, definitely, definitely. Been suffering from it myself lately."

"Have you really?" Carla looked immediately intrigued. "You must tell me about it. It's very helpful to talk to someone who *understands.*"

Guinevere knew the subtle emphasis on the last word was a small dig at her. She sighed, unaware that she had done so until Zac's arm slid off the back of the sofa and settled around her shoulders. Startled, she glanced at him. He smiled back blandly.

"I think we'd better be on our way, honey. I've got reservations for dinner, and we don't want to be late. You know how you like your food."

Guinevere, who had been so full on the two occasions when she'd had lunch with Zac that she'd been unable to eat anything else that day, glared at him. "I wanted to talk to my sister."

Carla looked up quickly. "Oh, don't worry about it, Gwen. We can talk later. Don't keep Zac waiting. Heaven knows you don't get out enough as it is."

"That's right," Zac drawled, getting to his feet and drawing Guinevere up beside him. "You should be grateful to me for providing you with an evening out. Just think, if it weren't for me, you might have spent this evening at home washing your hair or something."

"My gratitude knows no bounds."

But the muttered words were lost as Zac guided her away from the couch. Guinevere had a couple of second thoughts, then gave up and went along peacefully. There really wasn't much she could do. Carla hadn't wanted to meet her tonight in the first place, and now that she'd found a way to avoid the discussion, her sister wasn't likely to relinquish it. Her blond head was already bent solicitously toward Larry, who appeared to be equally involved in the developing conversation on depression.

"What's your sister's problem anyway?" Zac helped Guinevere forcefully into her red wool coat and then buttoned his own rather worn-looking suede jacket. He pulled up his collar as he guided Guinevere out into the chilly evening.

"A man," Guinevere informed him with heavy drama.

"She's seeing a psychiatrist because of a man?"

"I know it sounds ridiculous, but Carla's a very sensitive person. She was really quite devastated a few months ago because of— never mind. I'm sure you don't want to hear about my family's personal problems."

He considered that for a long moment. "Have you ever had therapy to help you get over a relationship?"

"Are you kidding? I'm a businesswoman. I haven't got time to wallow in melodramatic relationships. The city of Seattle is hardly going to sit around waiting for its business tax while I visit with a therapist. You of all people should understand that. You're the owner of a small business yourself."

"True. And I'd be the first to admit certain luxuries have to be kept to the bare minimum. The cash flow can get tight. Very tight. Sometimes just a couple of thousand will make the difference between staying in business or going under." Zac paused.

Guinevere ignored the obvious opening. She would be a fool to confide in Zac Justis about the ten thousand. If he thought she was going to provide him with an explanation for her activities in the

StarrTech computer a few months ago, he was sadly deluding himself. "Have you really got reservations for dinner, or was that just a ruse to separate me from Larry and Carla?"

"Why do you sound so suspicious?" Zac looked genuinely offended.

"Around you it comes naturally."

He shoved his hands into his jacket pockets and bent his head a little against the faint mist. "How about a bowl of chowder down at one of the places on the waterfront?"

"No, thanks, I'd rather go home and wash my hair. I knew it all along."

"Knew what?"

"That you weren't really going to take me out to a nice dinner."

"What's wrong with clam chowder?" Zac demanded. He was already walking her toward the waterfront. "Add a few crackers, and it's a meal in itself. Besides, we haven't got time for a long, drawn-out dinner."

"Why not?" Guinevere glanced at him in surprise.

"I've got plans for the evening."

"Include me out."

He took her arm as they crossed the railroad tracks and then Alaskan Way. "Don't you want to come with me to take a look at Cal Bender's house?"

"What?" In startled amazement Guinevere came to a halt on the sidewalk in front of one of the many shops that lined the waterfront piers. "Why on earth would you do that?"

"Partly because the only thing you've been able to find out while doing your Mata Hari routine is that no one knows why Bender hasn't been in to work and partly because I'm just naturally curious. Also, I admit I'm getting a little restless, and checking out Bender's house is at least a start. Gives me something to do."

"Sounds to me like a perfect example of the devil finding work for idle hands. Listen, whatever is going on at StarrTech, you can take my word for it that Cal wouldn't be involved. His whole goal in life is to strike it big with that software game he and Larry are designing."

"Come on, the best chowder place is on the next pier."

"Are you serious?"

"About the chowder or about having a look at Bender's place?" He sounded dryly patient.

"About the, uh, search. What if he's there? Zac, you can't just go into a person's home and—and start looking through his closets."

"No? People do it all the time."

"Not legally."

"No, not legally. You want large or small?"

"If we're talking prison sentences, I choose none of the above!"

"Calm down," Zac said. "I'm talking about chowder. Do you want the large or small size?"

"Small. I've lost my appetite."

"That's the best news I've had all week." Zac released her arm and went over to the sidewalk counter to place the order.

Guinevere watched him collect and pay for the Styrofoam cups of chowder. She wondered what on earth she was going to do now. It had never occurred to her that she would get this involved in Zac's investigation. Now that the possibility had been thrust upon her she was uneasily aware that she wasn't as averse to the idea as she ought to be. A strange curiosity was beginning to nibble at her.

Perhaps it was the natural result of being caught up in the situation. The questions Zac was trying to answer, after all, constituted the reasons he had blackmailed her in the first place. She was bound to be curious about them, and it was definitely in her best interests that the answers be found. When Zac had solved his riddles, she would be free.

"Do you have any logical reason to think that Cal Bender's

somehow involved in this mess?" She accepted her cupful of chowder along with the plastic spoon as Zac headed toward an open-air seating area. The half-enclosed space was filled with benches and tables and warmed by overhead heaters. Even though it was rapidly getting dark, sea gulls still wheeled and soared hopefully as they waited for the odd french fry or bit of fried fish. Sea gulls are not fussy eaters.

"No."

She eyed him warily. "I'm not sure that's sufficient grounds for searching his house."

"The first thing you learn in my line of work, Gwen, is that there seldom are sufficient grounds for doing things like this. If you had sufficient grounds, you wouldn't need to go hunting in the first place. You'd already have enough answers to work with."

"I can see there are several subtle nuances to be picked up on the job. Are you good at your line of work, Zac?"

"I'll find out when I file my income taxes at the end of the year."

"The bottom line." Guinevere sipped the hot chowder, aware of a sudden sensation of comradeship. She didn't like it and banished it at once. She knew she shouldn't allow herself to be drawn into the trap of feeling as though she had something in common with this man. "What did you do before you went into business for yourself here in Seattle, Zac?"

He slid her a curious glance. "Why do you ask?"

She shrugged. "Maybe it's just natural to want to know something about a man who's blackmailing you."

"I see your point." He opened several packets of crackers, pulverized them in one large hand, and dumped the remains into his soup. "I worked overseas a lot. The Middle East and Asia mostly."

"Doing what?"

"I was employed by a large firm that specialized in providing advice for U.S. companies doing business in other countries.

Hotels, construction firms, outfits like that. My business cards said I was a consultant."

In spite of her best intentions, Guinevere's curiosity grew. "What kind of consulting did you do?"

Zac concentrated on his soup. "I was supposed to analyze and assess security needs. Make recommendations. That kind of thing."

"Why aren't you still doing it?"

"Got tired of all the traveling. And I guess I got tired of working for someone else." He turned on her before she could formulate another question. "What about you, Gwen? What did you do before you set up Camelot Services?"

"You mean you don't know? Your investigation of me must have been somewhat limited."

"I didn't have time to do a thorough job," he said patiently. "I just found out what I had to know before I contacted you. I know you have one sister, your credit rating is good, and Camelot Services has been in business only a year. What did you do before that?"

"This and that." She could be succinct and laconic too.

"Gwen, I'm trying to make friendly, interested, comradely conversation. I know I'm not all that good at it, but the least you could do is encourage me. God knows you encourage everyone else to chat up a storm with you! Why not me?"

The harshness in his words jolted her. Thoughtfully Guinevere scooped up the last clam in her chowder, wishing she could read minds. Right now she'd give a great deal to find out what was going on in Zachariah Justis's brain. Something told her there was a lot she didn't know about her blackmailer. Perhaps far too much.

"Don't you think it would be best if we kept our, uh, association on a business level?" she asked politely.

He watched her in silence for a moment, eyes brooding and

speculative. "When you've finished playing with your soup, we can leave."

Grimacing, Guinevere got to her feet and tossed her Styrofoam cup into the nearest trash container. A sea gull that had been waiting with grave patience for the remains of the soup turned hostile as he watched the cup disappear beyond beak reach. With an angry rush of wings he hopped onto the railing and squawked his displeasure.

"She's not her usual friendly self tonight," Zac told the bird. "Here, have a bite. I know what you're going through." He tossed the bird a small piece of cracker. The sea gull grabbed it expertly out of the air and appeared somewhat mollified. Zac moved forward to take Guinevere's arm. "My car is parked across the street. Let's go."

"I was told never to accept rides with strangers."

"Sometimes you have to take a few chances in life. If you didn't believe that, you would never have opened your own business. You'd have stuck with your safe nine-to-five job with its group medical policy, company picnics, and retirement benefits."

She swung her head around sharply. "I thought you said you didn't know what I did before I opened Camelot Services!"

"I don't. I just assumed that like a lot of other people, you probably had a standard sort of job," he told her placatingly as they crossed the street and headed toward a parking lot. "What was it?"

She sighed, telling herself there wasn't much point in trying to hide totally unimportant information that he could find out easily enough if he tried. "I worked in an insurance firm. Before that I worked for a real estate development company. Prior to that I did time in a department store. Then there was the stint in microwave oven sales. Shall I go on?"

Zac smiled fleetingly. "I get the picture. Your résumé must look like a telephone directory. Couldn't hold a job?"

"I prefer to think of my past as a time spent gaining experience in a wide variety of fields," she informed him. "Very useful in my present profession. I can fake my way through almost any kind of job, and I can teach my employees to do the same. Most of the time all a client wants is a body sitting at a desk and looking efficient. That's easy enough to do for a short period of time."

"It looked to me as if you were genuinely working the other evening at the restaurant." Zac passed by a steel gray Porsche and a candy red Ferrari in the parking lot. He halted beside a dull cream-colored Buick that appeared to be about three years old.

"Sometimes duty calls." She scanned the unassuming Buick. "This is your car?"

"Afraid so. What were you expecting?"

"I'm not sure," she said, sliding into the front seat. It was the truth, she realized. She was still piecing together a composite picture of Zachariah Justis. "It might have made my first lesson in illegal entry more exciting if I'd been driven to the scene of the crime in something like that red Ferrari, though."

"The budget of Free Enterprise Security does not yet run to red Ferraris." He slammed his car door more heavily than was strictly necessary and turned the key in the ignition. "What's wrong?" He glanced narrowly at her as she slid farther into her corner of the car.

"Nothing. Just fastening my seat belt." The truth was she was feeling very crowded again. The front seat of the Buick was reasonably spacious, but Justis had a way of filling up available space. Guinevere made a small production out of the seat belt ritual. By the time she was finished Zac was pulling out onto the street and heading up the steep hills toward the interstate on ramp.

Darkness had settled completely over the city, and the lights in the downtown high-rises gleamed warmly through the persistent mist. The streets had emptied of the day crowd, and the first night denizens were beginning to make their appearances. The Buick's windshield wipers worked with stolid efficiency. A good night to be abroad with a frog, Guinevere decided wryly.

"What happens if we get caught, Zac?"

"We won't."

"How can you be sure?"

Zac checked over his shoulder before easing the Buick onto the interstate. "I wouldn't take you with me if I thought there was a chance we'd get caught."

"Thoughtful of you."

"I try. Relax, Gwen. The worst that can happen is Bender will walk in on us, and in that case I'm counting on you to explain the whole thing to him."

She whirled in the seat, staring at his profile. "Me! Are you crazy? You're taking me along to keep you out of trouble?"

"You're good at communicating with people," he pointed out.

She slumped in disgust. "I should have known. You're using me. That's what you've been doing from the beginning."

The line of his jaw tensed, but he kept his gaze on the traffic as he headed north. "I prefer to think of it as a case of your communication skills complementing my analytical talents."

"Bullshit."

He raised one eyebrow. "Is that an opinion or an assessment?"

"That's a sample of my communication skills."

Cal Bender's rented house was a small, aging structure of weathered wood set off by itself on an overgrown lot in the northeast section of the city. There was still a fair amount of vacant property this far away from the center of Seattle, and when she got a look at the rather decrepit structure, Guinevere assumed Cal must have gotten the place cheap.

"Typical hacker," she said with a faint sense of affection. "Puts his money into hardware, white socks, and junk food. Are you sure no one can see the Buick from the road?"

"I'm sure." Zac closed the car door. "Are you ready?"

"No."

"Good. Follow me."

"I've never believed in blind faith." She skipped a little to keep up with him as he headed around to the back of the house. Large, untrimmed bushes competed with weeds for control of the front yard of Cal's home. They also provided a lot of shadows. Guinevere tried to take advantage of the limited cover.

"What in hell are you doing?" Zac asked as he stopped and turned to look back at her impatiently.

"I'm trying to keep out of sight!"

"Watch where you step, you little idiot!" He reached out and yanked her off course. "Stay on the grass. You'll leave tracks if you get into that mud."

"Oh." Chagrined, Guinevere glanced down at the dark patch of ground she had been about to cross. In the dim night light it looked at first like a stretch of dry terrain. Then she saw the film of moisture. "Look, Zac, this really isn't my forte. Maybe I should wait in the car."

"No. I want you with me."

"But I don't know what I'm doing! I'm going to be more of a handicap than a help."

"Hush, Gwen. Consider it part of my blackmail demands." He had reached the rear of the cottage. A torn screen door hung limply on its hinges and squeaked when Zac opened it.

"Now what?" Guinevere eyed the wooden door behind the screen. "Is this where you show me your fancy breaking and entering technique?"

"Yeah." He held out a hand. "Got a credit card?"

"Are you kidding? You're not going to use my credit card for illegal purposes!"

"Gwen, I haven't got one of my own. I told you I've just applied to the bank. You said you'd already gotten yours."

Irritated, Guinevere leaned forward and put her hand on the doorknob. "You know what? Cal is very forgetful about everything except his computer projects." She twisted the knob, and it turned readily in her hand. "Just the type to forget to lock the back door." The door swung inward with a small sound of protest.

In the shadows Zac stared balefully at the open door. "Son of a—"

"Now what, fearless leader?"

"Don't look so smug. You've probably left prints all over the doorknob." He took out a handkerchief and wiped vigorously. "Don't touch anything else, understand?"

"Gotcha." On an unexpected wave of excitement Guinevere followed Zac inside the house. "Too bad we can't turn on a light."

"I've got a small pencil flashlight. Given what you've told me about programmer mentalities, I figure that if there's anything important to find, it will be around his home computer."

The route from the kitchen down the hall to the front room was an obstacle course dotted with candy wrappers, discarded socks, a towel, and several huge piles of computer magazines that were stacked precariously on the floor. The burst of excitement Guinevere had experienced as she stepped into the house faded into a more reasonable nervousness as she followed in Zac's wake.

The house smelled musty, as though it had been closed up for several days. It was also obvious from the odor that the garbage under the kitchen sink hadn't been emptied for a while. Then again, perhaps the homes of nerds always smelled this way.

The front room, revealed in brief glimpses under the gleam of Zac's small flashlight, appeared to have been done in postcollege-dorm decadence. Apparently Cal was still under the influence of the academic environment he had left behind only a year previously. Several advertising posters from software firms decorated the wall. The furniture was an eclectic combination of Goodwill discards except for the large desk that supported an IBM personal computer. It was a little difficult to spot the computer at first because it was nearly hidden beneath a maze of empty ice cream containers, magazines, operation manuals, and printouts.

Guinevere glanced around uneasily as she halted by the desk. "What a mess."

"Remember what I said. Don't touch anything."

"If you'd paid attention to those articles on modern management you claimed to have read, you'd know you're supposed to give orders in a positive, supportive manner, not a negative, bossy style."

"I'm still studying the subject," he told her absently as he scanned the surface of the desk. "Stay here while I take a quick look in the bedroom."

Zac moved off toward the hall on surprisingly silent feet. For such a solidly built man he moved very quietly, Guinevere realized. She stood in the darkness, watching him disappear, and came to the obvious conclusion that he'd done this sort of thing before. The thought was not vastly reassuring. She wondered why he had been so insistent on bringing her along tonight. Surely he could have moved more quickly and assumed fewer risks if he'd come out here alone. The small puzzle occupied her while she peered down at the shadowed desk.

There was just barely enough moonlight filtering in from the window for her to see a plastic box full of computer disks sitting amid the rubble. She was leaning across the desk to lift the lid of the box when Zac materialized at her shoulder. Guinevere jumped in spite of herself.

"Don't sneak up on me like that! You want to give me heart failure?"

He ignored the question. "What's that?"

"A box of disks. I was just wondering if any of the Elf Hunt material is stored in there. Larry has been sinking rapidly into a decline because he's had to wait for Cal to finish some piece of the game."

"Elf Hunt?" Zac's tone was sharp.

"Named after a close friend of yours, I'm afraid," she told him. "I gather Cal and Larry couldn't resist the play on Elfstrom's name. Shine your light in here."

"I told you not to touch anything." Hastily Zac pushed her hand aside and opened the box with the aid of the handkerchief.

The rows of neatly labeled disks popped into view. Carefully Zac began flipping through them, reading the titles. There were word processing programs, games, math programs, and several labels with titles in such obscure abbreviations that neither Zac nor Guinevere could guess what they meant.

"He's really into this home computer thing, isn't he?" Zac observed.

"Cal's brilliant. Don't forget he's the one who designed the inventory control program that turned up the problem of stray equipment shipments." Guinevere leaned closer to study the labels on the disks.

"I didn't know that. Damn it, Gwen, that's the sort of thing you're supposed to be reporting to me while you gobble down those expensive lunches you're conning me out of."

She tilted her nose, mildly surprised. "Sorry. Didn't realize you weren't aware of it. Does it matter?"

"At this point I don't know what matters and what doesn't. Kindly don't leave out such details in the future."

"Are you always this short-tempered when you're doing something illegal?"

With obvious effort he ignored the question. Instead, he continued to flip through the labeled disks. "Here you go," Zac finally murmured as he came to one that carried a hand-lettered label. "'Elf.' Think that's it?"

"Probably. Why don't I just take it with me? I know Larry would probably be glad to have it, and he and Cal are friends. Even if Cal gets back and finds out it's missing, he won't mind when he discovers Larry's the one who's got it."

"Forget it. We're not lifting anything. Our only goal tonight is to have a look around." With a grim snap Zac shut the plastic box and started opening desk drawers.

His authoritarian decision angered Guinevere. She was already aware of an unnatural tension assailing her senses because of the night's activities. Zac's short, crisp orders were not helping the situation or her nerves.

"I still can't figure out why in hell you brought me along. You keep telling me not to touch anything, and you won't let me take anything. For crying out loud, why didn't you just come out here alone? And don't give me that business about using me as a communicator in case Cal shows up!"

He half smiled in the darkness, bending over a drawerful of chewing gum packages, pens, and felt markers. "Haven't you figured it out yet?"

A new kind of apprehension made Guinevere whisper, "Figured out what?"

"I wanted you along on this little job tonight because it sort of cements our relationship."

She stared down at his dark head as he carefully flipped through a stack of folders. "Cements our relationship?" she asked ominously.

"Ummm. You're committed now, lady. You're an accomplice. I may not know much about management psychology, but I do know something about what happens between two people in cases such as this. They come out of the experience feeling they have to stick together for a while. A sort of partners in crime mentality. I wanted you involved, Gwen. Really involved. That way you're more likely to stay loyal to me."

It was probably the insufferable streak of arrogant satisfaction in his words that made Guinevere wait until he'd gone into the kitchen to check closets before she unobtrusively lifted the Elf game disk. She was very careful to shield her fingers with a tissue when she opened the plastic box and removed the thing.

It was no trick at all to drop the small object into her shoulder bag.

One had to vent one's hostilities against management somehow.

CHAPTER 4

The dark, heavily paneled hotel bar wasn't as cozily chic as the pub where Zac had found Guinevere the previous evening, but somehow it seemed more real in some ways. People here didn't play at wheeling and dealing; they really were wheeling and dealing. This was a place for refined, serious drinking by members of the upper echelons of the business class, both local and out of town. There wasn't a lot of lightweight beer and white wine sold here. The folks in dark pin-striped suits preferred real drinks: scotch, whiskey, martinis, and the occasional manhattan. This was a place to have *cocktails*: before-lunch cocktails, after-lunch cocktails, early-evening cocktails, late-evening cocktails, and anything in between.

The bartender had produced the tequila without comment, adding a side of lime and salt. But Zac wasn't fooled. He sensed that the straight tequila didn't fit into this atmosphere any more than it fitted into the yuppie bar in which Guinevere had worked as a waitress. This place might seem more real in some ways, but Zac didn't feel any more at home here than he did with the yuppies. He took a slow sip of the tequila and reflected on his fate in life. He really didn't fit in well anywhere.

He wasn't aware of feeling depressed or dissatisfied about the fact. He'd been living with it too long, for one thing. For as long as he could remember there had always been this odd sense of distance between himself and the rest of the world. His body had developed with a natural sense of coordination in high school, but he'd never quite grasped the concept of team spirit, so he'd never been successful in sports.

In the military he'd questioned orders frequently enough to earn himself a reputation as a troublemaker. He'd been promoted anyway but not into a position of leadership. An unusually perceptive commanding officer had seen the hard edge of stoic perseverance that underlined everything Zachariah Justis did and had recommended him for special intelligence training.

"You're like a dog with a bone, Justis. You just keep gnawing on something until you've digested the whole damn thing. And then you look around for the next bone. You need to work alone; you're too goddamned independent to be part of a team. But you're smart, and there's a certain ruthlessness in the way you approach bones. I think you're just what G group is looking for."

But he hadn't been quite what G group was looking for, Zac recalled wryly. Oh, he'd done all right for a while. The training had interested him, and he'd liked the prospect of being alone in the field. But in the military you never really were your own boss, regardless of how the system was set up. And once again he'd started questioning orders. Some of the bones he'd been given to gnaw inspired more queries than answers. And Zac was always looking for answers. But the military didn't always want all the answers uncovered. Zac and G group had parted company with a general understanding that he just didn't fit the profile of military intelligence personnel.

Life after that had not altered significantly. He'd had other assorted career opportunities, but although he'd usually gotten the jobs done, he hadn't always been thanked for the way he'd accomplished the task. He'd been slow coming to the realization that the role for which he was best suited was that of small, independent businessperson. Zac had another taste of the tequila and considered the fact that Guinevere Jones had been much quicker to understand her personal career objectives. She was doing at thirty what he'd waited until thirty-six to attempt.

That thought led him to recall the interesting little adventure at Cal Bender's house the previous night. The evening had been a revelation in some ways and a quiet affirmation of some inspired guesses in others. Most of those guesses had concerned the nature of Guinevere Jones. Zac's mouth crooked for an instant as he recalled the sense of excitement that had unwillingly emanated from her as she'd followed him into the cottage. He'd wanted to laugh at the time, but he hadn't dared. She would have assumed he was laughing at her when what he really wanted to do was let her know he shared the adrenaline rush.

Zac toyed with the tiny tequila glass and thought about how long he'd stayed awake after dropping Guinevere off at her apartment. He'd gone back to his own place and spent more than an hour speculating on the kind of excitement she would reflect in the heat of passion. His body had seemed tense and awkward for quite a while last night. The physical reaction was alarming in some ways. At his age he should be in better control of himself. But in other ways it had been curiously exhilarating. It had been a long time since a woman had affected him like that. He wondered if Guinevere had experienced any trouble getting to sleep.

Russ Elfstrom's approach through the shadowy bar cut off further speculation on the subject of Guinevere Jones. Automatically Zac glanced at his watch. Russ was only a few minutes late. He watched his friend coming toward him and thought about how little Guinevere liked the man. Not unnatural under the circumstances.

After all, it had been Russ who had finally caught up with her little scam on the StarrTech computers.

"Sorry I'm late." Elfstrom apologized as he took a seat. "Got held up with a conference in Starr's office. He wanted a report. I told him I'd be able to give him a more complete one after I'd talked to you."

"Is Starr getting restless?" Zac considered that possibility. The chief executive officer of StarrTech, Hampton Starr, was paying the tab after all. It would be unfortunate if he got impatient at this stage. Very unfortunate. Zac had been counting on the StarrTech fees paying the rent next month. He'd even entertained fantasies of buying another office chair.

"You know CEOs, Zac. They're always restless. They want answers yesterday." Elfstrom looked up as the waitress floated past. "Gin and tonic." He removed a pack of cigarettes from his pocket and shook one out as the waitress nodded and disappeared.

"Well, he's going to have to give me a little more time. Jesus, Russ, it's only been a few days!"

"I know, I know. I told him these things take time. Don't worry, I soothed the savage beast for you." Elfstrom snapped the flame on a stainless steel lighter and lit his cigarette.

Zac smiled. "I appreciate it."

"No problem. He'd like a meeting with you again, though. And soon." Elfstrom coughed hoarsely and frowned.

Zac shrugged. "Okay. I'm always available to the client. But I thought he wanted you to handle the, uh, interfacing." He was proud of himself for remembering the buzzword.

"He just wants a field report firsthand. Find out anything last night?"

Zac shook his head. "It looked like Bender hasn't been there for about a week. Wherever he is, he's not sitting at home hunched over his computer. Does he drink? Gamble? Use drugs?"

"Not that I know of. Never saw any sign of it at work. You think he's gone off on a spree?" Elfstrom drummed his short, stubby fingers on the table.

He did look a little like an elf, Zac found himself thinking as he watched his friend. Always in motion, hyper, intense. "I don't know what's happened to him, and I don't even know if it's got anything to do with StarrTech's problem. Bender's house was just a place to start looking." You had to start somewhere.

"Yeah, right." Elfstrom nodded quickly, speaking around the cigarette. "I'm not trying to push you, Zac. I understand how you work."

Zac winced. "Slow and methodical, that's me."

"You're thorough. That's what counts. The Jones girl give you any hard info yet?"

Zac wondered how Guinevere would like being labeled the "Jones girl." "No. I get the feeling no one in your office knows anything, Russ. I'm thinking of pulling her off the case."

"You're assuming she'd tell you anything she found out," Russ said half-accusingly. "Personally I'm not so sure."

"She'd talk, Russ. She'll keep her end of the bargain, believe me." But Zac realized he wasn't really so sure of Guinevere. In the beginning the straight blackmail had seemed simple and likely to be effective. Now he had his doubts.

"Well." Russ hesitated and then shrugged. "Your instincts were always pretty sound." His teeth gleamed in a fleeting smile as he caught Zac's eye. "This is just like old times, isn't it? You and me sneaking around in some bar to exchange information. Been awhile."

"Do you miss working for the company?"

"No. Life is short, Zac. Too short to spend it risking my neck in some godforsaken, backwater country advising some fool U.S. firm on how to do business with savages. When I heard you left the firm, I wasn't surprised. I figured you were getting your fill of that kind of consulting too. A little excitement goes a long way. That scene in Tallah was only one of many for you, wasn't it?"

Zac didn't like to think about Tallah. "About Hampton Starr . . ."

"Yeah?"

"Tell him I can meet with him tomorrow. I assume he wants the meeting to take place somewhere other than StarrTech offices."

"Oh, sure. I think he's getting off on the idea of playing boss of an undercover agent." Russ Elfstrom chuckled in rare amusement. "He gets a kick out of slipping around. Usually he has to make do with what he thinks are secret rendezvous with his little female conquests. This game is a nice diversion for him, I imagine. More like the big time."

Guinevere sat in front of the computer in the StarrTech IT department and stared unseeingly at the screen. She made no pretense of trying to continue with her input work. She had a far more worrisome problem on her mind than Elfstrom breathing down her neck. As of this afternoon there would be no one available to cover the offices of Camelot Services. Any potential client who called would get only the answering service. People didn't like answering services when they were in a hurry.

Guinevere had been quietly panicking since last night when she'd learned that Marilyn, her temporary assistant, would be unable to work longer than another half day. Damn Zachariah Justis and his strong-arm employment methods! She hadn't seen him since the night before last. That was the evening he'd fed her cheap chowder and made her a partner in crime. She shuddered.

There was no alternative. She would have to phone his office and inform him that she had to handle her own business affairs first. That meant leaving StarrTech at noon and not returning until she could figure out another way to install someone in the offices of Camelot Services. The nagging fear she felt as she thought about her deserted office was more than sufficient to keep her from doing Russ Elfstrom's stupid inputting.

"Hey, Gwen! How's it going?"

With a small shake of her head she pulled herself back to her current situation and turned to smile absently at Larry Hixon. He was sauntering into the office fifteen minutes late, but he was still way ahead of Jackson. Liz was down the hall meeting with a department secretary who wanted to schedule some work. Until Larry's arrival Guinevere had been alone in the office, free to panic in solitude.

"Hi, Larry. Get a chance to look at that disk?"

"I took it home with me last night and started checking it out. I owe you, Gwen. I was going buggy wondering what Cal had been doing to the game. I'm still going buggy wondering where Cal is, but at least I've got his work."

"Had he made great strides forward?" she asked teasingly.

Larry frowned. "No, but from what I've been able to tell so far, he's made some changes in the basic strategy of the game. I don't know why he messed around with that end of things. He was supposed to be working on the graphics. Tonight I'm going to load the thing and play it from scratch just to see what he's been up to. I can't believe you just went out to his place and picked up the game disk," he added admiringly.

"I was curious to see if he was home but just not answering his phone." The lie came easily, more easily than it probably should have, Guinevere realized. She was a little better at it than she felt she ought to have been. "When I found the back door open, I just walked in and looked around. The disk was labeled and lying near the computer. I couldn't resist picking it up for you. But don't tell anyone, okay?"

"Who am I going to tell? No one except you and Jackson and Liz knows I'm working on Elf Hunt. And I don't see any need to tell Jackson and Liz about your light-fingered tendencies!" Larry grinned malevolently as he dropped into his chair and switched on the computer.

"Larry, don't you dare call me light-fingered! If Cal gets mad when he returns, I expect you to get me off the hook."

"You know Cal. He never gets mad. He just gets more serious. He'll understand." Larry got back up out of his chair and poured himself a cup of coffee. He dropped enough sugar into the cup to make coffee-flavored fudge and asked with suspicious nonchalance, "How's your sister?"

"Fine." Her answer was rather short, but Guinevere couldn't help it. She had too many other problems on her mind. She didn't need any reminders of Carla's continuing depression.

"She and I had a long talk that night at the pub after you left with what's-his-face."

"Did you?"

Larry shook his head woefully. "Sounds like she's been through a lot lately."

"I'm sure she enjoyed telling you all about her hard life."

Larry seemed not to hear the sarcasm. "She really was nice, Gwen. I talked a lot myself. Told her about my plans for the future and stuff. I really felt down that evening. She seemed to understand."

"I'm sure she did."

"Too bad she's so bored."

Guinevere's head came up. "Bored?" she repeated carefully.

"Yeah. Sounds like she hasn't got anything to do all day long. Said she's been too depressed to work. But I've been thinking, Gwen. Sometimes it helps to work when you're feeling down. Know what I mean?"

Guinevere blinked, assimilating that bit of wisdom. "I know what you mean."

"But I guess she's just not up to all the drudgery of job hunting. That can be pretty depressing in itself, she told me."

Guinevere let the various and sundry lights flick on in her

beleaguered brain. "Not," she said slowly, "if there's a ready-made job just sitting there waiting for you to take charge."

Larry chuckled wryly. "How many jobs do you know that are just sitting out there waiting for someone? Oh, maybe us computer types have it fairly easy, but everyone else really has to bust his buns to find work these days."

"I just happen to know of one position available. Larry, would you mind if I used your name in vain?"

"Huh?"

"Never mind. Watch the hall, I've got to make a phone call. Let me know if you see the Elf on the horizon."

"He's easy to spot at a distance." Larry grinned. "Fluorescent light reflects real well off his bald head." He leaned out into the hall.

Guinevere pulled the phone toward her and quickly dialed her sister's number. She wasn't surprised when Carla's sleep-laden voice answered after several rings. Carla had been sleeping a lot lately.

"Carla? It's Gwen. Listen, I can't talk long, but I've just been having a fascinating discussion with Larry, and he's had an absolutely brilliant idea."

"Larry?" Curiosity and even a degree of genuine interest flickered in the weak question. "What idea?"

"Well, I was telling him how I haven't got anyone to cover the office this afternoon or tomorrow, and he suggested you could handle it for me." Guinevere held her breath, aware of the sudden, deep silence on the other end of the line. At the door Larry turned his head questioningly as he heard the heavily embroidered version of the truth. Then he quickly resumed his listening post.

"This was Larry's idea?" Carla finally said, sounding more awake.

"Carla, I'd really appreciate it. All you have to do is answer the phone and go through the list of temps to see who's free to take what jobs. It would mean I could finish the week here at StarrTech."

"I don't know why you're so determined to keep that contract," Carla said bitterly. "You've got plenty of others. And you wouldn't need to go out on the jobs yourself."

"Carla, please. I've told you this one is too lucrative to ignore." Yes, she really was getting fluent, Guinevere decided. The lies came more and more easily. She dragged Larry's unexpectedly magic name back into the discussion. "Larry thought it would be good for you to get out of the apartment, Carla. He's worried about you. This would be just the thing to take your mind off your problems for a while, don't you think?"

"Well . . . Did Larry really say he was worried about me?"

"We've just been talking about the matter. That's when I decided to call you and see if you'd do me this favor."

"Larry's a nice guy." There was another pause, and then Carla seemed to shrug. "What the hell. I guess I could go in for a few hours this afternoon."

"Thanks, Carla. I mean it. Thanks very much." The fervent gratitude in Guinevere's voice was not faked.

"Honestly, you worry so much about Camelot Services," Carla said plaintively just before she hung up the phone. "You'd think the business was your child or something."

Or something. On a wave of relief Guinevere put down the phone and turned to Larry. "Thanks, Larry. That was a great idea."

"You're welcome. But I'm not sure it was my idea. It'll be good for Carla, though." He straightened away from the door. "Here comes the Elf. Stopped down at the water fountain to pop one of those little pills of his."

Not only would working be good for Carla, but it was a darned sight cheaper than therapy, Guinevere added silently. She began to wonder how much longer she'd be forced to stay on the job at Starr-Tech. Zac was bound to realize before much longer that his stool pigeon wasn't learning anything important. Surely there wasn't much point in having her come back to StarrTech on Monday. Surely it was necessary for her only to finish out tomorrow, Friday, and then fade into the sunset.

Guinevere was astonished to realize that the thought of being free of Zac's blackmail didn't bring quite as much relief as she might have expected. That reminded her that he was going to pick her up after work. Unfortunately she wouldn't be able to soak Free Enterprise Security for an expensive meal tonight. She had to go into the office and work on her accounts. Having Carla cover the phones was only a stopgap measure. A lot of other things were quietly beginning to rage out of control in Guinevere's absence. She would probably have to spend the weekend in the offices of Camelot Services too.

The natural anxiety of an independent businessperson kept too long away from the shop fed on Guinevere's nerves all afternoon. The tension was broken once by a call from her sister around three o'clock. When Guinevere first answered the phone, she really panicked, afraid Carla had changed her mind, after all, about minding the office.

"Carla? Where are you?"

"At your office, for Pete's sake. Where did you think I was?"

"What's wrong?" Visions of irate clients and confused temps danced wickedly in Guinevere's head.

"Nothing's wrong except for the fact that your files are a mess. I need some time cards for one of your employees. Where do you keep them?"

Guinevere unclenched her fingers around the phone. "Top right-hand drawer in the red table."

"Okay, I've got them. You know you really ought to organize some of these files. They don't make much sense."

Carla hung up before Guinevere could explain that she had planned on getting the files reorganized in the near future.

By the time she was ready to leave StarrTech for the day, Guinevere could think of nothing else except getting to her office. She bade a hasty good night to Larry and Liz. Jackson had already sneaked out a half hour earlier after determining that Elfstrom would be tied up in a meeting for the rest of the afternoon.

She was hurrying through the StarrTech lobby, mentally outlining the things that had to be done at Camelot Services, when she nearly collided with Hampton Starr. He was striding briskly toward a silver gray Mercedes parked in the passenger loading zone at the curb, and it was obvious he and Guinevere both had been trying for the same revolving door.

"Excuse me," she muttered, and then realized the identity of the man she had nearly run down. Tall, with a wealth of prematurely silvered hair that matched the Mercedes, Hampton Starr was an imposing member of the business elite. He wore the pin-striped power suit with aplomb, and his handsome features were tanned to the proper degree of a healthy glow. That tan spoke of tennis and yachting in the summer months and European skiing in the winter. He carried his handsome head with the attitude of a king striding through his kingdom, an image that was fairly close to the truth. Starr ran his company with royal flair. He could be paternalistic at times, harsh at others. He was capable of great charm and ruthless discipline. He owned StarrTech and assumed, therefore, that he owned everyone in it. Fortunately the company was big enough that the average employee didn't come to his attention. For most he remained a regal figure to be viewed from afar.

Blue eyes that held all the arrogance and confidence in the world focused for a few seconds on Guinevere: the king encountering the dairymaid.

"In a hurry, miss?" The voice matched the rest of him, deep and resonant. "A hot date perhaps?" The blue gaze moved over her with swift assessment, apparently trying to determine whether she was the sort who had hot dates. He clearly expected her to be thrilled that he had condescended to crack a small joke with an employee.

Guinevere regarded him with cooling eyes. "Not nearly as hot as the one I'm sure you've got." She swung around on her heel and pointedly walked off to use another revolving door. She didn't look back.

Zac, who had been watching the near collision from a few steps away, hurried forward to catch up with Guinevere. "Hey," he called softly as he managed to slip through the door and take a proprietary grip on her arm, "what was all that about?"

Her head came around quickly, her face set in a cold expression Zac had never seen on her before. "All what?"

"That little scene with Starr." Zac moved his head to indicate the silver-haired man who was already sliding into the backseat of the chauffeured Mercedes. "I don't think I've ever seen you give someone the cold shoulder before, except for the time or two you've tried it with me. What gives?"

"My, you're an observant little investigator, aren't you?"

"Frogs have very sharp eyes."

Her mouth twisted briefly. "My opinion of Hampton Starr has nothing to do with your investigation. Forget it."

Zac thought about telling her of his tendency to gnaw on bones and then decided not to bother her with the insight into his character. He would worry the problem in private until he had the answer. "What's the rush?"

"I'm trying to get to the office. My real office. You know, the place where I try to make a living when I'm not being blackmailed."

"Jesus, you are in a charming mood this afternoon, aren't you?"

She came to a halt on the sidewalk, swinging around to confront him. "Look, Zac, I don't have any news flashes for you. Absolutely nothing happened in StarrTech's IT department today. Just as absolutely nothing happened yesterday and probably won't tomorrow. All that's being accomplished is a lot of inputting. Starr-

Tech is getting a lot of free work out of me while I sit there and have anxiety attacks, thinking about my own business's future. I'm bound to exhibit some resentment on occasion. Do you understand?"

He nodded, taking her arm again. "I understand. As a matter of fact, that's what I wanted to talk to you about tonight."

"Anxiety attacks?"

"I'm thinking of pulling you out of StarrTech, Gwen. You've been there several days now, and you haven't even picked up a glimmer of a rumor. The only thing you learned was what everyone already knew."

"The fact that Cal Bender still hasn't shown up?"

Zac nodded. "You confirmed that his best friend and would-be business partner doesn't seem to know where he is. That was an interesting bit of information. And of course, for what it's worth, you did discover Cal's remote connection to the inventory program that turned up the original discrepancies. But I get the feeling that's all you're going to learn."

She glanced at him suspiciously. "Does this mean you've come to the brilliant conclusion that I may not be a female version of James Bond?"

"It means I'm coming to the conclusion that there may not be a lot to learn in StarrTech's computer department. It was the logical place to start, especially since Russ was convinced that the missing shipments were being manipulated via the computer. But maybe it's time to explore another angle."

"What other angle?"

"Beats me." He smiled down at her. "I've been having some quiet talks with the people who work on the loading docks at StarrTech's warehouse. It's my job to worry about that, though. Not yours."

She gave him an assessing look. "I can see you making an impression at the loading docks." She smiled briefly. "You're being awfully generous and understanding this evening." Her suspicion and surprise were plain.

"Basically I'm really a nice guy once you get to know me."

"Says who?"

"I'm sure I could blackmail someone into saying it." Zac hurried her across the street and down toward First Avenue. "I've been curious to see your office from the inside."

"Why?"

"You're really in a confrontational mood this evening, aren't you? Maybe you need some food."

"Does the termination of the blackmail mean the termination of my free meals?"

"I think Free Enterprise Security can spring for a farewell dinner," he said.

"There's a great place out on Lake Union. Specializes in lobster. And it has a very extensive wine list."

"Are you serious?" He was going to miss her teasing, Zac realized. The thought made him restless.

"Unfortunately, no. I've got too much work to do tonight."

"Don't look so forlorn. I'll pick up some fish and chips down at the wharf and bring it back to the office."

She surprised both of them by saying, "Thank you," very politely.

An hour and a half later Guinevere leaned back in her desk chair and stretched luxuriously. Across the small room Zac glanced up from the business management magazine he had been reading. He watched the copper-colored silk shirt pull tautly over her breasts. She had discarded the trim suit jacket she'd been wearing, and her coffee-colored hair was straggling free of its coil. She was pleasantly frayed at the edges, and she looked ready for a warm brandy and a warm bed. He visualized her in a pair of flannel pajamas, complete with booties, and then decided to forget the pajamas. Zac was aware of an intense, almost overwhelming desire to be the one to tuck her in.

The remains of the fish and chips dinner had long since been deposited in the trash can, and he had lounged for the remaining time on the couch Guinevere had reserved for visitors. He had his feet planted on the coffee table, and he'd found himself quite content to spend the evening browsing through the magazines that had been stacked on the table. Once or twice Guinevere had asked him why he was hanging around, and he'd told her he didn't have anything better to do. It was the truth. He couldn't think of a single thing he'd rather be doing.

"How's it going?" He tossed the magazine down on the coffee table and folded his arms behind his head. His own jacket had been tossed over the back of the couch, and he'd loosened his tie before eating the fish.

"Not too bad, really."

"You sound amazed."

"It looks like my sister did a little work while she was here today. The time cards are ready, and the client schedules are all properly filled out."

"Is that so astounding?" He smiled at her look of incomprehension.

"On one hand, no. Carla used to be an executive secretary. She knows what she's doing in an office. But on the other hand, I never actually expected her to do more than cover the phones today."

"She must have figured that as long as she had to sit here, she'd put the time to good use. Be grateful."

"I am." The words were fervently spoken. "What about you, Zac? You must be getting very bored. I really don't need an escort home, you know."

"I thought we could have a brandy on the way back to your place." He kept the words casual, completely non-threatening.

With any luck she wouldn't see the hopefulness in him. Or sense the sexual tension.

Guinevere looked at him for a long time. "Are you really going to pull me out of StarrTech?"

He was annoyed at how easily she ignored his invitation for brandy. "I'll let you know tomorrow. I have a meeting with Hampton Starr in the morning. After that I'll make some plans. But, yes, I think I may set you free."

"And the Elf? He'll keep quiet?"

"You have my word."

"I don't see how you can be so damned sure of what he'll do," she said fretfully.

"He's my friend," Zac said simply.

"Someday," she announced coolly, "I'd like to hear the story of that friendship."

Zac felt the shiver of excitement and relief that went through him. It was the first time she had ever mentioned a future that even remotely involved him. "Someday," he said very carefully, "I'll tell you the story." He got to his feet. "Ready to go home?"

"Yes."

"About that brandy . . ."

She hesitated, reaching for her suit jacket. "I have some at home."

He let out the breath he'd been holding and thought about the first night he'd met her. "I remember." His hand closed aggressively around the doorknob, and he had to stop himself from slamming the door shut behind him too violently. The anticipation he felt was suddenly difficult to channel and control.

As she walked out onto the sidewalk beside him, Guinevere felt the strange tension that seemed to emanate from Zac's solidly built body. It fed her own uneasy sense of being at a crossroads. This was ridiculous. The relationship, such as it had been, was about to conclude. It sounded as though Zac had decided she wasn't going to be of much help in his investigation. This was the time to be slipping out of the Frog's clutches, she told herself firmly. So why was she inviting him home for brandy?

They walked the few blocks down to her apartment building in Pioneer Square without saying much of anything. She would not have made the walk alone at night, but with Zac as an escort Guinevere felt oddly safe. In silence Guinevere turned the key in her lock and let Zac in behind her. She tried to think of something suitably flippant and casual to say as she turned on the lights and found the brandy.

"Well, here's to my short stint as blackmail victim and undercover detective." She handed him his glass and raised her own in mocking salute.

Zac sat down across from her and warmed his brandy by cupping his large hands around the glass. "The end of what might have been a brilliant career."

"I doubt it."

He smiled briefly. "Oh, I don't know. You got a little rush out of that illegal entry the other night."

"A rush? I was terrified!"

"The terror's part of the rush, I think." He sounded as though he were just now thinking it through in his head.

"Believe me, I've no wish to repeat the experience." She shuddered delicately. "I'll stick to the daily terrors of getting temps to the clients on time. That's about all the excitement I can handle."

"Is that right? Coming from someone who was willing to risk draining ten grand out of StarrTech's benefits program, that's rather amusing."

Guinevere winced. "I suppose it must look a little as if I lack some scruples . . ."

"I didn't say that. It looks as if you've got some nerve. Just like you had the nerve to follow me into Bender's house the other evening. Here's to your nerve, Guinevere Jones." He took a deep swallow of the brandy and then set down his glass.

"Thanks. I think." She watched him closely, unsure of what was going to happen next. The tension in the air was rapidly turning electric. "Good luck to you, Zac. I hope you find your white-collar criminal."

"Sooner or later I will. Just another bone." He didn't take his eyes from hers. "But we're not quite finished, you and I, Gwen."

"No?"

"No. I said I'd make the decision tomorrow."

She nodded once. "Yes."

"That leaves us with tonight."

"Yes." Her fingers tightened fiercely around her brandy glass.

"Have you ever kissed a frog?"

"No. A few toads, I think, but no frogs." She was going to spill the brandy if she didn't set it down. Moving stiffly, she placed the glass on the table in front of her. The room seemed suddenly very close and crowded.

"Gwen . . ." But he didn't finish the sentence. He was already on his feet and reaching down to pull her into his arms.

Guinevere said nothing. She couldn't think of anything sufficiently brilliant or clever or witty. She flattened her palms on his shoulders, aware of the strength in him. He had his own unique, intriguing scent, she realized: warm; a little tangy, faintly musky with overtones of wool from his jacket. Not froglike at all. She lifted her face for his kiss before she could give herself all the reasons why she shouldn't.

His mouth was heavy on hers, surprisingly so. She sensed the urgency and controlled demand in him and was vividly aware of the way it sparked her own desire. Guinevere's fingertips sank into the nubby fabric of his jacket.

The large hands at her waist pulled her closer, testing her against strongly muscled thighs. Guinevere let her arms slip upward to circle his neck, and her mouth parted beneath the impact of his. The ribbon of tension and excitement she had been experiencing began to twist and turn around its own axis.

"Gwen, honey, you feel so good." His voice was a dark mutter of sound in her ear as he freed her mouth to nuzzle the curve of her throat.

She felt his hands slide down to her hips and curve over her buttocks, where his fingers flexed gently. She sighed, her lips skimming the line of his jaw, and then slowly, reluctantly, she pulled away to look up at him. She saw the question that was part demand in his eyes and shook her head a little. She touched his mouth with a fingertip.

"I don't think so. Not tonight. There are too many unknowns. Too many risks." Her voice was only a whisper.

"But you're a lady who has nerve. You know how to take risks." He probed the base of her spine, kneading the sensitive area deliberately.

"I think I've taken my share lately." She smiled tremulously. "Good night, Zac. It's been interesting."

"What's been interesting?" He looked half resigned and wholly frustrated.

"Kissing a frog."

"I guess I didn't turn into a prince, huh?"

"It doesn't matter. I wasn't looking for a prince. Good night, Zac," she said again.

"Good night, Gwen." He stepped away from her and walked slowly toward the door. With his hand on the knob he turned and glanced back at her. "I'll talk to you tomorrow. Lunch."

"To tell me I'm free?"

His eyes narrowed. She thought he was on the verge of saying something, but obviously he thought better of it. The door closed behind him.

Guinevere stood very still in the center of the room, staring at the closed door and wondering at the conflicting sensations pouring over her like waves. It would have been so easy to have him stay. And so very risky. What on earth was she thinking of even to consider the prospect of an affair with Zachariah Justis?

The ringing of the telephone cut through her chaotic thoughts. Automatically she went to answer it. The voice on the other end of the line was that of Larry Hixon. He was doing an excellent imitation of a nerd in the midst of an anxiety attack.

"Gwen? Were there any other disks near the computer?" he demanded agitatedly.

"What do you mean?"

"The disk at Cal's house. For Christ's sake, what other disk would there be? I want to know if there were any other disks that had 'Elf' written on the label?"

"I don't think so, Larry, but it was dark, and I was in a hurry. I may have overlooked something. Why? What's wrong?"

"I'm playing the game from scratch, just like I told you I was going to do, but it's screwy, Gwen. Cal has really edited this version, and I can't figure out why. We had already agreed on this part. We were satisfied with the basic strategy of the game. Gwen, he wouldn't have done this without a reason. Something's wrong. I mean really wrong. Either that or he's going to change Elf Hunt and market it all by himself. He wouldn't do that, would he, Gwen?"

"Cut you out? No, Larry," she said quietly. "I don't think he would do that. Can you tell me exactly what it is he's done to the game?"

"You'll have to see it for yourself. It's hard to explain. He's messed with it. For God's sake, I can't figure out why!"

A tiny flare of apprehension and excitement came to life in Guinevere's stomach. She remembered what Zac had said about adrenaline rushes. This was crazy, totally illogical. But she couldn't stop herself from saying the next few words.

"I'll be right over, Larry. I'd like to see exactly what Cal's done to your game."

CHAPTER 5

Guinevere found the house in the Wallingford district without too much trouble. She had never been to Larry's home before, but his directions over the phone had been given with a programmer's flair for accuracy. As she parked her small Laser on the street in front, she was mildly surprised to see that Larry's yard didn't appear as overgrown and weed-invaded as Cal's. But then Larry had always been the neater one at work.

It was hard to read the number on the front of the house because the porch light wasn't on. Neither was any other light, Guinevere realized as she walked up the shadowed cement path. It reminded her of the dark solitude of Cal Bender's house.

At the bottom porch step Guinevere came to a halt and frowned at the unlit structure ahead of her. It was nearly ten o'clock. Surely Larry would have some light on in the house. Granted, he might have forgotten to turn on the porch light or it might have burned out, but when you were expecting company, you had some illumination. Larry didn't appear to have turned on so much as a bathroom or kitchen light.

She had been in a rush since leaving her apartment. It had taken time to dig the Laser out of the apartment garage. She drove it rarely in the city, and it took awhile to warm it up. But it hadn't been more than half an hour since Larry had called. Why was everything looking so dark and abandoned?

A shot of chilled uncertainty went through Guinevere as she stood gazing up at the vacant porch. Memories of entering Cal Bender's empty house returned along with the knowledge that this sort of thing was easier to handle when Zac was along.

Guinevere took a deep breath and administered a short, pithy lecture on the subject of logic and keeping one's imagination under control. Then she boldly started up the wooden steps. Larry had called her only a short while ago. He must be inside.

The door swung open easily enough, and for the first time she saw light. It was the eerie glow of a computer screen in the corner, and it did nothing to reassure Guinevere. The small living room appeared to be empty. She groped for a light switch.

"Larry?" Her voice startled her by sounding unusually husky. She cleared her throat and called again. "Larry? Where are you?"

The overhead light revealed a reasonably neat version of a bachelor's living room. Larry was definitely not as sloppy as his would-be business partner. Here the tons of computer magazines were filed in bookcases, and the Twinkie wrappers were deposited in or near the trash can. Guinevere didn't even see any stray laundry lying on the worn hardwood floor.

There was no sign of Larry. The trickle of unease Guinevere was feeling metamorphosed into the first prickles of genuine fear. She was strongly tempted to back out the way she had entered, get in the Laser, and drive back to the safety of her own apartment. From there she could call Zac. Entering lonely, unlit houses was his idea of a hot evening, not hers.

But an innate sense of practicality sent her forward through the living room to peek into the darkened kitchen. It was a long drive back to her place, and after she'd roused Zac, she'd just have to turn right around and drive back out here. Besides, she told herself bracingly, what if Larry needed help? If something had happened to him, she shouldn't waste time running around finding someone else to handle the details.

The overhead light in the kitchen, once she found it, flicked on to reveal another empty room. Empty of Larry, at least. What appeared to be a year's supply of soft drinks was stacked along one wall, and there were dishes in the sink. The old-fashioned linoleum floor needed sweeping but wasn't nearly as far gone as Cal's kitchen floor.

The sense of emptiness was closing in on her, Guinevere discovered. It was becoming difficult to keep the fear from overwhelming the knowledge that she had to stick this out until she'd gone through the whole house.

It wasn't easy to push open the bathroom door on her way down the hall, but she made herself do it. By now her fingers were trembling. It was a vast relief to find the bathroom quite empty. That left only the bedroom. Grimly she made her way to the door, called Larry's name once more, and, when there was no answer, stepped into the room.

The sight of Larry's body flopped across the middle of the bed brought a scream to Guinevere's throat. In her sudden fear and panic the scream got locked behind her teeth and never emerged. Hand shaking in earnest now, she found the wall switch and held her breath as she turned on the light.

"Larry! Oh, my God, Larry!"

Part of her wanted only to turn and run. She never knew where she found the courage to go forward and touch Larry Hixon's shoulder. Guinevere only knew in that moment that one couldn't just run out the door in a situation such as this. One was obliged to assess the matter, determine whether or not any immediate help could be given. Then one called an ambulance and the police. One did what had to be done.

"Oh, dear God, Larry," she whispered. His head was turned away from her. Beneath the fabric of the blue work shirt he was wearing his skin still felt warm. Perhaps he was alive.

Frantically trying to remember her first-aid lessons, Guinevere slid her fingers up to the pulse under his jaw. It beat strong beneath her touch. He *was* alive. And perhaps not so badly hurt either. Gently Guinevere began running her hands over him. Good pulse and he was breathing. She didn't see any signs of blood soaking the bedding.

"What the hell?" Larry slapped halfheartedly at her hands and opened his eyes sleepily. "Jeez, Gwen. It's you. Sorry about that. I just wanted to grab a quick nap before you got here. Guess I really conked out." Stretching hugely, Larry sat up, yawned, and finally focused on her stricken face. "What's wrong?"

"What's wrong?" she echoed, her tone almost a squeak. "What's *wrong*? Good Lord, Larry, you just gave me the fright of my life. I thought something terrible had happened to you. The house was dark, there was no sign of anyone alive here, and that damned computer screen is just sitting out there glowing like a ghost out of a horror movie. What's wrong? I nearly collapsed into hysterics, that's what's wrong!"

"Jesus, Gwen, calm down," he said soothingly, getting to his feet. He yawned again and tucked his shirt into the waistband of his jeans. "I'm sorry. Didn't mean to scare you like that."

"Don't ever do that to me again!"

He smiled wryly. "Yes, ma'am."

The degree of her overreaction finally struck Guinevere, and she managed a weak smile of her own. "I'm sorry for yelling at you. I'm just not used to this sort of thing yet."

"Yet?"

"Never mind," she said quickly. "Tell me what was bothering you so much that you had to call me up and traumatize me like this."

Larry nodded, running a hand through his shaggy hair. "Oh, yeah. This way. I've got the game set up out in the living room. I was trying to play it before you got here. So damned frustrating, I finally gave up and tried for a nap instead."

"Why is it frustrating? I thought you invented the thing. You of all people should be able to play it." She followed him back down the hall to the living room and watched him insert disks into the two computer drives.

"I can get only so far and then the strategy goes screwy. Cal redid some of the crucial steps. He also reworked some of the graphics. But the biggest difference is that he switched the main character. Take a look."

Guinevere pulled up a straight-back chair and sat down next to Larry. On the screen little figures appeared. Behind them a cleverly designed landscape popped into existence.

"The idea is to steal the treasure from the evil elf who lives in Desolation Cave," Larry explained as he worked the keyboard the way a musician worked a piano. "There are all sorts of obstacles you have to overcome to find the treasure in the first place, and after you've discovered it, you have to escape the cave. This time the angry elf is behind you, springing all kinds of traps and sending monsters to stop you."

"And Cal's messed around with some of those traps and monsters? Made them act differently from your original plan?" Guinevere frowned intently at the screen as Larry made the small figure representing the player leave a castle and start toward the mountains.

"It's not just that. He's changed the elf character. Taken him out of the game entirely. The player is no longer trying to steal the treasure from the elf at all. It took me all day, but I finally figured out how to get into the heart of the cave. It should have been a snap because I did most of the work on that portion of the strategy, but Cal's set up a whole new series of traps. At any rate I got to the treasure this way."

He quickly manipulated the figure on the screen through a variety of lethal surprises until a graphic representation of a pile of gold and gems appeared.

"Now watch what happens." Larry made his character scoop up as much treasure as he could handle and start back out of the cave. Instantly a wicked-looking figure appeared on the screen, calling down a hail of poisonous arrows.

"What are those arrows supposed to be?" Guinevere asked.

"Acid rain. It eats away the treasure the player has just found. Cal wanted to put in a few social comments."

"I see."

"But that's not what's weird. See the figure that's supposed to be the guardian of the treasure?"

"Yes."

"It's not the original elf design. Take a look. We gave the elf a lot of Russ Elfstrom's characteristics: bald head, beady eyes, stubby little fingers—"

"Never let it be said programmers aren't people of imagination," Guinevere observed.

"Yeah, well, that character on the screen is not the elf Cal and I worked so hard to create. Take a close look."

"I see what you mean." Guinevere leaned forward to study the screen. "Beautiful graphics, Larry. Looks just like professional arcade animation."

"Thanks. But I didn't do that figure. Cal must have done it."

The figure pursuing the treasure hunter was not short or bald. Nor did he have stubby fingers. This character looked more like royalty. Tall, draped in robes with some sort of crown on its head, it was quite impressive.

"Okay, I admit it doesn't bear any resemblance to Russ Elfstrom." Guinevere tilted her head to one side and looked at Larry.

"The main characters in this little drama were drawn from real life. The treasure hunter is supposed to be a brilliant computer wizard—"

"Uh-huh. You or Cal serving as the model, I suppose?"

"Right. The evil elf was patterned on our illustrious department head. Liz shows up as a ghost lady who bars the way across a lake. Jackson is in here as a cyborg."

"I'm sure he'll be thrilled. He does have a kind of glassy-eyed look at times."

Larry didn't pay any attention to her comment. "If we assume that even though Cal changed a character, he would have kept to the basic premise of using StarrTech people as models . . ." Larry let the sentence trail off.

"Then that new character must be someone at StarrTech? Who would Cal use as a model for a king?"

"Who's the king of StarrTech?" Larry asked simply.

"Oh, hell. Hampton Starr."

Guinevere and Larry sat in silence, staring at the screen for a long time. Finally Guinevere asked, "Was Starr in the original version?"

"Yeah, but not in a very active role. He was the king of the castle. The one who sends the player out on the quest. I don't get it, Gwen. I just don't get it." Larry slumped back in his chair. "Why mess around with a perfectly good set of characters and a brilliant playing strategy?"

"I don't have the vaguest idea. But if we consider the fact that Cal's been missing for several days and that he left this drastically altered game program behind . . ." And that Cal had been the one who designed the inventory control program that had turned up the missing equipment . . .

"It just doesn't make any sense."

"I wonder if it might make sense to an, uh, associate of mine," Guinevere said slowly.

"Carla?"

"No. A frog." Guinevere made her decision. It wasn't much, but it was strange. "I know someone who likes to look into strange things. Would you mind if I discussed this with Zac Justis?"

"That guy you've been going to lunch with? No, not if he can keep his mouth shut. But why tell him?"

"It's a long story, Larry. I'd rather not go into it at the moment."

The working breakfast, as Zac had heard such meetings were called in business, had been an impressive affair. Hampton Starr had ordered a real power meal of steak and eggs, fried potatoes, and coffee. There was no sissy side of prunes or stewed figs. Zac had been forced to choose between equaling the macho breakfast or settling for a couple of poached eggs and toast. Not knowing which of them was going to pick up the tab had made the decision doubly difficult. He'd finally decided neither his stomach nor his pocketbook could handle steak for breakfast. When Hampton Starr had scooped up the check and announced that StarrTech was paying the way, Zac had had a fleeting wish that he'd gone ahead and ordered the steak. Opportunities such as that were rare. He realized how Guinevere must have felt when she was able to cadge a free meal off Free Enterprise Security, Inc.

But at least he had come away from the meeting with a better understanding of Starr. Russ had been right about the man. He did get a kick out of the corporate intrigue. Zac did his best to make his client feel as though he were masterminding a high-level counterespionage operation. He thought he succeeded to some extent. By the time he'd sawed through the steak Starr was looking pleased with himself. More important, he genially gave Zac the assurance that StarrTech had no plans to dispense with the services of Free

Enterprise Security. Zac relaxed a little as he realized next month's rent was safe.

After the meal Starr insisted on giving Zac a ride over to the high-rise that contained the office of Free Enterprise Security, Inc. Zac sat in the spacious backseat, enjoying the genuine leather upholstery and marveling over the built-in telephone. He wondered vaguely whether Free Enterprise would ever become successful enough to provide him with a Mercedes and a car phone. A brief image of himself sitting in the backseat of his own chauffeured car brought a fleeting, almost feral grin to his mouth. Then he realized that in the mental picture he wasn't sitting back there alone. Guinevere Jones appeared to be sitting beside him.

"I appreciate the update, Justis," Starr said easily as the heavy car slid silently to a halt in front of Zac's building. "Sounds like you're checking all the right angles. You saw nothing out of line at the warehouse?"

"I walked through the place earlier this week and asked a few questions. Told everyone I was a safety inspector. No one seemed to care how much I looked around or where I wandered."

Starr nodded with regal comprehension. "I see. Well, continue to keep me informed on a day-to-day basis via Elfstrom. Perhaps next week I'll want another personal report. In the meantime, remember what I told you about keeping this matter as quiet as possible. I don't want wild rumors leaking out to the stockholders. Not at this point. Bad for the image."

"I understand." Zac decided he must have done a fairly decent job of giving his presentation after all, even if he hadn't gone the full nine yards by ordering steak for breakfast. "Thank you, Mr. Starr. I'll keep you informed." He started to get out of the car.

"Oh, by the way, Justis, that woman I saw you leave with the other day?"

Zac froze for an instant. Up to this point the real reason for

Guinevere's presence in Elfstrom's department was a secret among himself, Russ, and Gwen. He didn't want to alter that. StarrTech was far too big an operation for Hampton Starr to know all his own employees, let alone the temporary people. Zac had wanted to slip Gwen in and out, no questions asked. Russ had agreed to go along with the arrangement.

"She's a temp who's working for a short term in one of your departments. We happened to know each other before she went to work there. Any problem?"

"No, of course not." Starr gave him a knowing man-to-man smile, the king sharing a bit of male bonding with a peasant, showing that on occasion he could be just one of the guys. "Merely curious. She and I nearly collided in the lobby, and I thought she reminded me of someone. What's her name?"

There was no point in lying. It might come back to haunt him later. "Jones."

Starr's smile turned into a brief grin. "Jones, hmm? You want to watch those Jones women."

"You know her?" Zac felt a tightness in his stomach.

"I don't think so although there's something familiar about her. But I enjoyed a brief affair with a woman named Jones a few months ago. She turned into a little tigress when the time came to break things off. You know how it is, some women just don't know how to take no for an answer." Chuckling richly, Hampton Starr closed the door and nodded to his driver.

Zac stood on the sidewalk, watching thoughtfully as the Mercedes disappeared into traffic. Then he turned and walked slowly into the building. There were three messages on his answering machine—all from Guinevere.

"Zac? This is Gwen. Can't you afford an answering service? Much better for the image. Machines give such a cold impression. Listen, I want to talk to you. Call me as soon as you can."

There was a click and a pause, and then the next message came through. "Zac? Where are you? This is important. Call me at StarrTech."

The third message was simple. "For crying out loud. Where the hell are you?"

Zac picked up his phone and dialed the IT department at StarrTech. Guinevere answered on the first ring. She launched into her topic without preamble.

"It's about time you called. Do you always sleep this late? Listen, I can't really talk here, but Larry's got something I think you might want to see. Are you free after work tonight?"

"Sure. I'll pick you up. What is it, Gwen?"

"Something to do with Cal." Her voice became a secretive whisper. He could just imagine her huddled over the phone as she finally got to do her spy imitation. The picture made him smile slightly. "You know that disk we saw that night at his place? The one labeled 'Elf.'"

Zac closed his eyes, afraid of what was coming next. "I remember."

"Well, I brought it back for Larry to look at, and he's found something interesting. It may mean nothing, but I think you should—"

Zac didn't give her time to finish. He exploded over the phone. "You did *what*? Brought it back? You lifted it that night? Damn it, Gwen, I told you not to touch anything that night. What the hell do you think you were doing? You little idiot! I'm going to strangle you! Of all the stupid, crazy things to do. Can't you even follow a simple order?"

Her voice became very frosty. "Well, if that's the way you feel about it, I suppose you're not interested in seeing the changes Cal made in the program. You wouldn't be interested in having it pointed out that Hampton Starr now plays a crucial role in the game—"

"Gwen, you're not making any sense." He'd like to get his hands on her, he thought disgustedly. How dare she disobey him like that? Did she think he gave orders for arbitrary reasons?

"I'll show you what I'm talking about tonight. *If* you're interested," she added far too sweetly before throwing the phone down.

Zac wondered if the magazine articles on effective employee management covered the problems inherent in managing someone such as Guinevere Jones.

It seemed to him that the rest of the day went by with excruciating slowness. Zac sat at his desk, wishing he hadn't had so much coffee at breakfast, and stared at the notebook in front of him. In it he had jotted down a variety of what seemed to be unrelated information. He tried to focus on the random thoughts and found images of Guinevere Jones flitting in and out of his head instead.

She'd had no business touching anything that night they'd gone to Cal Bender's house. But if she'd found something important, how the hell was he going to chew her out about it? In spite of himself, Zac had a strong sense of anticipation when he thought about this evening. This case needed something, anything, for him to start tying the loose ends together.

According to his notes, all he had to date was the fact that the thefts had taken place in the shipping system, Russ Elfstrom's suspicions that whoever was involved was manipulating the thefts through the company computer, Cal Bender's disappearance, and plenty of "Beats the hell out of me" types of answers from the people Zac had talked to at the StarrTech warehouse.

Zac's large hand fiddled with a ballpoint pen as he thought about his discussions with the warehouse and loading dock workers. A lot of StarrTech material was shipped through the major private carriers. Once a package had been put into the carrier's hands, StarrTech stopped worrying about it unless someone phoned to say it had never arrived.

Zac had explained that the other day during lunch with Guinevere. It helped to talk it out, he'd discovered.

"No irate clients are phoning to say they haven't received their orders," he'd explained. "There's no real way even to know which shipments are missing. It's crazy. If some bright-eyed wizard in accounting hadn't noted the small inventory discrepancies, Starr-Tech wouldn't even realize it had been ripped off."

"And if Cal hadn't modified the inventory control program in the first place, that wizard in accounting wouldn't have been able to make himself look so bright-eyed."

Zac's thoughts went back to that comment again and again as he sat staring at his small list of notes. Cal Bender's program had brought the discrepancies to light. And now Cal Bender was missing.

Zac wanted very badly to see what Bender had done to the infamous game program. Afterward he might still decide to tear a strip off Gwen, of course. That was his prerogative as the boss.

Guinevere knew Larry was nervous about showing Elf Hunt to Zac. But when she'd explained that he was quietly looking into Cal Bender's disappearance, Larry had relaxed. He was waiting for both of them when Zac and Guinevere arrived in Zac's Buick.

Zac had said little on the drive out to Wallingford. Expecting a lecture, Guinevere was relieved that he'd obviously decided to let the subject drop. Apparently he had more sensitivity than she'd credited him with.

"If what Larry has to show you seems promising, will you want me to continue going into StarrTech as a temp?" she asked as she climbed out of the Buick.

"We'll see."

She eyed him warily, wondering at the curtness of his answer. "I could manage another day or two. Carla doesn't seem to mind filling in for me at the office." Carla had agreed to hold the fort another day, much to Guinevere's astonishment. It had made things easier at StarrTech for her, knowing that someone was handling things at Camelot Services. With that off her mind Guinevere had found herself thinking more and more about the investigation Zac was conducting. It occurred to her that she was beginning to get into the spirit of the thing.

Larry appeared on the porch before Zac could respond. He had a large peanut butter sandwich in one hand and a can of cola in the other. "Come on in." He nodded toward Zac. "How's it going, Justis?"

"Gwen says you have something to show me on the game program you and Bender are designing?"

"The thing's been driving me nuts. I've spent every spare minute on it, and it's as though I'm having to learn it from scratch. Cal's changed all kinds of things. I'll show you." He turned to lead the way into the house. "You really looking for Cal?"

"I didn't start out to look for him, but things seem to be working out that way."

Two hours later Larry leaned back in his chair, frustration lining his face. "That's it. That's as far as I've been able to get. You don't know how tough it is to slog through this thing. None of the crucial turning points is the same as it was in the original version."

Zac nodded, staring thoughtfully at the screen. An hour earlier he had taken a turn trying to play the game under Larry's instruction. At some points he'd made a surprising amount of progress because he hadn't been operating under Larry's preconceptions of what was supposed to happen next. But neither he nor Larry got even close to winning. "Whose idea was it to use StarrTech personnel as character models?"

"Cal and I thought it would be funny. We figure no one's ever going to see the resemblance except us, so we won't get sued." Larry paused to jot down a few more notes in the tablet he had on his lap. He was documenting the result of every choice made while playing the game. He flipped the notebook shut and looked directly at Zac. "Gwen was telling me the truth when she said you'd keep quiet about the game, wasn't she? With any luck I'll be quitting in a couple more weeks, and then no one will be able to prove when or where Cal and I worked on the project. But until then I'd like to keep it secret."

"You think Hampton Starr would claim rights to it?"

Larry lifted one shoulder. "Probably not. StarrTech makes test equipment, not computer games. But who knows what management will do? Safest just to keep the whole thing quiet until after Cal and I are out of StarrTech."

"It's considered generally wise at StarrTech not to trust upper management." Guinevere got up from her chair. "Don't worry about Zac, Larry. He'll keep quiet." She was unconscious of the certainty in her own voice. "On to important matters. I'm starving."

Zac gave her a cool glance. "Is that a hint?"

"How about dinner on the way back downtown?" She could tell the innocent brightness of her tone didn't fool him for a minute. But he didn't argue.

They said good-bye to Larry, climbed into the car, and started back toward the center of Seattle.

"I was thinking of a rather nice fish place I know on the wharf," Guinevere began chattily.

"Uh-huh."

"You sound almost agreeable. What's the matter? Feeling sick?"

"I'm thinking."

She grinned. "Keep right on thinking. I'll point out the restaurant."

Half an hour later, well into her halibut, Guinevere decided she'd had enough of eating in peace and quiet. She waved a fork under Zac's nose to get his attention.

"All right, I give up. There's no sport in this. Like taking candy from a baby."

He regarded her mildly. "What's like taking candy from a baby?"

"Getting a free meal out of you when you're 'thinking.' No challenge. No fight. No spirit. It ruins everything for me."

"Sorry."

She made a disgusted little sound. "Forget it. Tell me what you're thinking about so seriously."

"Elf Hunt."

"What about it?"

Zac prodded his broccoli puree. "I wonder why they had to turn the broccoli into baby food."

"Vegetable purees are very fashionable at the moment. They add color to the plate. Forget the broccoli, and tell me what's going through your convoluted brain."

"The same question I had about the broccoli. Why mess with a perfectly good product and turn it into something else?"

Guinevere nodded quickly. "It's driving poor Larry out of his mind. He won't rest until he's worked his way through the rest of that game. You know what I find the most interesting?"

"What?" Zac tried a spoonful of the broccoli puree.

"That business of changing the wicked guardian of the treasure from the elf to the king," she said. "Larry's right. The figure of the king does have some Hampton Starr characteristics. And what happened to the elf?"

"It doesn't make much sense." Zac hesitated. "Until you consider the fact that it was Bender's inventory control program that was originally responsible for bringing the thefts to light."

"The next thing you know Cal's missing and all that's left behind is this altered version of Elf Hunt." Guinevere pushed aside her plate, propped her elbow on the table and her chin on her hand. "The guy in accounting wouldn't be a problem. He doesn't understand the computer programs inside and out. He just uses the results."

Zac looked at her consideringly. "But Cal Bender does

understand the programs. All of them. He could make those programs do anything he wanted them to do. And now Cal's gone. If
he was behind the shipping thefts and realized that things were
getting hot, I can see him skipping town. But why take the time to
alter Elf Hunt before he left?" There was silence for a moment as
Zac worked through a few more of his own thoughts. Then he went
on. "If we assume that when Cal altered the game program, he kept
to the basic theme of using StarrTech personnel . . ." His voice
trailed off again as he forked up a bite of his salmon.

"Go on." Guinevere discovered she was getting impatient.

"Well, maybe he did more than use StarrTech people in his
new version of the game. Maybe he decided to use a StarrTech
situation."

Guinevere slowly lowered the bite of halibut back to her plate.
She stared at Zac, fascinated. "The thefts?"

"StarrTech has tried to keep a low profile on the problem, but
there are obviously a few people who know what's happened."

"Sure. Russ Elfstrom, the guy in accounting who turned up the
missing shipments in the first place, a couple of vice presidents,
and Starr himself."

"With that many people aware of what's happening there's no
reason rumors couldn't have reached Cal."

"But Cal and Larry are practically business partners. If
Cal knew something like that, he would have mentioned it to
Larry. Unless Cal was guilty of the thefts in the first place. But
if Cal wasn't guilty and had a few suspicions about what was
happening—" Guinevere stopped abruptly, realizing where her
thoughts were leading. "Good grief! You don't think he left his
suspicions behind in the game?"

"I don't know what to think at this point."

"But why would Cal do it that way? If he wanted to confide in
Larry, why not just talk about it? Why go through all the trouble
of reprogramming the game?"

"I told you, Gwen, I'm not sure what to think just yet. I'm trying to organize things in my mind. Why don't you just eat your halibut and let me think in peace?"

"There's no need to snap at me!" Offended, Guinevere sank into a resentful silence, eating her way methodically through the halibut, the vegetable puree, and all the sourdough bread. She was considering dessert when another thought occurred to her. Her curiosity overcame her determination to keep quiet until hell froze over. "What about the king?"

With an obvious effort Zac pulled his attention away from whatever thoughts were occupying it and managed to focus again on Guinevere. "Hampton Starr?"

"Cal turned him into the evil treasure guardian. He's the ultimate menace now in the game."

"Interesting, isn't it?"

She glared at him. "It's slightly more than interesting. If we assume that the game somehow represents the StarrTech thefts, then Cal's reason for making Hampton Starr the bad guy is downright fascinating. Under normal circumstances he would have kept the elf as the bad guy. Cal really disliked Russ Elfstrom. Now the elf is out of the game, and we're left with King Starr."

"Yes."

"It doesn't make any sense. Starr is not exactly a sterling representative of the male species, but why would he be the bad guy in this? Was Cal implying he's somehow behind the thefts? The real source of the menace? If he was pulling a fast one on his own firm, why hire you? Because Elfstrom had realized what was going on and Starr figured he'd better make the appropriate moves?"

"I've told you," Zac responded flatly, "I don't know. I'm still trying to think."

"Well, pardon me for interrupting the natural flow of your brilliance. I think I'll have the chocolate mousse torte."

Something clicked briefly. "How much does it cost?" Zac remembered to ask.

"Don't bother yourself with such piddling details. Go back to being silent and brilliant. This lowly employee will nibble away while sitting humbly at her master's feet."

"That's an interesting image."

"Shut up and think, Zac."

CHAPTER 6

Zac remained immersed in his thoughts through the conclusion of dinner. He surfaced briefly when Guinevere waved the check under his nose, but after paying it with only minimal protest, he lapsed back into an austere silence.

That silence was beginning to bother Guinevere. She had never seen anyone withdraw so intently into his own thoughts except one of the programmers on occasion. Perhaps Zac was running a program in his mind, she decided with fleeting humor as she climbed into the Buick. Whatever he was thinking didn't seem to affect his driving. He guided the car back toward her apartment with an accuracy that was obviously second nature by now.

She wasn't certain what he was going to do when he parked the car, but it soon became clear he intended to follow her inside. Without a word he trailed upstairs behind her.

"Zac?" She fumbled with her key.

"Hmm?"

"Did you want a brandy or something?" She glanced at him uncertainly. "It's getting late. Maybe you should just head on home." It occurred to her that as many times as he had been to her apartment, she had never seen his. Brief curiosity flared in her for an instant. Someday she would like to see just what kind of lily pad the Frog inhabited.

"That sounds good." He stalked through the door and went over to the couch.

"What sounds good? The brandy? Going home? Zac, are you with me? Testing: one, two, three."

He turned his head to look at her as he sprawled back into a corner of the couch. For the first time Guinevere realized that the gray of his eyes reminded her of the color of a ghost. The thought made her strangely uneasy. There was a great deal she did not know about this man. Perhaps too much.

"I just want to think for a while, Gwen. Is that all right?"

"Well, yes, of course, but—"

"I seem to do it better when you're around than when I'm alone back at the office or my apartment."

"I had no idea I was such an inspiration." Guinevere tossed her oversize shoulder bag down on the nearest table and went into the kitchen. The brandy was becoming something of a ritual. She wasn't sure if that was such a good idea. Tonight she wasn't sure of a lot of things, including her own ambivalent feelings toward Zachariah Justis.

When she emerged a few moments later with the two brandies, he still hadn't moved. He had his feet up on the low table in front of the couch, and his eyes were half closed in deep contemplation. She wanted to say something flippant but changed her mind at the last second. Quietly Guinevere set his brandy in front of him, and then she took a chair. After a long pause, in which it became clear that Zac was not going to involve her in his internal dialogue, she picked up a best-seller she had been trying to finish for two weeks.

Time ticked past in the quiet apartment. Guinevere began to realize that the reason she had been unable to finish the best-seller was that it was intrinsically boring. Chances were she would never finish it.

Life in her living room wasn't particularly stimulating either. She glanced surreptitiously at the clock. Zac had been meditating for nearly an hour and a half. It was almost eleven. She considered setting off a small firecracker under his nose to get his attention so that she could tell him it was time to leave and then decided against it. She'd give him another half hour, and then she'd do something assertive such as kicking him out. Guinevere forced herself to go back to reading the best-seller.

When she glanced up again half an hour later, she saw that Zac's eyes had closed completely. He'd fallen asleep. Apparently the inspiration of her company had worn thin. His head was tipped back against the black leather of the couch, one large hand flung carelessly across the cushions. He appeared no less austere in sleep than he did when he was awake. His eyelashes were the only soft elements on the harsh landscape of his face. He had discarded the jacket, and the loosened tie at his throat gave him a rakish quality. With a sigh Guinevere put down her book and got to her feet. For a moment she hesitated.

She could shake him awake and stuff him into his car. Or she could get a blanket from the closet and cover him. The first choice was the logical one, the intelligent one. It was the only reasonable thing to do under the circumstances.

He looked exhausted, though, and she found herself reluctant to wake him. Where was the harm in simply letting him spend the night on her sofa? If he awoke before morning, he could see himself out the door.

Instinct told her that going to the closet to fetch the blanket was probably not an act of sound judgment, but Guinevere did it anyway. She tucked the edges of the red blanket around his shoulders. Her fingers brushed against the fabric of his shirt, making her aware of the warmth of his body. He didn't stir. Whatever he had been chewing on in his mind appeared to have zapped his energy completely. Either that or he had bored himself to sleep sitting here staring at her.

Guinevere stood back to examine her handiwork. Zac's feet stuck out beneath the blanket, but other than that he was nicely tucked in. She wondered what he would think when he awoke. Softly she moved around the room, turning off lights, and then she trailed down the hall to her bedroom.

It was strange for her to get ready for bed knowing there was a man sleeping in her living room. Guinevere considered just how strange that felt while she put her clothes in the closet and slipped into the comfortable flannel nightgown that hung from the hook just inside the door.

It was a myth that the average, single, professional working-woman had a scintillating, nonstop social life, an even bigger myth that said females frequently brought men home for the night. No one knew the truth better than the average, single, professional workingwoman, but for some reason the people who invented the myths seldom interviewed the people who lived the reality to check the veracity of the tales. The myths continued and the reality continued and rarely did the twain meet.

Friends and casual acquaintances of both sexes Guinevere had in abundance. But even though she knew that there was a shortage of eligible men and that she probably shouldn't be too choosy when it came to serious relationships, Guinevere found herself as discriminating in her personal life as she was in her career. There were worse things than spending evenings alone. Besides, Guinevere rather liked her own company.

So she climbed into bed and turned out the light and smiled to herself in the darkness at the thought of having an unreconstructed frog sleeping out in her living room. She went to sleep almost at once.

An unmeasurable length of time later she awoke from cluttered, confusing dreams of computer games and frogs that didn't turn into princes to find herself vividly aware of a change in the atmosphere. Without opening her eyes she tugged at the gray quilt, attempting to make herself more comfortable.

When that didn't work, Guinevere lifted her lashes to see the dark outline of a man lounging in her bedroom doorway. She froze. Her breath caught in her throat for the space of a few panicked heartbeats. Her mind seemed to go blank for a crucial instant. She should have bought a gun. Should have slept with it under her pillow.

"I've been thinking," Zac said, not moving in the doorway.

At the sound of his familiar voice memories of the evening fell immediately into place in Guinevere's head. Her lashes closed in a brief agony of relief. "Yes, I know," she whispered, her words husky with the remnants of her short-lived fear.

"It was your sister, wasn't it?"

She couldn't see his face in the shadows. Awkwardly Guinevere struggled to a sitting position against the pillows. "You'll have to excuse me, Zac. I'm a little slow at this time of the night. I think I've missed something in this conversation."

He shifted slightly in the doorway, straightening. "It was your sister who was involved with Hampton Starr."

Guinevere considered ignoring the question and then decided she probably wouldn't be allowed to do so. She pushed her tangled hair out of her eyes. "Is that what you've been dwelling on all evening? My sister and Hampton Starr? I thought you were trying to solve the case of StarrTech's missing shipments!"

"I was. But other things kept cropping up."

"Zac, none of those other things involves you or the case you're working on." She kept her tone resolute and assertive.

"I was worried for a while that it might have been you."

She wondered irritably if he'd even heard her assertive, resolute statement. "Wondered if I'd been involved with Starr? Not a chance. The man's a bastard."

"I knew you had something personal against him. And you risked so much just to siphon off ten thousand from StarrTech. It didn't make any sense until today."

"What happened today?" In a small, defensive gesture she drew up her knees and tugged the quilt to her chin. She wished she could see his face in the darkness.

"Starr gave me a lift back to my office and casually said you reminded him of someone. He asked me your name. I told him. Then he told me to be wary of ladies named Jones."

Guinevere caught her breath. "He knows who I am?"

"No. You just reminded him briefly of someone he used to take to bed. Someone who was also named Jones. Such a common name, Jones. Provides great anonymity, doesn't it? You didn't even have to worry about inventing a new name when you took that temporary assignment with his firm a few months ago. A big company like StarrTech always has a few Joneses on the payroll. Besides, whoever pays any attention to temporary clerical help? You remember that job, Guinevere. It was the one during which you sabotaged the benefits plan to the tune of ten thousand plus dollars."

"If that's the thorny little problem you've been working on all evening, you've wasted a great deal of time, Zac."

"I don't consider it a waste of time." He came forward. The dark bulk of his body reminded her of a ghost ship moving through a dark sea as he approached her through the shadows of her room. The fleeting fantasy vanished as he sat down heavily on the edge of the bed. The mattress gave beneath his weight. Zac was no ghost. He was very, very real.

"I suppose you're congratulating yourself on figuring it all out. Too bad there's no fee to collect for solving this particular mystery. Free Enterprise Security, Incorporated will go broke if you keep wasting your time on such trivial problems."

The bitterness in her words kept him silent for a moment. He was watching her intently, able to see her more clearly now that he had moved so close. She could see him more plainly, too, and the gleaming awareness in his gaze made her clutch the quilt tightly between her fingers.

"It was just a bone to chew on," Zac said. "I wanted to know what the connection between you and Hampton Starr was. Now I know. Your sister got involved with him, and when he lost interest, she was hurt. You took a little revenge on Starr by helping yourself to ten thousand dollars." He ran his fingers through his hair and yawned. "You must have been really upset by what he did to Carla."

Guinevere lost her temper and her self-control. "What he did to Carla has cost more than ten thousand dollars in therapy and Valium prescriptions, damn it. He just about devastated her. She was in love with him. For a while she even thought she might be pregnant by him. Thank God that turned out to be a false alarm. He told her he loved her, promised her marriage, led her to think that this time he was committed. Then one day he casually told her it had all been fun but it was over. Oh, and by the way, would she please turn in her resignation? He wanted someone new in his outer office. A change of scene."

"And you were furious on her behalf. Furious as only an older sister could be."

She lifted her head defiantly. "I figured the least Hampton Starr could do was pay for the therapy! Not to mention lost wages."

To her surprise Zac nodded agreeably. "Seems reasonable."

Having expected a scathing denunciation for her methods of revenge, Guinevere was plunged into a moment of confusion. She recovered quickly, wanting to explain further now that she had started. Or perhaps she just wanted to justify her actions in Zac's eyes, she realized.

"Does your sister know what you've done?" Zac asked.

"No. Dr. Estabrook thought it was best that she learn to stop dwelling on the past as soon as possible."

"So you took it upon yourself to balance the scales of justice along with your bank account." Zac seemed oddly amused.

"He had it coming. Hampton Starr uses people, especially women. Carla had worked in his firm for several months when he spotted her and decided she looked like an interesting diversion." Like almost everyone else in the Jones family, Guinevere had grown up with the idea that Carla was delicate. Carla needed protection. Guinevere had failed to protect her sister from Hampton Starr. So she had done the next best thing. She'd tried to avenge her.

"Starr is into intrigue." Zac undid the already loosened knot of his tie. Then he leaned down and tugged off his shoes. He yawned again and began unbuttoning his shirt cuffs. "He likes feeling as if he's manipulating people and events. Women who fall for him are undoubtedly easy prey. He gets off on the cloak-and-dagger bit. Probably missed his calling. Should have gone to work for the CIA."

"Zac, what are you doing?" She stared at him as he stood up to hang his shirt over the back of a chair. Under the quilt her toes curled as a flare of anticipation went through her body. If she wanted to stop what was happening, she had to act now. But her toes stayed curled, and the excitement in her veins made her feel flushed.

"You know," he remarked as he unzipped his trousers and stepped out of them, "I think a lot more clearly around you." The trousers were left folded on the chair. A band of white still cut across the darker shade of his skin. A moment later the Jockey briefs disappeared too. In the dim light the hard planes and angles of his body formed a sleek, utterly masculine shape.

Guinevere looked up at him, her own body taut with the intensity of her awareness. "I'm glad you're thinking clearly because I'm not sure I am. This is probably not a good idea, Zac."

"I can't think of a better one at the moment." He pulled back the quilt and slipped into bed beside her. "Can you?"

"No." Her answer was soft with sudden acceptance of her own desire.

"You didn't really give it a fair shot the other night." He reached for her, folding her into his arms.

"Give what a fair shot?"

"The effort to turn me into a prince. Maybe it takes more than a kiss." He put his thigh heavily over her leg, drawing her against his body, and then he covered her mouth with his own.

Guinevere let out the breath she had been holding. The cozy gray quilt created a deep intimacy that surrounded both of them. Within it she felt safe and warm and protected. The rest of the world faded into the distance. Zac's body was hard and fierce all along the length of hers. She closed her eyes and put her arms around his neck.

"Maybe it does take more than a kiss," she whispered against his mouth.

With a groan of anticipation and desire Zac pushed her gently onto her back. His shoulders loomed over her, blocking out the pale light that had trickled between the miniblinds. His leg got tangled in the soft fabric of her old-fashioned nightgown, his bare foot sliding along her calf. Guinevere felt the strength in Zac and realized she was luxuriating in it.

"God, you feel good." Zac buried his face in the curve of her throat, nuzzling the sweetness of her scent. His hand moved to the fastening of her flannel nightgown. "So good."

She felt the gown slipping from her shoulders, his large hands thrusting it out of the way with unexpected gentleness. Guinevere murmured softly, a wordless sound of growing wonder and need. She trembled as sudden shyness gripped her. When Zac pushed the gown down to her waist, she turned her face into his chest.

"Gwen, honey, I've been sitting out there thinking about you, wanting you. I've wanted to touch you like this for days." He drew the center of his palm down across one nipple. When the small nub went hard, he took away his hand and bent his head to her breast.

Guinevere shivered again, but this time not with shyness. Her fingers sank deeply into his bare shoulders and then moved upward to clench and unclench in his night-dark hair. The urgency in his body communicated itself to her clearly. She was aware of it on every level, and it fed her own flaring excitement.

"Zac, Zac, *please . . .*" She wrapped her foot around one of his legs, enjoying the crisp feel of the hair that seemed to be strewn all over him.

Her response to him seemed to delight Zac. She felt the delicate teasing of his teeth on her throat, and then he was taking her mouth once more. She parted her lips for him, and instantly he was inside, seeking to deepen the intimacy of the kiss. Even as he thrust his tongue between her teeth, he was flattening his palm on her stomach, pushing the nightgown down her hips.

"Lift up for me, honey," he said huskily.

She obeyed, arching her hips so that he could get the nightgown off completely. Zac groaned and slid his thigh between hers. The feel of him pressed so intimately against her aroused Guinevere further. She explored the contours of his back with her hand until she reached the hard planes of his hips. Then she moved her fingers around and down, wanting the feel of him.

"Gwen, honey, I swear to God, you've got magic fingers. I'm going to go out of my mind!" But he shifted his weight so that she could circle the heaviness of him, and then he was pressing himself eagerly into her palm.

He muttered something dark and fierce into her ear as she stroked him, and then his fingers, fumbling a little with passion, found the secrets hidden between her legs. Guinevere gasped as he touched her there, withdrawing slightly. Instantly he pulled her back against him, holding her tightly against his chest.

"No, honey, please. I want to touch you. I've got to. Can't you feel what you're doing to me?"

She wanted to explain that it was only the exquisitely unbearable excitement he was producing with his fingers that had made her pull away from him. She needed time to adjust to this kind of passion. It had sprung up so quickly, overwhelming her so completely that she wasn't quite sure how to deal with it. But there was no opportunity to go into a polite analysis of the situation. Zac was once more teasing the heart of her desire, this time allowing her no room to escape.

"Zac, Zac, now, please, make it *now*! I won't be able to last another minute." She felt the tightness in herself and knew that his hand must be damp from the warm liquid he had caused to flow so freely between her thighs.

"I'm the one who won't last much longer." He moved, coming down on top of her like a breaking wave. "I used to think I'd developed self-control, but around you . . ." He never finished the sentence. Instead, he thrust into her with an impact that sent tremors through both of them.

Guinevere felt the tautness in him and lifted herself to absorb the full length of his manhood. She felt herself stretched tightly around him, clinging with a hunger that was new to her. She shut her eyes, letting her mind drift freely into the never-never land of sensual euphoria and fantasy.

Zac clutched her shoulders, driving himself into Guinevere's softness as though he could make it his own by invading her. But every thrust served only to take him deeper into mysterious territory that invited yet challenged his sensual assault. She accepted him completely, urged him deeper, beckoned him so close to the fire that he had no choice but to get burned.

As Guinevere gave herself up to the shimmering tension, Zac surrendered the last claim he had on his self-control. He moved one hand down from her shoulder and slipped his fingers between their bodies. Guinevere felt him touch her one last time, and everything in her went over the edge. Zac followed her almost immediately, his body shuddering in climax.

"Gwen!"

The pleasant, satisfied aftermath held both of them in thrall for what seemed ages. But when Guinevere glanced sleepily at the bedside clock, she realized that only a few minutes had passed. Zac still lay sprawled on top of her, his weight crushing her deeply into the bed. She liked the feel of him, enjoyed the damp scent of him as his body relaxed after sex. Guinevere ran her fingertips idly down his side, counting ribs.

"Jesus, lady, that tickles." He didn't open his eyes. His head was resting alongside hers on the pillow.

"I didn't know frogs were ticklish."

There was a pulse of silence before Zac said very carefully, "Does that mean it didn't work?"

"What? The experiment to see if you'd turn into a prince? I don't know. It's dark. I haven't had a good look at you yet."

"Far be it from me to get up and turn on the light."

"Umm." She trailed her straying fingertip down to his hip. "Zac?"

"I haven't gone anywhere."

"I noticed." She could still feel him inside her. "Zac, were you really sitting out there in my living room, falling asleep while thinking about me?"

"Not exactly. First I thought a lot about that damn computer game Hixon and Bender created. Then I thought about your sister and Hampton Starr. And then I guess I dozed off. When I woke up, I discovered you'd very generously covered me up for the night. I realized all the lights were off and you'd gone to bed."

"That's when you first started to think about me?"

"It came to me in a flash that you were in bed only a few feet away. One thought just sort of led to another," he said proudly. He still hadn't opened his eyes.

"I'm not sure I like being last on the list."

His lashes lifted at that, revealing a gleaming gaze. "I'll reprioritize immediately."

Her soft amusement faded. "I'm still not sure this was one of the world's best ideas, Zac."

"I'll get to work right away on convincing you."

Saturday morning dawned chill and bright. Guinevere woke to the smell of coffee and the feeling that something fundamental had changed in the universe. When she opened her eyes, there was no sign of either a frog or a prince, but there were distinct morning sounds coming from her kitchen. She stretched hugely and then pushed aside the quilt. The coffee smell drew her, a fish to bait. She found a robe in her closet, belted it around her waist, and padded out to see what Zac was doing with the coffee.

She came to a halt in the kitchen doorway. He was standing in front of the sink, sipping from a steaming mug while glancing through the morning paper. For a moment she just absorbed the sight of him looking so much at home in a place where no man had ever really been at home before. He looked strong and vital standing there in the sunlight, and she remembered the feel of him during the night. He was dressed in the trousers and white shirt he'd worn yesterday, his hair still damp from a shower.

A feeling of uncertainty that was all mixed up with a distant sense of hope swept over Guinevere, keeping her silent for another moment. Then she took a firm grip on reality and stepped forward.

"Did you make enough coffee for two?" She walked barefooted over to the pot and peered at the contents. "Ah, lucky for you." She poured herself a cup.

"I'm not entirely without foresight, you know. I have more sense than to make only enough coffee for one in this kind of situation." There was soft, purring contentment in his voice—the voice of a very satisfied man.

Her knuckles went white around the handle of her mug. Guinevere looked intently out the window, studying the artist's loft on the second floor across the street. The artist wasn't up yet, she realized. Too bad. He was missing a lot of great light.

"You have a great deal of experience with situations such as this?" she asked with a calm that seemed unnatural.

Without any sound he was behind her, his arms going around her waist as he tugged her back against him. Guinevere felt his warm breath in her tousled hair.

"Gwen, I have very large feet, and sometimes I put them in my mouth. I didn't mean that the way it sounded. Some things are unique. God knows you're one of them. This morning is another. And last night was one of a kind. Please don't go cold on me."

She shook her head slightly, smiling a little as she relaxed. "Sorry. Guess I'm just a little tense."

"So am I in some ways. In others I feel very, very good."

They stood that way for a long moment, both gazing out into the new morning, neither knowing quite what to say next. And then there was movement on the other side of the huge, arched window across the street. A lean young man wearing only a towel wrapped around his waist wandered into the sunlit room and stopped in front of a canvas that stood on an easel. He ran a hand thoughtfully through his slightly long hair while he studied the half-finished painting. Then he turned around and waved at Guinevere. When he saw the man standing with his arms around her, he grinned and wandered back out of the room.

Zac went still. "Who the hell is that?"

"An artist. Can't you tell? See the paintings stacked around the room and the half-finished one on the easel? He keeps the windows uncovered so that he can get the maximum amount of light into the loft, I suppose. You know how artists are. They treasure light."

"He looked more like a Peeping Tom to me. You two stand here and wave good morning every day?" Zac released her and reached out to lower the miniblinds that he'd raised earlier. His annoyance was palpable.

"We think of ourselves as two ships passing in the night." For some reason Guinevere began to recover her normal cheerfulness as well as her sense of humor.

"Except that your ships aren't exactly moving, are they? Don't you know it's dangerous to encourage strangers in the city? What the hell's the matter with you?"

"We're talking mild fantasy here, Zac, not hard-core risk. He moved into that loft a few months ago and seems totally devoted to his work. You know how artists are."

"You keep saying that, but as a matter of fact, I don't know much about artists. And I don't think I want to. What have you got for breakfast besides dry cereal?"

"Not much."

"Let's go out then. I'm starving. I think I need protein to replace what I lost last night. Go hop in the shower, honey." He gave her a light slap on the rear.

"I'm on my way." She pinched his hard buttock quite forcefully as she went by him.

"Ouch!" He snagged her wrist and pulled her around to face him. "What was that for?"

"Just to let you know how those casual little love taps feel." She smiled challengingly up at him.

Suddenly Zac grinned and pulled her into his arms. "Let's start over again."

He bent his head and kissed her thoroughly until Guinevere forgot all about the morning's uncertainties and tension. By the time he freed her mouth she felt very satisfied with life.

"Now go take your shower," Zac murmured.

"Yes, sir."

She spun around. At the doorway she paused and glanced back. "You look the same, you know. Cute and green."

"I was afraid of that." Shrugging in resignation, Zac picked up the newspaper he had been reading. "Can't win 'em all."

"I think I've been conned."

He looked up. "Is that what you call it?"

"I'll be out of the shower in twenty minutes."

"Wonderful." He was already studying page two.

Smiling to herself, Guinevere trotted down the hall to the bathroom. Ten minutes later, thoroughly soaped and feeling infinitely more alive, she nudged the hot-water tap to a higher setting and prepared to rinse lavishly. There were a couple of places within walking distance where she and Zac could have breakfast.

She was trying to make up her mind about which one to recommend when the bathroom door swung open, sending a wave of cool air into the pleasantly overheated room.

"Zac, close the door!" She held her face up to the water.

"They found him, Gwen."

"What are you talking about? Found who?" She turned her head to let the water run down the back of her neck.

"Cal Bender."

That got her interest. She stepped back a bit from the water so she could hear him better. "No kidding? Did somebody just call? Where was he? On vacation in Bermuda?"

"Not quite."

There was an element in Zac's voice that made Guinevere peer around the curtain. He was standing on the red bathroom rug, staring intently at the newspaper in his hand. She had a sudden, uneasy premonition.

"Zac?"

He glanced up, his eyes not quite focusing on her as he followed some internal path of logic that only he could see. "The paper says some hikers found his body at the bottom of a ravine in the Cascades. Apparently he tried to do some rock climbing on his own not far from the highway."

"Oh, my God." The shower water seemed to have gone cold. Guinevere stood still, the curtain clutched in her fist, and stared at Zac's brooding face. Then her mind went to work on the implications. "Rock climbing? Cal? I didn't know he was into it. And aren't climbers supposed to go with a companion? Cal's closest companion was Larry."

"I think we'd better just have dry cereal after all, Gwen. I've got a lot of things to do this morning." Zac turned and started out the bathroom door.

"Zac, wait! What are you going to do?"

"Make some calls. Talk to some people." He gave her a wry smile. "It's what you do in this line of work."

"Are you going to contact Hampton Starr?"

"I don't think so. Not right away. There are some other questions I want answered first."

Guinevere thought about that. Then she said very softly, "I take it you don't think Cal's death was an accident?"

"Like I said, there are some questions that need answering. Don't stand too long in the shower. Your cereal will get soggy."

CHAPTER 7

The news about the unfortunate climber who had met his death in the mountains got only a brief spot on the radio that morning. The body had been discovered late the previous afternoon and had made the late-evening broadcasts in more detail. Guinevere poured herself another cup of coffee and listened to the radio spot alone. Zac was long gone. He'd wolfed down a few bites of cereal, kissed her in an absent yet possessive manner that should have annoyed her, and let himself out the front door. When the door closed, Guinevere was very much alone. The apartment, which usually seemed so cozy, felt unaccountably empty this morning.

It was obvious that whatever the night had meant to Zac, the morning had brought something more interesting: a new angle to the case on which he had been working. Apparently the call to work ranked higher than a discussion of an embryonic "relationship."

People to see, questions to ask. Business as usual.

Guinevere considered the folly of letting stray frogs spend the night, and then she started paying more attention to the radio. It would be, the announcer said soberly, several hours before the crew sent to retrieve the body would have it freed from the deep ravine. Initial identification had been made when a climber had scrambled down the jagged rock face and found Cal's wallet.

Guinevere raised the miniblinds again so that she could look across the street into the artist's studio and wondered about Cal Bender.

The man had been a loner as far as she knew. Larry had said he had no close family. It seemed that Larry had been Cal's only real friend, and that relationship had been primarily a business partnership. Bender hadn't been as outgoing or communicative as Larry was, so he hadn't enjoyed the easy, chatty friendship Larry had with the rest of the staff. But their joint interests and ambitions had drawn the two young men together, and their ability to communicate with computers had become the important factor in their association.

Guinevere thought of Larry and wondered if he'd heard the news. On a burst of empathy she reached for the phone and dialed his number. There was no answer. He'd probably spent the night working on Elf Hunt and had unplugged the phone so he could sleep in this morning.

The phone burbled just as Guinevere replaced the receiver, and she picked it up again. Her sister's voice greeted her.

"Hi, Carla, how are you feeling this morning?" Instantly she regretted the automatic words. That was always a risky question around Carla.

"All right, I guess." The lack of drama behind the response was surprising. Carla sounded almost uninterested in an inquiry she normally reacted to with grim detail. "I called to see if you've been to the office."

"I hardly recognized it." Guinevere smiled. "You've really made some changes. I've never seen the place so organized."

"It's a mess." Carla was adamant.

"It is?"

"There's a lot more to be done there, Gwen. If you don't get a handle on those client files, you're going to screw things up for yourself at income tax time."

Guinevere shifted uneasily in her chair and reached for her coffee mug. That sort of threat always had a traumatic impact on a small businessperson. "I thought I had everything in order."

"The whole setup is inefficient and amateurish."

For some reason that struck Guinevere to the quick. "Amateurish! I worked for hours setting up those files."

"Well, you should have hired a professional."

"A professional what? Professional file setter-upper? I didn't know there was such a being." Guinevere realized she was starting to get defensive.

"Calm down, Gwen. I'm only telling you this for your own good."

In a blinding flash of light Guinevere suddenly acknowledged what an about-face this was. She had been the one giving Carla lectures "for her own good" for months. Now the tables were reversed. "I appreciate the advice, Carla," she said stiffly, "but I don't see what—"

"Look, if you want, I can start going into the office on a regular basis for a few days. I could at least put things in order for you and show you how to run a good filing system."

Guinevere wondered if she was hearing correctly. "You could?"

"It's not as if I have a lot else to do."

"No, I guess not." Guinevere felt taken aback. "Well, I would certainly appreciate your help. I know I've let things get behind this past week while I've been handling that job at StarrTech."

"Gwen, that office was in trouble long before you went to work at StarrTech. We're not talking about a few unfiled items here. We're talking a basically poor filing system design. Filing is fundamental to a well-run office, Gwen. You're a decent typist, and you can answer phones, but that's about your limit. Filing is an art."

"I hadn't realized—"

"It's time you did."

"Yes." Guinevere felt humble. "It's very nice of you to offer to help, Carla."

"I'll start Monday."

"Uh, thanks."

It was only after Carla hung up the phone that Guinevere realized they hadn't discussed Valium deprivation or Dr. Estabrook's inadequacies.

Carla's words had left a load of worry and an odd form of guilt on Guinevere's shoulders. Or perhaps she was just feeling restless because she'd been abandoned by her lover before eight o'clock in the morning. Sometimes it was hard to identify the source of one's unease, Guinevere decided. Sometimes one didn't want to identify the source. Too many questions arose, questions such as whether or not last night had been a one-night stand or the start of a relationship.

Feeling pressed, with a need to do something, *anything*, Guinevere made the decision to go on into the office. After she'd dressed in a pair of jeans and a pumpkin-colored pullover sweater, she dialed Larry Hixon's number one more time. Still no answer.

At various points in the morning Guinevere continued to try Larry's number. She didn't know just when she actually began to worry about the lack of response, but sometime after lunch she sat back in her swivel chair and drummed her nails on the desk.

Perhaps Larry had already heard the news about Cal and had gone off by himself to think for a while. Or perhaps he was up but back at work on Elf Hunt and had forgotten to plug in his phone. Maybe he'd had a date the previous evening and had decided to spend the night. Heaven knew there were men these days who were not above wheedling their way between a woman's clean sheets and then blithely taking off in the morning without anything more than an absentminded farewell kiss. Back to business as usual.

It occurred to Guinevere that she was personalizing the issue.

She spun her chair around so that she could look out the window.

The offices across the street on First Avenue were dark and silent this morning. Everyone else in the neighborhood appeared to be home enjoying the weekend.

Maybe Larry had taken off somewhere for the weekend. She wondered if he would have mentioned such a trip to Carla. Out of curiosity she dialed her sister's number. Carla answered on the second ring.

"Larry? No, I haven't talked to him since yesterday morning. He called to see how I was doing running Camelot Services for you. Sweet guy."

Guinevere blinked at the implication that her sister had been doing anything more for Camelot Services than simply baby-sitting the phone. Then she forced herself to calm down. She had been on the verge of getting defensive again. "I just wondered if he'd said anything to you about going out of town this weekend."

"Nope. As a matter of fact, we talked about getting together Sunday afternoon for a picnic. It depends on whether Larry can finish playing that game of his. He seems totally committed to getting through it. I think it's become a challenge or something."

Or something. "Thanks, Carla. I'll talk to you later." Guinevere hung up the phone thoughtfully.

Carla was right. All indications were that Larry Hixon wouldn't abandon his computer until he'd hammered his way through the altered version of Elf Hunt. So why wasn't he answering his phone?

And what if Cal's death were something other than an accident?

Cal and Larry had been partners.

The vague disquiet that had been floating around the edges of her mind all morning drove Guinevere restlessly to her feet. She paced the small office once and then dialed Zac's number. It was no surprise that there wasn't an answer. After all, she thought irritably, he had questions to ask and people to see. The big-time investigator hot on the trail of discovery.

Reaching for her red wool jacket, Guinevere made up her mind.

She stalked out of the office, locked the door carefully, and then went out onto First Avenue. Striding briskly through Pioneer Square, she sidestepped a few panhandlers and made her way into her apartment garage. She fished the Laser's keys out of her purse. It was a short drive to the Wallingford district, and she knew she would feel better if she actually saw Larry sitting hunched over his computer with his cell phone beside him.

Just as she had on her first visit, Guinevere parked her car in front of Larry's house, and just as on her first visit she got the impression as she went up the walk that there was no one home.

She reminded herself of how her imagination had gone into overtime on her first visit and how ridiculous she'd felt when she'd walked through Larry's silent house and found him sleeping on the bed. Tentatively she knocked on the front door. There was no response.

Guinevere walked along the porch a few steps and tried to peer in through the window. The aging drapes had been drawn shut, however, and she couldn't catch even a glimpse of the interior. Guinevere trotted down the porch steps and went around to the back of the house. Her nerves were coming alive exactly as they had that evening she'd gone into Cal Bender's house, and she felt the adrenaline surge through her veins. She was also beginning to feel distinctly scared.

There were a hundred logical explanations for Larry's absence. But there had been a hundred logical explanations for Cal's absence too. And the answer in that case had been the one illogical explanation nobody had considered: death.

Guinevere shivered and stood on tiptoe to peek into the bathroom window. This sort of thing could get her arrested. Looking at your artistic neighbor across the street from a second-story window was one thing. Peeping into a man's bathroom window out in a quiet residential neighborhood was another.

She couldn't see any shadows moving behind the fogged glass.

Guinevere continued around the house. The back door was also locked, but Guinevere remembered how Zac had almost used a credit card to open Cal Bender's back door. She wondered how tricky an operation that was.

She flipped open her shoulder bag and dug out her prized charge card. It read "Camelot Services" in impressive gold letters. Guinevere hoped the bank wouldn't revoke it if it found out she was using the card in such a devious fashion. Glancing over her shoulder to make certain no one could see her, she slipped the card into the crack between the door and its frame.

After a few anxious minutes of jiggling and prodding she gave up. Whatever the trick with the credit card was, apparently it wasn't something you could pick up on your own in the field. It took some training and expertise.

With a sigh of defeat Guinevere started back around the house. She was crossing in front of the kitchen window when she realized it was partially open. She halted abruptly and wondered if it was also locked. It didn't appear to be.

Once again Guinevere glanced furtively over her shoulder, and then she tentatively tried to raise the kitchen window. It gave easily. For a moment she simply stood staring at it. All she had to do was crawl through the opening and she would be inside Larry's house.

The urge for answers overcame her usually sound judgment. Guinevere hoisted herself up onto the ledge and then fumbled her way through the window. A moment later she found herself on the counter beside the kitchen sink.

"Larry?"

The house seemed unnaturally dark. She supposed computer types throve in darkness. It was better for reading computer screens. She wandered down the hall into the living room. In the gloom caused by the drawn drapes she could see that there was no sign of anyone's being home. The place was cave-dark.

She stepped over to the computer and glanced down at the desk as she flipped on the light. The surface was much less neat than she remembered it. Larry had apparently spilled a little tea or cola and hadn't bothered to wipe it up before it dried. Not only had it stained the wood, but it had also spotted several sheets of paper and a magazine.

It took a few seconds before Guinevere realized that the stains on the desk weren't quite the right color for tea.

Her stomach tightened as she traced a fingertip over one dried pool. It wasn't sticky the way cola would be.

It didn't take a great deal of intuition to realize exactly what had caused the stains.

Women saw a lot of blood over the course of their lives. They cut themselves shaving their legs; they dealt with the monthly changes in their bodies; they patched up the wounds of little kids who fell out of trees. They knew blood when they saw it.

Zac took another swallow of the weak metallic-tasting coffee the waitress was pouring with a lavish hand and watched Russ Elfstrom work his way energetically through a moat of french fries that surrounded a hamburger. Zac thought fleetingly of the large breakfast he'd planned on enjoying with Guinevere before the news of Bender's death had intruded. So far he hadn't had a bite. He wondered what Gwen had done all morning. She'd probably had both breakfast and lunch by now.

"So everyone's convinced it really is just an accident?" Elfstrom paused to spread more mustard on his burger. A half-smoked cigarette smoldered in the ashtray beside his plate. "No signs of what the media likes to call foul play?"

"According to what I can find out, the authorities are treating it as exactly what it looks like: a climbing accident. They'll know more when they get the body out of the ravine and into a coroner's lab, but no one I talked to is expecting to find anything suspicious."

"Did you tell anyone why you were asking the questions?"

"Of course not. I just said I was making some inquiries on be-half of some friends who were concerned." Zac grimaced. "It's tough setting up new contacts in the right places, Russ. It's a whole new game here in the States. One has to establish a 'professional' relationship with the authorities. It was easier when the 'profes-sional relationship' consisted of a fistful of U.S. currency handed over in some dark alley."

"That tried-and-true method would probably work fairly well in a lot of places here at home." Russ arched one shaggy brow as he put down his burger and reached for the cigarette. He looked cynical.

Zac thought of the men he had talked to this morning. They had been serious, intelligent, and highly professional in their attitude toward their work. They had been polite but not overly helpful. They were more concerned with getting their jobs done than with accommodating him. Zac tried to imagine what would have hap-pened if he'd offered one of them a bribe for more information. He had a hunch the offer wouldn't have gone down well at all. "I don't think so. At least not with the kind of people I talked to today."

"Well, you found out what you needed to know. Everyone is sure Bender met his death while climbing some rocks."

"Gwen said she'd never heard of Cal Bender's doing any rock climbing," Zac said slowly. "And she said Larry was his closest friend. If Cal had taken off to do some serious hiking, why didn't he mention it to Larry?"

"Or ask Larry to go with him?" Elfstrom screwed up his face in the way he always did when he was thinking. The constant, under-lying urgency in the man seemed always to need some outlet. "She's right, you know. Bender and Hixon were buddies. They did a lot of things together. And they know the StarrTech computers inside out."

"You think Bender was involved in the missing shipments, don't you?"

Elfstrom's small mouth crooked wryly. "Yeah. It fits with the facts. He could have manipulated the shipping programs easily enough, and he disappeared about the time I realized something was going on."

"But he's dead, Russ. In a climbing accident. Why would a man on the run take the time to go rock climbing?"

Elfstrom looked at Zac. "No good reason I can think of. If it were me and I thought things were getting uncomfortably hot, I would have headed for Mexico."

"Unless, of course, you had a partner who didn't want you skipping town." Zac thought of all the directions his mind had gone last night when he'd been sitting in Guinevere's apartment, trying to get the pieces of the puzzle in place.

"Yeah, a partner who didn't appreciate his business associate's getting cold feet could be a problem."

"He might take his friend on a little rock-climbing expedition and leave him behind in a ravine. One guy told me this morning that it was just a fluke they found Bender's body. No one had reported him missing, and no one knew he had gone climbing. This time of year one could expect snow almost any day. Once the snow starts in those mountains, it will last all season. That body might not have appeared until next summer."

"What are you getting at, Zac?" Elfstrom waited with the patience of a man who had waited more than once for his friend's conclusions.

"Everyone keeps saying Hixon was Bender's best friend, his only friend."

Elfstrom shrugged. "It's the truth as far as I know."

Zac thought about Elf Hunt. "If Bender and Hixon had been involved with something illegal, they'd manage everything through a computer, wouldn't they?"

"It would be logical. It's the kind of thing they would know best. Guinevere Jones hasn't given you any information about Larry Hixon?"

"Not much," Zac said.

"I'm not surprised. She liked Bender and Hixon, Zac. And they liked her."

"Everyone in the office seems to have liked her."

"Yeah, but I'll tell you something. I don't think she could have pulled off her little scam with StarrTech's benefits program without someone's help. And I think Bender and Hixon liked her well enough to help her."

Zac felt a coldness in his stomach. He tried to ignore it. "Even if they did, what's that got to do with the missing shipments?"

"You tell me, Zac." Elfstrom shook his head sadly. "I suppose you're sleeping with her?"

Zac forced a smile. "You think my judgment might be impaired if I were?"

Elfstrom stared at him thoughtfully. "No," he said finally. "I don't think it would be. Not for long at any rate. You never let anything distract you for long, not when you've got a job to do. You know what they used to say about you in-house back when we worked for the company?"

"I'm not sure I want to hear it."

"They called you the Glacier."

"Oh, Christ."

"Slow-moving at times but unstoppable. And in the end everything gets covered."

"Not the most flattering image in the world." Maybe it was the unpleasantness of the glacier image. Whatever the cause, Zac's stomach felt even colder.

"I've got to tell you, Zac, the more I think about it, the more I'm sure Jones must have had help on her trip through the computer. And if she got that help from either Hixon or Bender, she must have been pretty close to one or both of them. Maybe she was sleeping with one of them."

Zac had a sudden, sickening memory of Guinevere's head bent intently near Larry Hixon's the afternoon he'd walked into the little pub. "Close enough for them to have told her what they were doing with missing shipments of StarrTech equipment? I doubt it, Russ." But she'd been close enough to one or both of them to be told about Elf Hunt. But she'd said that was no big deal. Everyone else in the office, except management, knew about Elf Hunt. Or so she'd said.

Zac forced himself to consider the possibility that Gwen had lied to him. People who lied about one thing tended to lie about others. He had to remember that she'd fleeced StarrTech to the tune of ten thousand dollars.

But she'd had her reasons, he told himself violently. She'd been seeking retribution on behalf of her sister. The motive had been revenge, a kind of freelance justice, not larceny. That thought led to another. He shook off his uncertainties and looked at Russ Elfstrom.

"Any chance of reaching Hampton Starr? I think he ought to know what's happening."

Elfstrom dismissed the possibility with a grimace. "Afraid not. According to what I heard, he left last night for another of his not-so-secret rendezvous on the coast. He didn't tell anyone which resort he'd chosen. That man goes through women like they were chocolates. Gobble one up and throw away the wrapper."

Zac remembered the figure of the king in Elf Hunt. It was the king who had been guarding the treasure in the new version of the game. Why had Cal Bender decided to change that key player's role? Larry Hixon hadn't wanted to rest until he'd figured out the answer to that question. Because the answer might provide information on something more crucial than a game?

It always came back to Elf Hunt. There was no reason why it

should, but there was also no denying that the damn game seemed to appear at every corner Zac turned in this investigation. The game and Guinevere Jones.

Zac stood up and scrounged in his pocket for some change. Russ Elfstrom looked up inquiringly. "Going someplace?"

"There are some more people to see. I'd better be on my way. We glaciers move exceedingly slowly, but we try to keep going. I'll call you later, Russ, and update you."

"Going back to your office?"

Zac shook his head. "No, I'll be out of touch for the next few hours. If you find out anything or if you figure out where Starr is, leave a message on my cell phone."

"Right." Elfstrom smiled grimly. "Good hunting, Zac."

Zac nodded shortly, remembering how many times Russ Elfstrom had said those same words during the years they'd been together at the company. Making certain he'd left enough for a minimal tip, Zac turned and walked out through the café.

His car was parked at the curb. The red violation flag in the meter popped up as he walked toward the Buick. A cruising meter attendant several yards down the street saw the flag at the same time. Zac told himself he would not run. He had time. All he had to do was lengthen his stride a bit in order to beat the meter attendant, who was gunning her three-wheeled motorized cart. He could hear the little engine straining mightily. The thought of having to pay the fine out of Free Enterprise's petty cash fund inspired Zac. His pace quickened into something suspiciously close to a trot. He reached the Buick and had the door open three seconds before the meter attendant braked to a halt. Quickly Zac turned the key in the ignition and waved briefly before pulling out onto the street.

The meter attendant glared after him, a small shark deprived of the whale on which it had intended to prey.

The small victory did nothing to lighten Zac's mood. He cruised

slowly toward Pioneer Square. It seemed important to see Guinevere and ask his questions face to face.

What good would that do? he wondered. She could easily lie to
him. How would he know? If she'd been lying all along and he'd
been unable to detect it, what would cue him into the truth today?
How badly would his judgment be affected by the fact that he'd
shared her bed last night?

In the past he would have agreed with Russ. He was capable of
separating his passion from his logic. But after spending the night
with Guinevere Jones, he was no longer so certain. She had been
the essence of feminine warmth and softness last night, taking him
into her with an eagerness that had made him feel like a conqueror.
She had been real and vital in his arms. There had been an intrinsic
honesty in her passion. He couldn't believe now that her excitement
had been anything but genuine. Or was it that his ego wanted to
believe in her response?

The fact that he had to ask the question at all alarmed him. He
should have known; in the old days he *would* have known whether
it was his ego rather than logic dictating his reactions.

He needed to see her, Zac realized. He had to pin her down and
get some answers. In the beginning he had promised himself that
he could ride the tiger that was Guinevere Jones. Now he had to
admit he may have been overconfident.

It took him several trips around the block to find a parking
place near Guinevere's apartment. It was early afternoon, and the
Pioneer Square shops and restaurants were doing a brisk business.
There was a home show in the Kingdome just down the street that
was drawing even more people than usual into the area. He had
been lucky to find any place at all in which to park.

At the locked apartment building entrance Zac pressed the button for Guinevere's apartment and waited in suspended silence for
the response. When there was no answer, he frowned and tried
again.

The apartment building door swung open at that moment, and two laughing young women stepped out onto the sidewalk. They paid no attention to Zac, who was standing with his finger pressed on the intercom button. Surreptitiously he stuck out his foot and caught the door just before it closed again. He stayed where he was, pretending to listen to the intercom until the two young women were out of sight. Then he opened the door and let himself inside the lobby.

Having taken the stairs two at a time, he arrived a few seconds later at Guinevere's door. Knocking got no more response than the intercom had gotten, however. Zac forced himself to face the fact that she wasn't home.

Then he began to wonder just where she had gone. He pulled out his cell phone and called the offices of Camelot Services. When there was no answer there, he dug Carla Jones's number out of information and tried it.

Carla answered almost at once. "Oh, hello, Zac . . . Yes, of course, I remember you. You were with Guinevere the other evening at the pub."

"I'm trying to find her, Carla. We were supposed to have lunch together. Any idea where she might have gone?"

"She called me from the office just a few minutes ago."

"Well, she's not there now."

"I think she said something about trying to get hold of Larry. She was worried about how he'd take the news of his friend's death. She'd been trying to call him all morning and hadn't been able to reach him. I wonder if she would have just tried driving out to Wallingford," Carla said musingly.

"Thanks, Carla. I'll check." Zac had to unclench his fingers from the receiver as he replaced the phone. Wallingford and Larry Hixon and Elf Hunt. And Guinevere.

A muttered oath slipped between his teeth as he reached the Buick. The tense coldness in his stomach was worse than ever. He wondered if small businesspeople kept supplies of antacid tablets on hand and whether or not they could be charged off as legitimate business expenses.

The Laser was parked on the street in front of Hixon's house. Zac found a place behind it, switched off the engine, and sat for a moment behind the wheel. One question was answered. Guinevere was here. He wasn't sure he wanted to hear the answers to the rest of his questions.

It took an effort of will to climb out of the Buick and walk up the front steps. His fist hesitated for an instant, and then he knocked loudly on the door. Glaciers just kept moving and dogs just kept gnawing on their bones. It was the way his world worked. The only way he knew how to work.

She opened the door on his second knock, and it seemed to Zac as he stood staring down at her that her eyes had never seemed so wide or so nearly green. She stood there, silent and still, looking up at him. And then she stepped forward and threw her arms around his waist, burying her face against his shirt.

"Zac, thank God you're here. I've been so scared."

He couldn't keep his arms from going around her, but his voice seemed harsh, even to his own ears as he answered. "Yeah, that's something I've been wanting to talk to you about, Gwen."

CHAPTER 8

Guinevere stepped back a pace, the rough edge on his words cutting through her fear and the relief she had felt when she'd opened the door and found Zac standing there.

"How did you know where I was?"

"Carla said there was a possibility you'd driven out here." He glanced past her into the darkened living room. "Where's Hixon?"

Guinevere shook her head, her anxiety evident in the new huskiness in her voice. "I don't know, Zac, and I'm worried sick. There's blood on his desk and I—"

"Blood! Are you sure?" He put his hands on her shoulders and forced her firmly out of the way. Then he stepped into the living room. "Have you been through the house?"

"Yes. He's not here, and there's no indication of where he might have gone. You can see for yourself everything looks in order except for the desk. What if the same thing's happening to him that happened to Cal Bender?"

"We still don't know for sure how Bender died." Zac stood by the desk, gazing down at the small dark stains. "The authorities are convinced so far that it was just what it looks like: a climbing accident." He glanced at the dried drops on the floor. "There's not a lot of blood. Whatever happened, no one bled to death here. Assuming this is blood."

"What else could it be?" Guinevere decided it must be her tension that was causing her to get defensive with Zac. She was reading too much into what was probably only his "professional" attitude on the job.

"There aren't too many other possibilities," Zac said in agreement. Absently he glanced at the small disarray of magazines on the desk.

"Shouldn't we call the police?" He knew it was blood, she realized. Why was he being so cool and calculated?

"I'm slow enough as it is. Get the police involved at this point, and things will grind to a complete halt. We'll never get any answers."

"Zac, I don't understand. What are you looking for now?"

"I just told you. Answers." He turned to look at her, his expression more remote than she had ever seen it. "And we might as well start with you. How well did you know Bender and Hixon, Gwen?"

"How well did I know them! I've told you, I worked with them for a while a few months ago. That's all. What is this?"

"Did they help you set up the benefits plan scam?"

"Zac, they had nothing to do with that!" She was really getting frightened now. "What are you trying to get at?"

"You've said yourself your skills in an office are limited mostly to typing and answering phones. You don't even have a computer in your own office. Where did you learn enough about computers to think you could get away with modifying StarrTech's benefits plan?"

"Zac, I don't understand any of this!"

"Neither do I." He stood like a wall of granite in front of her. "That's why I'm asking questions. If you want to get this over with fast, all you have to do is answer them."

"Why should I bother?" Good Lord, she mustn't get hysterical.

Not with Larry Hixon's dried blood all over the place. She had to stay calm. "You don't sound as if you're in a mood to believe anything I say anyway!"

"Try me, Gwen. Just try giving me some straight answers."

"I've told you, I played with that benefits plan myself. It wasn't hard. When I landed the contract with StarrTech, I didn't have any clear idea of how I was going to make Hampton Starr pay for what he'd done to my sister. I took the job hoping to learn something useful. I was put into the IT department. It was a friendly crowd of people, and everyone was more than happy to talk about what he or she did. Larry and Cal and Jackson and Liz were more than willing to answer any question I asked. I was assigned to do the inputting on a daily basis, and that covers a lot of territory. I saw all sorts of possibilities. But when I got the job of inputting some new names and addresses into the benefits program, I decided that was the easiest method. StarrTech is a big company. Who was going to notice a few checks going out to a Miss Jones? I even put in a cutoff date. I didn't take any more than what I thought it would cost to pay Dr. Estabrook."

"You don't have to sound so goddamned noble about it. In a lot of places they'd label that sort of thing outright theft!"

"I got the feeling you understood why I'd done it. Last night you gave me the impression you might have done something similar under the circumstances."

He rubbed the back of his neck as if trying to massage away tension. "What I said last night might not mean a whole lot today."

"Oh, that's just wonderful!" She was on the edge, Guinevere realized dimly. Both her temper and her nerves were frayed to the breaking point. "That's terrific. Vastly reassuring. Just what a woman needs to hear the morning after. I thought you were different, Zac. If there's a lack of nobility around here, you can lay first claim to it. You were right about one thing: You're no prince."

He ignored her accusation, nothing in his eyes wavering in the least. Gray granite. "You said the IT department at StarrTech was friendly, that Hixon and Bender and the others were only too happy to answer questions."

"It's the truth!"

"They even told you about that damned computer game."

"It wasn't that big a secret, except from management," she replied.

"What else did they tell you? What other questions did you ask? Just how friendly did you get, Gwen? Were you sleeping with Larry Hixon?"

"Good grief, no!" She felt a wave of pressure pushing at her, threatening to swamp her. Grimly Guinevere hung on to her sense of logic. "You'll have to be more specific. Tell me exactly what you want to know, Zac."

He took a step forward. "I want to know if you knew anything about the missing shipments. You were involved in one little scam; maybe you knew something about the other. You said it was such a *friendly* department, Gwen. Did Hixon or Bender tell you anything about the disappearing equipment?"

"Oh, my God." She stared at him, hardly able to believe what she was hearing. "You've decided that Cal or Larry is behind the shipment thefts? And you think I'm involved too?"

"I haven't made up my mind yet just what to believe."

Guinevere felt dazed and a little sick to her stomach. "When I think about the way I so stupidly let you stay last night—"

"Last night has got nothing to do with this."

"I can see that. A bad mistake on my part."

He took another step forward, and Guinevere had the impression he was having to restrain himself from taking hold of her. Instinctively she stepped backward. Zac halted when he saw her hasty withdrawal.

"Did you think that everything was going to be nice and simple after you had allowed me into your bed? Did you think I would be a lot easier to manage afterward? Did you think you could keep me from asking certain questions by sleeping with me?"

"Damn it, Zac, don't you dare accuse me of seducing you! You're the one who wandered into my bedroom in the middle of the night. No one invited you!"

"And no one turned me away after I got there," he said, reminding her.

Guinevere didn't know if she could take any more. She wanted to strike him and she wanted to cry. She did neither. Instead, she faced him proudly. "There's another way of looking at this, you know. From my side of the equation it looks as if you deliberately seduced me in order to get answers to your stupid questions. You used me, didn't you, Zac?"

"No, damn it, I did not use you!" He looked furious at the accusation.

"I think you did. But you're not handling this properly. You should have asked me all your questions last night when I was off guard."

"You think I should believe you, don't you? You've got the hurt, betrayed attitude of a woman scorned. Give me one good reason why I should trust you completely, Gwen. I had to blackmail you into this thing in the first place, remember? And I used your own little benefits scam to do it. You've hardly got an unimpeachable background."

Her throat was too dry. Guinevere had to swallow a couple of times before she could answer. Then she said dully, "You're absolutely right. Why should I bother to argue? You've made up your mind. All right, you're entitled to your conclusions, but in the meantime, what are you going to do about that blood on the desk? What are you going to do about the fact that Larry Hixon might be lying in some ravine?"

Zac watched her the way a predator watches prey. "I'll stand a much better chance of figuring out what's happened to Hixon if you'll answer my questions."

"I've already answered them!"

"You swear you knew absolutely nothing about the shipping thefts?"

"I swear it. But what good does that do? Why should you believe me? All we've got between us is a quick roll in the sack." She folded her arms tightly across her chest and stood stiffly in front of him.

A long, measureless pulse of time and tension passed between them, and then Zac seemed to shake off an invisible restraint. He moved, swinging around to open the box of computer disks that sat on the desk. "All right," he said coolly. "We'll take it from here." He began thumbing through the disks.

Guinevere eyed him narrowly. "What do you mean, we'll take it from here?"

"We'll assume that you're telling the truth."

She was too astonished to say anything for an instant. Then she found her tongue. "I can't tell you how thrilled I am."

"Don't try. Just help me find the game disk."

"Elf Hunt? You want the game?"

"Every time I turn around in this damn case I find that game somewhere in the vicinity. Cal was doing some serious modifications of the game before he disappeared. The last thing Hixon was working on as far as we know was that game. Now Hixon's gone. That's one coincidence too many. Ah, here it is." He pulled a disk out of the box and held it under the desk lamp to study the label. "Hixon was keeping a notebook that listed the changes Bender had made, remember?"

"I remember." Unwillingly, her anger and her hurt still in full sail, Guinevere walked toward the desk. "It's still there. I saw it a few minutes ago. What are you going to do, Zac?"

"Try to play the game again, this time looking at it from a different point of view."

"What point of view?"

"If we assume that Cal Bender got murdered, then we can assume he might have been killed because of the shipping thefts."

"You think there's a definite tie between the two?"

"It's the best guess I can make at the moment."

"You were making some guesses about me a little while ago. Maybe the conclusions you've come to about Bender are just as off base."

"Forget it, Gwen." He sat down in front of the computer and inserted the disk. "Pull up a chair, and help me get this thing started. Hixon showed us how to play the game up to a certain point the other day. We should at least be able to get that far this afternoon."

Guinevere reluctantly found a chair and pulled it into place. "What about this?" She looked at the bloodstains.

"Nothing in those bloodstains is going to tell us where Larry Hixon is right now. Maybe something in this game will."

"What did you mean when you said you were going to play the game from a different point of view?"

"Computer wizards tend to be sloppy in a lot of ways, but not when it comes to dealing with computers. If I've learned nothing else so far in this crazy investigation, I've learned that. You've seen the incredible detail Hixon and Bender have put into this game. And you've seen how hard Hixon's been working to figure out every single change his pal made. Take a look at that notebook. He's documented everything."

Guinevere flipped open the notebook and scanned Larry's notations. "So?"

"So if Bender was involved in the shipping thefts and if he was manipulating the thefts through the StarrTech computers the way Russ seems to think, then this game might have served as the documentation of the scam."

"For someone who doesn't know much about computers, that's a pretty interesting conclusion," Guinevere said.

"I don't know much about computers, but I do know something about human motivations."

"I remember. You knew exactly what to hold over my head in order to blackmail me, didn't you?"

He didn't answer, his whole attention on the first steps of the game. "Read me Hixon's notes one by one. We're at the drawbridge, and we've got three possible choices."

Guinevere glanced down at the notes. "Choose number three, the ax."

Slowly, making several frustrating mistakes that sent them back to earlier stages of the game, Guinevere and Zac slogged their way through a fictional wonderland of monsters, dwarfs, giant spiders, and menacing ghosts. Time crawled past as the character representing the player made his way deep into the mountains in search of the treasure. He reached the treasure hall and stole a packful of gems and gold. Then he started back down out of the mountains.

"This is the stage of the game Larry was at the last time we were here," Guinevere observed sometime later. "He was trying to figure out a way to get past the lady of the lake." She ran her fingertip down the list of notes on her lap. "Looks like he decided to try answer number four."

"Back up into the mountains? He just came from there. Why would he want to go back the way he had come? The king is pursuing him from that direction."

"Who knows? A programmer's logic perhaps."

"If I wind up getting bounced all the way back to the drawbridge, I'm going to blame you," Zac said mildly as he chose answer number four. "Damn, this thing is frustrating."

But the player was not sent back to the earliest stage of the game. Instead, he started back up the path into the mountains, still carrying the treasure. He dodged the pursuing king by hiding (answer number two) and then continued back toward the treasure hall.

"This doesn't make any sense." Guinevere leaned forward to study the screen. "The original point of the game was to escape the mountain stronghold and return to civilization with the treasure. Now Larry's notes are taking us back into the mountains."

"But the king went right by us and never saw a thing." Zac swore disgustedly. "Listen to me. I sound as if that's really us inside the computer trying to get away with the treasure. All right, what next?"

"'Confront giant spider again,'" she read.

"Instead of setting a trap for him? That doesn't sound right. Who would just confront a spider?" But Zac selected the option that specified confrontation.

The spider simply got out of the way as if it hadn't seen the intrusion.

"The spider is supposed to be the gate guard. Why didn't he react to our trying to get back inside the mountain?" Guinevere tapped the tip of her pencil on the pad. "Most of the characters are straight out of StarrTech personnel files, Zac. That's probably supposed to be a company guard."

"Who acts like he doesn't see a thing. Bribed?" Zac nodded. "Okay, what next?"

"There is only one more note, Zac." Guinevere chewed on her lower lip as she read the final direction. "After the giant spider let you through, you're supposed to choose answer number three."

"And go right back into the treasure hall? Okay."

Zac pushed the proper key and sat back as the graphics on the screen did a series of crazy gyrations.

"What the hell? The treasure hall doesn't look the same as it did the first time we entered." Zac examined the graphic display curiously. A light was flashing in the lower right-hand corner of the screen. "What's that?"

"The light? I don't know. There's no reference to it in Larry's notes. He must not have gotten any farther before—" She broke off, not wanting to finish the sentence. "What are the options listed for the next playing step?"

Zac read them slowly, "'Pick up treasure chest' is option number one."

"That doesn't make sense. We're already holding the treasure we wanted."

"'Go back to giant spider and negotiate.'"

Guinevere wrinkled her nose. "Who negotiates with a spider?"

"'Find another exit from the hall.'"

"Hmm. That's a possibility. There wasn't any other exit mentioned the last time we were in here. What's the last option?"

"It just says, 'Choose *D*.'" Zac's finger hovered over the letter *D* on the keyboard. "I think I'll try that one first. If it doesn't work, we can play the damn thing again and choose the new exit from the hall." He punched *D*.

The flashing light on the screen winked out. Instantly the graphics disappeared. In their place was an address.

"Good grief," Guinevere whispered, "why on earth would Cal have left an Alaskan address?"

Zac didn't move for a long moment, his gaze fixed on the screen. "Write it down, Gwen. Before it disappears or something."

Hastily she scribbled the unfamiliar Alaskan address. "Have you ever heard of Calliope Junction?"

"Nope. But that doesn't mean anything. I've never been to Alaska."

The address on the screen suddenly winked out. The first steps of the game reappeared.

"What now, Zac? Do we play it again? It's getting late. Almost dark." Guinevere slowly closed the notebook in her lap.

Zac carefully slipped the disk out of the computer drive and shut off the machine. "No, we don't play it again. It's taken us too long to get this far."

"But what about that other option? The one that offered a new exit from the hall."

He stood up and resheathed the disk in its envelope. "I'm a pragmatic man, Gwen. I'd much rather check out an address than continue playing games. Let's go."

"Go where? Zac, what are you going to do next?"

He was pulling out a handkerchief and wiping any surfaces he might have touched, including the computer. "What did that last picture of the mountain treasure hall look like, Gwen?"

"I don't know." She thought about it. "It seemed different. There wasn't any huge pile of glittering treasure. Just some stacks of boxes."

"Yeah. And where does StarrTech stack boxes in great quantity?" He glanced around, assuring himself the living room was in order.

"A warehouse." Guinevere followed him out the door. "What are you going to do, Zac?"

"Pay a visit to the StarrTech warehouse when there won't be anyone around but the night guard. Say, around ten o'clock tonight."

"What do you think you'll find? A box with that address on it? Zac, that's pretty far-fetched." She hastened down the steps in his wake.

"I don't know what I'll find. I just want to go looking."

"But what about those bloodstains? What about Larry?"

He turned around at the Laser, opening her car door for her. "Gwen, I'm playing some hunches," he said impatiently. "If I get lucky and play them fast enough, we may have a chance of finding Larry. If we do this formally and call in the cops, everything will go into a long delay. By the time it all gets sorted out the answers may have disappeared."

"On their way to Alaska?"

He smiled. "You know, sometimes you're not half slow."

She refused to respond to that. "I don't think you should go, Zac."

"But then you really don't have anything to say about it, do you? If I don't call you by midnight, go ahead and notify the police about Hixon."

He pushed her not ungently into the car and slammed the door. A moment later he was in the Buick, pulling out onto the street. He didn't glance back as he drove off toward town.

Guinevere sat for a few seconds behind the wheel of her car and thought that there was one more question she had wanted to discuss with him. Not only had the roles of the players been altered in Bender's version of the game, but one character was still missing from the game.

There had been no appearance of the elf at any point. Yet Cal hadn't changed the name of the game. The title on the screen had still been "Elf Hunt."

Guinevere wondered what would have happened if instead of pushing the *D* key, Zac had chosen the option that offered an alternative route out of the treasure hall. Slowly she put the Laser in gear and started home.

The questions in her head wouldn't go away. By nine thirty that night she was still fretting about the blood on Hixon's desk and the untried option in the last playing sequence of the game. When Guinevere wasn't busy worrying about that, she gave herself up to terrifying fantasies of Zac wandering alone around a deserted warehouse.

Except that he wouldn't be alone, she reminded herself. The night guard would be on duty. A night guard who, like a giant spider, wasn't doing his duty? Zac was the expert, Guinevere reminded herself. This was his line of work. She took some comfort from that and then asked herself why she was worrying in the first place about a man who obviously didn't have a lot of faith in her integrity.

She had been a fool to let him stay the night. Guinevere groaned silently as she paced her living room for the hundredth time. She glanced at the clock. In another half hour or so Zac would be inside the warehouse. Why had he wanted to go so late at night? Saturday was a quiet warehouse day anyway. Perhaps if some overtime had been authorized, there might be a few people around, but that was about all. He wouldn't have been bothered by a normal workday crowd if he'd just gone in early this evening.

Unless he not only wanted to avoid any stray overtime workers but had plans somehow to avoid the night guard too. Maybe after seeing the reaction of the spider in the game script, he was suspicious of the guards.

In which case he was *sneaking* into that warehouse, not simply going in on official business during the quiet hours.

Alarm flared along Guinevere's nerve endings. Cal Bender was dead. Larry Hixon was missing, and the elf had disappeared from the story script.

Bender and Hixon knew the StarrTech computer programs inside out. And so did the Elf. With a flash of intuition Guinevere wondered if it was the missing elf who would have been discovered if they had chosen the option that would have provided an alternative route out of the treasure hall.

Nervously Guinevere glanced again at the clock. From the beginning Zac had coordinated his investigation with Russ Elfstrom. It was entirely logical that Zac had informed Elfstrom of his plans to go into the warehouse tonight.

Everybody in the new game script had been assigned a role except the elf.

Guinevere felt herself grow very cold. She was overreacting. She didn't know anything about conducting an investigation. If she had any sense, she would stay out of it and let Zac play it his own way. He was the expert.

And then, one more time, she visualized his going through that warehouse on his own tonight, perhaps dealing with a hostile guard who took his orders from someone behind the scenes, say, a manipulative, intrigue-loving king or an unseen elf.

Guinevere gave up trying to rationalize herself out of panic. It was easier to succumb to it. She grabbed her leather bag, located the car keys, and let herself out of the apartment. After loping downstairs into the garage, she climbed quickly into the Laser. It was a long drive out to StarrTech's warehouse. It would take her almost half an hour to get there. And by now Zac would already be inside.

Getting past the guard had been unexpectedly easy. He had been nowhere around. Zac stored that interesting tidbit of information and then began his tour through the warehouse. He had a flashlight in one hand, and he was wearing a pair of what used to be called sneakers before they became fashionable. The dark cotton knit sweater and jeans gave him what Guinevere would probably think was a suitably commando-style air.

He thought of her as he drifted like a ghost through the stacks of packing crates and cartons. The knot of tension he'd felt this morning as he'd listened to Russ Elfstrom's logic had been inexplicable. He should have been able to deal easily with the possibility that Gwen was somehow involved in this mess. But it hadn't been easy at all to confront her. And he still wasn't sure he should trust his judgment. Christ! He'd been to bed with the woman only once. You didn't make fundamental decisions about whom to trust on that basis.

Trust was a factor that came into an association over a long period of time. It was something that came into existence when you'd worked with someone for a while, developed a rapport, done favors for the other person, and had him or her return those favors. Trust was something you had after someone had saved your neck and you, in turn, had saved his or hers.

Trust was a hard-won commodity and existed between very few

people. Trust, Zac knew, was one of the anchors in his friendship with Russ Elfstrom.

Sure as hell, Zac told himself, he was not obliged to trust Guinevere Jones after such a short period of time and one night in her bed. But maybe his judgment had been impaired. He'd let her off far too easily this afternoon. He should have pushed and pushed hard; he should have worn her down, prodded and pulled and pounded until she was in tears. She wasn't that tough. He could have broken her beneath a little well-applied interrogation.

But the hurt and defiance in her eyes had bothered him, made him feel ridiculously guilty. He hadn't wanted to be responsible for the pain. He'd wanted to comfort her, apologize for the questioning. He had just wanted to believe her and had let it go at that. So he'd trusted his instincts and backed off instead of pushing her until she cracked. The hell of it was, she probably didn't even realize how lucky she'd been.

Zac moved down a long aisle of crates. A part of him listened intently to the tiny noises in the darkness. He knew he was waiting for something, but while he waited he intended to have a look at the shipment holding area. A few minutes later he was in it, swinging the flashlight beam across the address labels on the crates and boxes waiting for shipment the following Monday. It was a long shot, of course. But offhand he couldn't think of anything more intelligent.

Cal Bender's body had been discovered. By rights it should have stayed hidden through the long, cold winter in the mountains. With any luck at all, it might not even have emerged in the spring. That ravine had been deep. Still, casual hikers had found the body. Bodies had a way of turning up, Zac reflected. They were hard to hide, harder than a murderer might think. Bodies decomposed and drew attention with the odor. Bodies floated to the surface of lakes, washed ashore on beaches, got dug up by gardeners, found by hunters. It was tough to hide a body.

One method was to ship it right out of the state.

Larry Hixon had disappeared this morning. The news about Bender's body being found had been on television late last night, and it had also appeared in the morning paper. Someone might have decided that things were getting much too dangerous and that it would be safer to take Hixon out of the game. The same someone might have decided to try an alternative method of hiding the body, perhaps a method that had worked successfully for hiding other things, such as equipment shipments.

StarrTech was saving money on its electric bill, Zac noted. Most of the warehouse was in deep darkness. A few fluorescent lights burned near the exits and threw long shadows down the aisles of boxes and crates, but here in the holding area it would have been impossible to read the labels on the boxes without the flashlight. As it was, Zac had to move slowly and carefully. On the positive side, he reminded himself, he was good at moving slowly and carefully. It was something he did well. A man had to take pride in whatever small talents he possessed.

In spite of his careful search, the crate with the label addressed to Calliope, Alaska, almost slipped past without Zac's seeing it. He had been leaning across it to read the large carton behind it. But when he stepped back, the odd name jumped into the flashlight's beam.

Zac felt the familiar, sudden surge of adrenaline that always seemed to hit him when he was close to an answer. Over the years he had learned to heed the warning. He examined the fastening of the crate. It would take a crowbar to get inside. That was okay. He'd already noted where the day crew kept its tools.

Zac moved quickly back through the aisles of cartons and crates, found a crowbar, and returned to the Calliope box. After balancing the flashlight on a nearby carton, he began to pry the top off the crate that had been bound for Alaska.

It was no surprise when he found Larry Hixon inside. The

amazing part was that Hixon was still alive. Unconscious, bound and gagged, but alive. There was a swelling on the side of his head, and there had been some bleeding, although not enough to seep out of the carton.

Zac was reaching inside the crate, on the verge of lifting out the unconscious man, when he heard the soft rustle of sound at the far end of the warehouse. Apologizing silently to the injured man, Zac let Hixon slide back down into the crate.

That soft noise was what Zac realized he had been waiting for. It meant that someone else had followed him to the warehouse. It could be only one person.

CHAPTER 9

The warehouse door gave easily when Guinevere opened it. Inside, there was a dim glow from an overhead lamp. The weak illumination spread out for a few feet and then disappeared into the darkness between the aisles of crates. No alarms sounded; no guard challenged her entrance. But Guinevere had the feeling she was not alone in the building. At this point she wasn't sure if that was good or bad.

She walked to the edge of the fluorescent lamp's ineffectual attempt to stave off the darkness and stood staring blindly into the shadows. She should have thought to bring along a flashlight. She almost called out to Zac to see if he was out there in the darkness but changed her mind when she considered what might happen if it wasn't Zac's presence she sensed.

Uncertainly Guinevere hovered on the border of the light, wary of moving into the shadows but convinced that having come this far, she had to keep going. Zac had seemed sure that there were secrets to be uncovered here, and she, in turn, was more and more afraid that he might be walking into a trap. Hesitantly Guinevere stepped over the edge into the dark. Slowly her eyes adjusted to the point where she could make out the dim aisles lined with crates and cartons.

It was a little too much like playing Elf Hunt for real: the inability to see what lay around the next corner; the persistent shadows; the conviction that there was a secret to be discovered. *Too real*, Guinevere thought as she slipped quietly along the concrete floor. *Much too real*. At least in Elf Hunt you had some clear-cut options. What she needed was an option.

As if by magic or computer sorcery, an option presented itself when she rounded the corner of a long aisle. A few feet ahead she could just barely see the outline of what appeared to be a workbench. Workbenches had tools. Carefully she threaded her way toward the metal table and shelves. Halting in front of it, she peered around until she found a long strip of heavy metal. It was a crowbar. She reached up and wrapped her fingers around the end of the object. It was heavier than she would have guessed.

Feeling at least minimally armed now, Guinevere turned to start back down another aisle. Her soft-soled shoes made little, if any, sound on the concrete, but she was certain anyone listening would be able to hear her breathing. That thought reminded her that she had to start listening for someone else's breathing.

Again she wanted to call to Zac, but once more she talked herself out of it on the grounds that she didn't know if there was a third party in the room. Her hunch was that there probably was. It seemed a good bet that said third party wouldn't be expecting her. She would provide an element of surprise, Guinevere told herself bracingly. Visions of acting as Zac's backup squad danced in her mind. Of course, he hadn't requested any backup, but that was because he probably didn't realize just how much danger he might be in tonight.

The illusion of being in the middle of Elf Hunt grew stronger as Guinevere traipsed slowly down one aisle. If the malevolent elf suddenly jumped out at her from behind a stack of crates, the fantasy would be perfect. The thought sent a shudder through Guinevere. Genuine fear began to replace the bravado that had been propelling her forward. She came to an uneasy halt at the end of one aisle.

This might not be the brightest way to approach things. Perhaps she should go back to the lighted area and think of a more brilliant strategy. Maybe she should do something simple and straightforward, like call the cops.

Guinevere didn't get a chance to go through the full list of possibilities. The force that struck her from behind cut off her thoughts as well as her supply of air before she even realized what had happened. The next thing she knew she was lying on the cold concrete, the taste of dust and grit in her mouth. A terrible weight seemed to be pressing her down. She couldn't seem to catch her breath.

There was a small snap, and then a glaring light burned on the other side of her closed eyes. The weight on her back shifted, and rough hands turned her onto her side. With an effort Guinevere opened one eye.

"Damn."

Guinevere dimly recognized the voice of the Frog even though she couldn't see Zac's face beyond the bright ring of light.

"My sentiments exactly," she mumbled.

"Christ, Gwen. It wasn't supposed to be you. What the hell—"

Before she could respond, another voice sounded from across the aisle. "Well," said Russ Elfstrom, "this is going to turn out very tidily after all. You always were very thorough, Zac. Slow, but thorough. I wasn't expecting Miss Jones, but she can be accommodated, I think."

Elfstrom stepped forward and switched on his own flashlight. It produced a powerful beam that cut a swath across the tableau of Guinevere lying on her side with Zac down on one knee beside her. There was enough glare to reflect back onto the Elf's satisfied expression. The light also clearly revealed the small handgun he held.

Guinevere decided that the harsh lighting effects made Elfstrom look very much like a character out of a very dangerous computer game.

Zac stayed where he was, studying the gun for a moment and then Elfstrom's face. "I was wondering when you were going to show up, Russ. When I heard Gwen, I thought it must be you."

Elfstrom nodded almost sadly. "I was afraid you'd figured it all out. For a while I had hopes of convincing you that Bender and Hixon and Miss Jones constituted the ring of thieves. I went to a lot of trouble to make it look that way. It would have made things easier, but it wouldn't really have altered the plan."

"Why did you get me involved in the first place?" Zac was calm, his voice even and controlled. He asked the question as if it had been generated by sheer curiosity.

Elfstrom shrugged. "Didn't have much choice. When that guy in accounting discovered the inventory discrepancies, he came to me first to check out the possibility of the problem's being caused by a computer error. He also talked to Bender, who swore the program was accurate. There was no way I could pretend it was a computer error, and I was sure the accountant was smart enough to know that. So I told him and Bender I'd take charge of the matter and go straight to Hampton Starr. I assured them management would handle it. That satisfied the eager beaver in accounting. And it kept him from going to Starr on his own."

"But it didn't satisfy Cal, did it?" Guinevere could barely get the words out. There was a fine trembling throughout her whole body.

"That bastard just kept digging away." Elfstrom gave an exclamation of utter disgust. "I told him to forget it, that everything was under control, but he just wouldn't let go. It was his program that had turned up the errors and you know how goddamned possessive programmers are about the stuff they've written. I was afraid he was getting too close to the truth. Then one night, after he'd gone home, I found the Calliope address. He'd written it down on a pad near his computer and torn off the page, but I could see the imprint on the next piece of paper. I left that address in the computer for only a period of twenty-four hours at a time. After a shipment left the warehouse, I always removed the address and any related records. But Bender must have been monitoring things, watching for any little hint. He must have rigged the computer to report back to him if there were any odd movements of information."

"Such as address information being inserted and then removed?" Zac asked.

Elfstrom nodded, his head moving in a short, jerky manner that registered his inner tension. "I knew I had to get rid of him. I followed him home, knocked him out, and used his car to drive into the mountains. I thought he'd stay in that ravine at least until next spring. By now he should have been under a couple of feet of snow."

"But the snow is late this year." Bleakly Guinevere recalled Jackson's complaints about the slow start of the ski season.

Zac eyed Elfstrom thoughtfully. "In the meantime, you were explaining things to Starr in your own way."

"I couldn't hide the situation, so I decided to camouflage it. You know the routine, Zac. A little misdirection and distraction can go a long way."

Zac paused before saying softly, "I know the routine."

"You should. I've seen you follow some incredibly mixed-up trails before."

"You thought you could keep me focused on the wrong trails this time, though, didn't you?"

The Elf smiled with a touch of resignation. "What can I say? We were friends. We went back a long way together. You owed me. You trusted me. And I'd done you still another favor by recommending that StarrTech hire you. Given all that, sure, I thought I could handle you. You should have heard the sales pitch I gave Hampton Starr, Zac. Described you in glowing terms. I didn't tell him that they used to call you Glacier, though. It wouldn't have gone with the image Starr wanted to hire. He had the impression he was getting an ex–James Bond. And he got to be the secret agent's boss. It was the ultimate intrigue for him."

"So everyone was happy. Hampton Starr was having fun, I got my first big client, and you got to keep pulling the strings behind the scenes."

Guinevere sucked in her breath as she struggled up on one elbow. Her side ached a little from the impact with the concrete. "Nobody seems to have considered my happiness in all this."

Elfstrom didn't bother looking at her as he answered. He kept his eyes on Zac. "You were just a means of focusing Zac's attention on certain areas. You'd already fooled around once with StarrTech's computers. I discovered that when I went through the system looking for red herrings I might be able to use. In a company the size of Starr-Tech there's always the possibility of a little computer fraud going on. Even a few simple errors could have been made to look like fraud. Then, if necessary, I'd have my scapegoat ready to throw to the wolves. Sure enough, there you were. I thought that sooner or later, with a few subtle suggestions from me, it would eventually occur to Zac that you might have been involved in the thefts. When everyone finally realized that Cal Bender's absence was definitely suspicious, I figured even Zac here would begin to put two and two together."

"The final player was Larry Hixon, right?" Guinevere winced as she sat up completely.

"I wanted the three of you, Bender, Hixon, and Jones, to stage a nice little drama for Hampton Starr's pleasure."

"And my role in the theatrics was to expose the scheme in the final act." Zac slanted a quick sideways glance at Guinevere before returning his attention to Elfstrom.

"Just before the final curtain," the Elf said, nodding. "Don't worry. Even though you didn't come to all the right conclusions, you're still going to go out a hero. Want to hear the complete scenario as Hampton Starr will hear it when he returns on Monday?"

"I can't wait."

"Bender is the victim of a falling-out among thieves. He was killed by his partner, Larry Hixon, when Hixon decided that a two-way split is better than a three-way split. Hixon and Guinevere, who have already pulled off a few side stunts on their own, such as draining ten thousand from the benefits program, proceed merrily on their way."

"Until I catch them one night in the StarrTech warehouse busily addressing a crate to Calliope, Alaska," Zac added.

Guinevere swallowed, aware of an unpleasant tightness in her throat. There was no rush of heady excitement circulating through her veins tonight. Where was the old adrenaline charge? She felt light-headed and frightened.

The Elf shook his head at Zac's ending to the story. "Not quite. You catch them in the warehouse, all right, but you find them quarreling. Hixon has just shot Miss Jones when you come upon the scene. He turns the gun on you. You get off one shot in true, heroic fashion, but Hixon also fires. Presto. All three of you are quite dead."

Guinevere's stomach threatened to rebel. Her shirt felt damp under the arms. Zac was nodding politely, as if appreciating the symmetry of the tale.

"And the security guard?"

"Received instructions not to report for duty this evening. Instructions that were generated by a computer and look quite official."

"It might work," Zac said.

"Oh, it will work. Misdirection and distraction. Very effective." Elfstrom looked pleased with himself but not particularly relaxed. His inner agitation simmered just beneath the surface.

"How long have you been rerouting equipment shipments, Russ?" Zac moved his hand along his thigh, as if his leg were getting cramped from the crouched position.

"Two or three years. It could have gone on forever if Bender hadn't decided to get fancy with the inventory program. It was a nice little scam, Zac. I simply rerouted some reasonably valuable equipment to folks who regularly prefer to buy from *discount* suppliers."

"None of the stuff StarrTech makes is high-tech enough to have an iron curtain market," Guinevere said, thinking of all the stories she had read of people selling technological secrets to foreign nations. "You don't even have to have a security clearance to work there."

"I'm not nearly that ambitious or that stupid, Miss Jones." The Elf looked at her briefly, as if she weren't too bright. "Sooner or later the government always seems to move in on that sort of activity. Much too risky. No, I preferred the safer, more sedate approach of dealing with the home market and the legitimate overseas market. There are plenty of small firms in the States and in friendly countries just getting started that are happy to purchase good-quality equipment at bargain prices. They're smart enough not to ask too many questions, and there is no paper trail to follow once the equipment leaves StarrTech. It simply arrives in Calliope, Alaska, where a certain party dispatches it on to the real destination, wherever that happens to be. StarrTech even winds up paying the freight bill to Alaska. The only expense I incur is the cost of forwarding the shipment on to the purchasers."

"Very neat." Zac ran his palm down his thigh again. "Until the computer system you were using caught up with you. I think there's a kind of justice in that somewhere, Russ."

"If one thinks ahead, one can misdirect justice along with everything and everyone else." The Elf smiled wryly. "You probably won't believe this, Zac, but I'm going to regret killing you."

"Are you?"

"Yes. I've enjoyed working with you on this project. It's been almost like old times."

"Almost."

Guinevere could feel the tension in Zac as he crouched beside her. As if she could read his mind she knew he was waiting for even the smallest opportunity to launch himself at the Elf. She looked at the gun in Elfstrom's hand and tried not to think of how the bullet would feel when it entered her brain.

"I think we've wasted enough time," Russ Elfstrom announced. He motioned ever so slightly with the nose of the gun. "On your feet, Miss Jones. You have to die over there near the holding area. People might ask questions if you were found in this aisle. Zac, you stay where you are until Miss Jones is in front of me."

He was going to use her as a shield to keep Zac from making any rash moves before reaching the holding area, Guinevere realized. She didn't make any immediate effort to climb to her feet. The Elf grew impatient.

"I said on your feet, you little bitch! You've caused me enough trouble."

Guinevere drew a painful breath and clutched at her side. "I—I don't think I can get up. I think I've cracked a rib."

"The hell you have." Elfstrom motioned to Zac. "Move back out of the way. Slowly, Zac. Very, very slowly. You should be good at that."

Zac inched backward unwillingly as the other man came forward. Elfstrom kept the gun and his gaze trained on Zac. Clearly he considered his old friend the greater risk. He set the large flashlight down on the concrete and then reached out to snag Guinevere's hand and yank her forcibly to her feet.

This was going to be her only chance. From out of nowhere the adrenaline exploded in Guinevere's system. She screamed as she stumbled to her feet under the impetus of the Elf's hand on her wrist. The scream echoed in the warehouse and caused the Elf, already clearly tense, to flinch. In her other hand she clung to the crowbar she had found at the workbench. It was supposed to provide an option. She swung it wildly.

Out of the corner of his eye the Elf saw the movement. He yelled as the metal bar caught him fiercely on the arm holding the weapon. The gun in his hand dropped to the concrete floor with a clatter. Zac was already moving, launching himself at the other man from his crouched position.

But in the last instant Elfstrom reacted. He still had hold of Guinevere's wrist, and he used it to yank her forward and send her spinning into Zac's path. Elfstrom's wiry strength was more than enough to lift her off the ground.

For the second time that night Guinevere felt the air being driven from her lungs. Zac swore, a muffled, infuriated sound that was cut off as he was pushed off balance. Guinevere tried frantically to roll to one side to get out of his way. She opened her eyes to find the glare of Elfstrom's flashlight full in her face. There was the sound of running feet disappearing into the darkness, and then she looked up to find Zac staring into the shadows, a gun in his hand.

It wasn't the same one that Elfstrom had dropped, she realized dazedly. That one still lay on the floor.

"A real Laurel and Hardy act," she muttered, staggering to her feet. Her hand went to her ribs. She was going to be very sore, although she was fairly certain nothing was badly damaged. "At least he's unarmed now."

"No." With a swift motion Zac leaned down and turned off both flashlights. "He's not unarmed. Elfstrom always carried a second gun. And we don't need these flashlights acting like spotlights." He grabbed Guinevere's bruised wrist. "Come on. Let's move."

"Where? Zac, shouldn't we—"

"Shush, Gwen. Not another word."

Fear returned in full force again as the temporary surge of energy faded from her bloodstream. Guinevere felt unaccountably cold and realized she was shaking slightly. Trying to be as quiet as possible, she followed Zac down the aisle. Her eyes began adjusting slowly once again to the darkness. She wanted to ask where he was leading her, what plans he was making, but she didn't dare break the silence he had imposed.

Straining to listen, Guinevere tried to catch the sound of a closing door, which might indicate that Elfstrom had left the building. There was no such reassuring noise. Zac rounded the corner of one aisle and started cautiously up another.

Perhaps Zac was heading for an exit, Guinevere theorized. There was a risk because over the exit doorways the fluorescent bulbs still glowed, the only lighted areas in the building. To get out one of the doors, they would have to pass beneath the light. If he were watching the right door, the Elf would see them. They'd be sitting ducks.

Apparently Zac had figured that much out for himself. He led the way down another aisle and over to the far wall, a section of the building that seemed to be in deepest shadow. Guinevere could see only a few steps in front of her now. Zac moved forward with more certainty. Perhaps he had come this way earlier and knew there weren't any unexpected objects waiting to trip them in the aisle.

Guinevere tried to tell herself that if she couldn't see far in the gloom, neither could the Elf. But the realization that he was out there somewhere in the shadows, stalking her and Zac, made her shiver again.

How long could this unbearable tension go on? Surely one of the players would have to make a move. For Pete's sake, Guinevere thought wildly, they all couldn't just spend the night in this place, wandering around in the dark until they blundered into each other. The thought was terrifying.

In the computer game of Elf Hunt at least one had choices to make, and there was the knowledge that the right answer did exist. All the player had to do was find it. In this real-life version of the game the possibilities didn't seem to be presenting themselves in any clear-cut fashion. And even if they did, choosing the wrong one would be choosing death.

Zac was heading for the far end of the warehouse, Guinevere suddenly saw. There was an exit down there, but it was illuminated, just as the others were. Maybe he planned to make a dash for the outside, hoping the Elf was at the wrong end of the room.

A soft sound from the next aisle over on her right made Guinevere freeze. Zac halted too. His fingers tightened reassuringly around her wrist, and then he released her hand. He pushed her down against the wall, into the deepest shadow. Then he crouched down beside her. She could just barely see the gun in his hand. The soft, gliding sound continued down the aisle. It had to be Elfstrom.

He was ahead of them now, Guinevere thought. It made her feel less vulnerable. Probably only an illusion, she told herself. Then she realized what had happened. The roles in the game had been reversed. She and Zac were now the stalkers. Zac rose silently, his head turned toward the direction in which Elfstrom had gone. Guinevere got up beside him, and this time Zac didn't take her hand. She knew his whole attention was on the hunt.

Guinevere eyed the approaching area of light, beginning to think in terms of predator and prey. It would be easy for Elfstrom to set up an ambush near the door and wait for them to walk into it.

There was a soft scraping sound from up ahead. Zac halted at once. For a long moment there was no movement from him, and Guinevere worried again about someone hearing her breathing. Then she felt Zac's hand on her shoulder, urging her down into a huddle at the foot of one long aisle. This time he was going to leave her, she thought in sudden anxiety. He was going to go after the Elf on his own. Hastily she grabbed at Zac's arm, trying to convey her disapproval of the action.

He ignored her. His strong fingers dug firmly into her shoulder for a few seconds, emphasizing the silent command to stay where she was. Guinevere surrendered reluctantly. This was Zac's area of expertise. She recalled how quickly the gun had appeared in his hand after the tussle in the aisle.

He left her there at the foot of the aisle and faded into the shadows. He was heading toward the lighted doorway. Guinevere peered after him. With every step closer to the door in the wall Zac's figure seemed a little more clear-cut, more visible. His shadow took substance and shape as he approached the weak light. If he was becoming more visible to her, she thought anxiously, then he was becoming more visible to Elfstrom. It was almost as if Zac were deliberately making a target of himself.

Then, even as Guinevere watched, shocked, Zac stepped sideways into the concealment provided by the end of an aisle of stacked crates. He just vanished. One moment he had become almost clearly visible, and then he had disappeared. He called roughly to Elfstrom.

"It wouldn't have worked, anyway, Russ. You must have hurried that business at Hixon's house after you heard the news about those hikers finding Cal's body. You hit Larry a little too hard. He bled a little. That living room was so dark you wouldn't have noticed. Probably had your hands too full to take a last look around anyway. You had to get him outside and into the car before dawn. But the first cop who walked in the door would have started asking questions about how someone the size of Guinevere could have struck Hixon that hard and then dragged his body outside to the car. It would have looked more like the work of a man. And that wouldn't have fitted with the scenario you had arranged here. Sloppy, Russ. But then you always tended to get nervous in the crunches, didn't you? Remember Tallah? Remember how you froze when that soldier pulled a gun on you?"

"Shut up, Justis. I saved your goddamned life in Tallah!"

"What are you going to do now, Elfstrom? This whole thing is coming apart around you. You're probably getting jittery, as usual. After all, this is the crunch. You know how upset you get when things go wrong. How are the nerves? You're smoking more than ever these days, Russ. Your hand started shaking yet? Is it shaking as badly as it did in Tallah?"

The tension and panic in the air seemed to beat down the aisles in waves. Before Guinevere could figure out what the conversation meant, there was a loud scrape of sound from near the door. An instant later Elfstrom appeared silhouetted in the overhead light. It gleamed off his bald head, just as Larry Hixon had once observed, and it made him, not Zac, the target.

"Damn you, Justis! You were supposed to be dead by now!" The frustrated shout was followed by the explosion of a gunshot.

Guinevere instinctively pulled her head down against her chest, huddling into herself. When she glanced up again, Elfstrom had disappeared. There was no sound except the echo of the gunshot fading into the gloom. It had been like watching a character on the computer screen appear and then disappear. Unnerving.

It seemed to Guinevere that there was a new element in the tense atmosphere. Impatience and fear and maybe something close to hysteria seemed to surround her, and the sensations weren't all emanating from her own highly charged emotions. The Elf was beginning to panic, she sensed. He was the one who was finding the game unnerving. He had lost his edge, been forced out of hiding. And now he was panicking.

There was another sound from the vicinity of the doorway. Guinevere looked around the corner of the aisle in time to see Elfstrom dart once more into the light and grab for the door handle. He was going to make a run for it. To cover himself, he fired two quick shots back down the aisle as he wrenched open the door.

"Elfstrom!" Zac moved out of the shadows. "Hold it, right there."

Almost out the door, Russ Elfstrom whirled and fired once again. This time there was an answering shot, and the Elf screamed as he crumpled to the cold concrete.

Ears ringing from the explosions of gunshots, Guinevere stared at the scene at the far end of the aisle. Even as she watched, Zac moved slowly forward into the light. He stood gazing down at the man who had once been his friend. Russ Elfstrom was breathing harshly, his hand clutching at his left shoulder. Vaguely Guinevere realized that he was bleeding from the right arm, not the left. The ringing in her ears receded.

"You were right, Russ. Most of the time I'm slow," Zac said. He sounded unbelievably weary. "But once in a while I'm fast."

"Like you were on the way out of Tallah." The Elf's voice was harsh and bitter. "It was all so perfect, Justis. I had it all planned. I was getting rich. And life is so goddamned short." He coughed and groaned.

Zac dropped to his knee. "You're okay, Russ. That bullet only caught your shoulder."

"It's not the bullet that's going to get me, Zac. Pills. Right pocket." Elfstrom had his eyes shut in agony now. He gasped for breath.

"Oh, Jesus," Zac whispered, clawing into Elfstrom's pocket for a small vial. "Gwen, find a phone. Get the police and tell them we need an ambulance. For two people."

"Two?"

"Hixon's stuffed into a crate headed for Alaska."

Guinevere raced for the phone near the workbench.

CHAPTER 10

Guinevere paused in the hospital room doorway and, through the array of brilliantly colored flowers she was carrying, studied the interesting sight of her sister comforting Larry Hixon. Carla seemed more than politely concerned with the small task of pouring Larry another glass of water. She was handing the glass to the man in the bed when she glanced up and saw her sister. She smiled. There didn't seem to be much residual depression left in that smile, Guinevere decided.

"Oh, there you are, Gwen. I was wondering where you'd disappeared to. I called your cell phone half an hour ago, and there was no answer."

"I stopped to pick up these." Guinevere moved into the room and found a place for the huge bouquet on the wide window ledge. "How are you feeling, Larry?"

"Like I'm gonna survive." He tried a weak grin. "Sorry I don't remember much about last night. My first clear image is of some medic calling into the emergency room from the ambulance. I wondered if I was watching TV, and then I realized I was the one he was notifying the hospital about. I think I woke up in that crate a couple of times, but I kept blacking out again. Doctor said that was common after a bad blow to the head."

"Believe me, you were better off sleeping through the main event." Guinevere walked to the bed. "I'd like to have done the same."

"The police have already been here. They said Elfstrom died in the emergency room last night. Massive heart attack. I gather I owe my life to you and Zac."

"Not me," Guinevere told him. "I was just part of the cheering section. Zac was the star player."

"And to think you used to call him a frog." Carla gave her sister an admonishing glance. "You said he was just like a large frog crouching all day long on a lily pad."

"Well, you know how frogs are," Guinevere said. "They sit there contemplating life for hours and days on end, and then, without any warning, they move. Very quickly, I might add. *Zap!*"

"We frogs always get our flies."

"Zac!" Guinevere swung around to see him filling the doorway. He looked haggard and worn, and his small attempt at humor rang hollow to her ears. She found herself wanting to put her arms around him and comfort him the way Carla was comforting Larry. Very firmly Guinevere reminded herself that her business relationship with Zachariah Justis was over. She had no idea what, if anything, existed between them now.

Carla looked at Zac. "Have you had any sleep?"

"A couple of hours this morning after I finished with the police." Zac came into the room and stood at the foot of Larry's bed. "How're you doing, Hixon?"

"Still got a headache, but my vision's cleared up. It was a little shaky for a while after I opened my eyes this morning. Like I'd spent too long sitting in front of a computer screen. I haven't had a chance to thank you, Zac. I never even heard Elfstrom sneaking through my kitchen window last night. The cop who was here earlier told me what happened."

"Forget it. You're the one who was responsible for putting the pieces of the puzzle together. If you hadn't played out Elf Hunt and left notes behind, we'd still be trying to figure out where the missing shipments were going."

"It was Gwen who got the new version of the game to me." Larry flicked her a half-sad smile. "I'm still having trouble believing Cal's dead. Murdered. Shit."

Carla broke in bracingly. "And you were slated to be next. It's over, Larry. You have to put it behind you. We all do."

"Still going to try to market the game?" Guinevere asked.

Larry nodded. "I think so. For a while I thought I'd have to rework the whole thing, but I finally found Cal's copy of the original game in his house. I'll make sure his name is on it somewhere."

Guinevere thought of something. "Does Hampton Starr know what's happened?" She glanced over at Zac.

He nodded once. "I've been in touch with my client. Finally. It was tough tracking him down. He was at some resort, drinking scotch in front of a roaring fire and enjoying the onset of winter along the coast. Very scenic, he tells me."

"I'll bet." Larry made a face. "Somebody in the printing department was saying just the other day how really scenic the new photocopy clerk is."

"I didn't ask him if he was enjoying the coast with the new photocopy clerk," Zac murmured. "We stuck to business."

"How very discreet of you." But Guinevere was watching her sister's face as Hampton Starr's name came into the conversation. Carla didn't appear to be paying much attention to the discussion. She was arranging Larry's pillows.

"Was the king surprised to find his wizard elf was the one who had been quietly ripping him off for the past couple of years?" Larry asked interestedly.

"He seemed . . ." Zac hesitated. "Very surprised. Yes."

Larry grinned. "Stunned, you mean. Starr likes to think he's an infallible judge of character."

"He also likes to think he's the one running all the little intrigues around StarrTech. He loves to plot and scheme," Carla put in unexpectedly. There was no real bitterness in her voice, only mild disgust. "It must have really startled him to find out that someone was running an intrigue against him right under his nose. Serves him right."

Zac glanced at Guinevere with an unreadable expression. "He recovered nicely. Right now he's orchestrating the press release. I get the feeling that it's going to look like trapping Elfstrom was all his idea. But I doubt if Hampton Starr has even the faintest idea of how many little schemes actually are hatched under his nose at StarrTech."

"Management is often blissfully unaware of a great deal." Guinevere smiled serenely. "Usually it's best for all concerned that they stay unaware. Mustn't bother the higher-ups with petty details." She turned back to Larry. "When you're up and about again, I'd like you to finish playing out Elf Hunt. I want to satisfy my own curiosity about one of the last options in the game." She explained the tunnel and her suspicion that when it was followed someone would find an elf at the other end.

"I'll check it out." Larry stretched and then winced, putting his hand to his head. Instantly Carla was busy soothing him. "I was playing the game when the lights went out," he continued. "I remember it was very late, maybe three or four in the morning. But you said the computer was off when you got there that afternoon?"

Zac nodded grimly. "Elfstrom was in a hurry, but he did take the time to shut down the computer. He didn't want any questions being raised about why you'd simply disappeared, leaving your computer on and a game in progress."

"It was dark in your living room, though. You had all the lights off, I suppose, while you worked on the computer," Guinevere explained. "So the Elf didn't notice the—"

Zac cut in before she could tell Larry about finding the bloodstains. "We'd better get going, Gwen." He glanced meaningfully at his watch. "I've made Sunday brunch reservations, and we'll be late if we don't hurry." He took her arm. "I'll be back later, Larry. In the meantime, get some rest, okay?"

"I'll see that he does," Carla said.

Guinevere found herself being escorted out the door and down the hall before she quite realized what had happened. She started to protest and then smiled wryly. "I take it you don't want me mentioning the bloodstains?"

"I left that detail out when I talked to the police," Zac told her. "If I'd mentioned it, they might have taken offense at the fact that we hadn't called them. As it was, I made it sound as if we were just pursuing some hunches and were as startled as everyone else when we found Larry and had Elfstrom walk in with a gun."

"Gotcha."

He slid her a speculative glance. "My small sin of omission doesn't seem to bother you."

"Heck, no. I've been involved in much bigger sins of omission myself." She reached out and punched the elevator button. "Believe me, I'm happy to keep the story straight." Then she eyed him with sudden wariness. "There are some sins I don't forgive easily, however. Have you really made brunch reservations?"

He shook his head. "No, of course not. I've had my hands full all day talking to the police, tracking down Starr, and getting over here to the hospital."

"I was afraid of that." She sighed. "I've been duped again."

He didn't respond to her melodramatic complaint. Instead, Zac lapsed into silence as he walked with her out onto the street.

"I took the bus," she said.

He nodded. "I grabbed a cab."

They could have caught the bus back down from First Hill. With so many of the city's hospitals and medical clinics clustered in that area of town there was plenty of good bus service. But somehow by mutual, if silent, consent they continued walking. It was a fairly long walk back downtown, but it was all downhill.

Guinevere made no further efforts to breach the silence. She sensed that Zac had had his fill of talking this morning. Talking and explaining and dealing with formalities were difficult when a part of you probably wanted to mourn a dead friendship. Zac had released her arm when they'd entered the elevator. Halfway back to town Guinevere impulsively reached out and took his hand. He twined his large fingers with hers and gripped her hand with a tension that made her wonder exactly what he was thinking. But he continued to say nothing.

They were almost down to First Avenue when Guinevere decided to take charge. "Come on," she said abruptly. "Let's go to my place."

Zac came up out of his reverie long enough to give her a questioning glance, but he didn't argue. He allowed her to guide him back through Pioneer Square to her apartment. The afternoon was wearing on. It was almost three o'clock.

Inside the apartment Guinevere pushed him gently in the direction of the sofa, and then she went into the kitchen and found the bottle of tequila she had bought several months ago when she'd decided to have a margarita and nachos party. There was still a quarter of the bottle left. In another cupboard she found a bag of potato chips.

She carried a couple of glasses, the tequila bottle, and the chips back out into the living room, set them down on the table in front of the sofa, and poured two short drinks. Then she handed him one.

Zac took it, staring first at the liquor and then into her face.

"You're supposed to say, 'Thanks, I needed that,'" she told him.

He took a sip and nodded. "Thanks, I needed that."

She let him drink in silence for a while longer, contenting herself with a few tastes of the raw tequila and several potato chips. Gradually the tension in Zac began to diminish. When he finally spoke aloud, though, Guinevere jumped a little. She'd grown accustomed to his brooding silence. It had reminded her of the evening he had been thinking so deeply and then fallen asleep on her sofa.

"He really did save my life once, you know."

Guinevere waited, saying nothing.

"It was in a dirty little hellhole of a place named Tallah."

Guinevere thought of asking exactly where on the globe Tallah was and then decided she could check out the geography later. Something told her just to sit quietly and let Zac talk.

"Things had gone wrong. Very wrong. The U.S. firm I was supposed to be advising badly misplayed its hand. In its infinite wisdom management had managed to mortally offend the honchos who ran the town. By the time I was sent in to consult on the problem, it was too late to do anything but try to get the U.S. personnel out of the area. I was able to get the firm's people out on a chartered flight. But at the airport the soldiers showed up and started demanding that the plane not take off. I stalled the soldiers while the pilot got the plane off the ground. In the end I was the only foreigner the Tallah authorities had left to punish for the big insult."

Silence hung again in the air, and Zac took another swallow of tequila. He hadn't touched the potato chips, Guinevere noticed.

"I found myself in a filthy jail cell waiting for a kangaroo court to be convened. And then Russ Elfstrom walked through the door, waving a hefty bribe and a lot of phony authority. Our company's head office had decided to try a quick grandstand play to get me out of jail rather than risk going through channels. Russ was the closest member of the firm who could be reached and coached on how to make the attempt. The soldiers weren't sure what to do, but in the end they decided the bribe looked too good to turn down. Russ was smart enough to tell them that the only way they could collect the money was at the border, where he had someone standing by to pay off. We got to the border, and the commanding officer decided to take both the money and me back to Tallah. Russ found himself looking down the wrong end of the gun and started to come apart at the seams. This had been a rather different job for him. He usually got the more civilized assignments. But that close to freedom I wasn't about to let that damned soldier take me back to Tallah."

Again Zac stopped talking, gazing out the arched living room window. Finally Guinevere dared ask, "What happened, Zac?"

"I jumped the guy. And I got lucky. I got him before he could kill Russ. Russ and I worked together off and on after that. Our areas of expertise were different. He was the electronics ace, the one they called in to deal with computer security and alarm systems. I got the more primitive kind of work. But it was a long trip back from Tallah. Crossing the border was only the beginning. And after that there was always a kind of bond between us. He left the firm three years ago to come back to the States."

When the silence descended again, it hung around awhile. Guinevere munched a few more potato chips while Zac worked on the tequila. She felt at a loss to know what to offer in the way of comfort. So she kept quiet.

The shadows lengthened in the living room. Outside, the sky was darkening early as rain moved in over Elliott Bay. Guinevere wondered if Zac had had anything at all to eat that day. He didn't seem even remotely interested in the chips. His eyes were filled with ghosts the color of the rain clouds overhead. Finally, at five o'clock, she got to her feet.

"I think we should go out and get a bite to eat," she announced.

Zac blinked, focusing on her as she stood assertively in front of him. "I'm not hungry."

"Yes, you are." She reached down and caught his hand. He rose reluctantly under the impetus and followed her tamely to the door where she found her jacket. "There's a little place just around the corner where we can get some good pasta. Tequila has its uses, but there aren't a lot of vitamins in it."

Downstairs and down the street she orderd the cheese ravioli for both of them, and after it had arrived, she stared pointedly at Zac until he began to eat. Once he'd started, she was relieved to see, he kept going. When the check came, she automatically picked it up. That finally got his attention. He gave her a small, quirking smile.

"What gives?"

"This is your lucky night." She paid the bill and took his arm to walk him back toward the apartment. At the door he came to a halt and looked down at her, frowning.

"I should probably go home," he said.

"Yes," Guinevere said. The rain had hit while they were at dinner, and its steady beat surrounded them as they stood under the shelter of the doorway.

"Gwen, I'm—well, thanks."

"For dinner?"

He shook his head. "For everything. For listening this afternoon. For being patient while I worked it through."

She smiled. "I thought maybe you were going to thank me for acting as your backup team last night."

Something flickered in his gaze. "And almost getting yourself killed? Forget it. Be grateful you're no longer working for me.

Otherwise, I would have ignored all those management articles on how to criticize employees in a positive and constructive fashion." He paused, considering the matter. "I probably should go ahead and tear a strip off you anyway. You scared the living hell out of me last night when I found out I hadn't tackled Elfstrom after all."

"You were expecting the Elf to show up?"

Zac nodded. "You and he were the only ones who knew I was heading for the warehouse at ten o'clock. I phoned him after I had put you into the car in front of Larry's house."

"I was afraid you might have notified him. At nine thirty I knew that Elfstrom was probably behind everything that had happened. There was no reason for Cal to have rewritten the game program leaving out the principal character unless that character was in a new role."

"Behind the scenes, pulling strings." Zac nodded again. "It didn't make any sense that the real menace was Hampton Starr. He could have been ripping off his own company for some reason, and he does like intrigues, but frankly, the guy's pure management."

Guinevere chuckled. "Exactly. He doesn't know a damn thing about computers. Besides, he enjoys his role as king of the empire. He prefers to rule in style. And he's terribly conscious of the image. It wouldn't have fitted the image for him to be running a black-market scam on the side."

"Right. And Cal and Larry were too wrapped up in their plans to make a fortune by selling Elf Hunt. Besides, just as Starr is pure management, they were pure programmers. And they were young. They came straight out of college into StarrTech. The odds were against their having the kind of contacts it would take to sell those shipments of equipment."

Guinevere went still. "And then there was me."

"Yes. And then there was you."

"Admit it, Zac. For a while you had your doubts about me. Did Elfstrom help plant them?"

"He worked on it." Zac lifted his hand to rub his thumb along the line of her jaw. In the overhead light his eyes seemed to have regained their brooding quality again. "But I didn't want it to be you, Gwen. Above all I didn't want it to be you."

"You put me through the third degree out at Larry's house."

He shook his head. "I barely touched you."

"Are you kidding? I felt as if I'd been put through the wringer!" Then Guinevere tipped her head to one side, studying him. It occurred to her that she had gotten off lightly after all. A real inquisition conducted by this man would have been endless and brutal. She knew that with a certainty that sent a small shiver through her, and she took a moment to thank her lucky stars.

"I didn't want it to be you, Gwen," he repeated.

"But you didn't want it to be your old friend either."

"No, but in the end I knew it had to be Russ. Like you, I realized that there was a reason the game had been totally rearranged with the major character left out entirely. Cal had, in typical computer nerd fashion, left the clues in Elf Hunt as he uncovered them."

"He probably wanted to make a grand announcement when he had everything pieced together. Cal would have enjoyed pulling the rug out from under the Elf. He disliked Elfstrom intensely. But Elfstrom moved in on him before he could finish the project."

They absorbed the implications of that, and then Zac made another halfhearted effort to leave. "I owe you, Gwen. I'd still be flogging this case if it hadn't been for your help. Shall I call you tomorrow with an update?"

"I'll be at the office."

He looked momentarily relieved, as though he'd been expecting her to tell him she didn't want a call. "Okay." He stepped back, his fingers falling reluctantly away from the side of her face.

Without giving herself time to think, Guinevere caught his hand. She took a deep breath. "I'm glad you didn't want it to be me, Zac."

"Gwen, I—"

She hushed him with her fingertips on his mouth. "Would you like to come back upstairs? Just nod if the answer's yes." She smiled tremulously.

Mutely he nodded. Mutely he followed her up the stairs. Inside the door of her apartment Guinevere put her arms around his neck. "I'm willing to try again."

"To turn me into a prince?" The gray eyes gleamed.

"Yes."

"Frogs are a bit slow at times," he said warningly, folding his arms around her waist.

"Sometimes slow is exactly the right way to do things." She lifted her face for his kiss.

Guinevere received two calls at the office the following afternoon. The first was from Larry Hixon. When she said his name with pleasure, Carla looked up expectantly from across the room, where she had several file drawers torn apart.

"Larry! You're home from the hospital already?" Guinevere smiled.

"I had to get home. Had to finish Elf Hunt. You were right, Gwen. Guess what you find if you go out the second exit of the treasure chamber?"

"The elf?"

"Yup. He's in there sitting at a computer console. The power behind the throne, I guess. He pulls all the strings in the game. Actually it's a brilliant twist to the ending. I think I'll keep it in the final version of Elf Hunt. I'm going to add a new character, though."

"A frog?"

"How'd you guess? Is Carla there?"

"Yes, she's here." With a smile Guinevere handed the phone over to her sister, who took it eagerly.

Guinevere had bought a paper earlier, and she reread the brief article while Carla chatted with Larry. When Carla hung up eventually, Guinevere sighed and tossed the paper back down onto the desk. "I can't believe it."

Carla grinned. "You're just mad because the reporter got your name wrong."

"Miss Smith. *Miss Smith.*" Guinevere groaned.

"You know how it is. Smith, Jones, who can remember? There are so many Smiths and Joneses in the world."

"You're awfully philosophical about it," Guinevere said.

"Frankly," said Carla, "it might be for the best that your right name and Camelot Services didn't get mentioned."

"You've got a point. Actually anyone reading that article is going to come away with the distinct impression that Hampton Starr stopped the Elf single-handedly."

Half an hour later the phone rang again.

"Gwen? It's Zac. The bank just called. It's approved a charge card for Free Enterprise Security, Incorporated." Triumph echoed in his voice.

"Congratulations. You can take me to dinner to celebrate."

"Uh, yeah. I could. But aren't you supposed to offer to take *me* to dinner to celebrate?"

"No, Zac. That's not the way it's done. You're the one who just got the card approved. Therefore, you're the one who uses it to pay for the appropriate celebration. This sort of thing generally calls for champagne instead of cheap tequila, by the way. You have a lot to learn about running a small business."

"I see. Well, in that case we'll make it a genuine business dinner, so I won't be questioned by my accountant when I charge it off as an expense."

"A business dinner?" For the first time Guinevere felt wary.

"Yeah. I've been thinking. You know, there are times when it's very useful to be able to put someone into a situation the way I had you in at StarrTech. I mean, with the cover of your firm as a background, you could go into all sorts of environments. Whoever questions a temporary clerk or secretary or receptionist? Especially one named Jones. I see a great potential for us working together in the future, Gwen. We can discuss it tonight over dinner."

"Not a chance!" she shouted into the phone. "Zachariah Justis, you listen to me. Camelot Services is not about to get mixed up in any of your future investigations. Do you hear me? We will not—"

But Zac had already hung up.

THE
CHILLING
DECEPTION

CHAPTER 1

Guinevere Jones discovered the gold-plated pistol in the men's executive washroom on the third day of her employment at Vandyke Development Company.

She went back to her desk in Edward Vandyke's outer office and sat brooding about her find for several minutes before she picked up the high-tech stainless steel phone and dialed the number of Free Enterprise Security, Inc. Zachariah Justis's response to the information about the gold pistol was predictable—Guinevere told herself she ought to have anticipated it.

"What the hell were you doing in the men's executive washroom?" he exploded.

"I'll tell you at lunch."

Offended by Zac's failure to perceive the significance of the gun in the bathroom, Guinevere replaced the receiver hard enough to make the listener wince on the other end of the line. The trouble with Justis was that he could be awfully one track; a slow-moving freight train that once started was generally unstoppable.

Guinevere smiled fleetingly to herself as she fed paper into the electronic typewriter. She was looking forward to lunch, even if she would have to spend fifteen minutes of the precious hour trying to explain what she had been doing in the executive washroom.

Half an hour later she arranged for calls to be transferred to another secretary's office, pulled the paper bag containing her new Nike running shoes out of the bottom drawer of the desk, and picked up her purse. Vandyke had still not returned from his strategy session with his managers, but it was twelve thirty, and he had told her to be sure to take her lunch hour on time. A very thoughtful employer.

Darting into the ladies' room halfway down the hall, Guinevere slipped out of her elegant high-heeled gray pumps and quickly stepped into the Nikes. Instantly she felt capable of jogging from the Kingdome to the Space Needle. She breathed a pleased sigh of relief and satisfaction. True, the shoes didn't particularly match the trim gray wool suit she was wearing, but that was of course the whole point.

Guinevere serenely joined several other women wearing suits and expensive running shoes in the elevator and jauntily made her way to the Fifth Avenue entrance of the high-rise building. She spotted Zac's solid compact form before he noticed her approaching. The tiny secret smile she often felt these days when she thought of Zac Justis curved the corners of her mouth. She was growing familiar with the irrepressible flare of pleasure and anticipation that came to life within her whenever she saw him, even though she couldn't fully explain the sensation.

The first time she had seen him she had thought him ugly. A frog, she had called him, and although she had kissed him more than once since that first eventful meeting, Zac Justis hadn't yet turned into a prince.

He wasn't really ugly, but there was something fundamentally different about Zac, Guinevere reflected as she approached him. Standing in the lobby of the office building he seemed separate, removed from the polished males in suits and ties around him. He was wearing the uniform—a dark well-tailored jacket and trousers, crisp white shirt, and subdued striped tie—but he didn't blend into the herd. Perhaps, given the rough unforgiving contours of his face and the remotely watchful quality of his ghost gray eyes, he would never truly fit in anywhere. Even his dark hair was different. It was cut short, not styled and blown dry. He was a man apart.

In that instant he saw Guinevere, and the remoteness in his eyes disappeared. It was replaced by a disconcertingly direct possessive expression that Guinevere found unsettling. She had been telling herself lately that she ought to discourage that look but she wasn't at all sure how to go about doing it. Deep down she wasn't certain she really wanted to destroy it, anyway. It did something to her when Zac regarded her in that way.

He stood waiting for her, his eyes assessing her neatly coiled coffee-brown hair, wide hazel eyes, and slender figure. She watched his gaze take in the chicly padded shoulders of her jacket, the nipped-in waist that didn't succeed in making her appear bustier than she actually was, and the gray skirt. She knew the very second he saw the new Nikes. Long dark lashes, the only softness in his hard face, lowered deliberately. Then he raised his eyes to meet her faintly smiling gaze.

"Something morbid happen to your shoes?"

"Wearing running shoes outside the office is very fashionable, Zac. It shows a concern for fitness, it's practical for running up and down Seattle's hills during one's lunch hour, and it's subtly, chicly amusing. Besides, they've been doing it in New York for a couple of years."

"That's no excuse. Everybody knows New Yorkers are weird." He shoved the revolving door and guided Guinevere through and out onto the sidewalk.

"You can be very useful to have around," she told him blithely as she buttoned her red coat against the perpetual Seattle mist. The mid-December chill was unrelieved by any sunlight.

"You're so good for my ego." He took her arm as they started across the plaza toward the sidewalk. "Hungry?"

"Always."

"I thought we could flip a coin to see who buys lunch."

"The last two times we did that you won. If we do it again, we use my coin."

"You've got a suspicious nature," he complained.

"Probably comes from hanging around people who conduct investigations for a living," Guinevere agreed cheerfully. "My mother warned me about bad company. How's business? Get that contract to do the security consulting work for that computer firm?"

They had reached the restaurant and Zac held the door open for Guinevere. "I think it's in the bag. Talked to one of the vice presidents this morning, and he wants me to start the project in January. Says his budget can accommodate my consulting fees after the first of the year."

Guinevere shot him a sidelong glance. "Can your budget accommodate the delay in income?"

Zac shrugged one shoulder fatalistically. "It'll have to."

"This isn't a ploy to make me feel anxious about the state of your finances and thus induce me to pay for lunch, is it?"

"Honey, you really have grown more suspicious lately. I'm worried about you."

Before Guinevere could respond the hostess came forward and showed them to a table for two. "We'll go dutch today," Guinevere announced as she picked up her menu.

"You're a hard-hearted woman." Zac bent his dark head to study his menu. "Okay, tell me what in hell you were doing in the executive john."

Guinevere chuckled in spite of herself. "I've never seen one before."

"A john?"

"An executive john. Big league, Zac. This is the first time my company has gotten a contract for a short-term secretary to fill in at such a high level. Usually temps are used at lower levels, to fill in for absent clerks. Executive secretaries generally have other executive secretaries in the same firm lined up to sub for them."

"Why did you take the job? Didn't you have anyone you could send out on the assignment?"

"This was the first time Vandyke Development has called Camelot Services for a temp, and I wanted to make a terrific impression. I didn't have anyone I could send who had ever worked as an executive secretary, except my sister Carla. I decided to take the job myself and have Carla baby-sit Camelot Services. She seems to be enjoying running my office lately anyway."

Zac's heavy brows were drawn together in a severe line. "So you raced out to take the job to see what life was like at the top?"

"Zac, we may both be at the top ourselves someday. I, for one, am going to know what to expect."

"Which was why you checked out the executive head." Zac nodded, satisfied with the interrogation. He put down his menu. "You're lucky you weren't caught."

Guinevere set down her own menu offhandedly. "Mr. Vandyke was tied up in a meeting with his managers. He's been pushing to get a proposal ready and I knew he wouldn't be back in the office until after lunch." She halted as the waitress came by to take their orders. "I'll have the black bean soup and the spicy noodle salad."

"Same for me," Zac murmured. "And coffee—plain coffee. None of that fancy espresso stuff." He waited with vast patience until the waitress had disappeared and began grilling Guinevere again. "Go on. Was it locked?"

"The washroom? Yes. A big gold key on a chain. Mr. Vandyke keeps it beside the door. It's more of a conversation piece than a real attempt to keep people out of the bathroom. His visitors find it amusing. The washroom entrance is a private one just down a small corridor from his office. In fact, you have to go through his

office to get to it." She leaned forward, aware of the amused enthusiasm in her own voice. "You should see it, Zac. All black and
marble with gold running through it, and mauve."

"Mauve what?"

"Mauve everything. Mauve toilet, mauve washbasin, mauve
towels. It's unbelievable. Marble everywhere—walls and floors and
countertops. Which was why I happened to notice the gun."

"It contrasted with the marble?"

"No, no, it wasn't on anything marble. It was in the drawer by
the sink."

Zac closed his eyes, clearly biting back another lecture. "Jesus,
Gwen, you went through Vandyke's bathroom drawers? I knew you
were a little light-fingered at times, I found that out during the
StarrTech affair, but I never thought—"

"I am not light-fingered!" Incensed, Guinevere straightened in
her chair, glaring at him. "Zac, this is important. If you can't listen
without interrupting, then I'll—" She broke off abruptly.

He appeared interested. "You'll what?"

"Never mind." She decided to rise above his taunting. Mouth
firm, she went on severely. "I noticed one of the drawers was partly
open. I happened to glance inside and I could see something gold.
So I just sort of eased the drawer out a bit more, and there it was."

"The gun?"

"Yes. And I don't mind telling you, Zac, it gave me a start."

"Maybe it will teach you to stay out of other people's private
johns."

The black bean soup arrived complete with a dollop of sour
cream in the center, and Guinevere discovered she was too hungry
to continue the argument. She spooned up the thick soup with
gusto. "Can you imagine, Zac? A gold gun?"

"Probably chosen by the same designer who did the head. Undoubtedly couldn't find one in mauve."

"Zac, this is not a joke."

"Honey, my guess is that it wasn't a real pistol. I'll bet it was one of those gadgets that lights a cigarette when you pull the trigger. Typical executive toy. Your imagination was no doubt in high gear."

"It looked awfully real, Zac." Guinevere became very serious. "And it worries me. Vandyke seems to be under a tremendous amount of pressure."

"You've only been working for the guy for three days. How would you know what kind of pressure he's capable of tolerating?"

She lifted her chin with unconscious arrogance. "I know people, Zac. He's worried and he's stressed."

He shook his head. "You feel sorry for people, you empathize with them. People confide in you because you're a good listener, and you can get along with a wide variety of personality types. That does not mean you 'know' people. Take it from me, Vandyke wouldn't be where he is today if he weren't capable of handling a fair amount of pressure."

"You've never even met the man!"

"Anyone who has a private marble-and-mauve washroom, let alone a private executive secretary, is basically made of sturdy stuff. Wimps don't get far in the business world."

Guinevere sighed. "You don't understand, Zac. I've been working very closely with him for the past three days. I had to take a phone call from his wife the first morning I was on the job. That call alone was enough to tell me he's on the edge. Vandyke was very upset afterward. And he's been upset every time she's called since."

"He's having marital problems?"

Guinevere nodded. "I'm sure of it. I think she's left him. And I'm sure he's still in love with her. I tell you, Zac, he was in bad shape after those calls."

"So you think he might be planning to kill himself in the executive washroom using a gold-plated pistol. His wife must be something else to warrant that kind of reaction."

Grimly Guinevere pursued her line of logic. "It isn't just the trouble with his wife. I happen to know that the proposal he's working on is a crucial one for the company. He's been wearing himself out getting everything in order for the big presentation to the client next weekend. I think he's afraid of someone stealing the documents. He's instituted very strict security in the office. In fact I think it was security reasons that made him hire an outside secretary instead of borrowing one of the vice presidents' secretaries."

Zac cocked an eyebrow, looking slightly interested at last. "He figured he was safer with an outsider who wouldn't know what she was typing?"

"Or who wouldn't have any contacts in the company. The selection of Camelot Services was probably a deliberately random choice. Vandyke doesn't have to worry about me already having established a foothold in the company as an industrial spy. I don't know anyone in the firm, and no one knows me."

"Your mind is a fascinating thing, Gwen," Zac said admiringly.

"You're not going to take this seriously, are you?"

"Not until I find out what all this is leading up to," he admitted.

Guinevere decided to play her ace. "It could be leading up to a job for Free Enterprise Security," she announced sweetly. "A little something perhaps to tide you over until that consulting assignment in January."

That got another raised eyebrow out of Zac. "What kind of job?"

Guinevere took her time answering. "Well, I'm not exactly sure what you would call it. I haven't discussed this with Vandyke yet either. But I've been thinking . . ."

"Lord have mercy."

She ignored him. "Vandyke is supposed to go to a resort in the San Juan Islands this weekend to make the presentation to his client. I'm going to go with him."

Zac suddenly ceased his methodical attack on the soup. There was an unexpected bleakness in his gray gaze when he looked up. "You're what?"

Guinevere decided not to let his too-quiet tone faze her, but it was easier said than done. Her throat seemed to need clearing and her appetite threatened to evaporate. This was idiotic, she lectured herself. Damned if she was going to let Zachariah Justis affect her this way. "Good grief," she managed dryly. "You'd think I had just announced I intended to run off for a quickie weekend fling with the boss."

"That's not what you're announcing?"

"Zac," she hissed, leaning forward, "I am discussing business. The trip to the resort in the San Juans is business. My association with Mr. Vandyke is business. Now if you'll climb down off your macho high horse, you and I will continue to discuss business. If you'd rather sit there and ruin a perfectly good lunch by glowering at me, then I'll let you eat alone."

"Where," he asked bluntly, "do I fit into all this *business*?"

"That's what I was just getting around to explaining."

"I can't wait."

Guinevere drew a deep breath, glad that his eyes had cleared a little. He had no right to react so possessively, she reminded herself. After all, it wasn't as if she and Zac had come to some sort of official understanding about their vague relationship. "I think Mr. Vandyke needs you."

"In what capacity? Chaperone for you and him?"

"Hardly. Mr. Vandyke is nearly fifty and very much in love with his wife."

"Who is presently giving him a hard time."

"Forget Vandyke's wife. I think he needs you to provide him with peace of mind, Zac. I'm going to have a talk with him this afternoon and see if I can't get him to understand that."

Zac looked at her blankly. "Peace of mind? What the hell kind of peace of mind am I supposed to provide him? Is he afraid his wife will find out he's run off to some resort with his new temp secretary? Gwen, you're not making a whole lot of sense."

"I am talking about his peace of mind regarding his proposal documents." Infuriated by his deliberate obtuseness, Guinevere set down her spoon with a snap. "Mr. Vandyke has several things preying on his mind at the moment. I am suggesting that he hire you to take at least some of the pressure off."

"You're going to tell him he should hire me to baby-sit his precious documents? Forget it, Gwen. I'm in the security consulting business, remember? I'm not a file clerk."

"For someone who's not going to see another consulting fee until January you're being rather uppity about this, aren't you?"

"I'm not starving to death. If I find myself in danger of it I'll ring your doorbell and beg for a handout."

"You'd rather beg from me than work for a living?"

A rare, wicked grin spread across Zac's face. "A tantalizing thought, isn't it? What would you give me if I came begging, Gwen?"

"A meal ticket down at the mission! Zac, stop making a joke out of this. I am genuinely worried about my client, and I think I've found a way to take some of the pressure off him and at the same time throw a little business your way."

"A perfect Guinevere Jones solution."

She gave him a challenging look. "Well, isn't it?"

"What do you envision me doing, Gwen? Running around for three days with a briefcase chained to my wrist? Who's going to steal the documents from him at the resort anyway? He's going there to meet the potential client, isn't he?"

"Yes, but he's not the only developer who will be presenting his bids to Sheldon Washburn. There will be two other companies represented. Those executives will undoubtedly be bringing along assistants or secretaries too. Any one of which might be a spy."

"The plot thickens."

Guinevere regarded him with lofty disdain. "Are you interested or not?"

"Not."

She was startled more than anything else. It hadn't occurred to her that Zac would refuse the offer of a job. It was Guinevere's turn to blink. "You mean that? You really don't want to pick up a nice check for three days' easy work?"

"I'm not sure it's good for the image," he said consideringly as their soup bowls were removed and replaced with plates of spiced noodles and chicken. "Briefcases chained to the wrist and all that. Kind of tacky. Smacks of courier boy or something. Low-class."

"I never said the briefcase would have to be chained to your wrist," she muttered. "And since when did you become so concerned with status?"

"You've been teaching me how important image is lately. It's all your fault." He spun a fork around in the noodles, expertly winding them neatly onto it.

Guinevere paused, thrown more off balance by his refusal than she wanted to admit. She'd had plans, she realized. The long weekend at the resort would have provided an opportunity to find some peace of mind for herself. "Well, I suppose if you feel that strongly about it I'll just have to think of something else."

"I not only doubt Vandyke needs a document baby-sitter on this jaunt, I also doubt he needs a private secretary," Zac went on coolly. "I see no reason for him to drag you along. Tell him your agency does not provide twenty-four-hour secretarial service."

Guinevere's eyes narrowed, resentment beginning to simmer in her. "I run Camelot Services, Zac. I'll decide what jobs to accept."

"Hadn't you better be concerned with your own image?" he shot back too smoothly. "If you get a reputation for taking out-of-town trips with businessmen you might find yourself swamped with more work than you can handle."

Resentment turned to fury, effectively killing her appetite. It took a fierce effort of will to control the angry trembling in her fingers as Guinevere carefully folded her napkin and got to her feet.

"Gwen?" Zac frowned up at her.

"Don't worry, Zac. I won't stick you with my share of the tab." She coolly slid the money out of her gray leather clutch purse. "That'll take care of my bill with enough left over for a tip. I'll have to trust you not to pocket the tip, of course, but I guess I don't have any choice." She reached for her coat.

"Jesus Christ, Gwen, what do you think you're doing?"

"Walking out before you can insult me any further." She smiled very brittlely. "I'm going back to the office—the man I work for happens to be a gentleman. Gentlemen are so rare these days."

"Damn it, Gwen, I wasn't insulting you. I was just trying to make a point. Now sit down and stop acting like a child. This is ridiculous . . ."

But Zac was talking to empty space. Guinevere had her coat on and was on her way out of the restaurant. In stunned amazement, he watched the scarlet coat flash through the door. Out on the street she turned in the direction of Vandyke's office building and vanished into the crowd. The problem with the new style in women's footwear, Zac decided, was that it allowed the wearers to move a great deal faster than they could in high heels.

Slowly Zac pulled his attention back to his half-eaten spicy noodles. "Damn temperamental female."

"Excuse me, sir. More coffee?" the waitress asked with a politely inquiring smile.

"No thanks."

"Will the lady be returning?"

"She had to leave," Zac mumbled, searching for a convenient excuse. It was humiliating to have a woman walk out on you in a public restaurant, he discovered, chagrined. "Business appointment."

"Of course. I'll clear her plate."

"Fine." It would be tacky to tell her to leave Gwen's plate of noodles so he could finish them, Zac decided morosely. Just one more irritation to chalk up to Guinevere Jones, he thought as he watched the excellent noodles disappear toward the kitchen. Not only did Jones abandon him in the restaurant, he couldn't even find a polite way to finish off the food she'd left behind. The lady was getting to him. Zac grudgingly acknowledged to himself that he wasn't accustomed to this level of uncertainty around a woman.

It seemed to him that he'd been alternately irritated, possessive, uncertain, and exhilarated since he'd first encountered Guinevere Jones a few weeks ago. The first time he'd gone to bed with her, he'd been aware of a feeling of rightness that he couldn't begin to explain in words. So he hadn't tried. Their relationship was at a very tentative stage. It could not yet be characterized as an affair, although Zac knew he would be irrationally enraged if he found out she was seeing another man. But surely they had more than a casual dating arrangement. At least, it felt like more than that to him. He'd like to get to the point where he could say he was having an affair with Guinevere Jones, Zac thought. The words sounded good to him. They had a nice, settled, *definite* quality. But as yet he hadn't dared say them aloud in Guinevere's presence.

Words in general seemed to be a real problem around Guinevere. Bleakly Zac finished his noodles and sat cradling his coffee cup in his large hands. Had he insulted her? He hadn't meant to. She must know that. He'd only been trying to point out that weekend jaunts with bosses might be frowned on in some circles—severely frowned on by one Zachariah Justis, as a matter of fact. Damn it, he'd only been giving her some good advice. She certainly spent enough energy giving him advice!

Of course, he reminded himself, perhaps she'd only been attempting to do him a favor. She'd tried to throw a little business his way. He'd been too busy jumping on her for scheduling that weekend trip with Vandyke to pay much attention to the baby-sitting job she'd suggested. Zac stared into his coffee cup and thought about her proposal. Normally the project would not have interested him in the slightest. He had no intention of hiring himself out to ride shotgun for executives who saw industrial spies behind every water cooler. He had deliberately structured Free Enterprise Security, Inc. to be a cut above that sort of mundane operation. His firm was a consulting business. He gave expensive advice, conducted highly discreet investigations, and generally aimed for a sophisticated security image. True, he was still Free Enterprise's only employee, but someday things would change. In the meantime he didn't want to jeopardize the image.

Zac was absently swirling the last of the coffee in his cup and wondering how to go about making amends for insulting her when it struck him that there was one irrefutable advantage to accepting Guinevere's job suggestion. It would enable him to spend a three-day weekend with Gwen at a classy resort.

Three days on an island with Gwen.

Stunned by the implications and wondering foolishly why he hadn't spotted them right from the start, Zac hurriedly fished out his worn leather wallet and matched the amount Gwen had left on the table.

Three days at a fancy resort with Guinevere Jones at the client's expense. It boggled the mind. What was the matter with him? He'd been so damn busy warning Guinevere not to go flitting off with another man that he hadn't even realized she was offering him a chance to be the one she spent the weekend with.

There was the unfortunate matter of having to safeguard a development proposal, but in his new excited mood Zac could anticipate no real problem with that element of the situation. The briefcase would be an annoyance, but he could deal with that. He headed back toward his office wondering if Gwen would let him handle the room reservations.

As soon as he reached the tiny cubicle he rented in the

downtown high-rise, Zac threw himself into the new chair he'd bought with the fee from the StarrTech case, reaching for the phone. Guinevere answered on the second ring. Zac half smiled as he heard what he called her office voice—husky, polite, and just distant enough to let the caller know that the lady was professional in every sense of the word.

"Gwen? Zac. Listen, I've been giving your job offer some more thought."

The polite quality left her voice, but nothing could banish the pleasant huskiness. "Don't strain yourself."

"I'm serious. I've decided you're absolutely right. I can hardly afford to turn down the work. Tell Vandyke that I'll be glad to baby-sit his proposal."

"You will?" She sounded startled.

"Sure. On one condition."

"What condition?" she asked, instantly suspicious.

"No gold handcuffs for the briefcase."

"You want silver or stainless steel?" A thread of humor finally melted the ice in her voice.

"I'll just clutch it with my bare hands. Oh, and Gwen?"

"Yes, Zac?"

He coughed a little, clearing his throat. "Have you made the reservations?" Visions of sharing a room for three days with Guinevere sizzled through his head. He felt his body tighten in instinctive response.

"No, not yet."

"I could handle ours," he offered as nonchalantly as possible.

"You don't have to worry about that, Zac," she assured him breezily. "Vandyke's travel department will handle everything."

"Oh."

Zac hung up the phone, determined not to let the small setback bother him. He would see this as an opportunity to be creative in the field.

Sitting in Vandyke's office, Guinevere stifled the unexpected burst of excitement that threatened to bubble up inside her. This would be a working weekend, naturally, but still . . .

She gathered her wayward thoughts and got to work on the problem of how to convince Edward Vandyke that Free Enterprise Security was just what he needed.

CHAPTER 2

Late Friday afternoon Guinevere stood at the window of the Camelot Services offices and moodily contemplated the rain that had evolved from an earlier mist. Rain had not been expected to continue into the afternoon, according to the news report. The forecast had been for the morning's light showers to give way to partial clearing. But in typical Seattle fashion the weather had made its own decisions without bothering to consult the local meteorologists. The guy on the evening news would have a brilliant explanation of what had actually happened. In the meantime everyone on First Avenue below Guinevere's window was getting wet.

When visitors asked Guinevere how she tolerated the long gray winters and the frequently damp summers of the Northwest, she was always a bit surprised. Sometimes she responded with statistics proving Seattle's legendary rainfall was actually quite moderate; sometimes she made a joke about having grown webbed feet. But the truth was she rather liked the changeable weather. Normally it was invigorating.

Today, however, the rain seemed intent on complementing her strangely ambivalent mood. She watched the people in the government office building across the street and decided they all appeared to know where they were going and what they were doing. They all appeared to be motivated by a purpose, a direction, a reason for existence. Perhaps they had finally found a way to balance the federal budget. Perhaps they were scurrying around in an attempt to keep themselves *in* the budget. Whatever the reason, Guinevere envied them. Most days she was guided by the same sense of sureness, but not today.

The door of her office opened behind her and Guinevere turned to glance at her sister as she entered. Carla was shaking rain off her fashionable pink and gray umbrella. She looked up, eyeing Guinevere critically, her green eyes speculative. Guinevere wasn't certain she liked the sisterly speculation but it was a great deal more pleasant than the tragic quality that had recently haunted Carla's face. She had recovered from the bout of deep depression brought on by a love affair gone wrong. But nothing would ever completely dispel the air of feminine fragility that Carla wore like an aura. Her blond hair, classically delicate features, and gently molded body made that impossible.

Carla wrinkled her nose in an unconsciously cute movement that called attention to a small sprinkling of freckles. Men were often fascinated by those freckles. They served the function of making an otherwise too attractive woman seem warm and approachable. "For someone who's about to leave on a three-day vacation, you're not looking particularly thrilled with life. What's wrong? Worried about Camelot Services?"

Guinevere shook her head. "Hardly. When I saw what you did to my files I realized the firm was in good hands. Besides, what could go wrong during a three-day weekend? You'll be fine."

"Is that what's worrying you? Am I getting a little too good at running your precious business?" Carla asked the question with a teasing smile, but there was an underlying concern. "The things I do for you are the things any first-class secretary would do. You should know that. You've hired enough first-class secretaries and you've been working as one yourself this past week. I certainly don't want the responsibility of actually owning and operating Camelot Services. I'm not cut out to be the entrepreneurial sort—takes a special breed, and I know it. Some kind of weird cross between a chronic optimist and a chronic worrier."

"Oh, Carla, don't be an idiot." Guinevere grimaced wryly. "I've been grateful for the help and you know that too. I'm fine, really. Just trying to see if I've remembered everything I have to take with me. This isn't exactly a vacation. I'm going to be working."

"Uh-huh. Is that why one of the things you're remembering to take with you is the Frog?"

Guinevere felt the flush in her cheeks, and it thoroughly annoyed her. "Zac is also going to be working on this trip."

Carla grinned cheerfully as she hung up her raincoat. "Sure. Working on getting you into bed. He's only having sporadic success, isn't he? What's the score add up to, four or five times at the most? You've got to admit, he's tenacious. A lot of other men would have decided the game wasn't worth it by now."

The stain on Guinevere's cheeks darkened. "For someone who was only recently having to see a therapist because of a failed relationship, you certainly sound casual about things now."

Carla's gaze softened. "Only because I know Zac is anything but casual in his feelings about you."

Guinevere turned stiffly back to the window. "You wouldn't be so sure of that if you'd heard the way he refused to come along on this trip to the San Juans."

"Is that what's wrong?" Carla demanded. "He isn't going with you and Vandyke after all?"

Guinevere shook her head. "No, he eventually agreed to take the job. But all I got in the beginning was a long harangue about how Camelot Services was starting to appear suspiciously like a rent-a-bedmate agency."

Carla giggled. "Oh, lord, I can just see it now. My heart goes out to the Frog. He put his foot in his mouth by jumping all over you for agreeing to accompany Vandyke, right?"

"Something like that." Guinevere sighed.

"Then he finally realized you were offering him a vacation fling with you, and had to backtrack like mad. Must have been painful for him."

"It wasn't exactly pleasant for me either. I thought he'd jump at the chance to go with me," Guinevere said wistfully. "Instead all I got was a lecture, until he finally realized he shouldn't turn down the job. Zac doesn't have any major consulting projects scheduled until January. Apparently he decided he could use the work. How do you think I feel, knowing he's only coming along for business reasons?"

"If you think that, you're not bright enough to be running Camelot Services."

Guinevere glanced up, eyes narrowed. "Well, how would you interpret it?"

Carla sat down behind Guinevere's desk. "Simple. His initial reaction was sheer jealousy. It was only after he'd calmed down a bit that he realized you were offering him a weekend fling."

"I am not offering him a weekend fling, Carla!"

"Then you can't blame him for going with you purely for business reasons, can you?"

Guinevere groaned and leaned her forehead against the cold glass. "It must have been a lot easier in the old days. Back when a woman could simply ask a man if his intentions were honorable."

"Men lied in the old days as easily as they lie today." Carla's voice was laced with memories of her own recent experience. "Besides, the definition of 'honorable' has changed. It used to mean marriage. Is that what you want?"

"I've only known him a few weeks!" Guinevere said with barely suppressed desperation. "Of course I don't want to get married. I don't want to marry anyone. You know that. I've got my hands full putting this business on its feet and I've gotten very used to my independence. I like being my own boss, Carla, both in business and in my private life."

"Okay, so you don't want marriage. What do you want?"

"Damn it, *I* don't know. I just know I don't like this foggy, undefined kind of relationship. I'm a businesswoman. I like things clear-cut, rational, comprehensible. He's a businessman. I thought he'd want the same clarity in his personal life."

Carla's mouth curved gently as she studied her sister. "What would make your relationship with Zac clear-cut, defined, and rational?"

"I wish I knew." Guinevere thought about the question. What did she want from Zac? "I just wish I knew." She straightened away from the window, forcing a determined smile. "And on that note, I guess I'd better go home and pack. Vandyke wants to leave first thing in the morning."

"You're really concerned about him, aren't you?" Carla asked shrewdly. "Not good to get emotionally involved with a client, Gwen. No wonder Zac was annoyed when you announced you were running off to the San Juans with Vandyke."

"I'm not emotionally involved," Guinevere said bluntly. "Not in the way Zac first thought. But yes, I am worried. You would be, too, if you saw Vandyke. He's tense and nervous, constantly drinking coffee and making little notes to himself. This proposal is a big one for his company. On top of that he's got problems with his wife."

"Have you met her?"

"No. But I've answered the phone every time she's called. And she calls him every day. I can't figure it out. She sounds so lonely, so unhappy. Vandyke sounds the same way when he finishes his conversations with her. But if they're both lonely and depressed being apart, why on earth *are* they apart? Mrs. Vandyke seems pleasant enough, but what can you tell on the phone? At any rate, I figured if Vandyke could at least stop worrying so much about somebody trying to steal his proposal documents, he might be able to relax sufficiently to make a good presentation to Washburn this weekend."

"Zac is supposed to guard the documents?"

"That's what I suggested to Mr. Vandyke." Guinevere went to collect her coat and shoulder bag. "He wasn't too keen on the idea at first, but I gave him a really brilliant presentation of my own."

Carla glanced up warily. "How brilliant?"

"Well, I convinced him that Zac was the best private security to come along since James Bond. I painted quite a glowing picture of the intrepid man of action. Vandyke finally seemed to think it would be a good idea if he hired Zac."

"Does Zac know about your little sales job?"

Guinevere shrugged into her coat. "Naturally, I didn't tell him in detail what I said to convince Vandyke," she said lightly. Discretion was the better part of valor in this instance. Zac would have been furious if he'd found out what a swashbuckling image he now had in Vandyke's eyes. "But Zac seems happy enough with the idea of the job now."

"Have Zac and Vandyke met?"

"Yesterday, in Vandyke's office." Guinevere paused, remembering the meeting. It had gone fairly well. Vandyke had asked Zac several questions about his past work and had seemed satisfied with the answers. Alone with Guinevere, Zac had been downright casual about the job, but he'd managed to put on a politely concerned front in Vandyke's presence. He'd agreed to go along in the role of Vandyke's personal assistant.

"Well, sounds as though it should be an interesting weekend," Carla decided. "Have fun. I'll see you Tuesday morning. Maybe by then you'll have achieved clarity, rationality, and a sense of definition in your relationship with the Frog."

"Why does that sound like a contradiction in terms?" Guinevere asked as she went out the door.

Saturday afternoon Guinevere again stood at a window watching an endless rain. But, she reflected, this time she at least had the advantage of standing in a luxurious hotel room, and the view was of tiny mist-shrouded islands dotting a stormy sea rather than clock-watching government office workers. The dozens of green islands off the coast of Washington that made up the San Juans comprised an exotic bit of Northwest paradise. The ferry system serviced the larger islands, such as the one on which the resort was located, but most of the smaller islets were accessible only by private boat or seaplane. Many were tiny and uninhabited. It was even possible to own your very own island. Guinevere smiled briefly at the thought. Her very own island. Now that was class. Almost as good as having one's own executive washroom.

The phone beside the bed rang. She gave a small start and went to answer it.

"Are you unpacked?" Zac asked without any preliminaries. His temper had been a bit unpredictable since their arrival that morning, and after he'd discovered he'd been given a room next to Vandyke and that Guinevere's room was several doors down the hall, he'd begun to show signs of grave uncertainty.

"Just finished. Vandyke said he wouldn't need me until after this afternoon's meeting with Washburn. How about you?"

"I finally convinced him that the documents were safe enough with him during the meeting." Zac sounded distinctly irritable. "Hell, I thought he was going to make me accompany him right into the sessions with Washburn. I told him I'd be standing by to collect the documents at four o'clock, when the meeting is scheduled to end. When I pointed out that not much could happen as long as he was closeted in the hotel conference room he reluctantly agreed. The guy really is a nervous wreck, isn't he? I wonder if Vandyke Development is in some sort of financial trouble."

"I wouldn't know. I've only worked for him a week. But I agree the poor man's on the verge of a severe anxiety attack."

"Yeah. Well, that's his problem, I guess. I'm not licensed to prescribe tranquilizers. What do you say you and I get out of here for a couple of hours. We can take a walk."

"In the rain?"

"Unless you can think of another way to take a walk today."

Guinevere held the phone away from her ear for a moment, glaring at the receiver. "I'll take a walk with you if you'll promise to remain civil," she said into it again. "You've been acting like a frustrated buffalo ever since we arrived."

"Frustrated may be the key word. I'll pick you up in five minutes. Somebody must have worked hard to find you a room as far away from mine as possible. It couldn't have happened by sheer luck."

The phone clicked in Guinevere's ear. Slowly she hung up, thinking about Zac's mood. He definitely sounded annoyed because the Vandyke travel department hadn't put her in a room next to his. Well, perhaps it was better this way. She hadn't intended these three days to be a sexy vacation fling. She envisioned instead a series of intense meaningful discussions. After all, she wanted to clarify the relationship.

Zac showed up four and a half minutes later. He had a waterproof windbreaker on over a heather-colored wool sweater and casual slacks. His eyes were the same color as the rain, Guinevere realized in faint surprise as she opened the door.

"Be ready in a second." She reached for her rakish red trench coat, belting it on over her pleated khaki pants and green pullover sweater.

"Trench coats are supposed to be khaki," Zac noted.

"You're such a traditionalist."

"At least you've found something else to wear besides sneakers." Zac eyed her fashionable rain boots.

"So glad you approve," she retorted coolly as she walked out the door with him.

Zac hesitated and then took her arm. "Sorry," he muttered. "I didn't mean to snap at you."

Guinevere heard the sincerity beneath the rough apology. "Perhaps Vandyke's tension is rubbing off on you," she suggested.

"Nope. That's not it at all."

"I see."

"Let's take the car into the village. We can walk around there. Maybe have a cup of coffee and look at the marina."

"Okay." Relieved that he wasn't going to launch an in-depth discussion concerning the reasons for his short temper, Guinevere allowed Zac to guide her out into the parking lot. He and Vandyke had each brought their own cars on the ferry. Vandyke's was a new Mercedes. Guinevere had come with Zac in his three-year-old Buick.

The small village, crammed with tourists during the summer, was quiet on a rainy winter weekend. It was easy to find a parking space near the marina and even easier to get a cup of coffee at a nearby café. Guinevere sensed Zac relaxing a little as the time passed.

"This is more what I had in mind," he announced as they left the café.

"Really?" Guinevere glanced up at him with a tentative smile. "Could have fooled me. I thought you were opposed to this trip."

His arm tightened around her shoulders. "Only until I started thinking of the possibilities." He started to say something else and then halted, glancing at a man who was opening a car door across the street. "Isn't that Springer?"

Guinevere peered through the rain at the young man dressed in slacks and a suede jacket. "I think so. I only met him once this morning after we arrived. He's Washburn's assistant, isn't he?"

"Yeah. Guess they decided they didn't need any extras at the first meeting. Looks like he's headed for the marina. Maybe he's got a boat."

Ambling along in Toby Springer's wake, Guinevere and Zac watched the man make his way past the rows of boats tied up in the marina. He was headed toward an old tin boathouse at the far end of the wharf. A single-engine seaplane bobbed on floats in the water next to the boathouse. Near the plane another man was crouched down over a twist of rope on the dock.

He must have said something to Washburn's assistant, because in the next moment Springer turned and saw Zac and Guinevere. He waved invitingly.

"I'm not interested in a ride in that silly little plane," Guinevere hissed to Zac as he started forward purposefully.

"You'll love it."

"Not a chance."

"Come on, Gwen, where's your spirit of adventure?"

"It hasn't recovered from the StarrTech case. It may never recover."

Zac wasn't paying any attention. He was busy greeting Washburn's assistant. "I see you escaped for the afternoon too. I was afraid for a while there that I'd have to sit in on the meeting."

Springer laughed, nodding politely at Guinevere. He was a clean-cut man in his midthirties with well-styled hair, designer clothes, and a sense of his own future worth. But he was also very charming. "I know what you mean. When Washburn told me we were getting three days in the San Juans I knew there were going to be a few catches. How are you, Miss Smith?"

"Jones," Guinevere corrected automatically. "I'm fine. Zac and I decided to sneak off for a tour of the town. I just love islands in winter."

"Personally," growled a soft masculine voice behind her, "I prefer other islands in winter. Islands with plenty of sun and sandy beaches. This sure as hell isn't my idea of paradise." Laconic, laid back, slightly world-weary and coolly cynical, the voice contained a hint of a Southern drawl. "A man who got himself stranded on one of these little uninhabited rocks in winter would probably wake up dead."

Guinevere turned. Although Zac was merely glancing back over his shoulder in response to the new voice, his fingers tightened a bit on her upper arm as he eyed the speaker. The man who had been crouched over the coils of rope was getting slowly to his feet. Guinevere watched him rise, admiring the perfection of a legend brought to life. A slow smile lit her eyes. It wasn't every day a woman got to see this sort of thing in the flesh.

The man rose to his full height. He must have been at least six one. Maybe six two, she decided. And he could have stepped out of an adventure film. More particularly, a film featuring a dashing, raffish, danger-loving pilot with plenty of "the right stuff." He was even wearing a genuine beat-up leather flight jacket complete with a scruffy fur-lined collar. His khaki pants were tucked into worn, scuffed boots and there was a wide leather belt around his lean waist. As she watched he very coolly stripped off his leather gloves and extended a hand to her. It was a picturesque gesture.

"The name's Cassidy," he drawled, blue eyes running over her in slow appraisal. He appeared to be in his midforties, but his dark brown hair was still full and had just the right touch of shagginess. His face was as lean and hard as the rest of him.

Entranced, Guinevere put out her hand and immediately felt the strength of his grip. "Cassidy," she repeated. Even the name sounded perfect. "My name is Guinevere. Guinevere Jones."

"I wish to hell my name was Lancelot." His eyes ceased their perusal and he met her gaze, grinning. "Lancelot was the one who finally got Guinevere, wasn't he? My history's a little rusty."

Zac's fingers were definitely digging into Guinevere's shoulder now. She moved slightly, trying to encourage him to loosen his grip, but he didn't seem to notice. "It wasn't history. Just a story," he responded to the other man's comment. "Nobody ever gets the facts right in those old stories."

Cassidy switched his gaze to Zac. He shrugged good-naturedly and held out his hand again. "I get the picture. Don't worry; I know private property when it's marked."

"I'm glad. Zachariah Justis." He accepted the other man's hand, ignoring Guinevere's gathering irritation. The handshake was polite but short. Neither man seemed anxious to prolong the civilities. "You fly the San Juans?"

"I do a little charter work."

Zac nodded toward the bobbing plane. "The One Eighty-five is yours?"

"Yup." Cassidy smiled in bland satisfaction. "Me and that Cessna have been through a lot together. But I don't think she's any more used to this cold weather than I am. Guess we haven't gotten acclimated."

"Where were you before you came here?" Guinevere asked interestedly. She would speak to Zac later about his rudeness, she decided.

"Worked the South Pacific," Cassidy said. "Sight-seeing trips for tourists, a little mail, some cargo. You name it. Thought it was time for a change, so I threw some darts at a map and came up with the San Juans. Soon as I got a taste of that cold dark water I began to have doubts."

"It's cold, all right," Guinevere agreed. "Hypothermia is a real problem around here in boating accidents. During winter a person can't last long in the water."

Cassidy sighed. "Back where I come from a man could swim from one island to another as far as those out there and feel like he was in a bathtub the whole way." He indicated the handful of mist-shrouded islets in the distance. "But around here a pilot's got to carry all kinds of survival gear just in case he does something dumb and winds up in the water."

"Hey, don't go into a long lecture on the perils of flying the San Juans, Cassidy," Toby Springer interrupted with a laugh. "I'm down here to see about arranging some tours for Mr. Washburn's guests. Gwen and Zac here are two of your potential passengers. Be careful, you'll scare them off."

Cassidy grinned engagingly, his eyes dancing over Guinevere. "Well now, I surely wouldn't want to risk that. Don't you worry about a thing, Miss Jones. I'll keep you nice and warm during the whole flight."

"Gwen doesn't like flying in small planes," Zac said smoothly, conveniently forgetting his earlier comments regarding her lacking spirit of adventure.

Cassidy looked crestfallen. "Ah, hell, I didn't mean to scare you off, Miss Jones. Safe as houses up there. That old Cessna practically knows how to fly herself by now."

"A cheerful thought. Just the same, I think I'll do my touring by boat or on foot. Zac's right. I'm not big on dinky little planes."

"Dinky!" Cassidy was theatrically offended. "That One Eighty-five is a real workhorse. She can carry six passengers, or a whole mess of cargo."

Guinevere laughed. "I didn't mean to insult the plane. Have you been a charter pilot for long?"

"Since I got out of the army. A long time, Miss Jones. More time than I want to add up." He stepped around her to where he'd coiled the rope, and as he moved Guinevere saw he had a distinct limp. She just knew there would be a good story behind that limp. Old war injury? Plane wreck? Enraged husband? "Hope you change your mind about flying with me, Gwen," Cassidy went on easily as he bent down to collect the rope. "I'd sure love to show you the sights."

"I'll bet," Zac muttered. "Come on, Gwen, it's getting late," he added more loudly. "I promised Vandyke I'd be back by four." He nodded crisply at Cassidy and Springer. "We'll see you later."

"Right," Springer agreed. "Probably in the bar. Good-bye, Miss—uh, Jones."

"Good-bye, Mr. Springer." She didn't have a chance to do more than nod briefly at Cassidy. Zac was already hauling her back along the plank dock. "Zac, what's the rush? It's only three thirty."

"Somehow," Zac observed caustically, "I get the feeling the entire world is conspiring against me."

"Sounds like a clear case of paranoia."

"All I know is, this trip isn't turning out to be what I expected."

"You have to be flexible, Zac."

But all Zac seemed intent on flexing at the moment was a little muscle. Guinevere found herself back at the Buick before she had a chance to catch her breath. Turning to glance once more toward the marina she saw Springer in deep conversation with the man called Cassidy.

It was during dinner, which she and Zac shared with Edward Vandyke at his insistence, that Guinevere learned she was not alone in her dislike of small planes. Vandyke fully concurred with her feelings.

In the week she had known him Guinevere had come to like the slightly balding, slightly paunchy, earnest, hardworking Vandyke. She knew there was intelligence and ambition beneath the sincere manner, as well as a willingness to work hard for his objectives, and she admired that. As she sat across from him at the dinner table she wondered what was causing the anxiety she sensed eating him. It seemed out of proportion to the business he was here to negotiate with Sheldon Washburn.

Washburn, a thin well-dressed man in his fifties, and his assistant Toby Springer were seated on the other side of the dining room. The two other businessmen and their assistants who were there to make presentations to Washburn were also eating. Everyone had been quite civilized over cocktails earlier, Guinevere reflected in amusement. You'd never know from looking at them that there was so much money on the line, she thought.

"I know exactly how you feel, Miss Jones," Vandyke said in response to her comment about seeing the small plane in the marina. "I did some charter work myself in my wild and misspent youth. It would suit me perfectly never to get near anything smaller than a Seven Twenty-seven again in my life."

Zac prodded his red snapper. "You did some flying?"

Vandyke nodded. "At the time it seemed very adventurous and it certainly made for some great cocktail stories over the years. But to tell you the truth, most of what I remember is the unpleasant aspects. Running a shoestring charter service is no picnic. Still, I suppose I shouldn't complain. It provided me with the stake I needed to start Vandyke Development."

"Did you operate alone?" Guinevere asked.

Vandyke concentrated on his salad. "No. I had a partner for a while. There was an accident, and he was killed. It was one of the things that made me decide I'd pushed my own luck far enough. I was sick of flying around, under, and through tropical storms; landing on dirt roads, or in places where there weren't any roads at all; trying to collect for deliveries from people who could have cared less about their credit ratings. And then Gannon got himself killed. . . ." Vandyke paused for a long moment, his dark eyes distant and full of fleeting pain.

Empathic as usual, Guinevere immediately wished she hadn't asked the question. Zac, however, seemed oblivious of Vandyke's unhappiness. Tearing off a chunk of sourdough bread, he asked, "Tropical storms? Where did you do your flying?"

"The Caribbean. What about you, Zac? Has your varied background included a bit of flying?"

Zac shrugged. "Some. Not much. It was a long time ago."

"Ever yearn to go back to it?"

"Nope. I feel the same way you do. For me the old adage applied: hours of boredom broken by moments of stark terror. Basically I'm a quiet businessman at heart. I prefer to—ouch!" He glowered at Guinevere, who had just kicked him under the table.

Guinevere smiled sweetly at Vandyke, who was looking curiously at Zac. "Zac tries to downplay his more adventurous activities. He's always pretending that everything he does professionally is just business as usual. Actually, some of his tales make your blood run cold. But you have to get him fairly drunk before you get the truth."

Vandyke managed a small chuckle. "I see. I'm not surprised. I suppose most men who have lived action-oriented lives like yours, Zac, become very casual about the risks they take."

"Until they get kicked under the table," Zac muttered.

"Well, I, for one, am very glad I took Miss Jones's advice and hired you to come with us this weekend. I shall sleep a lot better knowing you're nearby in case of need." Vandyke paused. "Do you carry a gun, Zac?" he asked in a low tone.

Guinevere jumped in to answer before Zac ruined the image she had so carefully created. "Of course he carries a gun, Mr. Vandyke. But he prefers not to mention it at the dinner table."

"I understand."

"I'm glad somebody does," Zac observed.

Later, after joining the others for a nightcap in the lounge, Zac decided he'd done his social duty. The first day of his long weekend with Guinevere was almost over, and thus far it had offered such highlights as an aging macho pilot in a Goodwill flight jacket who had made a pass at Gwen, dinner with a man who had a hard time hiding his personal anxiety beneath a layer of business charm, the discovery that Guinevere's room was quite a ways down the hall from his own, and a bad choice of wine at dinner. The last had been Vandyke's fault, but since the older man was picking up the tab it had seemed crass to complain. Zac had kept his mouth shut and gone back to tequila as soon as dinner was over. You were always safe with tequila.

A roaring fire burned on the huge hearth in the resort lounge. The businessmen who had gathered at the hotel were well into a late-night drinking siege, and Guinevere was beginning to look pleasantly sleepy. It was definitely time to go back to the room. Zac reached out to touch her hand.

"Let's go, honey. It's late, and you're half asleep."

"Okay," she agreed easily enough. Smothering a small yawn, she obediently got to her feet and said a polite good night to Vandyke, who glanced up and then rose.

"You two are going to your rooms?" he murmured, looking directly at Zac.

"That was the plan." Zac arched one brow inquiringly. "Any objections?"

"No, no, of course not. I just wondered . . . That is . . ." Vandyke coughed a little in embarrassment and leaned forward confidentially. "Look here, Zac, I hired you to keep tabs on, uh, things. I hate to sound priggish, but the fact of the matter is I would appreciate it if you stayed in your own room tonight. So I'll know where to find you if I need you."

"I hadn't planned on leaving the hotel." Zac shot a sidelong glance at Guinevere, who was saying good night to Toby Springer. She couldn't hear what Vandyke was saying. "Don't worry, Mr. Vandyke. I'll keep tabs on your briefcase."

"Yes, well, thank you, but I'd like to know where you are at all times. Do I make myself clear?"

Zac thought of the connecting door between his room and Vandyke's. It was locked, naturally, but that didn't mean much. The resort was old, the walls badly insulated. A man on one side of that goddamn connecting door would certainly be able to hear any sounds made by the occupant of the other room. A woman's soft cry of passion would be unmistakable. And Guinevere had her image to maintain. She wasn't likely to make love within earshot of her current client.

Without a word Zac took the precious briefcase from Vandyke, collected Guinevere, and left the lounge.

It occurred to him that maybe it was time to find out what it was about the development proposal being presented to Washburn this weekend that made Vandyke so damn edgy. The man was acting as if he needed a bodyguard, not just a baby-sitter for important papers.

CHAPTER 3

"What do you mean you're going to have a look in the briefcase? You can't do that, Zac. Those are my client's private business papers. Besides, it's locked." Guinevere shut the door to her room as Zac strode across the carpet and set the briefcase down on the bed.

"He's my client too. Remember? And he's acting weird."

"I told you he was very anxious about a lot of things."

Zac crouched down in front of the briefcase to study the locks at eye level. He fished a paper clip out of his pocket and straightened it. "He was the one who had the hotel give me a room next to his, Gwen. With a connecting door, no less. I asked the desk clerk this afternoon if there was any way of getting a different room, and was told that the present arrangements were per Mr. Vandyke's personal request. And just now Vandyke ordered me to sleep in my own room."

Guinevere flushed. "Yes, well, perhaps he was just trying to look after me. He's very much a gentleman, Zac. He might feel obliged to, er, protect me from unwanted advances. Or something."

"Bullshit. Vandyke is making it clear he wants a bodyguard, not a baby-sitter. But he won't come right out and say it. I'm starting to get curious." Zac fiddled delicately with the locks on the briefcase. "He's not as concerned about where the briefcase is as he is where I am. He was upset this afternoon when he got out of his meeting early and found us gone. I got the feeling he expected to find me standing right outside the front door of the conference room with my trusty machine gun slung over my shoulder."

"Maybe he has a right to be upset." Guinevere went to stand beside Zac, eyeing his efforts curiously. "After all, he is paying us to be on call this weekend. Where did you learn to do that?"

"Correspondence school." There was a tiny ping, and one of the locked clasps sprang open. Zac turned his attention to the other.

"Amazing what you can learn at home these days." Guinevere leaned closer. "Is it hard?"

"Only when someone's breathing over your shoulder."

She leaned closer. "You have to learn to work under pressure, Zac."

"Pressure," he announced as the second clasp popped open, "is something I'm learning a lot about this weekend."

"We've only been here one day."

He opened the briefcase. "Don't remind me." He stood up and examined the contents. Folders, several thick documents with *Vandyke Development Proprietary Information* stamped all over them, and a number of letters were neatly arranged in the case. There was also a small silver flask tucked into one corner. Zac reached for it.

"You didn't tell me the guy was a closet drinker." He unscrewed the top and sniffed. "Cognac."

"He has been under a lot of pressure lately, as I keep reminding you. Maybe he feels the need of a nip now and then; how should I know? He certainly handled his alcohol all right this evening." She broke off consideringly. "Of course, it would have been hard to drink very much of that wine at dinner."

Zac replaced the flask. "You can say that again. Tomorrow

evening we'll have to work it so that one of us gets to choose the wine."

"It'll have to be me. Anyone whose regular fare is tequila can't be trusted to pick good wine." Guinevere carefully probed the contents of the briefcase. "I've seen most of these at one time or another during the past week. He had me do some of the final revisions. He didn't even want some of these documents sent out to the word processing pool."

"That's a normal precaution when there's a major deal at stake. Routine company security." Zac lifted out a few of the papers and set them on the bed. "But Vandyke isn't acting routine."

Guinevere examined a cost analysis. "Are you sure you're not overreacting because he as good as ordered you to spend the night next door to him instead of, uh, wandering the halls?"

"Wandering the halls," Zac repeated thoughtfully. "Is that what you call it?" He didn't wait for an answer. "Let me see that envelope."

Obediently Guinevere handed it to him, watching as he opened the manila envelope and drew out a single sheet of paper. It was a badly photocopied document, she saw. Head tipped to one side, she peered at the grungy gray page. "That wasn't done by me. I would never have accepted such a bad print. In fact, I don't think the printing department at Vandyke Development would let any of the machines get that bad. They keep them in excellent condition."

Zac held it up to the light. "It was done on one of those cheap little machines you sometimes see installed in out-of-the-way places. You know, the kind of store that sells gas, cigarettes, condoms, and booze."

"A real service-oriented sort of place." Guinevere tried to get a look at the page. It appeared to be a form that had had various blanks filled in by hand. There was a column of scrawled names with spaces opposite for times and dates. At the bottom there was a signature. "What is it, Zac?"

He studied it thoughtfully for a long moment. "A page out of a pilot's logbook," he told her absently.

"No kidding? Let me see." She reached for the paper and he handed it to her. "These are the destinations? The places he flew? And these are the times and dates?"

"Yeah."

"I don't recognize too many of these towns."

"That's because most of them are names of places in the Caribbean and the West Indies." Zac peered over her shoulder. "The dates are all from nineteen seventy-two. The last one is May ninth. It says the pilot made a round-trip from Saint Thomas to some little island off the coast of South America. The trip back to Saint Thomas apparently took place several weeks after the trip out. Let's see . . . the first hop was in April. The return trip was on May ninth."

"Vandyke said he used to have a charter service down there some years ago. But that's not Vandyke's signature at the bottom of the page." Guinevere was positive of that—she'd seen her client's signature on enough papers during the past week to be certain. "It's hard to read. Shannon? Bannon?"

"Gannon," Zac said suddenly with finality. "L. Gannon." He took the paper back from Guinevere with a snap and replaced it in the envelope. "That was the name of the man Vandyke said was his partner, remember? The guy who got killed in an accident."

Guinevere shuddered. "It seems morbid to carry that kind of keepsake around, doesn't it? After all these years, I wonder why he does?"

"You'll notice he's not carrying around the original." Zac shoved the envelope back into the briefcase and replaced the rest of the documents. He relocked the case.

"So?"

"Don't look at me like that. I don't know the answer. All I know is that I'm being asked to stick very close to a man who's on the verge of having an all-out nervous breakdown."

Guinevere sat down on the edge of the bed, staring out the window. She could hear the rising wind heralding an incoming storm. "I'd hoped having you along would calm him down a bit, but it doesn't seem to be working. He's under so much pressure, Zac. I feel sorry for him."

There was silence behind her and then the lights went out as Zac flipped the switch. Guinevere didn't move, although she felt a sudden surge of tension. With the room lights off the gardens outside the window were faintly revealed by the discreetly placed outdoor lighting.

A moment later the bed gave beneath his weight as Zac sat down beside her. She hadn't heard him cross the room, but that didn't surprise her. When he wanted to, Zac could move very quietly. He reached out to fold her hand into one of his.

"How about feeling a little sorry for me, Gwen."

"Is it sympathy you want from me?"

He exhaled heavily. "No, not really. But I am suffering."

"Are you?"

"This trip isn't going quite the way I had imagined it would. Christ, I feel like Cinderella. I've got to be back in my own room by midnight or Vandyke will be pissed."

Guinevere turned her face against his shoulder. "I'm sorry, Zac. I sort of hoped it would be different too," she confessed tremulously. His arm tightened around her and she could feel the welcoming strength in him.

"Did you?"

Mutely she nodded, her face still tucked against his shirt. She loved the warm male scent of him, she realized. There was something comforting and deeply intriguing about it. She felt him reach up to loosen his tie, and then he cradled her face in his palm.

"I'm glad, Gwen."

His mouth came down on hers, heavy and warm. Guinevere shivered and let her fingers creep up around his neck. This wasn't quite the way she had planned it, she reminded herself. She had wanted them to talk this weekend to get a few things out in the open. A part of her needed to analyze the relationship that was growing between herself and Zac, and she had hoped that a quiet resort might provide the right atmosphere for that kind of delicate discussion.

The sensual side of their association was already powerful enough. On the few occasions when she had allowed it to take the dominant role Guinevere had had plenty of proof of that. Zac's effect on her senses was almost overwhelmingly intense. The passion sprang up so easily between them. Guinevere was starting to worry that it came too easily. She had been trying to keep it in perspective, not allow it to take over.

"Gwen, honey, I've been aching for you all day. We have a little time. Vandyke's probably still down in the bar. . . ." Zac's soft murmur was charged with sexual tension. The urgency he was feeling was being clearly communicated to her. Guinevere felt his hand against the sensitive nape of her neck. His fingers slid around her throat to the buttons of her yellow silk blouse.

"Zac," she whispered huskily, "I've been thinking about us. I wanted . . . well, I wanted to know if you've been thinking about us too. I mean . . ." Good grief. Even to her own ears she sounded like a tongue-tied teenager. This wasn't the way she had planned it.

"Jesus, honey. I think about you all the time," he said hoarsely. The buttons of her blouse slipped open beneath his fingers and he groaned softly against her throat as his hand moved down over her breast. "All the time."

"You do?" She gasped as he pushed his hand up under the lacy camisole she was wearing. His thumb found the exquisitely throbbing nipple and gently coaxed it forth. Her own fingers sank languidly into the hard muscles at the back of his neck.

"You must know by now what you do to me." He caught one of her wrists and dragged her hand down across his chest to his thigh. "Feel me, sweetheart. If you need any evidence, just touch me. All I have to do is watch you walk across a room and the next thing I know I'm in this condition."

"Oh, Zac," she breathed as his hand guided hers to the waiting hardness of him.

"I feel like I'm going to explode." He released her fingers and went back to stroking her breast with slow tantalizing movements. Gradually his hand traveled lower and with his arm around her shoulders he eased her down onto the bed. Guinevere felt the teasing thrill of excitement that flared in her lower body and knew she was rapidly nearing the point of no return. Already she was softening under his touch, yearning for the heavy weight of him, and she sensed Zac was well aware of her reaction. She had never known what it was like to literally ache for a man's possession until she had met Zac.

The urgency and immediacy of his physical effect on her was one of the things that made her wary and uncertain of the relationship. It was one of the things that had to be put aside so that a genuine dialogue could take place. Belatedly Guinevere remembered her own plans for the weekend.

"Zac?"

"We haven't got much time, honey. Here, lift up so I can get your skirt off."

"Zac, wait a minute, I think—"

"It'll be okay, sweetheart. Damn it, I didn't want to rush this." He fumbled with the zipper of her skirt.

"Zac, please, listen to me." Her fingers closed over his fumbling hand at the fastening of her skirt. "I wanted—I wanted to talk."

"We'll talk in the morning, I promise. Right now we haven't got enough time to talk and make love."

"Then we'll have to make a choice, won't we?" she said heatedly as some of her determination returned.

He agreed instantly. "Right. We'll talk later. Right now I'm going to lay you down on this bed, take off every stitch of clothing you've got on, and let you wrap yourself around me the way you do when you finally let go. God, I can't get enough of you when you come alive under me, Gwen. You're so soft and hot and clinging, and it's been so long since we've been together."

"Fourteen days," she reminded him grimly. "That's hardly a lengthy separation."

"Feels like a lifetime." He sprawled across her, locking her securely under him with his thigh. His fingers traveled up under the hem of the skirt he hadn't yet succeeded in removing and Gwen flinched passionately as he probed purposefully under her panties.

She planted her palms firmly on his shoulders, telling herself that she had to take a stand now or she would be lost beneath the tide of passion. "Zac, please. This isn't the way I had planned it. I want to talk. We *have* to talk."

He stilled above her, finally sensing her determination. She looked up into his shadowed face and saw the gleam of his hungry gaze. For a moment Guinevere faltered before the fire in him, but the need to settle the fundamentals of the relationship was stronger tonight than even her physical need of him. Settling things was the reason she had maneuvered him into this trip, she reminded herself. She must be strong for both of them.

"You want to talk," he repeated roughly, staring down at her.

Guinevere nodded, moistening her lower lip with her tongue. "Yes. Please. It's very important."

"Obviously." Zac sighed heavily and eased himself to a sitting position. "Somehow I knew things were going to go wrong. I think I'm under a curse this weekend."

"This is serious, Zac. It's important to me." Guinevere sat up slowly, a part of her already missing the warmth of his touch. Awkwardly she began refastening the buttons of the yellow silk blouse.

"What exactly do you want to talk about?" He sounded resigned.

She gathered her courage. "I think we should discuss the status of our relationship," she said very formally.

"Oh, hell." He let his head sink into his hands.

Guinevere looked at him worriedly. "Don't you agree, Zac? I mean, we've just been sort of floundering along for several weeks now and I think it's time we put things in perspective, so to speak. I think we should assess exactly what we each want out of this association of ours and determine the boundaries. I've been feeling very confused lately, Zac. Very unsure of what's going on between us. We need to clarify matters."

"You sound as if you've been reading a lot of magazines lately."

She stiffened, hurt by the sarcasm in his voice. "I don't think I'm asking too much."

"What are you asking?"

"I just told you!"

"Well, I don't know what you mean by clarifying matters. I thought things were fairly clear a few minutes ago when we were lying down."

"I see. That's all our relationship means to you? A convenient source of sex?"

His head came up and his eyes glittered in the darkness. "Hardly what I'd call convenient. I can count on the fingers of one hand the number of times you've let me get that close. I can't figure out why you're always moving just out of range. I know by now that I can make you want me. I know I can satisfy you. What's wrong, Gwen? Why the shadow dancing? Come to think of it, I'd like a little clarification in this relationship too. I'd like to know if I'm going to have to worry about every fast-talking executive you have for a client. I'd like to know if you expect a relationship in which you can feel free to flirt with every joker who comes along in a leather flight jacket. And I'd like to know what the hell you think you're doing leading me on here on your bed and then throwing cold water on everything by announcing it's discussion time!"

Guinevere winced at that, but then she brightened. "I think this is very healthy, Zac. I think this is exactly the sort of talk we need to have." She was about to continue when her eye was caught by a shadowy movement outside the window.

"Healthy!" Zac said, outraged. "You call this *healthy*? Christ, lady, you've got a strange sense of—" He broke off, seeing her stare past him. "What's wrong?"

She gestured uncertainly. "I'm not sure. I could have sworn I just saw Vandyke walk through the gardens. He was heading toward the cliffs." Guinevere slid off the bed and went to the window.

"In that weather? It's blowing up for a storm out there."

"I know. And it's very cold. I wonder why he would be taking a walk now?" Guinevere tried to make out Vandyke's disappearing form. Zac was standing behind her, watching the man's movements as he left the garden and vanished in the direction of the cliffs.

"That sea will be really kicking up out there by now," Zac mused.

"Oh my God, Zac. What if he's had a few too many drinks and decided to do something stupid?"

"You're thinking about that gold-plated pistol you found in the executive washroom, aren't you?"

She nodded, feeling his hands close reassuringly on her shoulders. "I can't quite see Vandyke as suicidal, but there's been so much bothering him lately. Zac, if he fell into that sea in this stormy weather he might not be able to get back out in time. He'd die in that cold water, even if he could keep himself afloat."

"You mean if he jumps into that sea, don't you?"

"I've never known anyone who might be suicidal, Zac. I'm not sure of the signs. Carla went through a severe depression after her affair with Starr, but she never got to the point of threatening to kill herself."

"Vandyke hasn't threatened it either. But maybe he wouldn't. Maybe he'd just go ahead and do it, if things got bad enough." Zac released her. "I guess I'd better go bring in the sheep."

She spun around to see him pick up his jacket and head for the door. "You're going after him?"

"Why not? I haven't got anything else to do, except sit here and chat until it's time to go back to my own room."

Guinevere's mouth tightened. "There's no need for sarcasm."

"It provides a modicum of relief. God knows I could use some relief. Good night, Gwen." He slammed the door with subdued violence as he left the room.

Zac made his way down the hall with long, deliberate strides, pushing open the door at the far end to step out into the chill night. Shoving his hands into his tweed sports jacket he bent his head against the wind and wished he'd gone back to his room first to collect a real coat. It was colder than hell out here. Much warmer back in Gwen's bed, even if she was intent on having a discussion about their relationship.

On one level he was forced to admit that he agreed with her. He, too, had been frustrated by the ambiguities and uncertainties in their association. Zac knew he wanted to get some things ironed out and clarified. But he'd been sure it would be simpler and more straightforward to have the necessary discussion after a blissfully passionate weekend at a luxurious resort. Or to put it somewhat more bluntly, he had sensed the talk would be better conducted after a couple of nights of concentrated sex. Guinevere was always so soft and warm and amenable after he'd made love to her. Relationship discussions with her were undoubtedly safer when held while her defenses were down.

The truth was, he was not anxious to sit down and hammer out the details of their relationship with Guinevere when she was in full command of herself. It would be too much like negotiating a business arrangement. She was a strong independent woman, and when she was in top form she was formidable. Much better to reason with her after she'd been softened up a bit, Zac told himself. With a woman like Gwen a man had to resort to strategy on occasion.

He was pursuing that line of thought when he caught a shadowy movement out of the corner of his eye. There was someone else in the garden. Even as he watched, the other night-walker vanished behind a hedge. Maybe someone trying to walk off a few alcoholic fumes before bedtime, Zac decided. He continued on through the gardens and into the grove of windblown firs that lined the cliffs above the sea. The moon obligingly slipped between clouds, providing some temporary illumination. In its pale gleam Zac saw Vandyke's figure hunched forlornly at the edge of the cliff.

Zac halted at the fringe of trees, aware of a deep uncertainty. He didn't know a damn thing about dealing with suicidal types. If Guinevere was right about Vandyke's state of mind, this was going to be tricky. Suddenly Zac wished Guinevere had come with him. She had an instinctive way of handling people that would make her much more useful in the present circumstances. Gritting his teeth against the cold and the task that lay before him, he started forward again.

In that same instant another figure arrived at the edge of the trees a few yards away. Zac's instincts immediately took command, instincts that had been nicely refined for survival. Obeying them was second nature to him. He leapt forward.

"Vandyke! Get down!"

The man at the edge of the cliffs turned slowly in bewilderment and found himself knocked flat on the craggy surface. He was quickly rolled behind a small heap of scruffy shrubs and boulders.

"What in hell . . . ?" Vandyke struggled to free himself.

"Hold still." Zac kept him pinned with one arm while he scanned the trees. There was no movement now. "Someone in the trees. He was watching you."

"Watching me? But I don't understand. I—Is that a gun you have?" Vandyke stared keenly at the object in Zac's hand.

"Unfortunately, no." Zac tossed aside the rock he had grabbed a few seconds earlier. "Should it be?" he asked in a level voice as he allowed Vandyke to sit up. Whoever had been there had gone now, Zac was certain of it.

Vandyke shook his head. "I don't know." He sounded vague, disoriented. Zac saw him give himself a small shake as if taking a grip on his nerve. "It's just that Guinevere said something about you going armed."

"Gwen sometimes exaggerates. She's very conscious of business images. You want to tell me what's going on, Vandyke?"

Vandyke glanced up nervously and then looked away. "Nothing's going on. I came out here to take a little stroll before going to bed. Probably whoever you saw was doing the same thing."

"Probably." Zac let the patent disbelief show in his voice. "Well, whoever it was, he's gone now. Let's get back to the hotel. A man could freeze out here."

"Yes. Yes, it's very cold, isn't it." Vandyke stumbled to his feet. "I'm sorry about this, Zac. I didn't mean to alarm you."

"Do you always go out walking in storms without bothering to put on a coat?"

Vandyke exhaled slowly. "I just had a call from my wife. It was upsetting. I wanted to think for a while. How did you know I was out here?"

"I saw you from Gwen's window. She and I were just saying good night."

"I see." Vandyke seemed embarrassed. "And the other person?" he asked Zac as they started back toward the hotel. "The one you said you saw in the trees?"

"I couldn't tell who it was. Just a shadow. You might be right, he might simply have been out taking a late-night stroll too. Amazing how many people go walking on a night like this."

"But you said he was watching me?"

"That's the feeling I had. Look, Vandyke, how serious does this business get? Just how valuable are the documents in that briefcase?"

Vandyke was silent for a long moment. "They could mean a great deal of money to any of the other developers here tonight. The cost data alone would be worth a hundred thousand."

"But I'm the one with the briefcase tonight. Everyone in the lounge must have seen me leave with it. Why follow you?" Suddenly Zac felt light-headed as the facts hit him. He swore. "Oh, *shit,* Gwen's alone back in her room with the briefcase. Come on!"

Vandyke tried weakly to protest, falling into an awkward run as Zac yanked him back through the gardens. The older man was puffing heavily by the time they reached Guinevere's room.

"Gwen!" Zac pounded once on the door. It opened immediately. A wave of relief went through him as he watched her look first at him and then at Vandyke. "Gwen, are you okay? The briefcase—"

"The briefcase is fine," she assured him absently. "Mr. Vandyke, are you all right?"

"Just a little out of breath. Zac here was very anxious to get back to you."

Zac was in no mood for more conversation. "Hand me the briefcase, Gwen. Vandyke and I are going back to our rooms. We'll see you at breakfast."

Guinevere eyed him thoughtfully. Without a word she turned around, went and got the briefcase, and brought it back to Zac at the door.

"Good night, Gwen," he said as she handed it to him.

"Good night, Zac."

"Swell evening, huh?" he couldn't resist drawling in ill-concealed disgust.

"You really know how to show a girl a good time."

He couldn't think of an adequate response to that, so he closed the door very politely in her face and started down the hall with Vandyke, carrying the briefcase.

CHAPTER 4

If there had been any polite way of refusing the boat tour that was announced at breakfast on Sunday morning, Guinevere would have done so. But after a jovial Sheldon Washburn dropped by Vandyke's table to inform him he'd arranged a special excursion—by boat instead of plane, because he'd heard Miss Jones didn't care for small planes—Guinevere's social options were narrowed. Vandyke had cordially accepted on her behalf.

"Very thoughtful of you, Sheldon. I'm sure my secretary will enjoy herself. I'm afraid I'm going to need Zac here, though. Who else is going along?"

"Toby Springer and two or three others who aren't needed at this morning's session." Washburn beamed at Guinevere, who tried to look properly grateful. "Miss Jones will be the only lady on the boat, but that shouldn't be too hard to take, eh, Miss Jones?"

Guinevere sighed. "I'll manage."

Washburn slapped Vandyke on the shoulder and went on to inform the others of their good fortune. Vandyke glanced uneasily at Zac, who had stoically continued to eat grapefruit during Washburn's announcement.

"You don't mind remaining here for this morning's session, Zac?"

"I'm sure Miss Jones will be able to handle a boatload of administrative assistants, won't you, Miss Jones?" Zac gave her a bland smile.

Guinevere refused to rise to the bait. "I'm certain it will be a lovely tour. And we're in luck. We've even got a bit of sunshine."

"Yes indeed," Zac agreed. "Luck is just overflowing around here today. Can't remember when I've felt so lucky."

Guinevere waited until after breakfast to corner him. She pinned him down in the rustic lobby, where he was patiently waiting for Vandyke. The briefcase was at his side.

"What happened last night, Zac?" Guinevere dropped down onto the sofa beside him, her brows in a straight demanding line.

"I got cold. In more ways than one."

"I'm serious. What went on out there on the cliff?" she hissed. "Was he really trying to kill himself?"

Zac sighed. "Beats the hell out of me. I can't read minds. But someone else was out there watching the whole scene."

"Someone else was outside in that storm?"

"Yeah. I guess I overreacted. I didn't know what was going on, so I tackled Vandyke and dragged him behind some cover. You'd have been proud of me, Gwen. I really did a nice job of reinforcing the old commando image. At least, until my client realized all I had in my hand was a rock, not a gun. But whoever had followed him didn't hang around. Very anticlimactic."

Guinevere examined his jacket intently. "Where is your gun?"

"Back home in Seattle."

She was shocked. "You didn't bring it with you?"

"I was under the impression that all I had to do this weekend was keep sticky fingers out of a briefcase. I had a couple of other items on my agenda, too, but none of them required a weapon." He sounded aggrieved.

Guinevere bit her lip, torn between sympathy and amusement. Impulsively she put a hand on his sleeve. "You can't come with us on this harbor jaunt?"

He looked at her. "You heard Vandyke. Not that it makes much difference. Everything else about this weekend is getting fouled up, so I might as well earn my pay. You're right about your client, Gwen. He's scared to death. I think he'll feel a lot better if I stay close to him. And since I've decided to actually work this week-end, I think I'll make a couple of phone calls."

"To whom? About what?"

"I love it when you get excited. The only problem is, you're picking the wrong time and place."

"Zac! Quit baiting me. Tell me who you're going to call."

"Someone who used to work for my old firm. He had the Carib-bean region during the seventies. He quit the company in nineteen eighty to devote his life to rum and writing the great American novel, but he stayed in Saint Thomas. I thought I'd see if he can dig up some info on the accident."

"What accident?" Guinevere asked, momentarily lost. "Oh! You mean the plane accident that killed Vandyke's partner."

"It's not normal to carry around a page out of a dead man's log-book, Gwen."

"You can say that again. It's downright morbid." Guinevere gave the matter some thought. "Maybe I can weasel out of this scenic tour."

"Forget it." Zac glanced over her shoulder at Vandyke, ap-proaching across the lobby. "It will take Sol a while to dig up any real information. That's assuming I can get hold of him in the first place." He got to his feet. "Have fun," he whispered into her ear, quickly brushing her nose with a kiss. "Sorry about that. I know it's bad for the image, but I couldn't resist." He was gone be-fore Guinevere could tell him wistfully that she didn't really mind the small kiss in public.

Two hours later she found herself in the back of the fair-size cabin cruiser Sheldon Washburn had hired for the occasion. Three of the other assistants had also been freed by their employers to take the trip. The surprise passenger was Cassidy. When he'd stepped onto the boat, grinning at her with charming wickedness, Guinevere had experienced a small twinge of guilt. Utterly ridiculous, of course, she told herself. She was certainly not to blame if Cassidy blithely chose to crash the cruise party. There was no way on earth Zac could take her to task for it. Besides, she didn't owe Zac undying fealty. They hadn't even had the big relationship discussion yet. And she was hardly contemplating anything resembling betrayal in any case! The whole situation was simply, clearly, undeniably not her fault. But she was secretly glad Zac didn't know who had joined the small group on the scenic tour. Some things were better left unmentioned.

Cassidy's grin grew decidedly broader as he chose the seat next to hers. He stayed there during the entire trip, one booted foot braced against the seat in front of him, his left arm casually draped across the back of Guinevere's chair. In a laid-back laconic manner he supplemented the travelogue the boat's pilot was giving.

"Have you flown to most of these little islands?" Guinevere asked politely at one point. In the rare morning sunlight the gems of lush green seemed to have been sprinkled in the water by a careless hand.

"No point flying to some of them," Cassidy told her. "No one lives on them. And some you couldn't beach the Cessna on anyway. They're just tree-covered rocks, without any natural coves or bays."

"I've heard some of them are privately owned."

Toby Springer caught the comment and remarked, "Washburn is thinking about buying one." There was a touch of pride in his voice. Springer clearly admired his boss's success.

"Really?" Guinevere asked, interested. "Near here?"

"Over there, I think. Isn't that the one, Cassidy? You took him there once in your plane."

Cassidy nodded, showing a supreme lack of interest. "Yeah."

"Does he have a home on it?" Guinevere peered at the small, thickly forested island.

"He's considering building one, but he hasn't gotten around to it," Springer told her. "No one lives there right now. It would be strictly an investment."

One of the other men who had been freed for the day joined the conversation. He was a young intense man with round preppy glasses and a thin face. His name was Milton Tanner. "Your boss has done pretty well on his investments. He'll probably find a way to turn that one into a fortune too."

Springer nodded. "Washburn's done okay."

Milt Tanner's face relaxed in a brief smile. "You can say that again. I got the job of researching him for my boss before we decided to make the proposal for the resort. He seems to have come out of nowhere in the mid-seventies and has managed to keep a low profile, but there's a lot of money behind him."

"He's smart and he knows land values." Springer grinned. "Why do you think I work for him? He's tough, but I wanted to learn from the best."

"How long have you been with him?" Guinevere asked, aware that Cassidy was growing restless beside her. He didn't appreciate the conversation having taken a turn that more or less left him out of it.

"A year," Springer said. "Another cup of coffee?"

"Sounds great." Guinevere smiled. "There may be sun out here today but it's downright chilly."

"I can take care of that little problem," Cassidy drawled, blue eyes glinting with meaning.

"Uh-uh." Guinevere smiled. "I think I'm safer with the coffee."

"People who always want to be safe miss a lot in life, Guinevere Jones. You don't really live unless you take a few chances." Cassidy's voice was soft, pitched for her ears alone. "It would be a shame if a woman like you missed too much along the way. I get the feeling you were born to take a few risks."

Guinevere tilted her head to one side, considering that. "I think you've made a slight miscalculation, Cassidy. The only risks I was born to take are those involved in running a small business, and I have to take more than enough of those."

He shook his head, eyes narrowed against the watery sunlight. "Trust me, honey. I could make you change your mind."

Guinevere smiled. He really was amusing. That kind of man often was. But a wise woman didn't expect anything more than superficial entertainment from such a man. It was all they were capable of providing. If you looked for anything else you were doomed to disappointment. There was something missing, something a perceptive woman couldn't always put her finger on but that she sensed was lacking. Guinevere knew that if she went looking for a complete man beneath Cassidy's flashy exterior she wouldn't find one.

The breeze seemed to turn colder as the boat headed back toward the marina.

The weather, however, was not nearly as cold as the expression in Zac's gray eyes as he stood on the dock an hour later waiting for the returning boat to be made fast. Guinevere hadn't noticed him until the last minute, and when she did she groaned inwardly. So much for small discretions. Cassidy was standing behind her, big as life, and she sensed his amused satisfaction as he solicitously helped her ashore.

"Anytime you want a private tour you just let me know, Gwen," he murmured as Zac came forward. "I can always squeeze you into my schedule. And you can see a hell of a lot more from the air."

"Thank you," she said lamely, aware of Zac's bleak expression.

She turned to him with a deliberately cheerful smile. "Oh, hello, Zac. I didn't know you'd be able to meet me. Did the conference get out early?"

"No."

"I see. Well, we had a great tour of the area."

"I can imagine. You ready to go back to the hotel? It's almost time for lunch."

He wasn't going to be gracious or understanding about this, apparently. A small flame of resentment started to uncurl within her. Damn it anyway, she told herself. Who was Zac Justis to make her feel guilty over a social situation that had been totally beyond her control? She didn't like the feeling and she didn't like the fact that Zac could induce it. This relationship she was involved in had to be clarified, and soon. She knew she was glowering as Zac opened the Buick's door and unceremoniously all but shoved her inside. The others were driving back to the resort in Springer's car.

"It wasn't my fault, you know," she muttered, and immediately resented the fact that she'd felt obliged to defend herself. "Cassidy just showed up at the last minute and hopped aboard."

"How fitting. Hopalong Cassidy."

"It's not nice to make fun of a person's disability."

"Did he regale you with the tale of how he managed to collect such a romantic limp? I'll bet it's a great story, full of heroism and danger." Zac grimly turned the key in the ignition.

"No, he did not. As a matter of fact we discussed the local islands, and then some of us talked a bit about Washburn's success. He's thinking of buying one of those empty islands out there, you know."

"No, I didn't know. But I'm not surprised. What's that got to do with anything?"

"Well, nothing. I just thought you were asking for a blow-by-blow account of the cruise, so I was trying to give it to you."

"Spare me. If I want the account, I'll ask for it."

"Yes, sir. You certainly are in a good mood, sir, if I may say so, sir. Did anything interesting happen between Washburn and Vandyke at the conference?"

Zac's mouth hardened. "I think Vandyke's going to get the deal."

Guinevere glanced at him. "Really? That's great. Maybe that will make him relax a little."

"It's not final yet, and Vandyke doesn't seem any more relaxed." Zac turned the corner onto the narrow road that led from the small village back to the resort.

Guinevere sought for more neutral conversation. "Did you get hold of your friend?"

"Sol? Yeah. He was sleeping off a hangover. Said he'd look into it when I told him I'd send along a check to cover his expenses. His great American novel hasn't yet found a publisher, I gather."

"So we don't know any more than we did this morning?"

"Nope."

"Where's the briefcase?"

"Vandyke has it. I think he felt guilty about asking me to stick so close when that wasn't really what he'd hired me to do. He told me to take off for a few minutes to collect you. We're meeting him for lunch."

Wonderful, Guinevere thought morosely. Zac was right. The weekend wasn't working out at all. At least not the way she'd hoped it would. She propped her elbow on the padded door and leaned her chin on her hand, gazing out the window at the tree-lined road.

"Zac?"

"Yeah?"

"Are you really upset about Cassidy being along on that cruise?"

There was a beat of heavy silence. "I shouldn't be, should I?" he asked grimly.

She slid him a sidelong glance. "No. You shouldn't. For one

thing, I had nothing to do with it. And for another, we haven't . . ." She faltered.

"We haven't had that little chat you want, have we?" he finished for her.

"Well, no."

"Is this chat of ours going to include some kind of agreement regarding outside relationships? Is that the right expression?"

She drew a deep breath, concentrating fiercely on the narrow winding road. "I had thought it might."

There was another heavy silence. Then Zac said slowly, obviously choosing his words with care, "Gwen, I am not normally a possessive man."

That surprised her. "You aren't?"

"It's worked reasonably well over the years, since women do not tend to get possessive about me."

"I see." She felt an immediate surge of sheer undiluted feminine possessiveness. The thought of Zac taking someone else out to dinner and discussing such things as a business image and IRS deductions for small firms was enough to make her stomach tighten, she realized suddenly. Until now she had only considered the situation from her side. She had been wary of what she had thought was his growing demand for exclusivity. Now she was forced to take a hard look at her own feelings for him.

"It's different with you, Gwen," he finally said. He sounded very grim about it.

She turned her head. "It is?"

He kept his eyes on the road. "I think so."

"You only think so?" She felt incipient panic.

He exhaled slowly and said very steadily, "Gwen, it's hard enough not knowing what you're doing or who you're with on the nights when you're not with me. If I thought you were sleeping with someone else— It would rip me apart."

She caught her breath at the stark honesty of the statement. "Oh, Zac. I didn't realize . . . I didn't know . . ."

He ignored her. "I know you're used to being free, totally independent. So am I, for that matter. But with me it was kind of a moot point. My social life isn't exactly hectic."

"Neither is mine," she said quietly. He had been honest with her. She decided it was time to take the same step herself. "Zac, I'm not seeing anyone else. I haven't dated anyone else since I met you."

He did glance at her then, gray eyes full of urgency. "No one?"

"No one."

He chewed on that for a moment. "For what it's worth, neither have I," he said.

"Zac?"

"Yeah?"

"It's worth a lot."

There was a great deal of silence for the remainder of the short drive, but it wasn't an unpleasant silence. Guinevere was aware of the tentative commitment that had just been made between herself and Zac. It wasn't exactly a formal declaration of the status of their relationship, she decided, but it was a step in the right direction. It was also a little scary, for reasons she didn't want to consider.

Vandyke was waiting impatiently for them when they returned. He seemed relieved to see Zac. He also had work for Guinevere. She spent the afternoon typing up some modifications to one of the proposals, which effectively destroyed any possibility of more time with Zac.

By dinner she was resigned to the inevitability of the failure of the weekend from a personal point of view. It was obvious that Zac had reached the same decision and had decided to give the client what he wanted. He kept unobtrusively within sight of Vandyke most of the time and after dinner he followed his client into the lounge.

Guinevere accompanied them, but by eleven o'clock she decided there was no point stretching out the evening any longer.

She politely said her good nights, smiling tentatively at Zac. He gave her a long, level look and shrugged fatalistically. She knew he was going to stay in his own room that night. What really bothered her was that he didn't show any signs of inviting her to stay with him. She must have really frozen him out last night with her insistence on a dialogue.

"Think I'll turn in too," Vandyke announced, rising with Guinevere. "What about you, Justis?"

"Doesn't seem to be much in the way of alternatives. One thing about these resorts in the winter—they're restful."

Guinevere saw Vandyke's brief expression of commiseration but the older man made no move to excuse Zac from guard duty. Twenty minutes later Guinevere was alone in her room, wondering where she'd gone wrong when she'd first schemed to drag Zac along on the trip to the San Juans. She sat down on the edge of the bed to take off her pantyhose.

"Ah, well, the best laid plans—oh, damn," she finished, reacting to the bad snag her fingernails had just made in the upper left leg of the pantyhose. "Zac's right. Nothing is going properly this weekend." She marched over to the wastebasket beside the dresser to drop them into it, but reconsidered. The snag was high on the leg. She wouldn't risk wearing the pantyhose under a skirt but she could get away with wearing them under slacks. Guinevere wadded them up and went to put them in the left-hand side of her suitcase. The good pantyhose were in little bundles on the right-hand side, and she didn't want to get them mixed up. In the morning she wasn't always perfectly alert to such details as snags.

That high-level decision made, Guinevere puttered around the room a while longer, changing into her long-sleeved cotton nightgown, brushing her teeth, and generally killing time preparing for bed. Then, very much aware of the empty bed, she picked up a paperback and tried reading for a while. But her thoughts kept straying to the cautious discussion she'd had with Zac in the car. Outside another high wind announced that a new storm was on its way. So much for the brief sunshine the San Juans had enjoyed that morning.

By midnight Guinevere gave up trying to read. She put the book down beside the bed and slid out from under the covers. Switching off the light, she went to the window and opened the drapes to stare out into the darkness of the incoming storm, leaning against the window frame and contemplating the new era of relationships between men and women.

Life was definitely not simpler in the modern age.

Why hadn't Zac made some attempt to convince her to come to his room tonight, if it was true he felt obliged to stay there because of Vandyke? Perhaps he felt rebuffed after last night. Guinevere winced. She hadn't handled last night very well. It was understandable if Zac felt she had been holding him at bay—in a sense she had been doing exactly that. And she wasn't sure she could explain quite why, even to herself.

Restlessly Guinevere moved around the room, picking up objects off the dresser, fiddling with the thermostat, listening to the gathering wind. It was when she found herself trying to reread the same page of the paperback that she finally came to a decision. This was a new era, she lectured herself. Zac hadn't invited her to his room, but nothing said she couldn't invite herself.

With a sudden sense of determination she yanked off the nightgown and stepped into her jeans without bothering to put on any underwear. She skipped a bra, too, when she reached for her wide-sleeved, oversize poet's shirt. She wouldn't bother with shoes. No one was likely to see her in the hall and even if someone did, the ballet-style slippers she was wearing were fine. Taking a grip on her resolve, Guinevere opened the door to her room, glanced both ways, and started down the empty corridor to Zac's room.

He was right. It did seem a very long way, especially at this hour of the night. She heard voices in a few of the rooms as she passed the doors, but she saw no one. When she reached Zac's door she raised her hand to knock. Suddenly she was overcome by a thousand second thoughts.

The door opened before she could commit her knuckles to the knock.

"I thought I heard someone out here," Zac muttered in a low growl. "What the hell are you doing here?"

He was wearing a pair of slacks and nothing else. Guinevere swallowed a little uncertainly. She looked up at him, appealing for understanding. "I came to say good night. No, that's not quite right. I came to spend the night."

He stared down at her. "The hell you did. Guinevere Jones, how can you do this to me? I'm going to spend the rest of the night in agony."

That shook her. "Agony?" Her eyes widened unhappily.

"Because you can't stay, you little idiot. I've told you, there's a connecting door between my room and Vandyke's. It's nothing more than a thin sheet of plywood, for crying out loud. Now get your sweet tail back down that hall before I lose my perspective on your business image."

Guinevere touched his bare shoulder with her fingertips. "I'll be very quiet, Zac. I promise."

He closed his eyes briefly in despair. When he opened them again there was a new element swirling in the gray depths. Guinevere knew that element. She'd seen it before. It sent a tremor of excitement through her. It also gave her courage.

"I want to stay, Zac."

"Honey, I'd give my right arm to have you stay. But for your own sake—"

"I'll worry about my own image." She smiled gently and went past him into the room, turning to watch as he slowly closed the door behind her. When he met her eyes she knew he had lost his small inner battle. Without a word he held out his arms, and she went into them just as silently.

"Zac, I'm sorry about last night," she said after a while.

"Hush, honey. Please hush." He stroked her head, his body strong and urgent against hers. Then he buried his lips in her loose, slightly tangled brown hair and inhaled deeply. "Christ, I want you. I want you so damn much. . . ."

She clung to him, her fingertips digging into the sleek skin of his broad shoulders as he unfastened her jeans.

"You forgot something," he murmured, discovering she wasn't wearing any panties.

"I dressed in a hurry," she admitted in a tiny whisper.

"I'm glad."

His palms cupped her full hips as she stepped out of the jeans. Luxuriously he gripped her, lifting her against the warmth of his lower body. His mouth moved urgently on hers and Gwen parted her lips to allow his tongue to enter deep inside. She could feel him hard and aroused against her and it sparked the excitement in her veins. Her arms wound around his neck.

She felt herself lifted off her toes and carried to the turned-back bed. Zac settled her in the middle and straightened to unzip his slacks. His eyes never left her as she lay there waiting for him, and when he finally stood naked before her she could already feel the beginnings of the delicious tension he created. He switched off the light and lay down on the bed. She felt his heavy thigh move across her languidly twisting leg, the hairy roughness of it making her moan softly.

"Shush," he muttered and covered her mouth with his own.

She ignored him, sighing into his mouth. How could she worry about the thinness of a connecting door when her whole body was starting to clamor for the satisfaction it knew it could get only from this one particular man? He drank the small sound she made, his hand stroking down over her breast. She could feel the faint trembling of anticipation in his fingers and gloried in the knowledge that he was barely able to hold himself in check. Being wanted this badly by Zachariah Justis was a powerful aphrodisiac, one she knew she was becoming addicted to. Her body lifted against his probing touch, seeking the vital masculinity of him. He pressed against her hip and she could feel the eagerness in him.

"Ah, Gwen, my sweet, soft Gwen." The words were as thick and sweet as honey as Zac reluctantly tore his mouth from hers and began to nibble hungrily elsewhere.

She clenched her fingers in his hair as his lips and tongue forged a sizzling path down to the peaks of her breasts, hovering there for a moment until she caught her breath and tried to urge him closer. Then he was moving lower.

His body was an enthralling seductive weight on her own as he sprawled over her. She felt the damp heat of his mouth in the small dip of her stomach, and then he was using his teeth with exciting gentleness on the inside of her thigh. He held her legs apart with his big hands and began a slow tantalizing trail of kisses back up to the part of her that was already damp with desire.

Guinevere moaned, turning her head into the pillow. Her knees flexed upward as the tension within her grew to overpowering proportions.

"Zac . . . Please, Zac. I want you so."

Slowly he made his way back up the length of her. He was hard and taut with his own need, and in the shadowy light she could see the fierce hunger in his eyes. His face was tight with the force of the urgency driving him. He lowered himself deliberately down onto her, holding her knees in their raised position. He teased her, probing slighty and then withdrawing, until Guinevere thought she would go out of her mind.

"Zac!" Heedless of anything but the need to have him fill her completely, Guinevere clutched at his back. "I can't wait any longer," she whispered into his neck.

"Neither can I." He surged against her, driving deep into her tight silken core.

Guinevere cried out, but he must have been expecting the husky sound because he once more sealed her mouth with his own. The soft feminine sob of excitement was lost in his throat. She could feel the groan of desire that rippled through his chest in response.

Quickly he established the primitive rhythm, drawing her with him down the spiraling trail. She wrapped her legs around him, abandoning herself to the thrilling ride and feeling the tightening of his muscles as he forged toward his own satisfaction. Guinevere was lost in the sensual whirlpool. The universe narrowed until it was filled only with Zac and the night. When the tension within her finally burst free of its bonds she cried out again.

Zac held her shivering body, trying to trap the delightful sounds of her climax even as he gave way to his own. In the end he knew he could not have successfully concealed Guinevere's presence in his room from the man next door.

The only thing that saved them both was the ringing of Vandyke's telephone just as Guinevere went over the edge. Zac hoped the noise had masked the final sounds of satisfaction. It was odd, he reflected vaguely as the phone next door was answered. He collapsed in a damp sprawl on Guinevere's equally damp body. On the one hand he wanted to shout to the world that this woman was his. On the other he felt a fierce desire to protect her. He knew how carefully she maintained her business image. He hadn't wanted to jeopardize it for her. But there was no way on earth he could have held out against her tonight.

At first Guinevere didn't know if the phone was ringing on the table next to Zac's bed or in Vandyke's room. By the time she surfaced far enough to figure it out, she could hear Vandyke's soft muffled voice.

"Cathy," Vandyke muttered.

Guinevere's eyes opened as she heard the name. "His wife," she whispered to Zac.

Zac shook himself a little, apparently trying to clear his head. He lifted himself away from Guinevere. "Good. That will keep him occupied. He won't hear you leaving."

"But, Zac, I don't want to leave."

"Move, woman. I should never have let you stay. Get dressed and get out of here." He gave her a small push and then pulled her back for a quick hard kiss before shoving her to the edge of the bed.

Resentfully, Guinevere did as she was told. A part of her recognized that it would be best if she exited from her own room in the morning. People talked, and while the times had indeed become more liberal, people still loved to talk most about the affairs of others. Small-business persons did not need too much of that kind of gossip.

Fumbling, she got back into her pants and shirt. Zac opened the door for her and she darted a quick glance down the hall. It was empty.

"Go," he hissed softly, but his eyes were gleaming with remembered passion.

She went, making it back to her own room without incident and falling into bed, convinced she wouldn't be able to sleep. She slept like a log. It wasn't until she was putting on her pantyhose the next morning that she realized someone had searched her room while she had been with Zac.

CHAPTER 5

He didn't feel like a frog the next morning, Zac reflected in lazy contentment. But then, he never did after a night that included Guinevere Jones in his bed. He yawned hugely, pushing back the blankets, and went into the bathroom. Guinevere had called him a frog the first time they had met. Of course, he reminded himself tolerantly, she'd had reason to view him in a somewhat negative light. He'd been blackmailing her at the time.

Zac leaned into the shower and turned on the water full blast. While he waited for the water to get hot he stretched, aware of the pleasant aftereffects of Guinevere's sweet passion. He always felt good the next morning. Strong, healthy, brilliant—and sexy as hell.

She had a way of making him feel this good. Zac didn't fully understand it and saw absolutely no need to try. It was a fact. A smart man made a grab for the good things in life and didn't waste time questioning them or tearing them apart to examine them analytically.

Guinevere, on the other hand, seemed to want to talk lately. Zac stepped into the shower, wondering if yesterday's conversation in the car on the way back from the marina had been sufficient for her. He'd gotten what he needed out of the chat. He grinned a little to himself as he applied soap to his chest. She wasn't seeing anyone else. She hadn't seen anyone else since she'd met him. Zac realized his idiotic grin was widening. He shoved his head under the spray.

She was late coming down to breakfast that morning. Zac joined a subdued Vandyke for coffee and a platter of bacon and eggs. Guinevere still hadn't appeared by the time Washburn took Vandyke and the other two business executives into a conference room for what was to be the last round of presentations. Vandyke hesitated before following the others, glancing worriedly down at Zac, who was still drinking coffee.

"You're going to stick around in case I, uh, need you later, right, Justis?"

"I'll be here. Good luck with the presentation."

Vandyke nodded brusquely and turned to go. Zac watched him leave, feeling helpless to reassure the man. He understood now why Guinevere was worried about her client. Vandyke was a man walking the razor's edge.

The conference room door closed behind the high-level executives just as Guinevere entered the coffee shop. Zac watched her scan the small crowd, which consisted of Toby Springer and the handful of other people who had accompanied their bosses to the resort. He waited with a sense of pleasant anticipation for the moment she spotted him sitting by the window.

She managed to look both chic and casual against the gloom of another rainy morning. The sweater she was wearing was a rich bronze color trimmed in black, and the pleated black pants had a wide band that emphasized her small waist and the full flare of her hips. Zac remembered the feel of her in the night and exhaled slowly.

She had wanted him badly enough last night to risk her image. That realization threatened to go to his head like hot brandy. The idea of Guinevere Jones sneaking down a hotel hallway just to be with him was enough to get him aroused all over again. He drew in another breath and again let it out with slow control. Sophisticated business security consultants did not allow their bodies to embarrass them in public restaurants. At that moment Guinevere turned and caught him watching her. She started toward him purposefully.

"I need to talk to you," she announced in a low tone as she sat down across from him. Her hazel eyes were narrowed and steady. The mouth that had been so soft and warm during the night was firm with resolve.

Zac groaned. "I was afraid of that."

Her brows came together in that funny way they did when she was about to deliver a lecture. "Zac, this is serious."

"I can tell."

Guinevere's frown deepened as she realized he wasn't ready to show the proper concern. What was the matter with him this morning? She leaned forward intently. "Zac, somebody searched my room last night."

He stared at her.

"Well, at least I've got your attention." She sat back, satisfied.

"Searched your room?" He looked dumbfounded.

She nodded with grave certainty. "Must have happened while I was . . ." She glanced away. "With you," she finished, looking at him again.

"You were only with me about half an hour." He ignored her flicker of embarrassment. "Gwen, are you sure? Why didn't you come and get me? How do you know you were searched? Were things messed up?"

"Oh, no. It was a very professional job."

"No offense, but how would you know if your room had been professionally tossed?"

She wrinkled her nose. "Tossed?"

"Forget it." He glanced up as the waitress approached and

waited impatiently while the woman poured coffee and Guinevere ordered cereal and fruit. Then he folded his arms in front of him on the table. "Tell me what happened," he said deliberately.

Guinevere sighed inwardly. She had known it would be like this, of course. Zac would want a blow-by-blow account, complete in every detail. He was a careful thorough man who tended to take his time about this sort of thing. He himself admitted that he worked slow. When he'd worked for the international group of private security consultants, she knew, his co-workers had nicknamed him "the Glacier"—slow-moving, but in the end everything got covered.

"I just realized what had happened this morning when I put on my pantyhose."

He blinked slowly. "Pantyhose?"

"I'm wearing a pair under these pants. They provide some extra warmth," she told him impatiently.

"I see."

"No, you don't. The first pair I put on had a run in them. On the left leg, above the knee."

"Tacky."

"Zac, you're not paying attention."

"I'm paying attention, I'm just not following the gist of this conversation. Tell me, in one-syllable words, the significance of your pantyhose having a run in them."

She made a small exclamation of disgust. "Zac, last night when I was getting ready for bed I snagged a pair of pantyhose."

"Okay, I can follow that. Go on."

"Don't be condescending. This is crucial evidence."

"I'm listening," he told her gravely.

"I didn't want them to get mixed up with my clean *un*snagged pantyhose and I didn't feel like taking the time to wash them out. So I put them in my suitcase on the left-hand side. The clean unsnagged ones are on the right. Got it so far?"

"Clear as crystal."

"Good. Well, this morning I reached for a pair from the clean side of the suitcase."

"The right side?"

"Precisely." She looked at him with faint approval. "And I got the pair I had put in on the left side last night. Whoever went through my suitcase didn't realize I'd know the difference, I suppose. Or else he was in a hurry." She waited with a gleam of triumph in her eyes.

Zac continued to gaze at her with level speculation. He was silent for a long moment. Finally, he said, "You're basing all this on one snagged pair of pantyhose? Nothing else appeared to have been touched?"

"No, it was a very careful job."

"Gwen," he said patiently, "why would anyone search your room? I'm the one who has the briefcase at night. Vandyke's the one who might have important papers to hide. You're, pardon the expression, just a secretary, as far as anyone around here is concerned."

"I don't know why someone would do it, Zac. You're the authority on business security, you tell me. Secretaries often have important notes and papers lying around. Maybe somebody was looking for something I might have left out after doing that typing for Vandyke yesterday afternoon."

"Gwen, if they went into your room during the short period you were with me, that means someone was keeping a close eye on your activities."

She shuddered. "Spooky, isn't it?"

"Also unlikely. Honey, I don't mean to let the air out of your balloon, but there's no logical reason why someone would search your room instead of mine or Vandyke's."

"How do you know they haven't searched yours?" she demanded.

He shrugged, picking up his coffee cup. "I'd know."

She saw the certainty in his face and concluded he probably would. "What about Vandyke? He's acting so strange lately I'm not sure he'd notice if anyone had been through his things."

"Or tell us if he did notice," Zac finished. "You're right there, but somehow I don't think it's happened."

"Then why me?"

"I'm not sure you were searched. One little pair of snagged pantyhose found on the wrong side of the suitcase is kind of slim evidence, Gwen. It would have been easy for you to forget which side you tossed them into. After all, when you were undressing last night you must have had your mind on . . ." He paused deliberately, and a slow satisfied smile lit his eyes. "Other things."

"Egotist."

He paid no attention. "Did you see anyone in the hall on the way back to your room last night?"

"No," she admitted, "but that doesn't mean anything. Someone could have come and gone before I left your room. Or he could have entered my room through the balcony."

"Eat your breakfast and we'll go have a look."

"You're just trying to placate me, aren't you?"

"No, I'm just trying to make sure one way or the other."

But they could find nothing else to verify Guinevere's suspicions. Zac went through the room carefully without finding anything to support the idea that someone had searched it. He shook his head and put his arm around Guinevere's shoulders. "Honey, I think it was your imagination at work. There's just no logic to it."

By now Guinevere was beginning to doubt her own discovery of the pantyhose. She sorted through the remaining pairs. "I don't know, Zac. I could have sworn the pair I put on first this morning was the pair I had deliberately put into the left side of the suitcase. Now you've got me wondering."

He ran a fingertip down her nose. "I told you, last night you had other things on your mind." His eyes gleamed for a moment with the memories, and she tried to glare at him.

"I knew I was never going to hear the end of it." She moved away from him. "What's the schedule for today?"

"I promised Vandyke I'd stick around the lobby in case he needs me. I just wish to hell I knew what he thought he might need me for. He's got the briefcase in the conference room. This is the last round of presentations, and Washburn's promised a decision by this afternoon. We'll all get to go home early this evening. Frankly, I can't wait."

"Did Vandyke look nervous?" she asked.

"No more so than usual."

"How long did the conversation with his wife last?"

"Not long. About ten minutes after you left."

Guinevere eyed Zac thoughtfully. "I don't suppose you could actually hear what he said to her?"

He smiled. "What a little snoop. No, I couldn't catch most of the words. Just her name occasionally. The connecting door isn't that thin—thank God. It means he might not have heard you. At least, he didn't make any reference to you being in my room last night."

Guinevere considered that. "I'm not sure he would. He's really quite a gentleman."

Zac paced to the window, running a hand through his hair. "Well, one way or another this whole thing should be over this afternoon. We'll catch the ferry back to Seattle and that will be the end of my commitment to Vandyke. What about you? How long are you supposed to cover for his secretary?"

"She'll probably be back on the job tomorrow."

"Good. I can't say this little jaunt hasn't been interesting in some ways, but I'll be glad when it's over. What are you going to do today?"

"I have some typing to take care of for Vandyke this morning. Then I guess I'll pack and get ready to leave."

Zac glanced back at her as he stood in front of the window. His eyes were the same color as the overcast sky. "Do you think we might try this again sometime?"

"A wild weekend fling?"

"Yeah."

Under his deliberate gaze she felt the warmth rising in her cheeks. "That might be nice."

"Next time we won't try to combine business with pleasure. It's too damn frustrating."

Guinevere hesitated. There were other things that were frustrating. "We still haven't had a chance to really discuss things between us, Zac."

He went to her, gripped her shoulders fiercely, and planted a hard kiss on her mouth. "Personally, I thought we'd made terrific strides."

"Do you really think so?"

The phone rang just as Guinevere was waiting in an agony of hope for her answer. With a disgusted sigh she went to answer it. She listened to Vandyke's hurried instructions and hung up with a regretful sigh.

"That was Vandyke. He wants me to hurry up with that typing. Guess I'd better get busy doing what I'm being paid to do. I'll see you at lunch, Zac."

"And I'll go do my duty in the lobby," he groaned as he stalked to the door.

Guinevere watched the closed door for a long moment before she went to the typewriter that had been set up in her room. So much for all her plans to define the relationship.

Washburn's announcement shortly before lunch caught both Zac and Guinevere completely by surprise. From their client's general attitude of depression and uncertainty, they would never have guessed Vandyke Development had been selected to do the Washburn project.

"Congratulations," Guinevere said sincerely over lunch. "It's a wonderful deal. You must be quite pleased."

Vandyke nodded, but he didn't look particularly thrilled. "It's definitely a load off my mind."

If that's the case, Guinevere thought, he certainly doesn't *look* very relieved.

"I'm glad it worked out," Zac said politely, watching the older man carefully. "The announcement came sooner than expected. When do you want to leave for Seattle?"

Vandyke looked at him questioningly, seeming suddenly to realize something. "Oh, I forgot. Washburn wants us to stay over one more day to finalize things. The others are going back this afternoon, but I guess I simply assumed you and Miss Jones would be available for one more day." He glanced worriedly at Guinevere. "Can you manage? I'm going to need you to handle the final letter of agreement. Washburn and I will rough it out this afternoon."

"We had planned on getting back today," Zac began firmly, but Guinevere cut him off.

"I can manage one more day," she assured her client. "What about you, Zac?"

He glanced at her, sighing. "Yeah, I guess I can squeeze in one more day."

"I'm very grateful to both of you. Why don't you take off after lunch and do some shopping or something, Miss Jones? I'm not going to need you until this evening, actually. It will take Washburn and myself several hours to hammer out the details. He wants to get everything wound up by tomorrow so he can get back to his offices in California. Zac, I'd appreciate it if you could hang around here?"

"Sure," Zac murmured. "Why not? Nothing I like to do better on a wild weekend."

"Zac!" Guinevere hissed warningly. Fortunately Vandyke didn't appear to have heard. He nodded vaguely, apparently satisfied, and excused himself. "I'll stay here with you," she went on to Zac, who immediately made a negative motion with his chin.

"Forget it. I'm not going to be good company and you'll enjoy hitting those little shops in town. Take your time. I'll just read a good book or something."

"What good book?"

"How about *A Thousand and One Erotic Fantasies of the Small Businessman*?"

Guinevere grinned. "Is it a best-seller?"

"It probably will be after I write it."

It was drizzling rain by three o'clock that afternoon when Guinevere finally decided she was not going to find the perfect pottery vase or an undiscovered painter in the town shops. She treated herself to a cup of hot tea and a scone at a small café and stared out the window at the rain-slick street. A few other tourists who favored the San Juans in winter were scurrying from one shop to the next, trying to avoid the gentle rain. A few cars made their way down the street with windshield wipers swishing languidly.

Guinevere thought of Zac, whom she had left sitting in the hotel lobby with a magazine, and decided she'd rather be sitting beside him. True, his good mood of the morning had disintegrated when he'd discovered they were going to have to stay another night, but she'd rather be with him in a bad mood than here by herself.

It was an odd realization. Guinevere thought about it some more while she had another scone. She was accustomed to being by herself. She liked her privacy and she liked her own company. It was strange to sit here and realize she'd rather be leafing through a magazine and listening to Zac grumble than shopping on her own.

Damn it, where was this relationship going? More important,

what was it doing to her ordered satisfying life? And what on earth had sent her sneaking down the hotel hall last night?

The answers to those questions continued to elude her, and she hadn't had much success in pinning Zac down about them either. Guinevere nursed her tea and continued to gaze out the café window. By now the other executives and their assistants would have checked out of the hotel and would be on the ferry heading home.

Maybe it would be nice to take one more walk down by the marina before she drove Zac's Buick back to the hotel. Guinevere paid her bill, left the tip, and tugged her red trench coat on. Outside on the sidewalk she opened her black umbrella. It wasn't really pouring, just drizzling as she made her way briskly down the street toward the marina. It was nearly empty of people, but the boats were always intriguing, especially when they bobbed on a gray sea against a gray sky. An artist would enjoy the scene, Guinevere reflected. She recalled Vandyke saying once that his wife dabbled in painting.

In the distance she could see Cassidy's Cessna tied up next to the old metal boathouse. She wondered if he ever flew on days like this. Probably. A guy with the right stuff flew in just about any sort of weather. She shook her head at the thought. Being in a small plane was bad enough; flying in one in bad weather seemed sheer stupidity, not to mention terrifying. But she supposed men like Cassidy thrived on terror.

She was gazing at the plane in the distance when she saw a familiar figure climb out of a car in the parking lot and start toward the boathouse. Toby Springer had apparently also been freed for the afternoon by his boss. Idly Guinevere started after him, deciding she'd kill a few more minutes saying hello.

As she watched, he ducked into the boathouse. By the time Guinevere reached the far end of the dock he hadn't reappeared. Maybe Cassidy was also inside the boathouse. Or perhaps Springer was going to take out a boat. She paused, wondering if she should go any farther. If Springer had business with Cassidy, she might just be a nuisance.

Guinevere changed her mind about saying hello. Turning, she started up the ramp. There was an old public toilet on her right. A worn sign on the side nearest her read LADIES in capital letters, and an overflowing trash can guarded the entrance. Guinevere angled around in front of it, following a path that would lead her back toward Zac's car.

As she walked past the far end of the building she glanced back at the boathouse. Cassidy and Springer had both emerged. They were facing each other, and although she couldn't hear what was being said Guinevere got the distinct impression they were arguing.

She also got the impression Cassidy was winning the argument. In fact, she decided as she stood watching them in the shadows of the rest rooms, she would have said Cassidy looked very much like a man giving orders. His hand moved in a flat, negative gesture, and Springer appeared to look resigned. He nodded once, stiff with obvious resentment, and then he swung around and started back toward the parking lot.

Curious, Guinevere switched her gaze back to Cassidy. He was watching Springer, but when the younger man climbed into his car he turned around and walked over to the bobbing Cessna. Opening the craft's door he stood under the high wing and looked around inside the cabin for a moment. Then he shut the door.

As he walked back along the floating dock toward the boathouse Guinevere realized he was carrying a gun. He held it unobtrusively against the right side of his body. No one watching from the marina would have noticed. But from the shadows of the rest rooms Guinevere could see the black metal of the barrel.

She was so startled that she failed to move until Cassidy reappeared from the boathouse. He no longer seemed to be carrying the weapon, unless he'd concealed it somewhere in his clothing. As she watched he ambled leisurely up the ramp and turned left, heading for a small coffee shop that catered to the boating crowd. He had the collar of his flight jacket turned up against the rain but he hadn't bothered with a hat. Dashing—and dangerous.

Guinevere stared at the boathouse and the plane for a very long time. It was getting late, and at this time of year the days were exceedingly short. By four o'clock it was going to be growing dark. There wasn't time to run back to the hotel and convince Zac that he ought to take a look inside that boathouse. If the job was going to get done, Guinevere told herself resolutely, she would have to display a little of the right stuff herself and do it.

She felt the odd little frisson of excitement that she had first known when she'd followed Zac one night during a search he had made of a private house. It was compounded of one part fear, one part adrenaline, and one part thrill. It was heady stuff, but she knew it was also very dangerous. Zac was to blame for having introduced her to it.

Could she make it down to the plane's dock without Cassidy spotting her from the café where he'd gone for coffee? The question was taken out of her hands when Cassidy suddenly emerged from the café and started up the street toward the center of the village.

It was now or never, Guinevere told herself. She emerged cautiously from the protection of the rest rooms and made her way down to the dock. Once on the dock she felt naked and exposed. Anyone who chose to come in this direction from the marina would see her. Halfway along the gently shifting planks Guinevere's heady sense of excitement became two parts fear and one part adrenaline. The thrill was gone.

She couldn't turn back now. She was only a few feet away from the old boathouse. A moment later her hand was on the door. She opened it and quickly stepped through into the dark interior. It took a moment for her eyes to adjust to the dim light seeping through the cracks. In another half hour she wouldn't have been able to see at all, and she wouldn't dare turn on a light if there was one.

A small cabin cruiser was tethered inside the boathouse, but that was all Guinevere could see. Disappointment welled up in her, mitigating the fear. She didn't know what she had expected to find, but she sure hadn't found it. The door closed behind her as she walked over to the cruiser. In the shadows it appeared to be a sleek craft, obviously built for speed.

Guinevere listened for a moment, but all she heard was the rain on the tin roof. Would she be able to hear the sound of approaching footsteps on the dock outside? Even if she did it would be too late to do anything about it. She would be trapped. The only way back to shore was along that narrow dock.

As long as she was here, Guinevere thought, she would just take a quick look inside the boat's cabin. It was a pity to waste the adrenaline. Carefully she eased herself into the boat and made her way to the neat cabin. There wasn't much to see. It looked exactly the same as the cabin of any other small boat. There was no gun casually left lying on the seat.

But then, she told herself, Cassidy wouldn't casually leave a gun lying on the seat. He'd put it somewhere safe. Perhaps a small cupboard or shelf that would be conveniently within reach of the boat's pilot. Remembering to use a handkerchief, Guinevere began cautiously opening doors. She didn't see anything that appeared to be dangerous or incriminating, but in the dim light it was difficult to be sure. She was about to give up when she eased open one last drawer built into the pilot's console. A flat black wallet lay folded inside. She pulled it out and flipped it open.

Luke Cassidy
Drug Enforcement Administration

She barely had time to examine the official-looking identification, which included a picture of Cassidy, when her question about being able to hear footsteps on the dock was answered.

Cassidy's slightly uneven stride was unmistakable, even over the sound of the rain on the roof. Guinevere was trapped, and she knew it. She shoved the leather wallet back into the small drawer and scrambled out of the boat.

And then the excitement that had driven her this far metamorphosed instantly into outright panic.

CHAPTER 6

The only exit from the boathouse was through the door, unless one counted the water as a potential way out. Guinevere froze on the dock, aware of the deceptively gentle slap of the chilly water against the boat and the wood planks beneath her feet. When she looked down all she could see was endless darkness. The thought of going into that was enough to make her dizzy.

The shock from an unplanned immersion into the cold water would be almost unbearable. The thought of trying to explain her presence in the boathouse to Cassidy was just as unthinkable.

Cassidy's footsteps paused just outside the door.

Summoning up what seemed an incredible amount of will-power Guinevere managed to tiptoe around the dock to the far side of the small cruiser. Its bulk now loomed between her and the door. She crouched in the shadows, praying that Cassidy would not enter the boathouse—or if he did, would not do more than glance casually around. Very little light was seeping into the old structure now. The shadows were welcome.

There was no sound at all from outside the door. Guinevere took several deep breaths and tried to crouch down even more. She was on her knees on the other side of the cruiser. The wooden planks, she discovered to her dismay, were wet, and the dampness was already penetrating the fabric of her pants. The water suddenly seemed very close. The sharp tang of it filled her nostrils.

She ought to get to her feet, march to the door, fling it open, and calmly announce her presence, Guinevere decided resolutely. After all, it wasn't as if she were doing anything terribly illegal. A person could wander into the wrong boathouse by mistake, couldn't she?

Possibly, she answered herself, and then she remembered the brief glimpse of Cassidy's identification. When the boathouse belonged to a man whose profession was hunting drug traffickers, one's explanations had better be pretty damn good. And offhand, she couldn't really think of a damn good explanation.

The image, she reminded herself grimly. She must remember the importance of her tiny but growing, and thus far pristine, business image. It would not be helped by being dragged into a drug smuggling case. Besides, for all she knew Cassidy might not even be willing to listen to explanations. He was obviously working undercover, and the discovery that someone was prowling around his boathouse would be enough to rouse suspicions in even the most even-tempered government man. If only Zac were here. He'd know how to confront Cassidy.

Cassidy's footsteps sounded again. Guinevere heaved a sigh of relief as they moved farther down the dock toward the plane. Hurry up and get what you came for, Cassidy, she thought. I'm getting cold.

There was a large ripple of movement beneath the dock, and water came splashing coldly up between the planks. Was the tide coming in, or was that just a small wave? Guinevere huddled into herself, her hands and feet wet now, as well as the front of her slacks from knee to ankle. She shivered again, and this time it was from something other than fear. The cold water was like ice against her skin.

Stiffly Guinevere changed position slightly, trying to pull the hem of her trench coat around under her knees. It didn't do much good. More water splashed up between the planks. By now, she knew, the sun must have almost disappeared. It was very dark inside the boathouse. A marina light was switched on outside.

There were more sounds along the dock. Cassidy had apparently finished his business with his plane. Leave, Cassidy. Go have a cup of coffee or a beer. Aren't you hungry? Almost dinnertime. His slightly uneven footsteps paused again outside the boathouse door. Guinevere almost tried to make herself invisible by closing her eyes, but forced herself to realize that wasn't going to do the trick. Taking a deep breath she stretched out flat along the planks, praying that the bulk of the boat was high enough to keep him from glancing over onto the other side if he opened the door. She rested her cheek on the dock, and promptly got a splash of icy water in her face. The shock almost made her cry out, and at that moment the door opened. Instinct took over. Guinevere went as still as a newborn fawn hiding from a predator.

A dim unshielded bulb blinked into life overhead. Cassidy came into the boathouse. Guinevere closed her eyes and told herself it was too late now to jump up and yell, "Surprise!" Nothing she could say would make her look innocent. Damn it, Zac. This is your line of work. You're the one who's supposed to be here in this mess, not me.

Another shudder went through her, this time such a mixture of anxiety and cold that she couldn't sort out one sensation from the other. Guinevere waited in an agony of suspense, wondering what it would be like in that instant when Cassidy walked around the dock and found her lying there. She had delayed announcing herself long past the point where she could have made a halfway reasonable explanation. It was too late.

Too late.

The light clicked off and the boathouse was plunged into

darkness. At first Guinevere wasn't sure what had happened. She heard the door slam shut and cautiously opened her eyes. Another ripple of water beneath the planks drenched the front of her trench coat and slacks. The cold seemed to be sinking into her.

Cassidy's footsteps dissolved into the distance as he walked back toward shore. Guinevere got painfully to her knees and tried to stand, not sure her legs would hold her. From out of nowhere she remembered that hypothermia didn't result only from immersion in cold water. You could lose body heat to a dangerous degree just by getting yourself damp in weather like this. Her fingers were feeling numb.

She found out how useless numb fingers were when she tried to brace herself against the side of the gently rocking cruiser. When she realized she couldn't feel the fiberglass hull beneath her hand Guinevere almost panicked. Frantically she shook her fingers, trying to generate some sensation. Then she began to worry about her damp feet. She should have worn her boots instead of the casual leather shoes she'd chosen.

Grimly she forced herself to calm down. She was all right. She was shivering a little and her fingers were numb, but she was okay. All she had to do was get back to the Buick and turn on the heater. By the time she arrived at the resort she would be toasty warm. She could have a nice hot cup of tea and perhaps a shot of brandy.

That pleasant scenario required that she first get out of the boathouse, however. Uncertainly Guinevere edged her way around the front of the cruiser and over to the door. She paused a moment, listening intently, and then decided she had to act. Cautiously she opened the door and slipped outside into the chill of early evening. The wind was brisk and it startled her when it struck through the dampness of her clothing. She shivered again, more violently. Light rain slashed at her as she ran for the shelter of the overhang of the rest rooms. From there she tried to peer into the shadows of the parking lot. Was Cassidy out there somewhere keeping an eye on his plane?

She couldn't wait any longer to find out. She was too damn cold. Taking a deep breath, Guinevere ran across the parking lot to the street where she had left the Buick. The physical activity didn't seem to warm her any. It only made her feel more miserable.

She reached the stolidly waiting Buick without incident and fumbled in her purse for the keys. A few moments later she had the car in gear and the heater going full blast. It seemed to take forever to get warm. Guinevere drove away from the village, following the meandering road that led back to the resort.

It was almost completely dark by the time she left Zac's car in the resort parking lot and made her way around to a back entrance. The thought of going through the lobby in her present condition was too much. She would feel a fool.

The car's heater had helped some, but she was still wearing her damp clothing and as she hurried down the corridor to her room Guinevere realized she was still too cold. She had begun shivering again when she got out of the Buick. Feeling a little frantic, she dug the room key out of her purse and twisted it awkwardly in the lock. The phone rang just as she went through the door. She picked up the receiver, knowing who it would be before she answered.

"Jesus Christ, lady, where the hell have you been?"

"Zac, it's a long story, and I'm so cold. Let me get into a hot shower and get warm. I'll meet you in half an hour down in the lobby."

"The hell you will. I'll be right up." He slammed down the receiver without waiting for an answer.

Sighing, Guinevere went into the bathroom, stripping off her wet clothing. She had the shower on and was just stepping under the blessed warmth when the bathroom door swung open. Guinevere glanced around the curtain to make sure it was Zac. One glance was enough. He was furious.

"How did you get back into the hotel without me seeing you? I've been pacing that damn lobby for forty-five minutes!"

"Please don't yell at me, Zac. I've had a hard afternoon."

"Shopping? Until after dark. When you knew I'd be waiting for you?"

"It's not that late, Zac." She turned her face up into the hot water, considering the nature of his anger. He really had no right to be this upset, she decided. "Worried about your car? It's fine, really."

"I was worried about you." He pushed back the curtain and ran his eyes assessingly over her nakedness. "Your hair looks like hell. What have you been doing?"

She kept her back to him. "Zac, you sound like an irate husband."

"So?" he challenged evenly.

"So back off a little. My patience is just about exhausted. And I'm not accustomed to having men yell at me when I come home a little late."

"I'll bet you're not. You're so goddamn used to doing exactly what you please, when you please, that you—"

"Aren't you?" she interrupted quietly.

To her surprise, that stopped him for a moment. She felt him staring at her, but she didn't turn around. She couldn't turn around, actually. The hot water was finally beginning to warm her. Nothing had ever felt as good as this shower.

"Yeah," he finally said. "I guess I am. I guess we're both accustomed to setting our own rules." He drew a long breath. "Okay, Gwen, I won't yell. But that was my car you disappeared in. I think I deserve an explanation, don't you?"

"I hate it when you get reasonable. Takes all the fun out of arguing with you." But she knew her voice lacked any real sting of flippancy. She sounded as weary as she suddenly felt. "Zac, could you order me a cup of tea from room service? I really did get cold. A little too cold, I think."

He must have sensed the seriousness of the situation. With a last assessing glance he dropped the shower curtain, and a moment later she heard the bathroom door close.

Zac was just pouring a cup of hot tea as she emerged from the bathroom swathed in her robe. He swung around and strode across the room, thrusting the warm cup into her hands.

"Here. Drink this."

She sipped gratefully at the tea, feeling its warmth heating her from within. "Stop glowering, Zac. I'm okay. And I'm sorry you were worried. Am I really that late?"

"Considering the fact that I was expecting you sometime between three and three thirty, yes. I was about to borrow Vandyke's Mercedes and come looking for you. What the hell happened? How did you get so cold?"

Wearily Guinevere sank down onto the edge of the bed, her teacup cradled in her hands. "It's going to sound silly when I tell you. Promise me you won't start yelling?"

He sat in the chair across from the bed, gray eyes pinning her. "I never make promises I can't be sure of keeping. Talk. Was it an accident with the car?"

"Your precious Buick is fine. The truth is, I got trapped in Cassidy's boathouse."

There was a split second of silence that seemed as heavy as lead. The gray gaze was unwavering. "With Cassidy?"

Realizing his conclusion, Guinevere hastily shook her head. "No. Zac, you're not going to like the way I did it but I think I've got some answers. I took a little walk down to the marina shortly after three. Guess who I saw talking to Cassidy?"

"Who?"

"Toby Springer. But this time it didn't look as if they were arranging an outing. They seemed to be arguing."

"Where were you that you could see that much?"

"Standing in the shadow of the public rest rooms. Exciting,

huh? I had no idea this investigative business was so glamorous. At any rate they both left, and—"

"Together?"

She shook her head. "Toby left first and then Cassidy. I assumed they were gone for the evening so I decided to have a quick look around that boathouse."

Zac closed his eyes, apparently pleading silently for patience. "I should have guessed."

"It's your fault. You're the one who taught me these devious little tricks."

"I've created a monster," he groaned. Then, curiosity getting the better of him, he asked reluctantly, "Well? Find anything?"

"A boat."

"Not an unlikely object to find in a boathouse."

Guinevere paused for effect. "There was a leather wallet in the boat, Zac."

"Oh, hell. You went through the boat?"

"It seemed like the logical thing to do. I said to myself, what would Zac do if he were here? You were my inspiration."

"Okay, I can see you're dying to spring the surprise. What was in the wallet?"

"I.D. for one Luke Cassidy. He's government, Zac. Drug Enforcement Administration."

"Shit."

"I felt a little nervous myself. I was about to make a strategic retreat when I heard him returning along the dock. I made it to the other side of the boat and crouched down behind it. That's how I got so cold and damp. The water kept splashing up between the planks. And when he came into the boathouse and turned on the light—"

"He found you?" Zac's gaze was riveted to her face.

"No. I nearly panicked. It was a horrible sensation, Zac. Only the thought of the image kept me from jumping up and throwing myself on the mercy of the government. Can you imagine? How would I have ever explained my snooping around in the boathouse of a government agent? Camelot Services would have undoubtedly come under all sorts of suspicion. It would have been embarrassing and humiliating and I might have ended up in jail or something. I can just see the headlines: Owner of Small Temporary-Employment Firm Linked to Drug Case."

"So you stayed put and managed to get yourself chilled to the bone instead? You were willing to risk hypothermia for the image?"

"I know it sounds dumb now, but at the time . . ." She morosely let the sentence trail off and took another sip of tea. She was finally beginning to feel comfortably warm again.

Zac got to his feet, shoving his hands into his hip pockets. Restlessly he stalked to the window. "You may have been right. Staying out of sight may have been the best option under the circumstances. But, Jesus, Gwen!"

"I know."

He turned to face her, his expression hard. "So he's DEA?"

"That's what the identification said. Had a little picture of him and everything."

"Damn."

"You're doing a lot of swearing tonight."

"Yeah. I'm feeling put-upon." He glanced back at the darkness beyond the window. "We're in the middle of something, Gwen, and I don't like it. Best option for us right now is to get the hell out of here."

She studied him worriedly. "Middle of what?"

He sighed, swinging around once more to confront her. "I heard from Sol late this afternoon."

"Your friend Sol in Saint Thomas?"

Zac nodded brusquely. "He said a man named Gannon and one named Edward Vandyke were partners a few years back in a small charter operation that was based on Saint Thomas. The business was closed shortly after Gannon was killed."

"All right. That fits with what Vandyke told us." Guinevere eyed Zac curiously. "So what's the catch?"

"According to the information Sol dug up, there was a suspicion that the Gannon-Vandyke charter service made money flying more than passengers and cargo."

Guinevere bit her lip, guessing what was coming next. "Drugs?"

Zac paced back to the chair and sat down slowly. "The authorities never uncovered any proof, and no charges were ever brought. Sol said it was just speculation. A lot of people with airplanes come under suspicion down in the Caribbean. There are a lot of pilots in that part of the world involved in the South American drug chain. The runs are extremely lucrative. A couple of big ones and a man would have a nice bit of capital. He might have enough cash to invest in a legitimate business, for instance. A business such as Vandyke Development."

"Or he might get killed," Guinevere said slowly. "The way Gannon did?"

Zac looked at her for a moment. "Actually, the way Gannon got killed raises some interesting questions."

"Didn't Vandyke tell the truth?"

"Sol says that according to the reports in the local paper, which he found in the library, Gannon went down in April of nineteen seventy-two. Apparently he dumped the plane in the water off some little island called Raton. It's an uninhabited place, a chunk of rock in the Caribbean. The authorities eventually found traces of the wreckage. The body was never recovered."

Guinevere frowned. "Okay, it all still fits."

Zac watched her through narrowed eyes. "Not quite. Remember the photocopied page of Gannon's logbook? The one we found in Vandyke's briefcase?"

She nodded. "I remember. What about it?"

"It shows another flight, in May of that year. One month after Gannon is supposed to have disappeared."

"Oh my God, that's right. I'd forgotten." Guinevere sat stunned, absorbing the implications. "And that last entry was filled out in the same handwriting as the previous entries, wasn't it? At least, I don't remember thinking at the time that it appeared to be different handwriting."

Zac inclined his head once, leaning back in the chair with his big hands linked together under his chin. The gray gaze was almost remote now. Guinevere had seen that look before, and it made her uneasy.

"So," he went on almost musingly, "we have one very nervous ex-partner of a man who may not be dead. And the partnership may have been involved in drug smuggling. We also have a dashing pilot running around who apparently is familiar with Toby Springer and Washburn. Said pilot is carrying DEA identification."

Guinevere shivered again, but not from cold. "I think you're right, Zac. I think we are in the middle of something. Something messy." She paused a moment, her mind skipping ahead. "Do you think it's the fact that Gannon might be alive that's upsetting our client?"

"He's running scared from something. If he'd been under the impression that his ex-partner was dead all these years, and then someone sends him a page out of a logbook with a flight filled in *after* the one that should have been the last . . ."

"You think Gannon's materialized from Vandyke's past and is going to blackmail Vandyke?"

Zac shrugged. "It's one possibility, and it would explain a lot. Vandyke's straight these days. He's built up a good business. He's about to conclude a very important deal."

"Rumors of a past spent smuggling drugs could ruin him in the Seattle business community," Guinevere concluded thoughtfully.

"Talk about having your image tarnished."

"Yes."

They sat in silence for a while, considering the situation. Finally Zac spoke. "I don't think it's the documents he's worried about. I think he's been trying to get bodyguard service without telling me that's what he really needs. He only seems to be concerned about the briefcase when I remind him of it. The rest of the time he's distracted and nervous, and he doesn't like me to get too far out of sight."

"A bodyguard? To protect him from a blackmailer?"

"A possibility."

"And in the meantime the Drug Enforcement Administration is breathing down his neck?"

Zac winced. "Poor Vandyke. He's got more reason to be nervous than he even knows. You said Toby Springer was arguing with Cassidy?"

Guinevere nodded thoughtfully. "It's not the first time I've seen them together. Remember when we first saw him standing on Cassidy's dock?"

"Yeah." Zac idly rubbed his thumb along his jaw, eyes distant. "If Toby Springer is working with Cassidy then we have to assume someone is setting a trap."

"But for whom? Vandyke's been legitimate for years. Would they really waste a lot of time and money coming down on him now?"

"The government never needs an excuse to waste tax dollars, you know that," Zac replied impatiently. "But you're right. It would seem more likely they'd be interested in a current case, not one that was over a decade old."

"I can't believe Vandyke is currently involved in smuggling dope!" Guinevere was incensed at the notion. "He's a nice man, Zac. He's got a wife he cares about, a good reputation, a successful business—"

"That business may have been founded on the proceeds of his

last smuggling venture," Zac reminded her bluntly. "He may have decided to go back to his old line of work for new capital."

"I refuse to believe it!"

"That's because you don't want to believe it. You like the guy."

"What's wrong with liking him?" she fumed.

"In your case, it tends to cloud your reasoning. You're too empathic, Gwen. You let your emotions dictate your loyalties."

She stared at him, infuriated. "What a chauvinistic thing to say! Just because I tend to trust my judgments of people, that doesn't mean I let my emotions sway those judgments! I like Edward Vandyke, and I don't believe he's involved in drug smuggling—whatever he may or may not have done in the past."

"Your faith in your client is touching. But it doesn't solve our immediate problem."

"What is our immediate problem? Warning Vandyke about Cassidy?"

Zac gave her a dryly amused look. "If you think Vandyke is an innocent honest businessman, why are you concerned with warning him about Cassidy? Why would he even need to be warned about him?"

Guinevere flushed, aware of the trap he was setting. "He's a client of mine. I feel obliged to help him. And you should feel the same, Zac. Vandyke's your client too."

"One who hasn't been straightforward with me."

"He's scared!"

"That's not my problem, unless he chooses to be upfront about the situation and unless he hires me to do something about it. Even at that point I'm not obliged to worry about it unless I decide to take the case. Gwen, as far as I'm concerned, Vandyke hired me to baby-sit a briefcase full of documents. So far nothing has happened to that briefcase. I've done my job. And you've done everything you were obligated to do. I have a feeling it's time for both of us to get the hell out of Dodge City."

"What do you mean?"

"I mean you and I should be on the next ferry back to Ana-cortes." He glanced at his black metal wristwatch. "It leaves in an hour. If we move, we can make it."

Guinevere set down her teacup, alarmed. "Zac, we can't just leave like that. We've got to talk to Vandyke."

"Honey, we don't have the least idea of what's coming down here. Cassidy might be planning some kind of raid. He might be setting a trap. And who the hell knows where Toby Springer fits into all this?"

A thought struck Guinevere. "What if Springer is a plant?" she asked, her eyes wide. "Maybe he's working for Cassidy's outfit as an inside informant."

Zac looked exasperated. "Wonderful. And where does that lead us? Do we then assume that Sheldon Washburn is cooperating with the government? Helping Cassidy set up Vandyke?"

Guinevere bit her lip. "Not necessarily. Washburn and Vandyke are going to be partners after the final contracts are signed," she went on slowly. "Maybe they've been partners before."

Zac considered that. "You think Washburn might be Gannon?"

"Why not? It's a possibility, isn't it? Washburn and Vandyke are in similar lines of work these days—real estate development. They've both emerged on the business scene since nineteen seventy-two, and they both seem to have had a good chunk of cap-ital with which to get started. It would be easy enough for them to pretend in front of the rest of us that they've never met before."

"Oh great, Gwen. Now you're not only convicting your own client, you're saying Washburn's in on it with him. Make up your mind."

She stood up. "I can't make up my mind. I don't know what's going on. And neither do you. We can't just leave Vandyke in this situation, Zac. We've got to at least talk to him."

"No we don't."

Guinevere glared at him over her shoulder as she crossed the small room to her closet and began searching for something to wear to dinner. "He's our client, Zac."

"We're not doctors, priests, or lawyers. Our relationship with a client is hardly sacred."

"Do you mean to sit there and tell me we're going to do absolutely nothing for Vandyke? Just hop on the next ferry and get ourselves safely out of the picture."

"It would seem," he said, "the most advisable course of action at the moment. I don't have any desire to be blithely sitting in the middle of this mess sipping tea when Cassidy comes through the front door, six-guns blazing. As you discovered in the boathouse, the prospect of explaining our innocence to the government is about as enthralling as explaining our tax returns to them at an audit."

Guinevere studied his face, seeing the resolve in his eyes. "Vandyke's a client, Zac," she said quietly, reaching into the closet to pull out a black wool dress. "I think we owe him the courtesy of offering him your services."

Zac looked as if he hadn't heard her correctly. "What's this? We owe him the courtesy of offering him *my* services? In what capacity, for God's sake? I'm a consultant, not a hired gun. And above all I will not allow you to get further involved in this damn situation."

"Zac, all I'm asking is that we talk to him. Tonight. We can leave in the morning after we've fulfilled our obligations."

Zac threw up his hands and surged out of the chair. "You're a stubborn, idiotic, emotional, bleeding-heart female who doesn't have the common sense she was born with. What's worse, you're trying to drag me down with you. If *I* had the sense I was born with I'd bundle you up, stuff you into the car, drive you onto that ferry, and say the hell with it."

Guinevere looked at him hopefully. "We'll talk to Vandyke?"

"*I'll* talk to Vandyke. You will keep your charming little ass out of this, or I will not be responsible for what happens. When it comes to security matters that turkey is my client, not yours. Got it?"

"Thank you, Zac." Guinevere demurely lowered her eyes so that he wouldn't see her satisfaction. She scurried into the bathroom to dress for dinner.

CHAPTER 7

There were times, Zac reflected a few hours later, when he'd give anything to have Gwen's winning way with people, when he would find it very useful to have them confide as easily in him as they often did in her. Theoretically he should have had Gwen with him when he tried to pin down his anxiety-ridden client. She always had a soothing effect on people. But the truth was he didn't dare get her any more involved in this crazy situation than she already was. Furthermore, if Vandyke was enmeshed in some drug-running scam the last thing Zac wanted was for his client to think he and Gwen were aware of it. People who ran drugs were inclined to be defensive on occasion. Downright hostile, in fact. The simple truth was, people who ran drugs were often willing to kill to protect their lucrative secrets. No, Zac decided, if Vandyke was innocent, and genuinely needed help, the man was going to have to volunteer more information.

By ten thirty that evening Zac had to admit that thus far the gentle art of subtle interrogation was not going well. He was fairly good at the straightforward pin-them-to-the-wall style, but he lacked the finesse needed for the more diplomatic strategy. He ordered another tequila and watched Guinevere dancing with Toby Springer. The sight annoyed him, but he had to admit it kept her occupied and away from the table while he was trying to corner Vandyke. Beside him Vandyke watched the pair on the dance floor broodingly. Washburn had retired a half hour earlier. Zac decided to make one more attempt with Vandyke.

"With your competitors gone, and now that you and Washburn have signed the development deal, I can't see any further need to worry about that briefcase, Mr. Vandyke. I think I'll let you keep it tonight."

"Fine." Vandyke sounded uninterested. He was still watching Guinevere and Springer.

"I thought Gwen and I could catch the first ferry out in the morning."

That caught Vandyke's attention. "You're going back early? I thought we agreed you'd stay until I'm ready to return to Seattle. I was planning on leaving around noon. Actually, I had planned to discuss the possibility of your continuing to—"

"I've got a business to run, and it really doesn't look as if you need me any longer," Zac said ruthlessly. He looked at the older man. "I'm not sure you ever needed me in the first place. No one so much as winked at that damn briefcase."

Vandyke shifted his glance back to the dance floor. "Having you along was just a precaution."

"Against what?"

"You know. Theft, industrial espionage, that sort of thing. You can't be too careful these days."

Zac held on to his patience. "Why don't we level with each other, Vandyke. If you're in trouble, tell me. You're my client. I'll do my best to help you. But don't give me any more bull about that damn briefcase. You were never all that concerned about it. You just wanted me nearby. Somehow I can't believe you were simply looking for companionship."

Vandyke stiffened. "Nobody's paying you to ask questions, Justis."

"I know. I'm being paid to stick close. Not to the briefcase, but to you. Why don't you be honest about that part, at least? Normally I don't hire myself out as a bodyguard. It lacks class."

"Now listen here, Justis—"

"But since I'm already on the scene, I'll do what I can—if you'll tell me what it is I'm supposed to be guarding you against," Zac concluded coldly.

"I don't have the vaguest idea what you're talking about."

Zac wanted to slam the man up against a wall. His fingers tightened around the small tequila glass. "If it's blackmail, Vandyke, there are ways of dealing with it."

Vandyke's eyes widened for an instant and then narrowed. His voice was tight. "You're way out of line even suggesting that I'm being blackmailed. What the hell gave you that idea? I have absolutely nothing to hide. I resent your implication, Justis."

Zac cradled his tequila in both hands, his elbows on the table, studying the older man for a long moment. This was getting nowhere. "All right, Vandyke. Have it your way. You hired a babysitter for that briefcase for three days. You've had your money's worth. I'm leaving first thing in the morning and I'm taking Gwen with me."

"I was under the impression Miss Jones was an independent businesswoman," Vandyke snapped. "She doesn't work for you."

"No, but in this situation she'll do what I tell her."

"Why should she do that, Justis?"

"Because if she doesn't I'll pick her up and carry her on board that ferry tomorrow morning. I'm not leaving her here with you when I can't figure out what the hell is going down."

"Does Miss Jones know your intentions?" Vandyke murmured sarcastically as Guinevere and Toby Springer approached the table.

Guinevere smiled, her eyes bright with charming inquiry. "Does Miss Jones know what intentions?" Springer pulled out a chair for her before Zac could get to his feet. Then the younger man sat down beside her. Zac felt his irritation rise.

"I was just telling Mr. Vandyke that you and I will be leaving first thing in the morning." He watched Guinevere coolly, silently challenging her to defy the edict.

Guinevere hesitated, and Zac saw the concern in her face. She knew he had failed. For a moment he thought she would refuse to cooperate, but she smiled ruefully at her client. "I'm afraid Zac's right. I've already stayed longer than I should. I promised my sister I would be back in the office tomorrow morning, and I won't be able to get there until tomorrow afternoon as it is."

"I'm paying you for your time, Miss Jones," Vandyke said huffily. "I don't see the problem."

"It's a scheduling problem," Guinevere explained quite gently. "My sister is only helping out, you see. She isn't a full-time employee of Camelot Services. I really must get back. And Zac has a business to run too. He took this job for you as a favor to me, but he made it clear from the outset he couldn't commit to more than three or four days. Isn't that right, Zac?"

"Right." He was vastly relieved that she didn't intend to fight him on this. "We'll leave in the morning." He glanced at his watch. "That first ferry is a very early one. We'd better head for bed." He got pointedly to his feet and waited for Guinevere. Toby Springer looked dismayed.

"Hey," Springer protested, jumping up to pull out Guinevere's chair. "How about one last dance?"

Zac already had his hand under Guinevere's arm. "I think Gwen's as ready for bed as I am, aren't you, Gwen," he answered for her.

"Well, actually, it is only ten thirty, and I"—she gave a small cough as Zac tightened his hold on her arm—"I did have a busy afternoon. I think I will retire. Good night, Mr. Vandyke. I probably won't see you in the morning. Have a good trip back to Seattle, and congratulations on concluding the deal with Washburn." She nodded politely at Toby Springer and allowed herself to be hauled forcibly out of the lounge.

"Really, Zac," she muttered as he marched her down the corridor to her room, "there's no need to be so heavy-handed about this."

"Probably not. But it comes naturally to me."

She shot him a swift glance as he took the key from her hand and turned it in the lock. There was a new remoteness in his eyes. It was the expression she'd seen during the last stages of the Starr-Tech case. She'd mentally labeled it Justis in Deep Think. He was just going into it now, and if she didn't catch him quickly he would be too far gone to deal with.

"No luck with Vandyke?" she demanded as she preceded Zac into the room.

"No."

The monosyllabic answer was not a good sign. Zac was further gone than she had thought. "Did you confront him with what we knew?"

Zac stood by the door, staring thoughtfully at the blank television screen across the room. "We don't know much."

"I realize that, but did you imply we knew he might be in real trouble?"

"I asked him if he was being blackmailed."

Guinevere perked up. "What did he say?"

"Denied it."

"Did you tell him about Cassidy?"

"No."

Impatiently Guinevere tossed her purse onto the dresser. "Well, why not?"

"If Vandyke's running drugs, I don't want him knowing we know. Not unless he's willing to confide in us first."

Hands on hips, Guinevere faced him, but first she had to get between him and the television set. "I see. A standoff, is that it? You wouldn't tell him how much we knew, so he decided to play it cool too. The result is that neither of you got anywhere because you wouldn't take the risk of confiding in each other. I knew I shouldn't have left the confrontation to you, Zac. I should have handled it myself."

Zac's eyes focused long enough to meet her irate gaze. "Don't be stupid, Gwen. There's more at stake here than trying to help a client who doesn't want too much help. We're better off out of this, and you know it."

Guinevere lapsed into silence herself after that. Zac was probably right, she realized morosely as she drifted around the room packing her suitcase, lost in a sensation of uneasy regret. Still, it just didn't seem proper to be abandoning Vandyke to his fate this way.

It was when she was getting ready to brush her teeth that Guinevere finally became aware that Zac was showing no signs of going back to his own room. He was still sprawled in the chair he had sunk into shortly after arriving, and his attention was still focused on something she couldn't see.

"Zac?"

No response.

Guinevere crossed the room to stand in front of him. "Zac? Aren't you going to go to bed?"

He blinked and looked up at her briefly. "No. I'm just going to sit here and think for a while."

"All night?"

He shrugged and went back to thinking.

Guinevere sighed and headed for the bathroom. When she emerged in her nightgown a few minutes later he hadn't moved. Tentatively Guinevere switched off the light. There was no word of protest from Zac. Deep Think had taken over completely. Either that or he was asleep. Guinevere gave up and crawled into bed.

She didn't look at the clock when the bed gave beneath Zac's weight a long time later. Guinevere stirred, feeling the pleasant heat of his body as he curled against her, and went back to sleep. Her last fleeting thought was that there was a deep sense of comfort to be found going to sleep in Zac's arms.

It was still dark when the ferry left shortly after six the next morning. Zac must have set an alarm, Guinevere decided, although she hadn't heard it. Of course, at that hour she would have been lucky to hear the Seattle Symphony if it had been playing right there in the hotel room. She was still yawning as she followed Zac up from the ferry's car deck and stumbled into the cafeteria.

"Sit here and I'll get us some coffee. Do you want anything to eat? We've got nearly a two-hour trip ahead of us." He frowned down at her as she slipped into a booth.

Guinevere shook her head. "Just bring on the caffeine."

He nodded and left, returning a few minutes later with two plastic cups. "Here you go," he said, and set one down in front of her.

"You weren't kidding when you said this ferry left early. It's still the middle of the night outside." She sipped the coffee gratefully. "Ah, that's better. Come to any momentous conclusions last night?"

Zac looked at her. "Not really. Just a lot of questions. Nothing new about those. I've had them all along."

"It still doesn't feel right."

"Ditching Vandyke?" Zac grimaced. "I know. I hate to admit it, but it does feel wrong somehow. I sort of liked the guy. But that's the thing about criminals, Gwen. They're incredible con men. If they weren't, they wouldn't get away with everything, up to and including murder."

"Vandyke is no murderer!"

"I was just making a generalization, honey. Calm down."

Silence prevailed for another few minutes as they drank their coffee. Then Zac said carefully, "I did some thinking about that wild hypothesis you had. The one about Washburn possibly being Vandyke's old partner, Gannon."

Guinevere felt a flicker of interest. "Did you?"

"With all those papers you were handling for Vandyke you didn't by any chance happen to end up with anything that might have Washburn's handwriting on it, did you? Notes he might have made, or his signature?"

Guinevere's eyes widened in admiration. "Zac, that's a brilliant idea. We could compare his handwriting to the handwriting on that page from Gannon's logbook." Her face fell. "If we still had the page from the logbook."

There was a significant pause from the other side of the table. "We've got it."

"We do? Zac, you copied it?"

He shrugged one shoulder a bit too casually. "I had a lot of time on my hands at certain points during the weekend, and the hotel had a self-service photocopy machine. Yesterday while you were playing hide-and-seek with Cassidy I got bored enough to use the machine."

"Let's see the page." Eagerly Guinevere leaned forward.

"First we'll need a sample of Washburn's handwriting."

"Oh, right. Got it here, I think." Guinevere rummaged around in her oversize shoulder bag for some stray envelopes and documents she had collected during the stay at the resort. "I have his signature on some of the drafts of the final letter of agreement he drew up with Vandyke. Here!" Triumphantly she pulled an envelope out of her purse.

Zac reached for the letter, opening it with slick efficiency. "Have you ever emptied that purse since the day you bought it?" he asked.

"I never empty a purse completely until I buy a new one. Let's see that page from the logbook."

He pulled a folded sheet of paper from his jacket pocket and spread it out on the table. "You realize this isn't exactly foolproof? I'm no handwriting expert. We won't be absolutely sure, even if the writing does seem similar."

"Stop being a pessimist. Let's have a look."

But one glance was all Guinevere needed. She looked at the flamboyant scrawl in which the logbook had been filled out, and then at Washburn's neat precise signature. "Well, so much for that brilliant theory. There's no similarity at all. No one's handwriting could change that much in the course of a decade." She frowned. "Or could it?"

Zac didn't look up from studying the two samples. "It's possible, if he made a deliberate attempt to alter his handwriting. But I don't think that's the case here. It would take an expert to be sure, though. On the face of it, I'd have to conclude Washburn is not Gannon."

"Ah, well. It was an interesting idea. What could we have done even if we'd decided he was Gannon?"

Zac's mouth crooked. "Not much. It would have been one more reason for staying out of Hopalong Cassidy's way."

"Because it would have meant Vandyke and Gannon had decided to go back into business together?"

"Mmm. And that Cassidy has probably set them both up for a fall."

"Now what do we conclude? That Cassidy has probably set up just our client?" Guinevere downed the rest of her coffee, aware of a deep feeling of anger. "I think we should have warned Vandyke."

Zac did a short staccato drumroll with his fingers on the table. "If the guy's running drugs, Gwen . . ."

"I know. But I don't think he is. He just isn't the type."

"Gwen—"

"I *know* he isn't. His wife is too nice and he's too worried about saving their relationship. A drug runner wouldn't give a damn about that sort of thing, would he? He'd just replace the wife with a cute teenybopper or something."

Zac's brows shot upward. "No kidding?"

"I'm serious, Zac."

He sighed. "So am I."

"So what do we do?" she asked challengingly.

Zac did the drumroll with his left hand. "That's what I've been asking myself all night."

Guinevere felt a spark of hope. "Let's go back and talk to him, Zac."

"We're halfway to Anacortes. It will take us another hour to get there and then nearly two hours to get back on the next ferry."

"We'll call him from Anacortes."

"Gwen, I'm not sure he wants our help. That's what's worrying me. I get the distinct impression the guy wants us to back off."

"We have to tell him about Cassidy," Guinevere said with grave resolution. "We owe our client that much, Zac."

Zac groaned and surrendered. "Okay. I'll call him when we reach Anacortes."

But an hour later when they drove off the ferry in Anacortes and found a telephone, the Good Samaritan project went down the tubes.

"There's no answer, and the front desk says they tried a page." Zac stepped out of the phone booth.

"Then we'll have to get right back on that ferry," Guinevere announced, feeling committed now.

"It would make more sense to try phoning every half hour," Zac pointed out.

"I think we should go back." She faced him determinedly. "I want to talk to him in person."

"I know I'm going to regret this," Zac murmured.

The return trip seemed to take forever, but three and a half hours after they had left the island Zac was driving the Buick back off the ferry. He took the first turn to the left and started toward the resort. He had said very little during the return trip, but he did glance casually at the marina as they drove past the dock where Cassidy kept his plane.

"The Cessna's gone."

Guinevere peered out the window. "What do you suppose that means?"

Zac abruptly increased the speed of the Buick, saying nothing.

By the time he finally parked in front of the resort Guinevere was more than uneasy, she was downright nervous. Zac quietly reached out and took her hand as they walked into the lobby.

"Hey, settle down. It's going to be okay. We'll deliver our grand message and then leave. We'll have done our duty by our client."

"I'm worried, Zac."

"So am I," he admitted. He released her hand and headed for the front desk. The clerk looked up in surprise.

"Oh, Mr. Justis. I thought you'd checked out this morning."

"I did. I'm back. I'm trying to locate Mr. Vandyke. Have you seen him this morning?"

The clerk nodded. "A couple of hours ago. He checked out too."

"Did he?" Zac leaned forward, his hands on the polished countertop. "Did he sign the bill?"

"Well, not exactly. Mr. Springer checked out for both Mr. Washburn and Mr. Vandyke."

"They left a couple hours ago? That wouldn't mesh with any of the ferry schedules."

The clerk was looking increasingly confused. "I believe Mr. Springer said that Washburn and Vandyke were in a hurry to get back to the mainland. They were going to hire a charter flight."

"Really? And what did Vandyke intend to do with his car?"

Confusion turned to nervousness mingled with belligerence on the clerk's face. Zac's relentless, undiplomatic approach was beginning to have its usual effect, and Guinevere decided she'd better step in. Smiling brilliantly she went to the counter.

"Don't pay any attention to him," she advised the clerk. He blinked warily. "He gets a little overbearing at times. We're trying to find Mr. Vandyke because something very crucial has arisen. A business matter. It's imperative that we find him. You say he and Washburn intended to fly out this morning?"

"That's what Mr. Springer said." The clerk kept an eye on Zac, who was still glaring at him.

"Then I guess we've missed him." Guinevere turned away from the desk. "Thanks for your help," she added over her shoulder, making a grab for Zac's arm and leading him out of earshot. "So much for that. There's no sense hounding him, Zac. He doesn't know anything."

"Vandyke told us he doesn't fly in small planes anymore," Zac said, looking down at her.

"I remember," Guinevere whispered.

"But the clerk thinks he hired a plane with Washburn this morning," Zac continued flatly.

"And Cassidy's plane is gone." Guinevere twisted her hands together as she wandered over to stand in front of the lobby fireplace. Zac followed slowly. A few other guests were lounging in chairs, reading and sipping coffee. It was a warm and peaceful winter scene, but Guinevere did not feel at all peaceful. "If Cassidy has moved in on our client already," she murmured, "would he have flown Vandyke someplace after arresting him? Wouldn't he have called in the local authorities?"

"Who the hell knows. Cassidy seems like the independent type. Not an overly cooperative sort. He'd want the excitement and glory of the kill." Zac rested a hand on Guinevere's shoulder as he stood staring down into the fire. "But he'd probably dump Vandyke into the laps of the local cops. The lion bringing in his prey so that everyone could admire him. He'd just want to be certain he got all the credit."

Guinevere slanted a curious glance at Zac. "You don't think much of Cassidy, do you?"

"He's a hot dog." Zac moved abruptly, taking Guinevere by surprise. "Come on."

"Where are we going?"

"To the marina. I want to have a look in that boathouse. If Cassidy's got his plane in the air this should be a good time to have another look around."

"But, Zac—" Guinevere began, but stopped as she noticed the clerk at the front desk signaling her. He had a phone in one hand and he was beckoning her with the other. "Miss Jones?"

Hastily Guinevere went forward. "What is it? Is that Vandyke on the line?"

Holding his palm over the receiver, the clerk shook his head. He looked anxious. "Mrs. Vandyke. She insists on speaking to her husband. I've told her he's gone, but she says—"

"I'll talk to her." Guinevere took the phone. "Mrs. Vandyke? This is Guinevere Jones, the temporary secretary your husband hired this past week. I spoke to you briefly on the phone on a couple of occasions."

"Yes, Miss Jones, I remember. Where is my husband?" The woman's voice was laced with concern. She sounded tired and more than a little scared.

"I'm trying to locate him myself. The front desk says he hired a plane this morning to take him back to Seattle."

Catherine Vandyke jumped on that announcement. "A plane? What sort of plane?"

Guinevere took a breath, her eyes meeting Zac's intent gaze. "A small plane, we think. Perhaps a Cessna One Eighty-five."

"That's impossible. My husband would never set foot in such a small plane. He hates them. Used to fly them, you know."

"I believe he did say something about it once."

"Well, he doesn't fly in them anymore. He must be around there someplace, Miss Jones. Please find him. Besides, he couldn't want to fly back to Seattle. What would he do with the Mercedes? He told me he was taking the ferry to the San Juans."

"Yes, Mrs. Vandyke, he did. Listen, I wonder if you could tell me—" Guinevere broke off in surprise as the phone was deftly removed from her hand.

Zac held the receiver to his ear, one hand braced against the desk. "Mrs. Vandyke, this is Zachariah Justis. I've been employed by your husband for the past few days. He hired me to do some security consultation. . . . Yes, that's right. . . . No, I don't know why he would need someone like me. I do have a few hunches. I thought maybe you could tell me. . . . Are you absolutely certain your husband wouldn't willingly fly in a small plane?" There was another pause while he got the short, apparently affirmative response. Zac drew a breath. "Okay, I've got a couple of questions. They're going to seem a little off the wall, but if you'll answer them I might have a shot at locating Vandyke."

Guinevere stirred restlessly, frowning. She should probably be dealing with the woman, she decided. Zac could be so heavy-handed at times.

"Were you married to your husband when he had that charter operation down in the Caribbean, Mrs. Vandyke? . . . I see. Do you remember his partner, a man named Gannon?" Zac listened for a moment and then held the phone away from his ear. Helplessly he held it out to Guinevere. "She's gone hysterical on me."

Guinevere took the phone. On the other end Catherine Vandyke was in pieces. There were tears and fury in her voice. "What are you talking about? How do you know about Gannon? This is ridiculous. I insist you put my husband on the phone, or I'll call the police. Do you hear me?"

"Mrs. Vandyke, this is Guinevere again. Please listen to me. Zac is only trying to help. We know your husband is in trouble, but we don't know what kind."

"But he can't be in trouble," the other woman wailed. "Gannon's dead. He's been dead all these years."

"We have reason to think he might be alive. If he were alive, Mrs. Vandyke, would he be a threat to your husband?" Guinevere looked at Zac to see if she was asking the right questions. Zac was furiously scribbling a note on a pad of hotel paper.

"Oh, God, I don't even want to think about it." Mrs. Vandyke sounded terrified now.

"Listen to me, Mrs. Vandyke. You've got to think about it. You've got to help us, or your husband might wind up in real trouble. Zac can help him. It's his business. But he needs some answers. Please tell me about Gannon."

There was a sob on the other end of the line, and then Mrs. Vandyke caught her breath. Guinevere could almost see her pulling herself together, rallying to meet the crisis.

"Gannon was my husband's partner."

"We know that much."

"He . . . he used to claim he loved me."

Guinevere said nothing, listening to her strengthening voice.

"That was a long time ago," Mrs. Vandyke whispered. "We were all much younger then. More reckless. More adventurous. But Gannon was more than that. He was—well, wild in some ways. Always living an adventure. Bigger than life. He thrived on danger and excitement. And he thought he was irresistible where women were concerned."

"I understand," Guinevere said softly.

"He never could see why I preferred Edward. Edward was the

businessman of the two. The one who kept the records, got the contracts, met the schedules. Gannon took the chances. Edward was quieter. And I knew Edward loved me. A woman could never be first in Gannon's life. Do you know what I mean, Miss Jones? Gannon would always put himself and his need for adventure first. And he could be vicious."

Guinevere felt herself grow suddenly cold. "Vicious?"

"I'll tell you something I've never told anyone else, Miss Jones. The truth is, the day I learned Gannon had gone down I felt an indescribable relief. He had been so angry the day he left. Edward and I had just decided to get married, and we made the announcement the night before Gannon's last flight. I'll never forget the way Gannon stormed out of the little restaurant where we'd all gone for dinner. Early the next morning before he left he found me. I worked in a little boutique there on Saint Thomas. He walked into the shop, dragged me out from behind the counter, and told me that when he got back things were going to be different. He swore I was going to marry him, not Edward, and he'd make sure of it, regardless of who got in the way. I was scared, Miss Jones. There was something in his eyes that morning. I knew he wasn't really so madly in love with me that he couldn't bear to think of me marrying another man. It was his damn pride that was hurt. Gannon was so . . . so supremely . . . what do they call it these days?"

"Macho." Guinevere shuddered. The picture forming in her mind was not at all reassuring. She knew another man who fit Mrs. Vandyke's image of the mysterious Gannon.

"Yes, macho. He frightened me that morning, Miss Jones. I began to worry about what he might do to Edward when he returned. But he never returned."

"Mrs. Vandyke, how old would Gannon be now?" Guinevere read the question off of the notepad Zac was holding up in front of her. But she was very much afraid she already knew the answer.

"A few years younger than Edward. Midforties. Miss Jones, do you really think he—"

"Do you remember anything else about him? The color of his hair? His eyes?" Guinevere quickly scanned the other questions on the notepad. Zac was getting impatient but he didn't try to yank the receiver away from her. "Did he have a limp?" she asked, reading the last scrawled question wonderingly.

"No limp," Mrs. Vandyke said with certainty. "His hair was dark. Do you know something? I can't remember the color of his eyes. It was a long time ago, Miss Jones. Mostly I remember my impression of him, a certain daredevil quality. A kind of boyish wickedness, except that I think it went deeper. He used to carry a gun. Claimed you never knew what you were going to get into. He kept it under the front seat of his plane—said it was his emergency backup. I sometimes wondered if he wasn't carrying something else besides the regular cargo and passengers. But I was always afraid to ask." Mrs. Vandyke hesitated before summing up Gannon. "He could have stepped out of a film. Do you know the type?"

"I think so, Mrs. Vandyke." I'm very much afraid I know exactly the type, she thought as she glanced at the last note Zac had written.

Cassidy?

Mutely, Guinevere looked up at him. She nodded.

CHAPTER 8

"Except for the limp."

Guinevere trotted after Zac as he made his way to a quiet corner of the lobby. He came to a halt, staring at the floor, lost in thought. "Mrs. Vandyke's description does sort of fit Cassidy except for that limp of his," Guinevere repeated.

"A lot of time has gone by since she last saw him. Hell, he might have injured that leg when his plane went down."

"True." Guinevere thought for a moment. "Too bad we don't have a sample of Cassidy's handwriting. We could compare it to that page out of the logbook, the way we did Washburn's."

"We might be able to find something at the boathouse." But Zac sounded vague, his mind obviously on something else.

"Zac, what do we do next? This is your area of expertise. I want to hear something brilliant from you. It's beginning to look as if our client may have been kidnapped."

"I don't know about that. It's possible Cassidy really is with the DEA. He might have decided that a career catching dope smugglers was as exciting as running dope himself. It's still possible this whole thing is a legitimate agency action."

"Hah!"

Something suspiciously close to amusement flashed in his eyes. "Oh ye of little faith."

"Yeah, well, I'm a businessperson, remember? I operate on facts, not faith. And one clear fact in this whole mess is that Mrs. Vandyke is scared of the man she knew as Gannon. She implied he was just this side of crazy. Zac, what are you chewing to pieces there in your mind? I know I don't have your full attention."

"The car."

Guinevere wrinkled her nose. "Vandyke's car?"

"This is a small island, Gwen. They can't just leave the Mercedes sitting around on a back road. Someone would be sure to notice it. And once the cops find Vandyke's car abandoned they'll start asking questions—assuming that the cops don't already have Vandyke."

"I think we should assume they don't," Guinevere said staunchly. "I think we should assume foul play. Very foul play."

Zac let a minute of intense concentration pass before saying, "I think you're right." He sighed.

"So what do we do?"

"Go back to the marina. We might be able to find someone who saw the plane leave. If we get lucky, that someone can tell us if our client was a passenger. We can also check to see if Cassidy conveniently left anything floating around with his signature on it. It would be nice to verify that he really is Gannon."

"Right." Guinevere spun around, but Zac clamped a hand on her shoulder, halting her abruptly.

"There's one more thing I want to check here before we go racing off."

"What's that?"

"I'd like to see if one of the grounds keepers or a maid or even a guest noticed who drove off in Vandyke's Mercedes. It's not in the parking lot." Zac released her and started purposefully back to the front desk. The desk clerk saw him coming and tried to retreat.

It didn't work. Zac cornered him and told him what he wanted. Making no attempt whatsoever to hide his disgust at having to oblige, the desk clerk checked with the manager, who agreed to summon some of the gardeners and maintenance people.

They got lucky with the man who trimmed the hedges. He'd noticed the Mercedes being driven off about forty-five minutes earlier.

"A yuppie dude," he told Zac with the disdainful air of a man who has a degree in philosophy but who has deliberately chosen to work with his hands. "A dressed-for-success type. Know what I mean? Italian sunglasses. I remember thinking the glasses were a bit much, considering that there's no sun today."

Guinevere caught her breath. "Toby Springer."

Zac nodded his thanks to the gardener. He reached out and tugged Guinevere's arm, but she didn't budge.

"Come on, Gwen. We've got to get moving."

She leaned close and hissed in his ear. "You're supposed to tip your informants."

Zac stared at her. "Where the hell did you get that idea?"

"I've read detective fiction. I go to films. I know about this sort of thing."

"Yeah? Then you tip him."

"You should consider tips part of your business expenses."

The gardener appeared oblivious of the low conversation, but he kept within sight.

"Damn it to hell," Zac muttered, dragging out his wallet. "Do I tell you how to run Camelot Services?" He didn't wait for an answer, but walked briskly over to the gardener and thrust a couple of bills into the man's hand. The ex-philosophy student apparently had read a lot of detective fiction and seen some films himself. He thanked Zac but he didn't seem terribly surprised.

"Satisfied?" Zac grabbed Guinevere's arm and led her toward the Buick. "If I can't get reimbursed for that by our client I may take it out of your hide."

Guinevere didn't deign to respond. "So what about the Mercedes," she demanded as she slipped into the front seat of Zac's car.

"They've got to get it off the island, and if Springer just drove it away from the resort forty-five minutes ago he can't have gone very far with it. My guess is he'll be waiting patiently in line for the next ferry."

"Which leaves when?"

"Not for another hour. We've got time."

"To check out the boathouse?"

"Right." Zac swung the Buick out of the parking lot and headed back toward the marina.

The first thing Guinevere noticed when she and Zac parked the car and approached the deserted dock where the Cessna had been tethered was that someone had dug up a lock for the boathouse door. "There was no lock when I came down here yesterday," she said, disappointed.

"Maybe Cassidy figured there was no reason to lock it while he was in the vicinity." Zac glanced around, but spotting no one nearby he went to work on the padlock with a small wire. Guinevere watched in admiration as the lock gave in his hands.

"Incredible," she murmured, pushing on the door.

"It's nice to be loved for my mind." He followed her inside, flipping on the light.

Guinevere let the remark pass. The cruiser was still tied up at the dock. "I found the wallet on board."

Zac stepped onto the boat and systematically went through all the drawers and cupboards. He found nothing. The wallet with Cassidy's DEA identification was gone.

"It was right there in that little drawer by the pilot's chair," Guinevere insisted, peering into the cabin.

"Well, it's gone now. And there's nothing else here that has a sample of his handwriting. Come on."

"Where to now?"

He led the way outside and started toward the old public rest rooms.

"Zac, do you really have to use the facilities now? We're in a hurry, in case you haven't noticed. You should have gone before we left the resort." Guinevere watched him stride up the small incline.

"The real nuts and bolts of investigative work," Zac began in a lecturing tone, "consists of going through garbage. A lot of gar-bage. Why do you think I label myself a consultant? I'm trying to stay out of the lower end of this kind of work. I'd like to perfect a more sophisticated image." He lifted the lid off the trash can that stood in front of the rest rooms. "But thanks to you I'm stuck with going through garbage on this job. Come here and give me a hand."

Guinevere inhaled sharply as she viewed the contents of the trash can. "Yuk."

"Mustn't be squeamish."

"What are we looking for?" She leaned over fastidiously to re-move a fairly clean-looking scrap of paper.

"This is the nearest trash can to Cassidy's dock. He may have tossed all kinds of junk in here. And it sure doesn't look as if it's been emptied for a while. Our best bet would be a receipt for fuel. Nobody pays cash when they fill up an airplane. Costs too much."

They found the receipt stuck to a gum wrapper. There was grease on it and something sticky, and a smear of gum in the mid-dle. There was also a scrawled signature: *Cassidy.* Zac pulled out the logbook page, and there was no doubt about the similarity be-tween the two samples of handwriting.

"Okay, so now we know we're right. Where does that get us? We're wasting time, Zac."

"Gwen, you've worked with me before. You know I'm not the fastest thing on two feet."

She grinned briefly. "But you're thorough." And when the chips were down, she had learned, Zachariah Justis could be very fast and very thorough indeed. She shuddered at the memory of the conclusion of the StarrTech case. She would never forget the sight of blood seeping from a dying man onto a cold concrete floor.

"I try to compensate." Zac dropped the lid back on the trash can. "Let's go talk to some locals who might have seen Cassidy's plane leave."

Zac moved slowly along the docks, asking casual questions of the boat-owners and maintenance people. Yes, they'd heard the plane leave a while ago, but no one had paid much attention. Cassidy always came and went at odd hours; charter pilots operated that way. No, no one had noticed whether or not he had a passenger. Time passed and Guinevere began to glance more and more frequently at her watch. Finally she tugged at Zac's sleeve.

"What about the ferry? It'll be leaving soon."

"Fifteen more minutes."

"But, Zac, what are we going to do if we find Toby Springer sitting in the Mercedes, waiting to drive on board?"

Zac shrugged. "We'll be assertive."

But when it came to it Guinevere decided "assertive" didn't quite cover it. Walking casually along the line of cars, they saw Vandyke's Mercedes sitting between a Toyota and an Audi. She watched completely astonished as Zac walked around to the driver's side, opened the door, and without any warning shoved a startled Toby Springer across the seat.

"Hey! What the hell—?" Springer's mouth fell open as his head bounced against the upholstered door. "Justis! What are you doing here?" He struggled upright, rubbing his head, and his gaze flew to Guinevere, who was standing in the aisle between parked cars. No one seemed to notice Zac's actions.

"Gwen? What's this all about?" Springer started to appeal to her, but realizing Zac already had the car in gear and was forcing his way out of the line, he changed his mind.

Horns sounded behind the Mercedes as Zac made it plain he wanted room. Irate drivers grudgingly tried to back up or pull aside. Guinevere trotted over to the side of the road, ignoring several upraised middle fingers. Zac ignored them too. Within a minute he had the Mercedes out of the herd waiting to board the ferry.

"Let's go, Gwen!" He halted the car momentarily and she scrambled into the backseat. Then he headed toward the marina parking lot.

"Jesus, are you two crazy?" Springer stared from one to the other. "I've about had it with crazy people."

"Dealing with a lot of them lately?" Guinevere asked, leaning over the back of the front seat.

"It seems like it. Come on, Gwen, what's going on here? Who does Justis think he is? Is he dangerous?"

"No," Guinevere assured him, seeing the genuine anxiety on Toby's face. "He's just a big teddy bear. Don't worry about him, Toby. We only want to ask a few questions. We're very concerned about—"

She got no further. The big teddy bear had parked the car in the shadow of the rest rooms and was already out the door. By the time Toby Springer realized Zac was coming around to his side of the car it was too late. Zac yanked open the Mercedes door, reached inside, and ripped Springer out of the front seat.

"Zac!" Guinevere reacted with horror as Toby Springer found himself slammed against the wall of the building. "What are you doing? Don't hurt him!" She scrambled out of the car.

But Zac wasn't paying any attention to her. With one hand on the other man's throat Zac held Springer pinned to the wall. He leaned close. "Where is Vandyke?"

Springer shook his head. "I don't know. I mean—"

"You've got his car."

"Yes, but that's because Washburn ordered me to drive it back to the mainland. I'm supposed to meet him in Seattle." Springer swallowed and made a visible effort to get control of himself. "Look, I don't know what the hell you think you're doing, but unless you've got a good explanation for all this, I'm going to call the cops. You can't just jerk people around like this. I was only following my boss's orders!"

"I'm here on business, too, as it happens. Just like you." Zac's hand tightened slightly on his victim's throat. "Vandyke is my client. I want to know what you've done to him."

"I haven't done anything to him. For Pete's sake, I'm trying to do him a favor by taking the Mercedes back to Seattle. Washburn said Cassidy was going to fly Vandyke back to the mainland because he didn't want to waste time on the ferry."

"Did you see Vandyke leave with Cassidy?"

"No. But that was the plan, and the Cessna's gone, so I assume—"

"What about Washburn? Where is he?"

"Washburn took an earlier ferry. He left me behind to cover the hotel tab and take care of Vandyke's car."

"So how did Vandyke get to Cassidy's plane? Did you drive him to the marina?" Zac asked.

Toby shook his head. "No. I guess Cassidy came and picked him up. I haven't seen Vandyke all morning." Springer cast another appealing glance at Guinevere. "Can't you call this guy off? I don't know what the hell's happening. I swear it. I'm just doing what I'm told by my boss. Jesus, try to do a guy a favor so he can fly back to the mainland and save some time and what do you get? Another crazy man."

Guinevere frowned and stepped forward, putting her hand on Zac's arm. "Let him go, Zac. You're hurting him."

Zac raised his eyes in silent supplication, but his hand dropped from Springer's throat. "What do you mean, *another* crazy man?" he asked as Springer warily straightened and tried to smooth his Pierre Cardin sports jacket. It was Guinevere who answered.

"Are you talking about Cassidy?" she asked with sudden insight as she turned to face Springer. "I almost had the feeling Mrs. Vandyke was on the verge of calling him crazy. She referred to him as a little wild. Bigger than life, perhaps dangerous."

"He's a two-bit pilot who thinks he's auditioning for Hollywood." Springer sounded thoroughly disgusted. "I don't know why Washburn was always so—" He broke off, glaring at Zac.

"So what?" Guinevere went forward to gently help straighten Springer's tie. Her concern seemed to have a soothing effect.

"I don't know," Springer muttered. "It was like Washburn took orders from Cassidy, instead of vice versa. It was Cassidy who told Washburn when to go look at the island, for example. It was as if Washburn was supposed to make his schedule bend to fit Cassidy's or something."

"That island you said Washburn was interested in buying." Guinevere glanced at Zac, who said nothing. His eyes were intent on Springer's face.

"Yeah. I heard him say it was the same size as some place called Raton."

"Raton?" Guinevere gave the word the Spanish pronunciation. "The same size as Raton Island?"

"I guess. Damned if I know. Cassidy wasn't what you'd call real communicative with me. He always treated me like I was Washburn's secretary, not his personal assistant. Like I was shit. I argued with him about his attitude yesterday. I was sick of it."

She smiled wryly. "What else made you think Cassidy was crazy?"

"I don't know. You met him. It was like he wasn't quite real or something." He paused and then added bitterly, "Maybe women like that sort of thing."

"Only in movies," she assured him, thinking of Catherine Van-dyke's instinctive preference for the quieter man she had married. "Women tend to find men like Cassidy . . ." She hunted for the right word. "Incomplete. Empty in some way." She was aware of Zac's glance of surprise, but she ignored it. "Did he ever tell you anything else about this island?"

Springer shook his head. "No, but I heard Washburn complain once about Cassidy being hung up on the subject. Said he was obsessed with it. Kept talking about how easily a man would die on an island here in winter. Look, are you two finished? I've got a ferry to catch."

"No you don't," Zac said, glancing at his watch. As if to confirm his words the whistle sounded as the ferry began moving slowly away from the dock. "You're stuck here for another hour or so."

"So are we," Guinevere pointed out worriedly.

"Not quite. We've got transportation."

"Are we going to charter a plane?"

"Not to go to that island Washburn was interested in buying. For that we'll use the boat Cassidy left behind. Come on, Springer, we're going to find some charts, and you're going to show me exactly where that island is."

Springer started to protest but changed his mind. He fell into step beside Zac, apparently surrendering to the inevitable. Guinevere hastened to follow.

Twenty minutes later Guinevere stood in the boathouse watching Zac. He was doing something intricate to the cruiser's ignition system. Springer was drinking coffee next door in the small café and muttering to himself about the heretofore unknown aspects of big business. Guinevere wondered if he'd go to the police as soon as he saw Zac start the boat. Zac didn't seem to care.

"I didn't know you could hot-wire a boat," Guinevere observed.

"An ignition system is an ignition system." The words were muffled as Zac continued to concentrate on his task.

"Is there no end to your talents?"

"This kind of talent isn't exactly the sort I was hoping to practice when I established Free Enterprise Security."

"I know. You wanted class, polish, sophistication. You wanted to be a consultant."

Whatever Zac said in response was lost in the cough of the engine as it sprang to life. He ducked out from the cabin and stepped onto the dock. She watched as he slid open the metal door that opened onto the water. The sky was still overcast but the rain hadn't started.

"I hope this isn't going to be a waste of time," Guinevere muttered as she got aboard the cruiser.

"We haven't got anyplace else to start looking. If the island proves a dead end we'll call in the cops. The hard part is going to be convincing them that Cassidy really has kidnapped Vandyke. We're not even a hundred percent positive ourselves." Zac took the wheel of the small cruiser and eased the boat out of its water-based garage. No one on shore paid any attention as he swung the bow around and headed away from the marina.

"What I don't understand is why Cassidy came back to terrorize his ex-partner after all this time," Guinevere said, pitching her voice above the roar of the engine as Zac opened the throttle.

"It's the time factor that makes me think this isn't going to be a simple kidnap-for-ransom deal. I have a hunch Cassidy isn't motivated by money, although I guess it's a possibility."

"Revenge? Because of Catherine?"

"Maybe. I have a feeling there's more to it than that, though."

"That's because you're a man. You don't want to admit a woman could drive a man to spend more than a decade plotting revenge," Guinevere declared with conviction. She held her wildly whipping hair out of her face.

Zac glanced at her, his eyes unreadable. "The idea is a little bizarre, but not totally inconceivable."

"What?" She frowned up at him, trying to understand his meaning.

"Forget it. In one way you're right. I'm inclined to believe there's more than a woman involved. Mostly because I don't see Cassidy ever letting a woman—any woman—get under his skin to that extent."

Guinevere's eyes widened in reluctant appreciation of his insight. "I think you're right. He's not the type to get that involved with any one woman. He hasn't got it in him to be faithful, let alone fall in love. That's what I meant when I told Springer that men like Cassidy seem somehow incomplete. It's as if something important got left out when they were put together."

She was silent for a moment, the thought striking her that she was finding herself increasingly attracted to Zac precisely because he was complete. He was solid in some indefinable way, as if there were a deep, substantial core in him. He was centered in a way Cassidy never would be. She knew it with a sure feminine instinct that she didn't bother to analyze.

"Zac?"

"Yeah?" He was watching the horizon, searching for the island.

She took a deep breath. "What do you think we'll find on that island? Vandyke's body?"

"I hope not. Dead men don't pay off their expensive consultants."

"Zac, please."

Zac shrugged, his mouth twisting wryly. "I don't know what we'll find. One thing's for sure, though. If that Cessna is anchored offshore, you're not going ashore with me."

"What am I supposed to do?" Indignantly she glared at him. "Sit in the boat and wait?"

"You should have brought along some knitting."

"Oh yeah? And what about you?"

"I should have brought along a gun," Zac said unhappily.

In the end they didn't have to worry about what each had not thought to bring. Zac circled the tiny islet that appeared on the chart as the dot Toby Springer had marked. There was no sign of a Cessna. There was no sign of anything or anyone, in fact. Guinevere glanced around worriedly as Zac eased the small cruiser into a tiny cove and as close to shore as possible. He shut down the engine.

"Do you think this is the right place?"

"It's as good a possibility as we've got. Does it look like the chunk of rock Springer pointed out to you during the tour you took?" Zac was wrestling with the postage-stamp-size inflatable raft he had found in the back of the cruiser.

"Sort of." Guinevere tried to recall the details of the small island that had been pointed out to her. "I think I remember this little cove. Other than that, it's hard to say." The islet was shrouded in a dense growth of windswept fir. It was impossible to see more than a few feet beyond the rocky shoreline.

"This cove is about the only place anyone could come ashore." Zac tossed the raft over the side. "Actually, we're close enough to wade onto the beach, but the water is so damn cold."

"I'd rather ride," Guinevere declared vehemently as she scrambled carefully into the raft. The new Nikes she was wearing would be soaked if she'd tried to wade ashore.

"Hold still."

"I'm trying!" She braced her palms against the sides of the small landing craft. "You're too heavy for this thing, that's the problem."

"All I ever get are complaints," Zac muttered, cautiously getting into the boat and picking up the paddle.

Guinevere shut up, instantly assailed by guilt. She didn't say another word as Zac paddled them to shore. She felt even more guilty when he jumped out to pull the raft all the way up out of the water so she wouldn't have to get her feet wet. His own sturdy wing tips got splashed.

"It's cold," she whispered, folding her arms across her chest, and immediately wished she'd kept her mouth shut. She didn't want Zac to think she was complaining again. But he didn't seem to have heard her. He was systematically walking the tree-lined beach. When he paused to study some object near a boulder she hurried forward.

"What is it?" she asked, watching him bend down to retrieve the small item. "Oh my God, it's a Vandyke Development Company pen." Her eyes flew to Zac's. "Vandyke must have dropped it."

"No wonder. Someone was really using some muscle to drag him through that underbrush." Zac nodded toward a scraggly jumble of shrubs.

Guinevere froze. "He was being dragged?"

"That's what it looks like. You stay here. I'm going to have a look." Without waiting to see if she intended to follow orders, Zac started into the trees.

Guinevere counted to five and then went after him. Her progress wasn't exactly silent and he must have known she was behind him, but Zac chose to say nothing. He seemed completely intent on following the signs on the ground.

Ten minutes later he emerged into a small clearing somewhere near the center of the island, and Guinevere nearly plowed into him before she saw what had brought him to such an abrupt halt. Edward Vandyke lay in a huddled heap on the ground. He seemed to be unconscious. Blood seeped through the makeshift bandage he had apparently tried to wrap around his left knee.

CHAPTER 9

Vandyke opened pain-glazed eyes as Guinevere and Zac knelt beside him. His face was drawn, the grim brackets around his mouth nearly white as he held on to consciousness. Guinevere saw the wariness in him as well as the confusion. Gently she touched his shoulder.

"It's all right, Mr. Vandyke. We've got a boat. We'll have you back to civilization in no time." Out of the corner of her eye she saw Zac shrug out of his black wool jacket.

"Help me get this around him. It looks like he took fairly good care of the leg before he passed out. The main thing we've got to worry about is exposure. It's so damn cold." Zac eased an arm under the wounded man's shoulders, lifting him so that Guinevere could tug the wool jacket into place.

Vandyke groaned but struggled to help them. "How did you know . . . ?" His voice was weak, his words a little slurred.

"We didn't." Zac was succinct, his attention on Vandyke's wounded knee. "Just followed some hunches. Uncooperative clients sometimes wind up in this sort of situation."

"Zac! For heaven's sake, this is no time to lecture him."

Guinevere shot Zac a furious rebuking glance, which he totally ignored. He was adjusting the makeshift bandage. It seemed to have been fashioned out of a handkerchief and the hem of Vandyke's white button-down shirt.

"He's right." Vandyke inhaled sharply as Zac did something to the wounded knee. "Should have explained."

"You can do the explaining later." Zac stood up. "Right now the main priority is to get you to a hospital. How long have you been lying here?"

"I don't know. Seems like forever. What time is it?"

"Nearly two o'clock."

"It was sometime around ten when he forced me to board the plane. He was waiting for me when I came out of the hotel. By the time I saw him it was too late—he had a gun in my ribs." Vandyke winced as Zac started to lift him to his feet. "Shit, that hurts."

"I'm not surprised." Zac braced him. "I assume there was something symbolic about the left knee?"

Guinevere moved forward to support Vandyke on the other side. She felt the trembling in Vandyke's arm and her concern increased. He was shivering from what was probably a combination of shock, pain, and cold. Not a good combination.

"Cassidy's left knee is bad too," she said, remembering the limp. She realized what Zac was implying. "Is that why he shot you there?"

Vandyke groaned, his head sagging weakly. "Said he wanted me to see how it was. Wanted everything to be just the way it had been for him. The bastard. I think he's crazy. Certifiably."

"That's what your wife thinks too," Guinevere said calmly as she and Zac maneuvered Vandyke toward the trees.

Mention of his wife brought Vandyke's head up for a moment. "Catherine? You talked to Catherine?"

"This morning. She called the hotel while Zac and I were standing around the lobby trying to put it all together. She helped us confirm that Cassidy was Gannon. We thought for a while it might be Washburn. Cassidy—or Gannon, or whatever his name is—is carrying DEA identification, by the way."

"DEA?" Vandyke made an obvious effort to concentrate. "Oh, yes. Drug Enforcement Administration. What a joke. I can see where that would appeal to his sense of humor."

Guinevere was about to ask him what he meant when a faint sound in the distance caught her ear. Even before she could properly identify it, her instinct warned her it was the drone of an aircraft engine. Frantically she looked past Vandyke and met Zac's eyes.

"Damn." Zac started to ease Vandyke back down to the ground.

"What?" Vandyke lifted his head with great effort, his gaze bleary as he tried to focus on his rescuers. "What's going on?"

"There's a plane coming," Guinevere explained softly, her eyes on Zac as they settled Vandyke in a sitting position against the trunk of a scraggly fir.

Vandyke understood at once. "Gannon?"

"I don't know yet. Until we can be sure we'll stay here in the cover of the trees. Christ, Gwen. Did you have to wear that red trench coat? You'll stand out like a sore thumb."

"Sorry I'm not appropriately dressed. The invitation didn't say black tie."

"Take it off until that plane's gone."

"If I've told you once, I've told you a hundred times, your professional manner lacks finesse." She unbuttoned the coat and scrunched it into a tight ball, which she then pushed behind the reclining Vandyke. Instantly she became even more aware of the chill air.

"It's Gannon," Vandyke whispered, closing his eyes wearily as he leaned back against the tree. "He must have found out you were looking for me."

"Springer?" Guinevere looked at Zac questioningly as she, too, huddled back under the branches of the tree.

"Possibly, but I doubt it. I think Springer was just a pawn. More likely Washburn. He might have been left behind to keep an eye on things. We assumed he'd gone back to the mainland but we didn't have time to make certain. He could have been watching Springer, or watching the boathouse."

The plane came into view, its floats clearly visible as the craft banked to circle the island.

"He'll see the boat." Guinevere thought of the little cruiser anchored just offshore. "Maybe he'll assume the game is over and decide to get out of here."

Vandyke moved his head in a weary negative. "The guy's wild. Over the edge. He wants his revenge and he's not likely to let it slip through his fingers now that he's this close."

"I think Vandyke's right. Cassidy's not going to give up now. The only question is whether he'll land and come ashore like a one-man assault team or go back for reinforcements."

"Reinforcements?" Guinevere asked, startled.

"Washburn." Zac glanced at Vandyke. "Was Washburn with him when Cassidy brought you here?"

"No. Haven't seen Washburn since this morning."

The plane made a low pass over the center of the tiny island, so low that Guinevere could see the figures in the cockpit. "Well, he's with him now," she whispered as she stared after the craft.

"Thank God for these trees. He doesn't dare get too low." Zac paused as the plane made another sweep around the island. "By now he's seen the cruiser and he knows you're not in that clearing," he said calmly to Vandyke. "My guess is he'll come ashore, but you know him better than I do. What do you think?"

"I think you're right. He knows I'm out of commission and he probably knows Miss Jones is the only person you brought with you. As far as Gannon is concerned she doesn't count. He'll only be dealing with one real opponent. No offense, Miss Jones, but I don't think he's likely to take you too seriously."

"No one takes secretaries seriously. One of these days the business world is going to regret it."

"Plot the revolution later, Gwen. We've got to make some plans."

"Such as?"

"You and I are going back to that cove. It's the only place Cassidy can land and come ashore." Even as Zac spoke the drone of the engine overhead altered purposefully. Zac looked up, but the plane was out of sight beyond the trees. "He's going to bring the Cessna down now. Let's go."

Hastily Guinevere made certain Zac's coat was secure around Vandyke, who appeared to be about to drift back into unconsciousness. Then she rose to follow Zac back through the trees. In the distance she could hear the last roar of the aircraft engine.

"What's he doing?"

"Taking the risk of beaching it."

"Beaching it?"

"Running the plane as close to shore as possible," Zac explained absently as he made his way through the trees. "It's a risk because that beach is rocky and he could puncture the floats. But I imagine Cassidy is in something of a risk-taking mood right now. I guess I should start calling him Gannon." He halted abruptly.

"Now what?" Guinevere kept her voice low. She was beginning to feel the chill through her wool sweater, and she knew Zac must be feeling it too.

"Over there behind that outcropping." Zac took her arm and pushed her in the direction he'd indicated.

Guinevere found herself amid a jumble of boulders that looked as if they had been tossed aside by a giant hand sometime when the little islet was being formed. Scraggly bushes clung to the rocks, defying the elements. The trees grew right up to the edge of the pile.

"Stay down," Zac whispered as he urged her into the protection of the rocks.

"What are you going to do?"

"Have a look." He released her and cautiously made his way up the broken jagged heap.

Guinevere watched, hardly breathing, as Zac climbed. He moved with a coordinated strength that seemed somehow out of place with his button-down collar and wing tip shoes. He didn't look very much like a sober IRS-fearing businessman right now.

Once before, at the culmination of the StarrTech case, she had seen Zac metamorphose from a conventional, deliberate, practical businessman into a hunter, and it had left her feeling as if she really didn't know him as well as she sometimes thought she did. That hint of something she couldn't comprehend was another of the elements that had kept her vaguely wary of the growing attraction between them. Perhaps it was impossible for a woman to ever completely know a man, she thought as she watched Zac disappear around a craggy chunk of rock.

Guinevere sat huddling, arms wrapped around herself, and waited for Zac to return. There was no sound in the distance. She shivered, wondering what Cassidy was doing—no, what *Gannon* was doing. When Zac eventually slipped back down the wall of rock she started violently. She hadn't even heard him. Her wide eyes flew to his.

Zac hunkered down beside her, his expression hard and infinitely remote. That sense of something unknowable in him was stronger than ever, Guinevere realized bleakly. Yet it was that very quality that might save her life today. She didn't have any illusions about what Gannon might be capable of doing. The man was not just slightly alien, he was crazy.

"He's ashore," Zac murmured bluntly.

Guinevere tensed. "Where?"

"He's circling around on the far side." Zac nodded in the direction behind her. "Probably going to work his way back to the clearing where he left Vandyke."

"Washburn?"

"Still in the plane. My guess is he doesn't like this any better than the rest of us. Probably starting to realize he's let Gannon push him into a somewhat awkward situation. I think he'll stay where he is and let Hopalong get the glory. Hell, Gannon prefers a one-man show."

Guinevere bit her lip. "Cassidy—I mean, Gannon's armed?"

Zac shrugged one shoulder. "You ever see a cowboy in the movies who wasn't?"

"Zac, what are we going to do? This is a small island. Sooner or later he'll find Vandyke, and then us."

"The trick will be to find Gannon first then, won't it? Gwen, I want you to stay here. If Washburn does come ashore, he'll probably head in the same direction as Gannon. Frankly, I don't think he will come ashore. You'll be reasonably safe as long as you stay out of sight."

"What about you?" But she already knew the answer to that. Zac was going after Gannon. Guinevere put an urgent hand on his shoulder. "Be careful, Zac. Please. I . . ." She broke off, trying for a fleeting smile. "Remember the image."

He surprised her with a quick, wholly unexpected grin. "I'll try not to get it any more tarnished than it already is. Stay put, honey."

Zac slipped away from the jumble of boulders, praying they would protect Guinevere. He felt decidedly naked without any sort of weapon. But damn it, he was supposed to be a real businessman these days. He was supposed to spend his time worrying about deductions, contracts, the prime rate—and how to talk Guinevere Jones into bed. He *wanted* to spend his time that way. He just knew he was cut out for it. He was a natural-born independent businessman.

When he'd started Free Enterprise Security he'd had no intention of taking jobs that wound up like this. He'd planned to be an expensive consultant, for crying out loud. A respectable, highly paid, report-writing consultant. How in hell did he come to find himself trapped on a postage-stamp-size island with a crazy man who shot people in the leg and left them to die of exposure? The next time Guinevere tried to throw a little business his way he would throw it right back at her.

Of course then he'd have to figure out a way of keeping Gwen from letting her overly empathic nature get her into trouble all by herself. All things considered, Zac decided, he'd rather be here than sitting at home in Seattle wondering what Gwen was doing. Hell of a choice.

He eased into place behind Cassidy-Gannon, who was prowling through the trees with an expert's skill. The problem in dealing with Gannon was, part of him—the dangerous part—was real, not some phony actor's pose. And Zac sensed his quarry wouldn't hesitate to use the revolver he held in his hand.

There was no way to rush him, not yet. Zac could keep him in sight easily enough, but he didn't see any possibility of moving in on Gannon. The man was too alert and too dangerous.

The breeze off the water was starting to pick up now, turning into a storm-bearing wind. The rain would follow soon. The sound was welcome cover for Zac's movements, but he began to worry in earnest about the effects of the cold on his client and on Guinevere. Vandyke was already sliding into shock, and without her coat Guinevere was going to be very chilled very soon. For now the adrenaline roaring through his own veins seemed to mask the direct effects of the cold, but Zac realized that was only a temporary effect. Only Gannon looked reasonably comfortable. The dashingly distressed leather flight jacket was no doubt good insulation.

Gannon was working his way around the island in a slow circle. Zac followed warily, wondering how long it would be before his quarry cut inland. The chief goal of this whole exercise as far as Gannon was concerned was to kill Vandyke. Sooner or later Gannon was going to want to know what had happened to his victim. If he was crazy enough, he might risk heading for the clearing before he'd taken care of any possible opposition. And if Gannon was convinced that Zac probably wasn't armed, he was likely to make his move fairly soon.

Zac waited with the patience that came naturally to him at times like this. He had that much on his side, he realized. He had hunted this kind of game before.

A few minutes later Gannon abruptly turned and started inland. There was a glint of blue steel from the heavy revolver in his hand as he headed through the trees. Apparently he had decided he couldn't wait any longer. He was going to find Vandyke and force the enemy's hand.

Zac froze into complete immobility until Gannon was far enough ahead again to make pursuit safe. Then he moved after the other man. There was no telling what Gannon would do when he reached the clearing and discovered that Vandyke was no longer there. The wildness in him made him more than a little unpredictable in some ways—in others it made him entirely predictable, however. Gannon would kill, Zac knew, without a second's hesitation.

"Damn you, Vandyke!"

Gannon's roar of rage as he reached the clearing startled Zac. He hadn't expected the man to lose control so quickly. Cautiously he moved closer. He could see him now, standing at the edge of the clearing, feet spread wide, dark hair whipped by the chill wind. The collar of the flight jacket was standing high around Gannon's neck. He swung around, crouching, gun steady in his hand, and for an instant Zac thought he'd been seen. Then Gannon continued to move in a circle, crouching low.

"You think you can hide, you bastard? Think that soft executive type you brought along as an assistant is going to help you? No way. I'm going to kill him, Vandyke. But I'm not going to kill you. You get to die the way you thought I'd die. I'm not gonna let you off easy."

Gannon moved around the perimeter of the clearing, peering into the trees. Zac stayed very still. He was on his stomach now, concealed by a clump of blackberry bushes. He could catch glimpses of movement from Gannon and tracked him until the other man was on the far side of the clearing. If Gannon went back into the trees in that direction he would probably stumble across Vandyke.

Gannon was confident and crazy. That volatile combination of factors was the only edge he'd get, Zac told himself. He inched forward, circling the blackberry bushes. His hand closed over a small rock.

"Give it up, Justis. You've got the girl with you. I'll let her go if you come on out. Hell, I might even let you go. Who knows? All I want is Vandyke dead. Come on, Justis. Take a chance. Make me an offer. I know you're not armed. Guys like you don't carry guns, do you? You're businessmen. Executives. Soft. Just like Vandyke. Bunch of wimps who don't know how to take care of themselves. You're easy meat for a man like me, Justis. Your only chance is to come on out and see if you can't make a bargain."

Zac waited until Gannon was a little closer. His fingers tightened around the rock. He was only going to get one chance.

"Hey, Vandyke, you awake? You listening to this? Or are you already dead? You've gotten soft, Vandyke. You're fat and soft now. I'll bet Cathy looks at you in bed and wonders what the hell she married you for. I'll bet she thinks about me when you try to get it up. You ever tell her why I didn't come back from that last run, Vandyke? You ever tell her the truth? How you set me up?"

Zac gathered himself. Gannon was only a few yards away and he was watching the trees in the opposite direction from where Zac lay on his stomach. It was now or never. Zac came to his feet in a quick smooth movement that flowed naturally into the throw, putting all his weight behind launching the rock at Gannon's back.

In the last split second some instinct must have warned the other man. He whirled, gun raised.

The rock caught Gannon solidly on the shoulder, and he stumbled backward, losing his balance on his weak left leg. There was a roar as the revolver in his hand was fired by his reflexive tug on the trigger. The bullet went wild.

Zac was out of the trees and on the other man before Gannon had a chance to recover his balance. With a quick chopping motion he brought the side of his hand down on Gannon's forearm. The gun fell to the ground. The momentum of Zac's rush carried both men down beside the weapon.

Guinevere's head came up with a jerk as she heard the muffled report of the revolver. For an instant she was paralyzed with terror. In her mind's eye she could already see Zac lying on the cold ground, bleeding to death. Awkwardly she struggled to her feet, her legs cramped and chilled.

A noise from the beach behind her brought her back to her senses. Washburn had apparently been startled by the shot too. Hastily she crouched down again, trying to see the cove through the clutter of rocks.

What she saw was the flash of movement as Washburn hurried along the plane's floats and jumped ashore. She held her breath as, not more than ten feet away, he dashed past her and into the trees. There was an expression of grim fear on his face. He seemed to be heading toward the clearing from which the sound of the shot had come. And he was waving a gun wildly in his right hand. Guinevere was certain that if Washburn had known how to fly the Cessna he would have had it in the air by now. As it was, he was virtually forced to go to Gannon's rescue. Gannon was his only sure means of getting off the island.

Even if Zac had escaped that first shot, Guinevere realized in horror, he wouldn't have much of a chance against a second armed man. Frantically she scrambled out from the clutter of boulders. The only instinct driving her now was the knowledge that she had to do something, *anything*.

She was almost in the trees when she remembered Catherine Vandyke's comment about Gannon carrying a backup gun hidden under the pilot's seat.

Was it the weapon he had taken ashore? Or was the gun under the seat considered a spare, something for an emergency? If the gun existed, she must get it. It was the only edge she would have. Guinevere swung around and dashed down the short pebbled beach. Her feet got wet as she scrambled onto one of the floats. Balancing precariously, Guinevere reached for the cabin door on the pilot's side and yanked it open. The interior of the plane felt a few degrees warmer than the outside air. Guinevere inhaled deeply. She shoved her hand under the seat and fished wildly. Her groping fingers touched a worn leather holster. She closed her eyes in fleeting relief, and pulled it out to find it held a vicious-looking snub-nosed revolver. The metal felt cold in her hand and she was surprised at the weight of the thing.

Clutching it fiercely, Guinevere maneuvered quickly back along the float and leapt for shore, groaning as another lapping wave caught her foot. She started running for the trees. Her feet squished softly in the Nikes but the shoes themselves didn't make much noise on the rough terrain.

The clearing wasn't hard to find, the island was so small that anyone who headed for its center was bound to stumble across it. She tried to approach carefully, hoping the running shoes would silence her footsteps. A few minutes later she knew that the man she was chasing had already reached the clearing.

Washburn stood at the edge of the small open space, his gun hand moving frantically back and forth. A second later Guinevere could see why he was so agitated. Zac and Gannon were locked in brutal combat on the ground, their bodies shifting too quickly to enable Washburn to get a clear shot. They were probably not even aware that Washburn was standing there with a gun. Shakily she raised the revolver she had taken from the plane.

"Hold it right there, Washburn. Drop the gun or I'll shoot. I swear to God, I'll shoot."

The older man froze. In that instant there was a heavy thumping sound and the two men on the ground in the clearing also went still.

Everything and everyone seemed to be frozen for a timeless few seconds. Then Zac moved slightly. He was breathing deeply, and there was blood on his face. He got slowly to his feet, his eyes on Washburn. Behind him Gannon lay limp.

"Throw the gun down, Washburn. She can shoot you before you turn around. Come on, throw it! Way over there. Do it now, Washburn!"

Something about the implicit violence in Zac's voice must have convinced Washburn that the woman behind him really was armed. He swore softly and tossed the gun aside. It fell several feet away. Then he turned slowly to face Guinevere.

Clutching the weapon in both hands, Guinevere held it on her victim as steady as she could, but the sight of Zac's bloody face unnerved her.

"Zac? Are you all right?"

But Gannon stirred in that moment and Zac turned back before answering. "Stay right where you are, hero. Gwen, don't let Washburn move an inch. At that distance you can't miss, and he knows it."

Washburn was staring at her, fear and impotent rage in his eyes. "Little bitch," he said through gritted teeth. He spoke over his shoulder to Gannon. "You fool, Cassidy. I knew I should never have listened to you. You're crazy, you know that? Out of your head, you dumb bastard."

"Shit," Gannon muttered, staring at Guinevere. "That's *my* gun. Get her, Washburn. That damn thing's not loaded! Take her!"

Washburn hesitated and then panicked, apparently deciding to take the chance. With a roar of outrage he leapt for Guinevere. Zac was on top of him like a ton of bricks before Washburn could reach her.

Guinevere never got a chance to pull the trigger but a shot rang out even as Zac and Washburn hit the ground. Zac pinned Washburn with ease and then glanced around. He saw Guinevere staring in the direction Washburn had tossed his gun.

Vandyke stood clinging with one hand to a low-hanging branch. He still had Zac's black jacket draped around his shoulders. His face was white with shock, but he clung steadily to the gun he had retrieved from where Washburn had thrown it.

Gannon lay on the ground in an appallingly still sprawl. Vandyke's shot had caught him halfway across the clearing while he had been trying to get to the revolver he'd lost during the fight.

Once more everything was deathly still. Only the increasing whistle of the wind broke the silence. Zac stretched out a hand to take the weapon Guinevere was still holding. "Here," he said with surprising gentleness. "Let me have that."

Mutely she started to give it to him, muzzle first.

"Damn it, Gwen, be careful." Hastily he plucked it out of her hand.

She blinked, too overwhelmed by events to think clearly. "Why? It's not loaded."

Zac shook his head wearily. "Of course it's loaded. You think a cowboy like Gannon would ever keep an unloaded gun as a backup? He just wanted Washburn to create a distraction. So he tried to send him charging into you while he made a play for the other gun."

"Oh my God." Guinevere started to shiver. She had been very close to pulling that trigger, she realized. And she would have done it, to save Zac and herself. The thought of how she would have felt after shooting a man at point-blank range was enough to make her sick to her stomach. Then she saw Vandyke sagging to the ground.

"Zac," she whispered, "we've got to get him out of here."

Zac's mouth crooked wryly as he took in her own stunned and chilled condition. "That's right," he said with suspicious mildness. "Let's take care of the client."

CHAPTER 10

"He thought I'd set him up all those years ago." Edward Vandyke exhaled slowly. He leaned back in his high-backed padded leather executive chair and looked at his wife across the top of the polished mahogany desk. Behind him the Smith Tower and the Kingdome were visible through the floor-to-ceiling windows. It was raining again.

Sitting beside Zac, Guinevere saw the look that passed between husband and wife. Memories of another time and place and all the shared years in between were in that look. It was a *married* look, Guinevere decided, the kind of charged exchange only a husband and wife could have. She wondered fleetingly if she would ever have that sort of exchange with Zac. The mental image of being with Zac ten or fifteen years from now was impossible to conjure clearly, but she found she could make a hazy picture of it.

Guinevere abruptly gave herself a small shake and pulled her attention back to the meeting taking place in Vandyke's office.

"He was always so wild, so . . . on the edge in some way. I think that in these last few years he must have gone completely over the brink." Catherine Vandyke waved one hand helplessly. Her delicately shaped artist's hand was set off by a very expensive diamond-and-emerald ring. She was a lovely woman in her midforties, with high cheekbones, a graceful throat, and hair styled in a very current fashion. Her off-white designer suit must be almost as expensive as the ring. She was also a very gentle woman. Guinevere liked her as much in person as she had on the phone.

Vandyke looked at Zac. "So Washburn was actually working for Gannon?"

"Washburn wouldn't admit it, but Gannon was the one in charge. We traced Washburn's financial background. As Toby Springer said, he emerged out of nowhere in the mid-seventies, buying and selling land. No one knew where he got his start. Now it's pretty clear that Gannon financed him. Washburn provided business expertise for Gannon; in exchange he managed the huge sums of cash Gannon was making. In short, Gannon made the money by running drugs and Washburn invested it for him. A nice arrangement for both of them."

"It makes sense. Gannon never had the interest or the patience it takes to handle money wisely. He got his kicks out of taking risks, and he liked the payoff, but that was all. On the other hand, he was too shrewd to let a fortune melt away because of poor management." Vandyke smiled a little sadly. "Poor Washburn. Probably never knew what hit him when Gannon picked him out of nowhere, walked into his life, and offered him that kind of deal."

"Well, apparently Gannon had done some research on Washburn," Guinevere said. "He must have known his hand-picked financial adviser had a rather shady background in commodities-trading fraud, because he used the information to keep Washburn in line. Washburn told the police that he'd been forced to engineer the deal that set you up this past weekend. The proposal to develop the resort, the competing business presentations—it was all window dressing. The main goal of the weekend was to get you isolated. Gannon had told Washburn he'd rip his new empire to shreds if he didn't cooperate. By then, of course, Washburn was used to moving in fast circles and he liked the big-time wheeling and dealing. He would have done a lot to protect his new world."

Vandyke cocked one eyebrow. "And Toby Springer?"

"Just what he claimed," Zac said mildly. "A young man on the fast track to success, or so he thought. He assumed he'd hitched his wagon to a very bright star when he became Washburn's personal assistant. My guess is that even now he doesn't know how close he came to having a fatal accident."

"An accident?" Mrs. Vandyke looked startled.

Zac nodded. "I doubt Cassidy—I mean, Gannon—would have let him live. Springer knew too much, although he hadn't yet realized it. He knew about the island, he knew Gannon had flown off with you that morning, and he tended to be talkative. It was an unhealthy combination for him."

"The island." Mrs. Vandyke pounced interestedly. "How did you make the connection? What made you realize that was where Gannon had taken my husband?"

Zac smiled bleakly. "We weren't sure. It was part hunch and part guesswork based on what we'd been able to piece together about Gannon. We knew Gannon had ditched the plane near an uninhabited island in the Caribbean several years ago. A place called Raton. He must have managed to swim to shore. We also suspected he had survived, although no one seemed to think so, including his ex-partner." Zac glanced briefly at Vandyke, who said nothing. "Thanks to chatty Toby, Guinevere had learned that Washburn and Gannon had taken a couple of trips to a deserted hunk of rock up in the San Juans, supposedly with a view toward purchasing it. Springer also told us that Washburn thought Gannon was hung up on that island. You gave us another clue when you said on the phone you thought Gannon might be not only dangerous but a little crazy. If he was out for revenge after all this time and if he'd gone to the trouble of setting up such an elaborate trap then it made sense he'd want the final scene to be equally bizarre. We took a chance and decided to try the island. Besides"—Zac shrugged—"at that point we didn't have any-place else to look. If Gannon hadn't taken your husband to the is-land we would really have been back at square one. We probably couldn't have convinced the police there'd been a kidnapping at that point. Nothing terribly suspicious had really occurred. No one was officially missing."

"How did you guess Gannon was still alive?" Mrs. Vandyke asked, her gentle eyes curious.

Guinevere cleared her throat delicately. "Zac made an inspired guess."

"The hell I did," Zac said bluntly. "I saw the page out of Gan-non's logbook, the one that had information filled in on a flight that had taken place *after* the flight during which Gannon was suppos-edly killed. A friend of mine in the Caribbean gave me the details." He looked at Vandyke. "I opened the briefcase that first evening."

Vandyke smiled. "I'm glad you did. Sorry I was so obtuse about your offers of help, but to tell you the truth I wasn't sure what was going on myself. I got that page out of Gannon's logbook several weeks ago and I didn't know what the hell to make of it. It just ar-rived in the day's mail with no return address. I realized it meant he might still be alive and that he might be coming after me, but I didn't know what to expect. He must have sent it as an act of ter-rorism. Until he made a move, I was walking on eggs." He glanced at his wife. "It occurred to me that he was out for revenge. I wanted you out of the way."

"And that's why you became so difficult? So many excuses, so many suggestions that I go visit my relatives." Catherine Vandyke shook her head ruefully. "I thought you were having an affair. Go-ing through the male midlife crisis or something. I was frantic and furious. You should have told me, Ed. And later, at the resort, when Mr. Justis here tried to offer help you should have told him exactly what sort of help you needed! When I think of how close you came to getting killed . . ."

"As it is it's going to be quite a while before I play golf," Vandyke drawled. His hand moved under his desk to gently massage his left knee.

"I've been wondering about that left knee," Guinevere said determinedly. "I take it Gannon was shot in the same place? That's the reason for the limp?"

Vandyke nodded. "That's what he told me when he kidnapped me and flew me to the island. Said he wanted everything to be the same as it had been for him. He dragged me to that clearing and casually put a bullet in my leg. Then he left."

Guinevere frowned. "But what did he mean?"

"About having everything the same?" Vandyke sighed. "He was in trouble with the people he was working with all those years ago. He'd been playing both ends against the middle, I guess, and had managed to make both his South American contacts and his Florida buyers angry. Gannon assumed he could outmaneuver everyone, but someone apparently realized he was skimming, keeping some of the stuff he was supposed to be ferrying from South America to the States."

"And after all these years he decided you'd betrayed him?" Zac asked.

Vandyke nodded. "As I said, he was really far gone there at the end. The truth is I had begun to suspect he was involving our charter service in drug running. I was getting nervous. If he went too far he could have gotten all of us killed." He shot a quick glance at his wife. "I confronted him with my suspicions and told him he'd better quit, or else I intended to fold the business. Gannon could never have run the charter service on his own. He knew nothing about running a business. He just wanted to fly. He was enraged. There were other things going on at the time, personal matters that—"

"I told Gwen that you and I had decided to marry just before Gannon took that last flight," Catherine Vandyke interrupted calmly. "I mentioned that in his usual egotistical fashion Gannon had taken offense."

"Yes, well, all in all Gannon was in a foul temper before he left on that last flight. When he kidnapped me a few days ago he told me there had been an ambush set at his rendezvous point. He'd been shot in the leg but he managed to get the plane back off the ground. Whoever was waiting for him apparently made a few direct hits on the aircraft, however. Got the fuel lines. At any rate, Gannon lost power near a small chunk of rock called Raton Island. He barely made it out of the plane, and when he did he found himself wounded and stranded on an uninhabited island."

"But he survived," Guinevere said softly.

"Gannon was good at surviving." Vandyke flattened his palms on his desk and stared briefly at his fingertips. "He assumed that under the same circumstances I couldn't have survived. He always said I was soft."

"Hardly the same circumstances," Zac pointed out. "An island in the sunny Caribbean isn't exactly the same proposition as an island in the San Juans in winter. On Raton, at least, he didn't have to worry about dying of hypothermia. How did he get off Raton, by the way? Did he tell you?"

"He got lucky after a few days—Gannon usually did get lucky. He built a fire with the cigarette lighter he had in his pocket when he ditched the plane. It caught the attention of a yacht that happened to be in the vicinity." Vandyke winced. "He made sure I didn't have anything with which to build a fire. And he seemed to know a lot about the effects of exposure. Figured I wouldn't last twenty-four hours."

"Where has he been all these years?" Mrs. Vandyke asked wonderingly.

"Playing games in the South Pacific," Zac responded. "The

police checked. Apparently he was still running drugs, but not under his old name. When he got back from Raton he discovered he was presumed dead by everyone, including the drug dealers he'd tried to cheat. He decided to take advantage of the fact to start over. Took a new name, moved to another part of the world, built up new identification. Found a new business partner, who didn't have as many scruples as Vandyke had."

"How did he get that DEA identification?" Guinevere asked.

"That was phony. He must have had it made up. Probably figured that in his line of work it might someday come in useful to bluff his way out of a sticky situation with the authorities. I imagine a lot of local cops on backwater islands in the South Pacific would have been just as impressed as you were with the DEA papers."

Guinevere wrinkled her nose. "I resent that. I only got a very quick look at it, you know. Hardly enough time to tell whether or not it was genuine."

Zac's mouth crooked. "I doubt that you would have been able to tell even if you'd had more of an opportunity to examine it. It was a good forgery."

Mrs. Vandyke shook her head sadly. "Imagine spending all these years plotting revenge. It must have eaten away at his soul."

Vandyke frowned thoughtfully. "I got the feeling from what he said that he didn't start thinking in terms of revenge against me until a couple of years ago. That's probably about the time when he really started to slip off into a world of his own. Until then I think he assumed the truth—his drug-running friends were on to him—and he was most concerned with what to do about it. But about eighteen months ago he began thinking about the old days, he told me. His mind started gnawing away at what had happened, and he suddenly decided I must have been behind the setup that nearly got him killed."

"I'm sure a psychiatrist would have something interesting to say about what happened inside Gannon's head eighteen months ago," Guinevere murmured.

"Probably even more to say about me, for being crazy enough to think I could handle this mess on my own," Vandyke said. "I must admit, Zac, that when Miss Jones insisted I bring someone along to keep an eye on the proposal documents, I began thinking it would be reassuring to have someone around who knew what he was doing in a touchy situation. I really wasn't all that worried about the documents, but Miss Jones made it sound as if you might be useful in other ways, so I let her talk me into hiring you. I want you to know how grateful I am to Free Enterprise Security. Needless to say, there will be a bonus in addition to your normal fee."

"That's not necessary," Zac said in a businesslike tone. "My normal fee includes all extracurricular activities. Besides—I, uh, had my own reasons for taking the job."

"I see. Well, I can only thank you once again. And you, too, Miss Jones. If it hadn't been for your suggestion—"

"I was wondering," Guinevere said brightly, "if I could show Zac the washroom."

Vandyke looked momentarily blank. "The washroom?"

"She means the executive washroom." Catherine Vandyke laughed in delight. "That ridiculous indoor marble-and-mauve outhouse you had put in last year."

Vandyke grinned in sudden understanding. "Pretty classy, huh? Impresses the hell out of my visitors. Go ahead and have a look, Zac."

"It's not really necessary," Zac began awkwardly. There was a trace of red on his cheekbones. But Guinevere was already tugging him to his feet and leading him down the short corridor to the executive washroom. "For Pete's sake, Gwen, this is embarrassing."

"This is incredible," she corrected, flinging open the door.

"Good lord." Zac stared in amazement at the gleaming black marble and gold fixtures. "You're right. It's incredible."

"Someday," Guinevere declared, "we'll have one just like it."

"We will?"

Guinevere ignored him as she caught sight of the partly open drawer. Her voice lowered to a whisper. "Look, Zac. There's the golden gun I told you about. The one that really started me worrying about Vandyke's state of depression."

Zac reached out and casually picked up the weapon, one brow arched. Just as casually he pulled the trigger. Instinctively Guinevere jumped. A small flame winked into existence from the barrel of the gun.

"Well, what do you know," Guinevere said in disgust. "On such tiny misjudgments whole cases for Free Enterprise Security are built." Head high, she turned and stalked back down the hall to Vandyke's office.

Several hours later Guinevere was still fretting about mistaking the gold cigarette lighter for a real gun.

"It looked like the real thing," she told Zac for the fiftieth time as she stood in the doorway of his kitchen and watched him toss the salad.

"I know, honey. Anyone could have been fooled."

He had apparently decided to stop teasing her about it and was now taking the consoling approach. It was hard to argue when someone was consoling you. Guinevere groaned and turned to amble out into the living room, wineglass in hand. Behind her Zac studied the salad, trying to decide what else to add. He opened the refrigerator door and took out some feta cheese.

"I guess it must have been Gannon you thought you saw in the trees the night you went to fetch Vandyke from the cliffs, hmm?" Guinevere peered out the living room window, waiting for Zac's response.

"Must have been. He was undoubtedly stalking his quarry. It

was probably Gannon who went through your things the night you traipsed down the hall to see me."

"Why would he do that?"

"Who knows. Maybe to see where you fit into the grand scheme of things. He might have wanted to know if you were Vandyke's mistress."

"His mistress!" Guinevere was shocked.

"Or perhaps he just liked going through women's underwear."

"Ugh." She was quiet a moment. "You know, I think Gannon was wrong about Vandyke," she said tentatively.

There was a beat of silence from the kitchen. "You mean his assumption that Vandyke was soft?" Zac asked calmly.

"Yes. There was nothing soft about the way Vandyke pulled the trigger on that island, Zac."

"No."

"You told me once that a weak man couldn't have gotten as far as Vandyke had gotten in business."

"Uh, Gwen?"

"Yes, Zac?"

"Don't dwell on that line of thought, okay?"

"Why? Afraid that I'll start wondering just how tough Vandyke might have been back in the days he was Gannon's partner? He came out of that business with enough money to start Vandyke Development. The charter operation must have been operating on slightly more than a shoestring." She thought about her own words. "Zac?"

"Don't ask, Gwen." But he sounded resigned to the fact that she would ask.

"Do you think Gannon might have been right? That he and Vandyke were running drugs and that Vandyke decided to set up his partner and get out of the business?"

"You said yourself that Vandyke's a good man. You like him and you like his wife. He's also a good client. Paid his bill right on time. I don't think there's any point in asking a lot of questions at this stage."

"You may be right."

In the sharply angled living room of Zac's modern high-rise apartment Guinevere stood at the windows and watched tugboats cautiously move a Japanese freighter into Elliott Bay. There was no doubt that Zac's view was better than hers, but Guinevere didn't particularly like the sober colors and conservative furniture of his apartment. She much preferred her own bright reds and yellows and dramatic touches of black to this serene climate of mellow wood and stone-colored carpet. Still, there was something solid and real about Zac's home, just as there was something solid and real about the man himself.

Guinevere swirled the wine in her glass and thought about her unsuccessful plans to pin down something solid and real about her relationship with Zac. From that point of view the previous weekend had been more or less a failure. True, they had quietly admitted to each other that neither was seeing anyone else, but that seemed insubstantial and tentative to Guinevere.

On the other hand, exactly what did she want with Zac? There was still that faint wariness in her, still a feeling that she didn't truly understand him. She had always assumed that a complete understanding of the other person was essential to a sound relationship. But there were times when she was not only aware that she didn't know him completely, she also wasn't sure that she wanted to know him that well. Once again she remembered the way he could shift from businessman into violent hunter.

It wasn't that the hunter in him seemed at odds with the more conventional side of his personality, it was simply that she didn't fully comprehend that aspect of him. As a woman, she mistrusted that element of his nature. And yet there had been moments when she had felt the thrill of adrenaline, the stark sensation of knowing one had to act or all was lost. Still, she had a feeling, based on brief glimpses into the more primitive side of her own personality, that for her the sensation was fundamentally different than it was for Zac. She couldn't explain it. Perhaps it was because she was a woman and he was a man.

Which brought her back to the question she had asked herself on that nameless island in the San Juans—can a woman ever completely know a man? Perhaps the question should have been: would any woman in her right mind ever really want to completely know and comprehend a man?

Out on the bay the freighter was nearing the loading docks of the Port of Seattle.

"Gwen?" Zac materialized behind her, his glass of tequila in his hand. "You were so quiet out here I wasn't sure what you were up to."

"Just watching that ship. Can you imagine spending your working life on a ship like that? Days on end of not being able to touch dry land. Tiny little cabins, storms at sea, tyrannical captains . . ."

"You're letting your imagination carry you away. I think people who go to sea do so because they like the work. Simple."

She smiled fleetingly. "You're probably right. Sometimes my imagination does carry me away. I tend to read too much into things, analyze them for hidden meanings, try to figure out what someone *really* meant."

"I know. Me, I'm much more straightforward." He looked down at her, gray eyes intent.

"Are you?"

"Gwen, do you want to try another weekend?" he asked abruptly.

She looked up at him through her lashes. "In the San Juans?"

"Anywhere. Do you want to try going away for a few days? Just us this time? No clients?"

"I'd like that." She smiled tremulously.

He looked strangely relieved. The intensity in his gray eyes lightened by several degrees. "Good. Good, I'm glad. Thanks, Gwen."

She'd show him how casual and straightforward she could be. "Is dinner ready?"

He looked momentarily surprised, as if his thoughts had been elsewhere. "Yeah, sure. In another couple of minutes."

"Good. I'm starving. And can you turn the heat up a little in here? I haven't felt really warm since we returned from the San Juans. My overactive imagination, I suspect." She wandered across the room to examine the thermostat setting.

"Uh, Gwen?"

"Yes, Zac?"

"You know, I've been thinking."

"Careful, Zac."

"I'm serious," he protested, watching her fiddle with the thermostat. "This past weekend you said you wanted to talk about our relationship."

"A momentary aberration on my part. Don't worry, I've since recovered. How about seventy-eight degrees. Okay if I set it that high?"

"Set it wherever the hell you want." Zac sounded as if he was getting annoyed. "Listen, Gwen, I'm sorry I didn't let you talk. To tell you the truth, the idea of discussing 'us' made me nervous."

"I said don't worry." She smiled very brilliantly at him. He didn't return the smile.

"All right, I won't. But I think we should get something settled." He glared at her.

"Such as?"

"I think we need to know where we stand. Gwen, we are not involved in a casual dating relationship."

"We aren't?"

"You aren't helping," he said accusingly.

"I'm not sure what you want me to do." She dropped her hand from the thermostat and faced him.

"I want you to agree that we're involved in a full-fledged affair," Zac declared aggressively.

Guinevere thought about that. Labels sometimes clarified things. Sometimes they made things more complicated. "Do you think you could term what we have together an 'affair'?"

"Yes, damn it, I do."

"Right. An affair it is. Can we eat now?"

He stalked after her as she started back into the kitchen. "Gwen . . ."

She turned and saw the frowning hesitation on his face. For a moment Guinevere thought he was going to do something wholly unexpected and out of character, such as begin a long in-depth discussion of just what it meant to be involved in a full-fledged affair. A deep, meaningful, analytical discussion about a relationship.

But he didn't. The frown vanished and his gray eyes gleamed. He grinned his rare wolfish grin and handed her the salad tongs. "Here. You can serve the salad. I'll get the steaks."

"That's what I like about you, Zac. You're simple and direct. You keep your priorities in order."

"I'm glad you're learning to appreciate my finer qualities."

Maybe she was at that, Guinevere decided, dishing out the salad.

Keep reading for a special excerpt from Jayne Castle's

SINISTER AND FATAL

THE GUINEVERE JONES COLLECTION, VOLUME 2

Coming in February 2014 from Berkley

The night had been a long one. No, that wasn't strictly accurate. It had been *lonely.*

Guinevere Jones glared at the stylish new coffee machine as it dripped with agonizing slowness. She could have bought a cheaper coffeemaker yesterday if she'd been willing to settle for a plain white or beige model. But this little sucker was an exotic import, and with its dashing red and black trim it had totally outclassed all the bland models on the shelf next to it at the Bon. Even the glass pot was elegantly different from an ordinary coffeepot. Definitely high tech. She hadn't been able to resist it. It lent such a perfect snappy note to her vivid yellow kitchen. Unfortunately it was proving to have more style than efficiency. Zac would undoubtedly have a few pithy comments to make when he tried it out.

If he ever gets around to trying it out, Guinevere reminded herself resentfully as she stood in front of the coffee machine, a yellow mug dangling uselessly from one finger. Zac had been very busy with a new client lately, a client who seemed to find that the most convenient time to consult with the head of Free Enterprise Security, Inc. was in the evening. The fact that the client was

Elizabeth Gallinger wasn't doing much to mitigate Guinevere's prickly mood. Guinevere's own firm, Camelot Services, which specialized in providing temporary office help, had had a short secretarial assignment a few months ago at Gallinger Industries. Guinevere had only seen Queen Elizabeth from afar, and then just briefly, but the memory of that regal blond head, classic profile, and aristocratic posture had returned in all its glory last week when Zac had mentioned the name of his new client.

Elizabeth Gallinger was thirty-two, a couple years older than Guinevere, and already she was running one of the most prestigious corporations in Seattle. Queen Elizabeth, as she was rather affectionately known by her employees, had inherited the position of president when her father had died unexpectedly last summer. Everyone had anticipated that Elizabeth would be only a figurehead, but everyone had underestimated her. Elizabeth Gallinger had very firmly assumed the reins of her family business. Four generations of old Seattle money had apparently not led to serious mental deficiency due to inbreeding.

Guinevere was beginning to wonder if Zac was the one with the mental deficiency. If so, it couldn't be blamed on inbreeding. Zachariah Justis had a pedigree as ordinary and plebeian as Guinevere's own.

Guinevere frowned at the slowly dripping coffeemaker. It occurred to her that an ambitious entrepreneur with no claim to illustrious predecessors or illustrious family money might find Elizabeth Gallinger a very intriguing proposition. Zac had never been overly impressed by money, but there was always a first time.

Damn it, what was the matter with her? If she didn't know better, Guinevere decided ruefully, she might think she was actually jealous. Ridiculous. The fact that Zac hadn't spent a night with her for almost a week was hardly cause to become green-eyed. She and Zac didn't live together. The affair they had both finally acknowledged was still at a very early, very fragile stage. Neither wanted to push the other too far, too fast. They were both carefully maintaining their own identities and their own apartments.

Fed up with the slowness of the coffeemaker Guinevere yanked the half-full glass pot out from under the dripping mechanism and quickly poured the contents into her yellow mug. Coffee continued to drip with relentless slowness onto the burner. Deciding she'd clean up the mess later, Guinevere hastily put the pot back on the burner and turned away to sip her coffee.

Through her kitchen window she could see the high arched window of the second-floor artist's loft across the street. This morning, as usual, the shades were up. Guinevere had never known the artist who lived and worked in the spacious airy apartment to close them. Artists were very big on light, she had once explained to Zac when he'd had occasion to notice the tenant across the street. She smiled slightly, recalling Zac's annoyance over the small morning ritual she went through with the anonymous man who lived in the loft.

Guinevere had never met the lean young artist. But she waved good morning to him frequently. He always waved back. When Zac happened to be in the kitchen beside Guinevere, the unknown artist tended to put a little more enthusiasm into the wave. Zac's invariable response was a low disgusted growl. Then, just as inevitably, he'd close the blind on Guinevere's window.

But Zac wasn't here to express his disapproval of the anonymous friendship this morning. He hadn't been here to express it for the past several mornings. So Guinevere sipped her coffee and waited for the appearance of her neighbor. Idly she studied the canvas that stood facing her on an easel tilted to catch the northern light. The young man with the slightly overlong hair had been working on that canvas for several days now. Even from here Guinevere could recognize the brilliant colors and dramatic shapes.

But there was something different about the painting this morning. Guinevere's brows came together in a frown of more than concentration as she tipped her head and narrowed her eyes. There was a large black mark on the canvas. From her vantage point it appeared to be an uneven square with a jagged slash inside. It didn't fit at all with the wonderful brilliance and lightness of the painting.

Guinevere went forward, leaning her elbows on the window ledge, the mug cradled between her hands. Besides the ugly black mark on the painting, she could see that something was wrong with the canvas itself. It was torn or slashed. Terribly slashed.

Slowly Guinevere began to realize that the huge canvas had been horribly defaced. Her mouth opened in stunned shock just as her unknown neighbor sauntered yawning into the brightly lit loft.

He was wearing his usual morning attire, a loosely hitched towel around his lean waist and a substantial amount of chest hair. Guinevere had decided that he always wandered into the loft just before he took his morning shower. Perhaps he had an artist's need to see how his work looked in the first light of day. He glanced at her window before he looked at his painting.

Across the narrow street his eyes met hers. Even from here she could see the questioning tilt of one brow as he made a small production out of looking for Zac. When she just stared back, her expression appalled, he finally began to realize something was wrong. He looked at her curiously. Guinevere lifted one hand and pointed, and the stranger turned and glanced over his shoulder. His gaze fell at last on his savaged canvas.

His reaction answered Guinevere's silent question as to whether he could have done the damage himself. The artist stood staring at the ruined canvas, his back rigid with shock. When at last he turned to meet Guinevere's eyes again, all trace of amusement had vanished. He just stared at her. Unable to do anything else, consumed with sympathy for him, Guinevere simply stared back.

How long she stood like that Guinevere wasn't sure. It was the artist who broke the still, silent exchange. Swinging around with an abruptness that conveyed his tension, he picked up a huge sketchbook and a piece of charcoal. Hastily he scrawled a brief message in fat letters.

The Oven. 10 Minutes. Please.

Guinevere nodded at once, then turned away to find her shoes, hurriedly finishing her coffee. She was already dressed for work in a gray pin-striped suit with a narrow skirt, and a yellow silk blouse. Her coffee-brown hair was in its usual neat braided coil at the nape of her neck. She slid her stockinged feet into a pair of gray pumps and slung a leather purse over her shoulder.

Quickly Guinevere made her way through the red, black, and yellow living room with its red-bordered gray rugs and high vaulted windows. The old brick buildings here in the Pioneer Square section of Seattle had wonderfully high ceilings and beautiful windows. When they had been gutted and refurbished, they made great apartments for the new upwardly mobile urbanites. The busy harbor of Elliott Bay was only a couple of blocks away, and although Guinevere didn't actually have a view of the water, just knowing it was close gave her a certain satisfaction. Many mornings she walked along the waterfront on her way to her First Avenue office.

Closing and locking her door behind her, Guinevere hurried down the two short flights of stairs to the security door entrance of her apartment building and stepped out into the crispness of a pleasantly sunny late spring morning. On mornings like this, one knew for certain that summer really was just around the corner. Another sure sign was the fact that several restaurants and taverns in the area had started moving tables and chairs out onto the sidewalks. The rain was due late this afternoon and would probably last awhile, but this morning the air was full of promise.

The missions, which were one of Pioneer Square's more

picturesque features as far as Guinevere was concerned, had already released the crowd of transients, derelicts, and assorted street people they sheltered overnight. Without much enthusiasm the ragtag assortment of scruffy mission clients were slowly drifting out onto the sidewalk, blinking awkwardly in the sunlight as they prepared for the day's work. Soon, either under their own power or aboard one of the free city buses that plied the short route, they would make their way toward the Pike Place Market, where the tourists would be swarming by midmorning. One particularly ambitious soul decided to practice on Guinevere. She smiled vaguely and shook her head, ignoring his outstretched palm and request for cash as she hurried toward the restaurant known as the Oven.

As soon as she opened the high doors the smell of freshly baked cinnamon rolls assailed her, reminding her that she hadn't had a chance to eat breakfast. A fire burning on the huge hearth on one side of the enormous old brick room took the chill off the morning.

Guinevere glanced around. She didn't see her neighbor anywhere, so she decided to throw caution to the winds and order one of the cinnamon rolls. It arrived with butter dripping over the sides. Of course, you couldn't eat a cinnamon roll without a cup of coffee. Something was required to dilute the butter. She was paying for both when the artist slid into line behind her.

"Hi." His voice was pleasantly deep, edged with a trace of the East Coast and laced with a certain grimness. "What a way to meet. Thanks for coming. I'm Mason Adair, by the way. I feel as if I already know you."

Guinevere smiled at him, liking his aquiline features and the large dark eyes. It struck her that he looked exactly like a struggling young artist should look. He was taller than she had thought, towering over her as she stood in line beside him. His height coupled with his leanness made him appear aesthetically gaunt. He was also younger than she had imagined. Probably about thirty.

His paint-stained jeans, plaid shirt, and heavy leather sandals fit the image too.

"I'm Guinevere Jones. Want a roll?"

"What? Oh, sure. Sounds good. I haven't had a chance to eat yet."

"Neither have I." Guinevere picked up her tray.

"Here, I'll take that." Mason Adair took the tray out of her hands and started toward a table in front of the fire. A little of the coffee in Guinevere's cup slopped over the side as he set the tray down on the wooden table. "Sorry. I'm a little clumsy by nature. Finding that canvas slashed this morning isn't improving my coordination. Shit."

Guinevere smiled serenely and unobtrusively used a napkin to wipe the cup as she sat down on one of the short wooden benches. The fire felt good, even if it was produced by fake logs. Mason Adair sank down onto the opposite bench and reached for his roll.

"I was shocked when I glanced out my window and saw that huge black square on your beautiful painting. At first I thought maybe you'd gotten disgusted with your work and had deliberately marked it up." Guinevere stirred her coffee.

"I've got a certain amount of artistic temperament, but I'd never do anything like that to one of my own paintings. Hell, I liked that one. Really liked it. I think it might have been inspired by your kitchen, by the way."

"My kitchen!"

"Yeah, you know. All that yellow. Every morning I look in your window and it's like looking into a little box of sunlight."

Guinevere smiled with pleasure at the unexpected compliment. "I'm flattered."

"Yeah, well, somebody wasn't." Morosely Mason chewed a huge bite of his roll.

Her pleasure disappearing as she recalled the reason she was finally meeting Mason Adair, Guinevere sighed. "I'm terribly sorry. Have you any idea who would do a thing like that, and how someone could have gotten into your loft?"

Adair hesitated. "No, not really. I asked you to meet me here because I wondered if you'd seen anything, or anyone. I never pull that shade and you usually have your kitchen window blinds open. I thought maybe you'd noticed something out of the ordinary last night. It must have happened last night. I was out all evening and I didn't look at the painting before I went to bed."

"Mason, I'm really very sorry, but I didn't see a thing. I did some paperwork in my living room. I do remember going into my kitchen for a snack around nine o'clock, but your window was dark."

"No lights on?"

She shook her head. "Not then."

"Whoever did that would have needed some light, don't you think?" he asked broodingly.

"It would depend on what time during the evening he did it. It doesn't get really dark until after eight o'clock now. I suppose someone could have gone into your studio and defaced your painting sometime before then without needing to turn on a light."

Mason took another huge bite of his roll, dark eyes focusing blankly on her concerned face. Guinevere had the impression he was trying hard to sort out some very private thoughts. She let him chew in solitude for a moment before she said, "That square that the vandal drew in black. It looked a little odd. Of course, I couldn't see it very well from my window, but there was something about the shape of it that looked awkward. Was it a child's work, do you think? Youngsters getting into mischief?"

"This isn't exactly suburbia. We haven't got a lot of children running around Pioneer Square. Just an assortment of street people, artists, and upwardly mobile types. All adults. At least physically. Mentally, who knows?" Mason chewed for another moment. "And it wasn't a square. It was a pentagram."

"A what?"

"A five-sided star."

Guinevere blinked. "I know what a pentagram is. What was the mark in the middle?"

"Just a zigzag slash." Mason looked down at his plate, still half absorbed in his own thoughts. "I think whoever slashed the canvas might have brought along his own knife. None of my tools appeared to have been touched."

Guinevere frowned, leaning forward. "Mason, don't you find it rather odd that whoever did that to your painting chose to draw a pentagram?"

"Odd? The whole damn thing is odd. Spooky, too, if you want to know the truth."

"Yes, but a pentagram? With a bolt of lightning in the center?"

He raised dark eyes to meet her intent gaze. "I said it was a zigzag shape, not a bolt of lightning."

Guinevere hesitated. "I always think of pentagrams as being symbols of magic."

Mason didn't say anything for a long moment. "Yes," he finally admitted. "I believe they are."

There was another lengthy pause. Finally Guinevere asked, "Was anything taken?"

Mason shook his head. "No. Nothing. Didn't touch the stereo or the paints or the cash I keep in the drawer of my workbench." He sighed. "Look, this isn't your problem, Guinevere. I shouldn't have bothered you with it."

"I don't mind—we're neighbors. Going to call the cops?"

"I'll report it, but I don't think it's going to do much good. What's a little malicious mischief these days, when the cops have their hands full with real live murders?"

"Real live murders," Guinevere repeated with a trace of a smile. "I think that may be a contradiction in terms."

Mason stared at her for a second. He laughed. "I think you may be right."

"Has anything like this ever happened before, Mason?"

The brief flash of humor faded. "No."

"What about the possibility of jealousy? Are any of your friends resentful of your success?"

"What success? I've got my first major show tonight down the street at the Midnight Light Gallery. I'll be lucky if someone offers me more than a hundred bucks for one of my pictures. That doesn't qualify as sudden success."

"Your first show?"

Mason nodded. "Yeah. I just hope I live through it. I've been kind of jumpy lately, waiting for it. Whoever did that hatchet job on my painting last night couldn't have picked a better time to rattle me. It's all I needed."

Guinevere drummed her fingers on the table, thinking. "You know, if there's anything more to this than a fluke case of malicious mischief, maybe you should do something besides just reporting it to the cops."

"What more can I do?"

"Hire a private investigator to look into the matter," Guinevere suggested.

Mason stared at her. "Are you kidding? When I can barely pay my rent? I don't have that kind of money. Forget it. There isn't much an investigator could discover, anyway. How's he going to locate a vandal?"

"How about the little matter of how the vandal got into your studio? Was the door forced?"

Mason's brows came together in a solid line. "No major damage was done—I would have noticed. I didn't see any pry marks and none of the locks were broken, but my apartment isn't exactly Fort Knox. It wouldn't have taken a lot of expertise to get inside. You sound like you've been watching a lot of TV lately."

"Not exactly. But I have been keeping some questionable company," Guinevere said blandly.

Mason's brows shot upward as he put two and two together. "Let me guess. That solid-looking guy with the dark hair and the superconservative business suits."

"Zac is trying to dress for success. He's learning the fine points of making a forceful statement in the business world while upholding the image of his firm."

"I see." Mason's dark eyes lit with amusement. "Unlike me. How's he doing?"

"At maintaining his image? Rather well, as a matter of fact. He's just landed a very nice contract with a local firm."

Mason nodded. "So he's doing okay maintaining the image. How about in the category of making a forceful statement?"

"Oh, Zac has always had a knack for making a forceful statement when he wants to," Guinevere said cheerfully. Memories of Zac hunting human game on a cold and windy island in the San Juans several weeks previously flickered briefly in her head. She had to suppress a small shiver. Zac was very, very good at making forceful statements on occasion.

"I'm not surprised," Mason murmured. "I think he's made one or two forceful statements in my direction recently. The last time he closed your kitchen window blinds I got the distinct impression he would have preferred to have his hands around my throat than the blind rod. So he's the questionable company you keep? What does he do in the business world that necessitates all this forceful personality and image-building stuff?"

"He runs a company called Free Enterprise Security, Incorporated. He does security consultations for business firms."

"How big is Free Enterprise Security?"

Guinevere swallowed a scrap of her cinnamon roll. "To date there is only one employee."

"Zac?"

"Uh-huh." She grinned. "But he manages to get things done. You know, this isn't exactly his line of work, but I might mention your situation to him and see if he's got any advice. He's terribly discreet. He has to be. Businesses don't like their security problems publicized. That's why they consult outfits such as Free Enterprise Security."

Mason looked at her askance. "I have a funny feeling he's not going to be overly sympathetic."

"He has no reason to be jealous and he knows it. I've already told him that you and I have never met."

Mason chuckled. "You won't be able to tell him that anymore, will you? I can't wait to hear his reaction when you tell him you've taken to meeting me for breakfast."

Zac's reaction was forthright and to the point. He looked up in astonishment from the plastic bucket of steamed clams from which he was eating and stared at Guinevere as if she had just announced she had made a brief trip to Mars. "The hell you did," he said, and went back to his bucket of clams.

Guinevere pushed her own lunch aside, leaning forward to get his attention. The lunchtime crowd was heavy down here on the waterfront. She and Zac were sitting in the corner of a small sidewalk café that enjoyed an excellent view of the harbor and the tourists strolling the broad sidewalk that linked the boutique-lined piers.

"Zac, you're not listening to me."

"I heard every word you said." He scooped another clam out of its shell. "You claimed you had breakfast with that artist you've been ogling for the past few months. There are laws against that sort of thing, you know."

"Having breakfast with an artist?" She was getting annoyed.

Deep down inside Guinevere wondered if she'd hoped to see at least a spark of romantic jealousy inflame Zac's smoke-gray eyes. All she was detecting was irritation.

"No, ogling artists." Zac forked up another clam. "Stop trying to bait me, Gwen. I've had a hard morning. You're just mad because I had to cancel our date last night."

Guinevere set her teeth very firmly together and spoke through them. "Contrary to what you seem to believe, I am not indulging in a fit of pique. I really did have breakfast with Mason."

"Mason?"

The name brought his head up again. This time there was something besides irritation in the steady gray gaze, and Guinevere wasn't sure she liked the too-quiet way Zac said the other man's name. She shifted uncomfortably in her chair.

"Mason Adair is his name. He's very nice, Zac, and he's got a problem."

Zac stopped eating clams. "Is that a fact?"

"Zac, I'm serious. This morning when I looked out my window I could see that the painting he's been working on had been terribly defaced overnight. Someone had drawn a huge black pentagram on it and then taken a knife to the canvas. Mason was shocked. He saw me looking just as shocked and held up a sign suggesting we meet at the Oven. You know, that place with the cinnamon rolls just around the corner from my building?"

"I know it," Zac said grimly.

"Well, he was rather shaken up, as you can imagine. Has absolutely no idea who could have done such a thing. He asked me to meet him on the outside chance I might have seen something from my kitchen window last night. He hoped I might have spotted someone moving around in his studio."

Zac's gaze could have frozen nitrogen. "Did you?"

"No." Guinevere sighed in exasperation.

"Good." Zac went back to eating clams. "That's the end of it, then. No more breakfast meetings with naked artists. Hell, Gwen, I credited you with more common sense than that. You've lived in the city long enough to know better than to agree to meet absolute strangers. What got into you? Were you really that upset because I had to cancel our date?"

"I hate to break this to you, Zac, but I did not rush out to buy cinnamon rolls for a starving artist this morning just because you broke our date last night."

"He made you pay for the rolls?"

"Speaking of broken dates," Guinevere continued stoutly, "how was your little business meeting last night?"

"All business. Elizabeth is a very impressive executive. She focuses completely on the problem at hand and deals with it. Great business mind."

"Does she know how much you admire her . . . uh, mind?"

Zac looked at her steadily. "Are you by any chance jealous, Gwen?"

She lifted her chin with royal disdain. "Do I have cause?"

"No."

Guinevere went back to the fish and chips she had been nibbling earlier. "Then I'm not jealous." The thing about Zac was that he had a way of dishing out the truth that made it impossible to doubt him. She couldn't ignore that tingle of relief she was feeling, though. It annoyed her. "Now that we've disposed of the personal side of this discussion, perhaps we could get back to business."

"What business?"

"Well, I told Mason I'd mention his little problem to you."

"Guinevere." He rarely used her full name. When he did, especially in that soft gravelly voice, it usually meant trouble. "What exactly did you tell Mason Adair?"

She concentrated on sprinkling vinegar on her french fries. "I just said I'd mention the incident in his studio last night. He's going to report it to the police, of course. But as he said, they won't be able to do much. Just another small case of vandalism as far as they're concerned. They might even write it off as a case of professional jealousy. Mason's going to have his first show tonight. It could be that not everyone wishes him well. At any rate, Mason's fairly sure it isn't something one of his acquaintances would do. And there's something odd about that particular kind of vandalism, Zac. I mean, that business with the pentagram and the bolt of lightning in the center. It wasn't just malicious or nasty. It was weird. Pentagrams are associated with the occult."

"You're rambling, Gwen. Get to the point. What exactly did you tell Mason Adair?"

"I told you," she said with exaggerated patience. "I said I'd mention the matter to you."

"And?" Zac prompted ominously.

"And maybe see if you had any advice for him," she concluded in a mumbled rush as she munched a french fry.

"Advice?" Zac ate the last of his clams and pushed the plastic bucket out of the way. He leaned forward, his elbows resting on the table, his hard blunt face set in a ruthless unrelenting expression that seemed to slip all too easily into place. His rough voice was softer than ever. "No, Gwen, I don't have any free advice for your starving artist. But I do have some for you."

"Now, Zac—"

"You will stay clear of him, Guinevere. You will not get involved with pentagrams, slashed canvases, or artists who run around in only a towel while they wave good morning to their female neighbors. Understood?"

Guinevere drew a deep breath. "Zac, I was asking for advice, not a lecture. If you're not willing to help—"

"But I am willing to help, Gwen. I'm helping you stay out of trouble. Or have you already forgotten what happened the last time you tried to involve me in a case I wasn't interested in handling?"

"Now, Zac, you collected a nice fee for that business in the San Juans. You can hardly complain about my involving you."

"Hah. I can complain and I will complain. Furthermore . . ."

Zac was warming to his topic now. The lecture might have continued unabated for the remainder of the lunch hour, if a small toddler in an emblazoned designer polo shirt and shorts hadn't come screeching down the aisle between tables and made a lunge for Zac's empty plastic clam container. The child, giggling dementedly, scrambled up onto Zac's lap, grabbed the container, and spilled the contents across Zac's trouser leg. Empty clamshells and the accompanying juice ran every which way, splattering the restrained tie and white shirt Zac was wearing with the trousers. There was a shriek of delight from the toddler and then the child was racing off to wreak more havoc and destruction.

Zac sat looking after the small boy, a stunned expression replacing the hard one with which he had been favoring Guinevere. In the distance two distinctly yuppie parents ran after their errant offspring. They had the same designer's emblem on their polo shirts that their son had on his. A coordinated family.

"Have you noticed," Zac asked in an odd voice, "how many small children there are around these days? Whatever happened to all those women who said they were going to have careers instead of babies?"

Guinevere tried to stifle a small grin. "I'm still keeping the faith."

Zac's gaze returned to her face. "It's the biological-clock syndrome, you know."

"Biological clock?"

"It's running out for women your age," he explained in that same odd voice.

Guinevere's grin disappeared. "Zac, what on earth are you talking about?"

"Babies," he said grimly. "My God, even Elizabeth Gallinger is talking about babies."

"Elizabeth Gallinger! Zac, what in the world were you doing talking to Elizabeth Gallinger about babies?"

But Zac was staring sadly at the clamshells strewn across his trousers. "I have the feeling this suit will never be the same."

Jayne Castle, the *New York Times* bestselling author of *Deception Cove*, *The Lost Night*, *Canyons of Night*, *Midnight Crystal*, *Obsidian Prey*, *Dark Light*, *Silver Master*, *Ghost Hunter*, *After Glow*, and *After Dark*, is a pseudonym for Jayne Ann Krentz, the author of more than fifty *New York Times* bestsellers. She writes contemporary romantic suspense novels under the Krentz name, as well as historical novels under the pseudonym Amanda Quick. She lives in Seattle. You can find her online at jayneannkrentz.com and facebook.com/jayneannkrentz.